A Note

dng. woman

My name is Suzanne Valadon and I was born in 1865, the illegitimate daughter of an alcoholic charwoman, a servant, who ran off with me in shame to Paris where she stumbled onto the Montmartre and where I grew up in the streets. I lived, sometimes rashly, sometimes foolishly but most of the time passionately; and I always felt myself to be unique. I regret not having achieved even more. Perhaps because I was a woman artist, I was automatically set apart from the others. Women's names in art were few for they were designated by society to marry, have babies and generally be an appendage to their husbands.

I fought for what I wanted and cracked the prevailing code for women. I lived and painted the way I desired and was accepted by Degas as "one of us" because Degas had considered me an exclusive property of the Montmartre, nurturing on it, and dying in it. I took lovers with the easy carelessness of a man, freely and completely without the usual games that women play. I believed that a woman who was a man's equal and gave herself to him because of what she felt, was more desirable to him than one who submitted in obedience. I couldn't accept artifice, only truth and I infused this into my paintings.

But the only great mistake I made was to die and end my work and bestow my son Maurice Utrillo's genius on *that* woman, his genius I alone cultivated. That was my most foolish act.

*A novel based on the life
of Suzanne Valadon, artist
and mother of Maurice Utrillo,
painter*

Suzanne

of Love and Art

a novelized biography by

ELAINE TODD KOREN

Maverick Books
Woodstock, New York

Painting on Front Cover: *Dance at Bougival* courtesy of the Museum of Fine Arts, Boston. Posed for by Suzanne Valadon.

Photograph on Front Cover: *Suzanne Valadon at Twenty* courtesy of Galerie Gilbert and Paul Pétridès, Paris.

Published by Maverick Books
Post Office Box No. 897
Woodstock, New York 12498

Copyright © 2001 Elaine Todd Koren

This is a work of fiction. Most incidents are based on fact using personages prominent in the subject's life. However, dialogue and some events and persons described are the fictional interpretation of the author.

All rights reserved. No part of this book may be reproduced or transmitted in any form or by any means, electronic or mechanical, including photocopying, recording or by any information storage and retrieval system without written permission from the author, except for the inclusion of brief quotations in a review.

Library of Congress Catalog Card Number: 98-68379
ISBN 0-9672355-2-9
Includes bibliographical references, notes and comments.

First softcover printing, January 2001
Printed in the United States of America

10 9 8 7 6 5 4 3 2 1

In Appreciation

IRVING STONE
I would like to thank the late Irving Stone for his encouragement and support when it was greatly needed. He was a true humanitarian. He inspired me by his writing of biographical novels of the Impressionist period in Paris with which I dealt. The artists Vincent Van Gogh in Lust for Life and Camille Pissaro in Depths of Glory served as fine and sensitive portrayals.

The following paragraph from his letter speaks for itself:

June 28, 1989
Dear Ms. Koren:

Suzanne Valadon is indeed a first-rate subject and I think in the long run you will sell it. Do not change it over from a biographical novel to a biography or any other form. You were right in the first place. I think you are going to have to go the same route I went. Seventeen publishers over a period of three years rejecting my manuscript of LUST FOR LIFE. The manuscript was finally accepted by a small publishing house, Longmans, Green & Co., a catholic house and one that had only published a single novel before mine. You just have to keep up the faith.

Irving Stone *

Irving Stone died on August 26, 1989, two months later.

* Reprinted by Courtesy of Jean Stone, his wife and editor.

*for my parents who left me the courage,
my children who believed
and to my husband, always....*

Preface

One is either captivated by Suzanne Valadon or irritated. One is never indifferent. In Suzanne, I began to explore a complex personality and she dominated me fusing my own traits with hers in my writing. Her agonies and frustrations in terms of her son and the impetus generated by each creative work grew more powerful as I wrote. And she spoke for herself in that writing, spoke to a son drenched with alcohol, spoke to an unfaithful husband, spoke to a tender lover. And when she spoke it was sometimes quietly, sometimes vehemently and sometimes lovingly. I merely wrote it down.

But how did it all begin? For myself, I was caught up in the early eighties when I stumbled upon a passage by Alfred Werner in his portfolio about Maurice Utrillo describing the artist's mother. Certainly, it could not have been the first time I read it, but it was the first time something clicked and hence my long odyssey into the golden era of French art began.

My journey through this novel was fraught with complications for few biographies existed about her life. Several biographies of Lautrec, who exerted a profound influence on her, hardly acknowledged her relationship with him at all. Certainly she had not the stature of Mary Cassatt or of Berthe Morisot in terms of exposure and recognition. There were also many contradictions.

She was a mythologist, constantly reinventing stories about herself and her relationships with Lautrec, Degas and others. I settled on time periods which seemed most logical. My gracious letter a decade ago from Irving Stone explains my considerations as to the novel's form. Finally, with a serious revision from third to first person under the influence of Faulkner's, "As I Lay Dying," I used seven voices to get inside the minds more fully of those who were close to her.

Almost all of the book is fact based, and I attempted to keep the dialogue probable. Some things were imaginary such as Suzanne stumbling on Eveline, her husband's paramour in the castle, the creation of Berthe Sourel, a cleaning woman and sometime prostitute, as a model for the painting, *The Blue Room*, the awful fate of Odette Poupoule, the prostitute painted by Lautrec and the locket given to Suzanne by Lautrec.

If all Suzanne Valadon had done was to have produced a son whom she instructed and literally moulded into a major artist, she would have earned a measure of glory; but to have achieved success as an artist in her own right, virtually self-taught was a major achievement. Suzanne Valadon stood apart in her art, intensely realistic, painting the world she knew about her without sugar coating and guise. At the start of my research I had attended an exhibit of Women's Art at the Brooklyn Museum, and when I entered, a huge painting confronted me. The woman depicted was painted stretched out on a divan wearing striped pants who nonchalantly regarded the world; she resembling either a whore or a charwoman. It stood apart from the others. But I knew. I felt that only Valadon would have painted it, only *she*. It was of course, *The Blue Room*, possibly her most mature work. It was her own aspect of life as she saw it.

Germaine Greer stated it very well in *The Obstacle Race*, "A woman who breaks the mould may make her own normality."

7 voices:
1. Marie
2. Henri Toulouse (midget)
3. Suzanne
4. Degas (master & painter) (the hog)
5. Grand-Mère
6. Maurice (son)
7.

Suzanne

Puvis de Chavannes (apt. #, old)
Renoir (girlhood)
Miguel Utrillo (father g Maurice)

A Street in Montmartre

How does one touch the infinite with a writer's tools,
Measured words which embrace a past century
and fall upon a Paris street on which
a child dances and holds a drawing fast

as time passes swiftly; and the woman
evolves before her childish tears are dried.
She feels that twentieth century shadow
touching with tepid fingers and with

quickened pace she moulds her artist son.
Her passionate brush and his palette knife
live side by side as their paintings whirl
in sequence to the mortal end of artists all.

Memories splay the air with drops of longing for
the warmth of Maman's ancient tea cups, crazed.
The silvered images pour into relentless time
shattering the marvelous swift glitter of youth.

How does one touch the infinite with a writer's tools,
Measured words which round out dim, bleak shadows
once lifeless, now there's pain and love.
                      How does one . . . .

ETK

Prologue

December 25, 1883
Paris, France

She was conceived and delivered in disgrace. Only a bastard after all, an artist's model, Marie Clémentine in her mother's eyes is no better than a common whore.

Panting by the bed in her labor, she accumulates a torrent of her mother's curses. She will suffer through the pain and be done with it and empty her belly of this uninvited infant. Who is this stranger who rents one's flesh so that one can scarcely breathe from the pain, a pain which cascades in waves and then recedes like obedient tides. For a few moments of pleasure? Insane! And to have the man go free and now be eternally tormented with the idiocies of childhood. She is only eighteen and her life has barely begun.

Maman Madeleine's husky voice accuses, "You run around the room like a crazy person. What a way to have a child . . . get into bed like a normal woman."

"No!"

"Of course you are *fou*. How could I expect anything else?"

Her own mother, a miserable drunk, her own mother who wails spraying the air with a cheap blend of brandy and venom.

The midwife, old Colette, comes hobbling in and places a huge kettle of boiling water atop a black coal stove. She deposits stained blankets on the bureau and then rubs her elbows covered with scabs from the strong lye of washtubs. A stale odor of heavy laundry soap oozes from her body. She examines Marie closely for a moment, and then falls into a monotonous chant as she fingers a rosary; sinking into an old rocker whose stuffing peeks out from a coarse blue linen covering. Another pain steals the young woman's breath and sprawls her down onto the iron bed. The midwife's seasoned gnarled fingers pat and knead her huge swollen abdomen as though to estimate the size of the baby. Her eyes scan Colette's stock of frayed towels scrubbed countless times, torn sheaths of muslin stained by the blood and excrement of past endeavors. Somehow the old woman's rosary beads calm her; between pains she traces the outlines of faded stains designing a white laundered apron.

Hoarse urgent sounds crackle from the midwife's throat. She wrenches Madeleine from her sleep and pushes her to fetch some warm towels. Madeleine, half dozing, staggers back to the bed, dumps an armload onto a peeling cabinet and looks down at her daughter. "To have a baby without a father like some *putain*," she croaks. She sways, and shakes her fist at unseen enemies. She lifts her skirt and pulls out a small bottle of brandy from a pocket sewn in her petticoat, frantically slurping its contents. She crosses herself, and sinks into a straw rocker, wipes her mouth with her sleeve and spews out oaths. Her eyes hold ancient pools of frustration.

The pains increase in severity until they are five minutes apart. *Merde*, so this is what it's all about, the young woman thinks. The midwife folds her legs back and has her grip the tarnished brass rungs of the headboard behind her. Old Colette calls out to bear down with each pain and the young woman moans.

"*Mon Dieu*, it must be fifteen hours," mutters Madeleine through a drunken haze.

"Have patience," says the midwife. "A first child . . . "

"My daughter is a whore," Madeleine croaks through the brandy.

"Shut up you drunken fool."

A dull snapping sound fills the room as the water breaks. The towels are flooded cradling Marie's buttocks. Madeleine sits immobilized as a dark head comes into view and then slurps frantically from the bottle. The yellow liquid sloshes down her chin in golden rivulets. Suddenly all is silent.

"Something is wrong," Colette whispers hoarsely. The contractions suddenly stop. It is now late in the morning of December 26. Christmas Day has passed and the snow comes down in thick curtains outside the window. A deathly stillness is interrupted from time to time by a low moan and a slow trickle of blood drips through the towels, pooling and soaking through the muslin sheet. The blood comes thicker and seeps through the mattress to the wooden floor.

Colette in alarm crosses herself. She throws on an old hooded cape and plunges into the stormy night to fetch the doctor.

Marie sees the doctor through flashes of consciousness, and hears muffled whispers when suddenly there is one gigantic bearing down as though her life were passing between her legs. Somewhere in the distance she hears herself shriek. A baby cries lustily, and a marvelous warmth is being placed atop her belly. Is that the baby? What day is it? Had Christmas come and gone? It seems an eternity has passed. And as though to answer her question, comes the midwife's voice.

"You don't have to worry. This little one was not born on Christmas day after all."

"Much difference it makes," Madeleine drones wearily.

The baby wrapped in swaddling clothes, squeals in the small basket.

Madeleine, drunk from brandy, slumps in folds in the rocker. The gasoliers begin to hiss softly, throwing cobalt blue shadows on the wall merging softly with an inky darkness.

Hours pass since the delivery. The doctor looks at the semiconscious figure, visibly shivers and shovels some coal into the large stove heating the room. He paces back and forth before the bed, examines her, and then examines her again.

"The hemorrhaging is subsiding," he mutters as he bends over Marie, slaps her cheeks and put spirits to her nostrils.

Madeleine stares at the figure on the stained sheets and scratches her sides. A trickle of amber liquid seeps from a corner of her mouth. She lifts herself out of the chair and bends over her daughter.

"Marie," she says this time very softly. "You have a son."

The young woman opens her eyes and looks toward the basket. The infant is sleeping contentedly.

"He's a quiet baby, Maman," Marie says wearily. "I think I'll call him Maurice . . . yes, I'll call him Maurice. I like that, Maurice . . . in honor of nobody . . . nobody at all." She falls into a deep sleep.

Several days later Madeleine goes to the *mairie* and registers the birth.

Maurice Valadon, born December 26, 1883, at 1:00 P.M. in the afternoon to Marie-Clémentine Valadon. Father, unknown.

Part One
(1865-1901)

"You are indeed one of us."
Edgar Degas

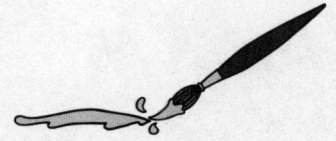

1

<u>Marie</u>

The Awakening

I felt nothing after the delivery. It was as though a searing pain had wiped out all feeling and I marveled that for all the pangs of childbirth and bouts of nursing, I felt little connection with the infant. Months later, I stood on the model's platform at Cormon's *atelier*, about to pose as a nymph in the Elysian Fields and paused to watch the strange tableau taking place before me at one of the easels. Émile Bernard, a young student, was being threatened expulsion from the Academy for having painted a nude in streaks of vermilion and emerald green. My eyes scanned the room while waiting to begin and I controlled a sudden impulse to pull my chignon under a cap and cover my breasts swollen with milk with a loose fitting artist's smock . . . and I would sit at an easel and call myself Marcel and draw as well as the best of them. And you, Professor Cormon would discover that your Marcel was really Marie. What great fun to have a woman slip into the Academy.

I usually posed in the nude, but today I was to be draped as a Greek statue and it's going to be a clever feat to hide my poor swollen stomach with the miserable drapery so worn it's shredding. I felt an icy chill which settled on the easels and stiffened the brushes, and I shouted to the *massier* to have him put more coal in the huge stove at the front of the room. Cormon rapped on a desk for me to begin posing and the students began to sketch me and murmured among themselves glancing at one another's work. I watched them from my modeling position in the center of that huge room, digesting some of their techniques. Some of the students judged my proportions through narrowed eyes, some were painting, some just drawing using greased pencils, taking care with hatching indicating shadows, and erasing and redrawing. All the same, I always had the thrill of importance standing before them on the model's platform with all eyes focused on me. This was what I waited for, this moment, this marvelous moment, as though I had almost arrived.

Look at that bastard Cormon sending out his usual lengthy warnings. "I am a member of the Salon Jury of the Academy des Beaux Arts and don't forget it. You will paint the way the finest of our artists painted in the true classical tradition." How his posture droops in his cutaway, and how he struts in his awful spats . . . and poor Émile Bernard seems to shrink as Cormon glares at him. The old goat gets pleasure from scaring the wits out of the students. He walks around their easels looking for the unmentionable terrible emerald green, and he waves Émile's painting about as a dreadful example. "And furthermore . . . I want no portrayal of lewd pubic hair, sensuality that is too graphic. A woman's body in its natural state without a hand covering the vital parts is crude, undignified. It should conform to the standards of antiquity which bare nature itself can scarcely match". I wonder if he ever had a woman, the worm. I say there's nothing wrong with painting a woman the way she really is with hair on her *vagin* and I'll do it many times because it *is* natural and I'll draw her with fat hanging from her arse and her breast if that's the way she is. I'm not a terrified stupid fool who trembles with every chalk line and dab of paint I put on the canvas.

Dieu, Cormon is trying to scare the daylights out of that newcomer. "I'll be kind to you, but I can bar you from the Salon as I shall do to Monsieur Bernard at the proper time. Just persist in demonstrations of flagrant color such as this. I told you all repeatedly to beware of that demon, *color*. Because you are new here, I'll be charitable and hope to see improvement in your work." But I must say that little one doesn't seem to care what Cormon says . . . he intrigues me. Why, he's a midget. Gauzi just called him, Henri . . . of course, it must be Gauzi's friend from Toulouse . . . he's a little one, alright, but I warrant he has a big cock on him . . . those small men always surprise you that way, but he paints with such glorious colors . . . *Mon Dieu*, he is small, but he does have nice eyes . . . who cares so I'd let him *foutre* me anyway if he would teach me how to paint like that . . . how he gets around on those little stumps, but what an artist, worth a dozen of the others . . . now look at Louis Anquetin sitting so smugly at his easel as though nothing happened between us . . . why was I ever with him when he talks about every woman he's ever had . . . good looking with golden hair and he struts about acting as though every woman would die not having him . . . now Guichet, the sailor, always knows what makes a woman feel good . . . I could have him this very instant, yes I could. I'm not like other women waiting for the man to make advances . . . if I want a man I make no bones about it and undress first like a free woman not a hypocrite like those simpering *jeune filles* I meet every day and of course there's the curse of another baby and that's why women are trapped as much as they think they are free . . . *merde*, I'm filling up with milk and I'll have to leave so Cormon is in for a great shock when his nymph steps down, the worm. Oh, listen to the devil . . .

"The delicacy and refinement of colour of centuries past have been desecrated and violated by such atrocities as cadmium and chrome yellow, pure colors of the spectrum slopped on canvases without dilution, without that subtle blending one calls art, paintings done by barbaric men in the name of art in the name of something heinous called *Impressionism*, the scourge of the art world . . . as I have said, beware of that demon, *color*, and . . ."

I stepped off the model's platform as the drapery fell to the floor and with rising voices from the easels he whirled about and just gaped and there I was as naked as you please . . . *Dieu*, let him stare at me, the fool . . .

"And where do you think you're going, Mademoiselle? Exactly where do you think you're going?"

"I have to nurse my child," I said with great innocence.

Laughter rose up from the easels.

He cupped his ear. "What are you saying? Did I hear correctly? And I asked for a draped nymph today so have the decency to cover your private parts when not modeling, woman."

But there I stood as naked as a babe. Of course his little nothing is probably standing at attention by now.

"Can you please repeat yourself Mademoiselle."

"You heard correctly . . . I have to nurse my baby. Did you never hear of a woman nursing, Monsieur? I'm very surprised," I said as sweetly, as I dared.

"You be still, woman!" Cormon's voice cracked. "Don't use that nauseating tone with me. You have too much to say for a model and I want no further comment from the students." He delicately wiped his lips with his trimmed handkerchief.

"I'll say what I think!" I retorted. Cormon's eyes swept my entire body as though looking for something, and then he turned his back on me. I imitated his motions while listening to the rising laughter coming from the students.

"And inform me why I couldn't employ props who don't talk back?" He said bitterly.

"I'm not one of your props and if I were one of your students, I would paint as I please, I assure you." I answered with great bravado but my heart beat wildly.

The laughter rose deliciously and some of the students were banging on their easels. Anquetin and Émile Bernard were delirious over the sudden twitching of Cormon's face. The midget beamed and swallowed nervously so that his huge Adam's apple bobbed up and down.

"Fortunately, my dear Mademoiselle, you will never have that opportunity to show us your dismal talent. And what delusion lets you think that a woman would ever be admitted into this Academy? Enough! Don't bother posing tomorrow. I'm not running a nursery, and incidentally I would learn how to speak in a proper fashion to your superiors or I can remove you from our model's registry. We have many models eager to replace you."

He reached into his ridiculous cutaway jacket and took out a small pill box. His hand was shaking. We all watched him lean his head back, drop a pill in his mouth, and then bend down and brush his spats. "Another thing," he said slowly, his eyes narrowing, fixed at something awful in the class, "if any of the students proves to be the father of one of *her* bastards, I will throw him out." His voice was calm flooding the room with guilt.

"Animal," I murmured bravely, retrieved my clothing, held myself very erect and vowed that I would never return. Cormon smiled, a mocking smile and turned his back. Maman waited for me outside the *atelier* with Maurice in the carriage, and we went to a sheltered square where I nursed him in a warming embrace. Cormon's students passed by holding huge portfolios. I waved and some stared, some laughed and some looked away embarrassed.

But on most days when I returned from modeling, the house was empty and silent. Maman was usually out with little Maurice. Each afternoon, she bundled him up, tucked him into his carriage and took him for an airing, sometimes in the bitter cold. And during that time I would wait. Oh, how I would wait. I would wait so long that I feared that I would cease to be. Was that possible, I wondered? Of course I was being punished for leading the life of the free woman as I called myself, and I was caught in the old trap, the trap of pregnancy. What did I expect when so many got into my culotte. *Merde*, I would not be destroyed by all of this. It wasn't meant for me to bear the drudgery of being tied to the infant and will go on with my life. That's the way it will be. *C'est ça!* And then I realized that for all my brave declarations of independence and my boasting about my free life I was tied to the infant. My carefree girlhood had ended.

I tried to reach out into past events and make sense of what had happened. And slowly like a gathering storm, I saw a whole host of impressions of the passing years which melded one into the other, and like a kaleidoscope there were flickering scenes, patterns and colors; they flared up and then faded in my memory.

* * *

I was younger, so much younger then. It was 1875, and I was just a child of ten looking down at the countryside and I thought

I heard the echoes of the husky tones of my mother, a drinker's voice, a voice which seeped through the rocks and played with the insects in the grasses of the Butte Montmartre; it filtered through the trees brushing the leaves with its hoarseness until it crept its way to the top. I can still imagine her voice calling . . .

"Marie-Clementine . . . where are you?"

I skipped along merrily swinging my hips from side to side. "I'm coming Maman." I'll simply skip right down the hills again just like this . . . two skips and one jump, two hops on the left foot . . . what a funny dance I made up.

And then I began to sing a dirty French ditty I picked up from a drunken artist where Maman scrubbed. I didn't understand the words but I chanted it anyway, chanting it as loud as the birds would allow. Perhaps I could shock someone, but nobody was listening. I paused and looked at the windmills turning lazily in the breeze. All Paris spread magnificently before me, a panoramic sea of dark roofs dotted with church spires. And I could see the Seine, a winding curving stream shimmering with light, dividing Paris. Everything flowed down to the valley of the Seine.

It was later in my life that I learned that the golden age of Montmartre was beginning then. The hill of Montmartre climbing high above the Seine, overlooked the colorful tortuous streets, picturesque and saturated in the Bohemian atmosphere filled with artists of all sorts, *artiste-peintres,* composers, sculptors and writers. Montmartre was a village which sat on a hill, drenched with the clear green color the impressionists used. *Dieu,* I had seen them paint, yes I had. And then there were the farmyards noisy with the scampering and squealing of chickens and pigs, and manure made dank dark trails down the walkways . . . yes, Montmartre was a country village in 1875, and I danced its crooked little streets which wound to the top. How marvelous it all was. And it was all mine, my own playground, and I hugged myself in joy.

I sketched a small kitten sitting on a rock watching me. I sketched with a pencil from my bag. "And that's enough of you, *petit chat,* funny little cat." I slipped the pencil back between the pages of the pad, placed the notebook into the pouch and then looked again at the windmills of Montmartre turning, turning, and it was all magic. I felt like a princess as I claimed it all as my own special territory, and then placed a hand on each hip and took a deep breath.

"How I love you Montmartre," I shouted. "How I love you my Montmartre! Do you hear me down there?" I flung myself down in the grass and looked upward at a marvelous sky.

I often wondered how Maman had ever come to such a wondrous place. I vaguely remembered the Commune and the Siege. I recalled that Saturday in 1871, when I was six years old, how a rumor spread about Paris that the government troops from Versailles were on the march against the capital. Suddenly I was in the streets being tossed about by a frenzied mob. Maman began to scream when she spotted me as she hurried home from washing people's floors, and some drunk threw me into the air. But I wasn't frightened. I took out a pencil and jabbed him in the balls and he dropped me in the street. I was almost trampled by a carriage. The drunken mob surged on and I gleefully saw bandits, prostitutes and two poor men dragged to rue du Chevalier de la Barre, stood against the wall and shot. *Dieu*, I just remember the blood, so much blood. I found my rag doll in a ditch trampled by carriage wheels and took it home. Its head was crushed and it was missing a leg. It was the only doll I ever owned.

But all this didn't frighten me because I knew *petit chat* that I would spend my life here in Montmartre and never leave.

How the nuns at the Convent of St. Vincent de Paul tried to keep me in school, but they couldn't hold me. I skipped and danced down these funny twisted streets and drew little pictures of the birds and the trees . . . what a wonderful world this was. I remained stretched out on the grass at the top of the Butte and closed my eyes, and I felt the soothing warmth of the sun with my cat sleeping by my side.

When I skipped along rue Lepic I saw a young artist and watched him paint; his face was so kind, so very kind, with strange light blue eyes which could go right through you; how beautiful he was and what lovely colors he used.

"You're very handsome, Monsieur. Are you an *artiste-peintre?*" Of course he was. I didn't have to ask.

"I can draw with pencil and crayon." I offered.

"*Vraiment!* And what do you draw?"

"Everything . . . mostly my cat, Monsieur."

"Well . . . isn't she a very pretty little sprite, Choquet?" the painter said to his friend.

"Why don't you sign your name to the picture, Monsieur, so I can always remember it. You paint very well and you should continue being an artist and that's my advice, *c'est ça!* Just remember I am Mademoiselle Villon, daughter of François Villon, the great poet.

The artist laughed and laughed and winked at this Choquet who laughed as well. "You're quite famous, Mademoiselle Villon," he said. "Thank you for your excellent advice and I'll sign my name on this canvas little one, just for you."

"Renoir," I read aloud. "Oh thank you, Monsieur. You see, Monsieur, I hardly go to school . . . the nuns are looking for me right now, but I can read. I'm very clever, you know. Well, goodbye, Monsieur Renoir, and don't forget me. Just be an artist and I'll remember you, forever and ever."

"You're a hard one to forget, mademoiselle," Renoir laughed.

"And I can't wait to grow up so I can love you."

"Well then, I certainly will look forward to it." Renoir laughed but went on painting. I surely thought he'd stop for me. *Merde*, he can see how very clever I am.

Maman stood at the entrance of the house on the Boulevard Rochechouart and scolded, "Well the sisters told me you weren't in school, so don't lie! What do you do all day? I scrubbed four floors for a rich old hag and you waltz about like a princess never learning anything. I'll always have misery. It's my fate." Then she went for a flask under her skirt and slurped her brandy.

"I'm in my playground, Maman. I skip and I dance and draw pictures, and today a most marvelous thing happened . . . I met a handsome painter."

"You are *fou* and you'll never amount to anything, and I can tell you I'm ashamed when you dance in the streets when you should be in school! What devil prompts you? Why can't you behave like a *jeune fille*, like the others?"

"Don't be angry, Maman . . . just look at the picture I drew for you," but my mother pushed me away.

"A pox on your father . . . how glad I am that he was crushed to death. Oh, how I would like to see him burn in hell!" She began to mutter about him in her funny whiskey voice. I guessed from the way she cursed him that my father must have been someone quite terrible falling off a bridge one day and crushed by a millstone on another . . . but all the same I made him the poet, François Villon, and I of course became his famous daughter, Mademoiselle Villon.

"You don't understand how I suffer, Marie," she always said.

But I tried to understand, at least some of it. Of course I was only two months old when late in 1865 we went to live in this one room on the Boulevard Rochechouart where Maman promptly became a charwoman. She carried a huge canvas bag at the bottom of which lay a bottle of brandy, and she would drink it on the job. I was so ashamed when she came back in a haze of alcohol, so ashamed! I saw her scrubbing the floors and cleaning the rooms of the Café Guerbois on the Boulevard Clichy. I knew there were painters and musicians there, and constant shouting as I crept closer and peeked in and saw and heard artists torn to shreds by the most marvelous of young men, and it fascinated me, but Maman scarcely understood them and did her work in her half drunken stupor.

How Maman ranted afterwards, how she ranted, for to be an artist was to be a lunatic. And to be a woman artist was as bad as being an artist's model or a prostitute. She raved about a new freedom in which there were women artists, a horror in itself. "A woman is not free . . . she is not free and everyone knows she has to be protected by a man and have his children, not be a dried up old spinster when she could well afford a dowry. What are the mothers of these lady artists thinking of?" Then she would finish it all off with a drink, always that damn drink . . . and how I hated Maman when she drank . . . with the odor of brandy which filled the air about her and filtered through her soiled muslin . . . and the smell which drenched my frock after I attempted to embrace her.

"You're getting drunk, Maman. Why must you drink? Why? My friends' mothers don't drink. I'm just not going to listen to your stories anymore . . . I'm not listening to a drunk and from now on, I'll go where I please. I hate, hate, hate you because if you cared for me you wouldn't drink you stinking woman!"

"And you're *fou* to go dancing up and down the streets like an idiot with your bare feet, so that everyone laughs at you; the *diable* possesses you for sure," and Maman crossed herself.

I held my ears and slammed the door behind me and skipped back to the Butte clutching a pad and pencil in my hand and did more sketching, and then sat with my face in my hands and felt sad and empty as I watched my cat stalking a worm. "Oh, my *petit chat*, how Maman is a chore to me. I hate her sometimes . . . how I really hate her. Doesn't she realize that the others at the convent can't draw the way I do? And why does Maman drink so much? Are you a clever cat who can tell me the answers? All you do is sit and purr and want me to stroke your back," and I smoothed his fur with my bare toes.

I lay in the grass and looked up at the tops of the trees, at the sunlight dancing on the leaves and all the sadness left. I felt warm and safe and I thought of what Maman told me about her life. I wondered how it felt to clean people's houses after having managed a whole household, a job that Maman said was very important. And so what if I'm a bastard . . . see if I care. I would just enjoy myself in this life and make up my own rules. I would never, never look like Maman, so dirty and ugly and I would never, never drink, and maybe, maybe, I would be married to a beautiful man like that *artiste-peintre* in rue Lepic.

"It's all quite marvelous," I called across the fields of the Butte and into the trees, and my voice came back on a balmy breeze which rustled the leaves of my drawing pad. "It's quite marvelous, all the same!" I hugged myself.

And I escaped the nuns at the convent as I perched high on a fence and sang my songs, and I decided that I would never be just like anybody . . . like the ordinary women in the streets with their big aprons and disheveled hair doing baskets of laundry, someone else's filthy laundry with sudsy arms, calling their small babies . . . endless babies. And husbands who came home so grimy, sometimes beating their wives. How can people make love, touch bodies when they act like this? Oh, I had found out about it all from Babette, my friend at school, how people make love . . . but I can wait. I would see about making love when I was older . . . yes, I would see and if I liked it I would do it many, many times and with men who were beautiful. "Oh, my little Villon, isn't it all so wonderful? Yes, I'll call you François Villon, my little cat. Then you'll be great."

My Villon sat curled up on a limb intently watching a bird.

When I dropped out of school I worked as a waitress, sold vegetables in Les Halles and then did a stint as a dishwasher in rapid order. The position as a dishwasher was a temporary one at La Nouvelle-Athènes, a restaurant where artists met in endless conversations. I did little dishwashing. Now that I was twelve, I could sit with them, yes, that's what I might do. How very clever I was. Why must I do those miserable dishes when they made my hands so red? How I would love to be one of the artists. I'll become one of them before the day is out and no one will know the difference, I thought that afternoon.

"You're fired," said Jacques, the manager smiling.

"What?"

"You heard me. You're fired," he said still smiling.

"I'm shocked, Monsieur, and deeply wounded," I said repeating a passage I had heard in a play in school. It was the way François Villon would have spoken.

"You are deeply wounded? You are *fou* and don't think you fooled me behind that pole. I've been watching you. Why do you stand and listen to the artists? Why are you so interested? You're supposed to be helping out in the kitchen, and that's all!"

"Pig! Give me my money and I'll leave, you . . . *bâtard!*"

"*Sacrebleu!* A mouth like this . . . oh, but you're a little slut, and a wicked one at that."

"Give me my money, you . . . you son of a bitch!"

He raised his hand as though to strike me but I stood looking as fierce as I could.

His eyes narrowed and then he shrugged his shoulders, reached into his pocket and handed me a franc.

"You promised me three francs."

"Three francs? You're not worth five sous. You think you're Marie Antoinette? You're Marie-Clémentine a worthless little runt."

I spat in his face. He wiped the spittle off and lunged at me. "Now you're going to get it!" he growled in anger. I kicked him in the groin and he doubled up. A proper looking man in tweeds got up and raised a cane in intervention.

"Monsieur Degas, please let me handle this bundle of evil. A gentleman like you, such a famous artist, shouldn't dirty your hands with this kind of garbage. She's rotten all the way through. Look at her eyes . . . like the eyes of the devil himself."

"I see unusual eyes," said this Monsieur Degas. "What's wrong, child?"

"He just fired me, that wicked one did, and now my family will all starve. We'll starve, and he'll burn in hell," I said borrowing one of Maman's oaths about my father.

"Don't listen to her. She's a liar, Monsieur!" Jacques shouted.

"Why did you fire her?" Degas asked.

"She does nothing, Monsieur, but stand around and listen to artists' conversations. Why she does, I don't understand. But she's worthless, worthless in the kitchen."

"I've worked for many weeks, Monsieur, like a slave for only a franc and now we'll have nothing to eat. I haven't eaten for three days and my mother is starving and my sister begs for a crust of bread. Surely you must have seen her selling herself with the other *lorettes* poor thing, and my five brothers are without shoes and my father beats me . . . oh, it's all too horrible." I cried into a handkerchief. "And that's not the end of my misery. My father wants me to sell my body like my sister on the street for a franc, may he burn in hell," I imitated my mother's wailing.

"Do you see what you're doing? You're paying her slave wages," said this Degas angrily to Jacques. "This child could become a hopeless whore because of you."

"Monsieur, this little saint has worked exactly four days out of five weeks. The child lives in the streets the rest of the time and is completely uncivilized . . . a liar and a cheat, and if you start with her, she'll chew you up and spit you out."

"Nonsense! She's only a child. How old are you, mademoiselle?" asked Degas.

"I am ten, Monsieur." I could lie so easily.

"Well, here are ten francs to feed your family, one franc for each of your years."

How stupid I was. I should have said I was twenty.

"You see . . . what did I tell you? She's an inveterate liar, Monsieur. She is twelve and has no brothers or sisters or father, a bastard for sure . . . and as for selling herself, even the pimps wouldn't put up with her. You've been taken, Monsieur, taken by this demon who passes as a child." He rubbed his groin.

"Is it true what he said?" Degas questioned me angrily.

"Look at her eyes, how shifty she is. Look at her eyes, Monsieur. She grins at you even now like a devil."

Degas stared but I turned and fled like the wind dashing along the tortuous path of the Butte with the ten francs of Degas and the one franc of Jacques in my pocket. I went a distance to the rue Clauzel where an artist's colour shop had opened two years before by a little man we all called Père Tanguy, and stared at its blue front.

When I entered the shop, Tanguy smiled at me. How very nice he was. I could easily fool him. I bought a new pad of sketching paper, my first pieces of red chalk and a wondrous box of pastels. Each pastel was like a jewel to me, and he wrapped each one in a magic tissue, and lay them in a wooden box which smelled delicious. I couldn't wait to use them.

"They are the best pastels in Montmartre, mademoiselle . . . I don't always carry them," smiled Père Tanguy. "But, mademoiselle, it's a wonder that you're not in school."

"Oh, I'm much older than I appear, Monsieur," I said. "I look twelve but I'm really eighteen and am a famous artist with a studio in Montmartre. My name is Marie-Clémentine Valadon. Surely you've heard of me."

"Oh, of course, mademoiselle . . . I'm sure all of Paris has heard of you." He believed me. I was so very clever.

"Well you can find me daily at la Nouvelle-Athènes with the

other artists . . . in fact I just sat at a table with Monsieur Degas, the famous artist, and had a glass of wine and he spoke . . ."

"Certainly, he spoke of your greatness," laughed Tanguy.

"*Exactement!*" What a fool this man was.

But Tanguy smiled, wrapped up my purchases and muttered to himself, "A little devil, to be sure."

And I returned to my home and drew a cat and a dog with the new red crayon, and several days later I gave Maman a nude pastel drawing of myself as a Christmas gift and she slapped me, "Have you nothing better to do but to take off your clothes and parade yourself? It's the devil in you that makes you do this," and she crossed herself with a grimy hand.

"I'll never, never, show you my drawings again!" I screamed.

But I did again and again, and there were interminable drawings of chickens and dogs and even naked people. And then I offered these scribblings to my mother who saw them as the work of idle hands and then drank half a bottle of brandy.

The years followed swiftly, one after another, and by my sixteenth birthday it amazed me when an artist described me as a headstrong lively creature, a wild gamine of the streets of Montmartre, with a saucy look, full ripe figure, sapphire blue eyes fringed with heavy lashes, and sun streaked reddish brown hair, a real beauty. Is that what I was like? It amazed me that he took notice of me. And I gazed at my reflection in a three way mirror, turning my head this way and that, marveling at the arrogance and defiance in my face, and was struck by my appearance. It was a sudden revelation. Yes, I thought, It's true. I am a beauty. But I stood motionless and looked into the glass with mixed feelings. Could I use my striking appearance in some way?

The big top of a circus erected by Fernando rose high near my home. I envisioned myself flying through the air on a trapeze as a circus acrobat, my supple body gracing the big tent. Sometime later I joined the Cirque Molier. But after a month my glory ended. I fell from the trapeze hurting my back badly. Fernando refused to take me back.

And then, by chance, a neighbor, a model, changed my life.

A thrill went through me, a glorious feeling I wanted to hold and recapture forever. It became one of my crystal moments, a moment of elation and perfection and a turning point. It was a taste of glory to forever savor in other moments of disenchantment. This was such a moment. Something miraculous was about to unfold forever. I was instructed to go to the fountain of the Place Pigalle and I quivered with anticipation. I had watched the models thronging about the fountain and now I would be one of them. If I had to pose in the nude it concerned me little. I only felt how very marvelous it all was. How very marvelous. I hugged myself in joy and the world opened before me.

* * *

It was delicious in the sparkling sunlight at the Place Pigalle when *The Marché aux Modèles* was held on Sundays beside the fountain. It was a loud and hectic market which was further complicated by the horse-drawn trams of the La Villette-Trocadéro line which added to the din. We arrived in the morning and waited beside the fountain for the painters to appear and choose, and the whole proceeding filled me with awe and excitement. It was a parade where one displayed her wares and now I knew I could match the best of them. And after my first sitting for a minor artist I said to myself, "This is it!" over and over again. I didn't understand why it was so important to me but I knew that I was somewhere at last.

That Sunday morning I stood with my neighbor, a tall voluptuous blond Amazon dubbed *la grosse* Adèle who became my immediate friend assuming a proprietary interest. "You had better learn the ropes, Marie, or they'll all take advantage of you; how lucky you are you have me. What did the last one pay?"

"Five francs."

"They cheated you. Don't let them pay you less than ten francs, and don't sit more than four hours. When you get more experienced you can ask for more. You'll make more if the artist is well known. Don't sit for a pig like my last one for five francs for a whole day's work and tried to put his cock in besides."

"Oh Adèle, *Dieu*, and did he?"

"I told him that I'm not a peasant from the country or one of those Italian whores coming over who will sit for five francs and sleep with you for a week. I'm a Parisian and this is 1882, not 1842. What did he take me for anyway? And then I spat in his face and walked out . . . the filthy pig. Oh you have to know the score. He would have fucked me if I stayed another minute."

"You're such a marvelous business woman, Adèle."

"Well the next artist was worse than that . . . the studio was so cold that I asked for more coal for the stove and he ignored me, so there I stood naked as you please with goose bumps all over my body, the swine, and then he began to take off his pants and I saw his cock standing straight out at attention staring at me and it was turning blue from the cold. Marie, I nearly died it was so funny. I never saw such a little one in all my life. That's when I grabbed my clothes and my five francs and ran out."

We giggled deliciously, embracing one another.

"Adèle, please tell me. Did you ever do it? I'll keep it as a bosom secret, I swear it. Oh, tell me, Adèle. I'm your best friend."

"Not yet, but once, almost. When it was time, it collapsed . . . that thing collapsed . . . he got nervous because I'm a virgin."

"It collapsed? Oh, Adèle, I don't believe you."

"But Marie, I haven't told you about my mad sculptor yet."

"Tell me Adèle, please tell me. A sculptor . . . it's so exciting."

"Well, he can't sculpt to save his life, I can tell you that. His name is Rodin and all he thinks about are sex and women. He's an old lecher, and over forty, at least."

"But Adèle, you're so lucky to sit for a sculptor."

"Well, he's really disgusting. This *fou* Rodin kneads my flesh all over before he models his damn clay, like I'm a piece of dough. I have black and blue marks all over my body. But I can tell you that when his damn hands squeezed my breasts for five minutes, I pushed him away, make no mistake. The models say he's crazy for women, the dirty old bastard."

"How simply dreadful. If he touched my body, I'd kick him in the balls. I'd kick him so hard that he'd never *foutre* anyone again. Nobody will get the best of me unless I want him to."

"Don't brag Marie. Anyway, it's worse than that. Before he sketches me, he has me walk around without a stitch on, so he can look at me from every angle. I told him that he should get a damn Italian model who will do anything for five francs. And anyway, I heard he made two models pregnant, the bastard."

"I can see, Adèle, his cock will get into you for sure."

"Never! I would never stoop to that."

"Stop putting on airs with me Adèle as though you're the Virgin Mary. If I like it, I'm going to sleep with every man in Paris."

"Of course your great friend, Céline, that whore, is giving you some of her wonderful ideas . . . that . . . that *putain.*"

"Well, that *putain,* my dear friend is modeling for a gigantic statue for America about their liberty . . . about to be sent over."

"*Tant pis!* So much the worse for America . . . who cares . . . just leave some men for me anyway, Marie."

We both squealed with delight.

"Well, I think that seventeen is quite old," I said. "My friend Babette did it at thirteen, took off her chemise and everything for Guichet, the sailor, and she had a baby."

"Take care that Guichet doesn't make you pregnant like your friend. He's already pulled the culotte off every girl in Montmartre. I can see you now with a big belly, then what will you do? I bet your mother will beat you good and proper."

"Oh Maman . . . who cares." I dismissed her with my hand. And anyway Adele, I'll just throw the baby away. I'm not going to ever care about anything."

"You won't ever even care about your child?"

"Of course not. My child will have to take care of itself."

"Oh how you like to shock. I know that you're not that heartless, Marie. You fool others but not me."

"Really? Do you want me to grow old like my mother? I just want to enjoy life. How marvelous this modeling is and how wonderful you're my friend." I kissed Adèle on the cheek. "Don't you feel just marvelous, don't you feel it?"

"All I feel is hungry."

"I'm not afraid of anything, Adèle . . . even making love . . . oh Adèle, look at that handsome one. I've seen him before. Isn't he an artist? Oh look, Adèle, he's that artist, Renoir."

"He's an old man." Adèle grimaced.

"He doesn't look so old."

"Well he's at least forty."

"I suppose that's old but I've always loved him and he's so handsome. Look at how friendly he is and how he laughs so easily. Oh, Adèle, how he makes me tingle."

"You are *fou*, Marie. You don't even know him and you already love him."

"Well I do so love him, yes, I do, Adèle . . . I just love him. Is he still standing there . . . I'm afraid to look . . . it's just too, too unbearable. Perhaps he'll be my first." I whispered.

"Well he can't be because he's gone home, my dear friend."

"*Merde!*"

One day, Adèle took me for lunch to the little restaurant, *"La Mère Bataille"* in the rue des Abbesses, where the painters were squeezed shoulder to shoulder. There were writers and business men in black derbies and young artists still in their smocks with wet canvases tied to their easels. *Dieu*, so much wine was consumed, all sorts of wines and absinthe . . . how the artists loved that absinthe. Sipping absinthe at the "green hour" was quite exciting. And afterwards, we stood again at the fountain and waited to be selected by an artist.

"I could always model for Cormon, that worm, and those students at the *atelier* think they know all about art. If I were one of them, I would show them a thing or two," I said.

"And what are you going to show them?"

"Why, how to draw, of course."

"Of course, you're the great artist, Marie-Clémentine."

"Well, I will be, you'll see. You're the only one I've told this to because you're my bosom friend, Adèle, so don't breathe a word."

"I don't know how you've time for drawing when all you think about is men. Look at that old one over there. Ha! Ha! He won't get me this time, the old goat."

"What?"

"I posed for him . . . he's greedy, that one. He's doing a big ridiculous mural with all kinds of gods and goddesses."

"*Dieu*, he swings his hips like a woman, that's for sure."

"Rich men all walk like that."

"Oh, Adèle, he's *pede*. You don't know anything about life."

"Who cares what he is. You should pose for him, Marie. His

name is Puvis de Chavannes and he's a well known artist, but you have to walk six miles to his studio in Neuilly and . . ."

"I'll never walk six miles to anyone's studio, rest assured."

"Don't be silly, Marie. He's rich, and you'll make money and maybe be his sweetheart, and he'll buy you things like a new gown. And he has a beautiful apartment, all gold and white in Rue Pigalle. Oh, Monsieur de Chavannes," she called out. "I want you to meet the most sought after model in Paris, the great Marie-Clémentine, who sat for royalty and the Premier of France. She wants to pose for the thousand figures in your mural."

"*Merde*, Adèle, what's wrong with you!"

"*Vraiment*," said Puvis, coming over to us. Puvis was tall, bearded, had a distinguished air and Adèle said he never forgot a slight. He smoothed his morning coat and dusted his white spats with his glove.

"Isn't she beautiful, Monsieur de Chavannes?"

Puvis stood dissecting me. He made me squirm. He held one hand under my chin, lifted my face and adjusted his pince-nez.

"A remarkable face," he muttered.

"What do you see, Monsieur, that you stare so?" I asked.

"Beauty, in one word, beauty," he smiled. "Do me the honor of posing for me." He adjusted his expensive bowler.

"I'm so sorry, Monsieur, but I, I have another engagement."

"Well then, some other time," he said graciously, making a graceful gesture with his long fingered hand. "Your name again?"

"Marie-Clémentine."

He said nothing but I watched him walk off into the distance, a tall man, so fussy looking, swinging his hips like a woman.

I modeled for Cormon and his young art students at the *atelier*. I disliked Cormon's ways intensely, a dislike which grew daily but at the *atelier* I received a bonus. I began to glean techniques from the artists' comments, and I would quickly observe the work in progress of each student. And when I relaxed in the intermission of my sitting, I felt something exciting forming deep within me . . . a door was opening. It thrilled me and pushed me forward, and suddenly my drawings changed and they astonished me. I compared the primitive pencil drawings I did as a child, to my drawings now made with a strange new sureness. It was familiar and foreign to me at the same time. I secretly compared my work to the students after modeling stints. I worked in pencil and pastel and felt comfortable in both mediums. Considering the little effort I gave to each work, I was completely amazed at the results, compelled as though my little sketches were an important part of myself . . . as though they were a miracle. Each time I posed at Cormon's, I learned something new which I added to my craft and part of the miracle was that it was all so simple. I was inadvertently drawn into the bohemian life of Montmartre. The thing which I so dreamed of as a child actually happened. I sat with the artists in La Nouvelle-Athènes, and listened to their ranting against the established; and their struggle to survive I knew in my gut was my struggle. I felt one with them.

Spring came and I looked down at the Seine cutting though Paris, dividing it in two. How very wonderful that I could still sit and sketch, my little sketches growing in number and drawn with all the passion I could gather until the very act of touching the paper with my chalk was a kind of muted delirium.

And in the springtime laundresses trudged from peeling doorways carrying baskets of laundry. These poor young women had scrubbed with relentless zeal at their tubs; and I watched older women already bent from standing hour after hour over the dirty laundry of Paris for several franks. It all disgusted me. It was something Maman did but I, Marie-Clémentine would not be a part of it. I wouldn't have my hands reddened and arms covered with scabs from the coarse lye in soapy vats. I just wouldn't sink to this. My poor mother scrubbed until her knuckles bled, and complained about her aching back, but it was all her fault.

Maman sent me to the Rue Pigalle to this Puvis de Chavanne's apartment with a basket of laundered linen she had slaved over. How marvelous to live here in the midst of this wealth, like a castle, just as Adèle had described it, all gilt with glittering chandeliers and with crystals dancing in the setting sun.

He was taller and more broad shouldered than I remembered. He was also carefully dressed as usual, and I liked his beard which gave him a rather dignified look. Was he really 57 as Adèle said he was? How old! I wondered whether he had a mistress. The men like to *foutre* at any age.

"*Merde*," I said breathlessly. "How marvelous it must be to live here." I put down my basket of laundry. "My mother sent this back."

"Your mother?"

"Yes . . . Madeleine Valadon."

"You are the model I saw at the Place Pigalle. I don't want to offend you, Mademoiselle, but there's no resemblance . . ."

"You don't offend me. Maman is a hag."

"Why do you stand and wait?"

"I've decided, Monsieur, to pose for you."

"And suppose I've changed my mind?"

"Then I'll leave. I have other sittings."

"My word, aren't you an independent one. But won't your mother be worried?"

"It doesn't matter. She won't know the difference by eight o'clock this evening."

"I don't understand."

"She'll be dead drunk by that hour, I assure you."

"Well you can stay the night and I'll have my cook prepare the dinner."

"I want you to know, Monsieur, that I'm not walking to Neuilly and my monthly came heavy today so I'll have to be draped."

"*Alors*, we'll take a carriage to Neuilly. Are you going to dictate all the terms of these sittings, Marie? It is Marie, isn't it? What other instructions are there?" he said raising his eyebrow.

"I'll let you know when it's time."

"And suppose I don't agree?"

"That's up to you, Monsieur. But I won't suffer anywhere."

"Don't go too far, Marie. Artists are an impatient lot and there are plenty of models."

"If you say so, Monsieur. But I'm not a usual one."

"I would agree."

I stayed with Puvis for about six months and Maman wailed over my ruin. When I visited intermittently I saw her in a semi-stupor, and she sat staring vacantly into space. Empty bottles of brandy were scattered about, and what she didn't swallow trickled down in a dark stream from the corner of her mouth onto her chin and neck. I could imagine her cursing her life each evening in her drunken state. It was nothing new.

Puvis took me daily by coach to his studio in Neuilly and sometimes we returned to Montmartre.

The studio seemed like a great barn to me where the wind swept through every opening. I thought of what Adèle said about standing with goose bumps over her body. The room was lit by several huge windows; there was a table with a basin, several old couches and a gigantic coal stove heated the room. Puvis' unfinished work took up a good part of one wall and his huge paintings of gods and goddesses, another.

I stood nude on the model's platform while Puvis finished his Calliope and then draped myself as he began another nymph. And I watched him paint fascinated by his prissiness. I couldn't bear it that not one drop of paint dirtied his hands and that he handled his brush with such delicacy.

And in the course of my modeling, he took me to bed and made love to me. And what a fool I was to have given in to that old goat. But I remembered long afterward that Puvis was gentle and considerate and surprised at my virginity. There was a dark red stain on the fine linen which Puvis, thank heaven, gave to a laundress other than Maman. I relaxed after a few days without pain. He certainly knew all the tricks as a lover, was sensual and tender and called me his voluptuous one. He was a marvelous teacher and I a willing pupil, and in spite of deriding him to Adèle, I found myself feeling pleasure giving in to him. *Mon Dieu*, I felt a kind of initiation which came over me like a fever. And I wasn't in love with him, something I knew from the outset. But one afternoon after making love, I foolishly believed I could confide in him. He scarcely understood.

"I'm going to confess something to you, Monsieur Puvis. I draw in secret but would like to be an artist someday."

"I think your talents are elsewhere," he smiled, kissing my nipple.

"Where do you think they are . . . between my legs?"

"I'll ignore your lack of delicacy, Marie. You can marry, a man with money perhaps, and have children. What more would you want?"

"Is that my life then, in your eyes?"

"Isn't that enough?"

"No, Monsieur Puvis, it's not. I want more."

"As long as you have your beauty, Marie, you really have nothing to worry about. I don't understand you."

"But can I always be young, Monsieur Puvis?"

"Everyone grows old, Marie, even I."

"Then what will be left for me? I'm not ordinary. I'll marry when I choose or never."

"Oh, nonsense. What's wrong with being someone's wife?"

"Nothing."

"Well then, it's a woman's lot . . . if she's lucky. And if she's fortunate he'll have a bit of money."

"How dreadful your ideas of women are . . . we are nothing."

"Marie, it's not good for young women to question so much; they lose their beauty . . . they frown and lines mar their faces. Be happy with your life."

"Do you know what I think, Monsieur Puvis? I think that women are thought of very badly by men. I'll make up my own rules and do what I want and I'll live as a free woman."

"A free woman? What in the world is that? You'll wind up in terrible trouble if you don't behave yourself, Marie. I'm speaking like a father. You think too much and it's very unladylike, and you deem yourself someone special, which, I'm sorry to say, you're not." His voice softened. "Don't you want to be a proper young lady? You'll marry someone who will take care of you. What do you say to that?"

"If I so choose to do. And if I choose to be a whore, that's my own decision."

"You're to speak like a proper female while you're in my bed!"

"I will speak as I choose."

He frowned and turned his back to me.

So I lay in bed with him and his flesh felt old, and I wondered if he was embarrassed by the firmness of my body in contrast to his own. I became increasingly annoyed by his phlegmatic nature and even prodded him in various ways to arouse his jealousy. Nothing worked. And then suddenly my work was over. He instructed me coldly that I simply had to return home.

"So this was only a business deal?"

"What did you think it was?"

I flung an expensive vase across the room. It shattered against the wall.

He flushed in anger, "You can break anything you please but just be careful I don't deduct it from your final wages!" His voice softened. "I assure you, Marie, I've thought about it . . . but a lasting liaison is impossible."

"How can you be so cold?"

"I'm not cold, just practical . . . a convenience, nothing more. You'll be generously compensated. Didn't you want that? Did you think you were the first?"

"You were the first for me!"

For the first time I saw him wince. "I have never forced you to do anything. It was all of your own choosing. It's a woman's responsibility to protect her virtue." He whispered the last word.

"I hate you, I hate you . . . with your perfect ways. Adèle was right to leave." I lay on the bed and pretended to weep.

"Save your tears and tantrums for another. They won't work."

I lay still on the elegant sheets. My mind whirled. This was not the way I imagined it would be. But in the space of a few months, I had gotten a taste of luxury, attending well known bistros, strolling with Puvis on the Boulevard and eating dinners in expensive restaurants. How proud I was that Puvis was so important. I could never be with an ordinary man. Perhaps it's because . . . because . . . I'm going to be a great artist in spite of what Puvis thinks.

But how beautiful the clothes were that he had made for me at the end. How marvelous to be rich. A seamstress made me a princesse styled dress with a train in gold and pink silk with a matching bonnet, and I looked into the glass and marveled at the amber lights in my hair. What an old woman he was as he fussed over the material rejecting the fashionable satin as too mature for me. And the new lace edged chemises from a quality lingerie shop sent little quivers up and down my spine. I would always feel the exquisite softness of the green velvet cape when I buried my face in it. But when we visited the cafés where artists thronged, I loved it best of all. It was the familiar feeling from my childhood. I was fascinated by their arguments, the bohemian atmosphere and the names and curses and insults about paintings bandied about.

But it was there, in La Nouvelle-Athènes restaurant, that he brought me to a table where artists were engaged in a heated discussion; it was there he shouted above the din to someone who looked up at me curiously. "I want you to meet my friend, a handsome gentleman artist who needs a model for, what is it? I'll never remember the name of your damn painting, Renoir." The introduction by Puvis certainly was a way to rid himself of me. I didn't care. I looked up at Renoir still with the eyes of that child of ten. I shivered.

* * *

I knew that Renoir was an Impressionist and that he was born in Limoges, as was Maman. He was the son of a poor tailor. In this our backgrounds were similar. Renoir was a good looking dashing figure with a jovial manner, a snub nose, curly black hair under an old felt cap who loved boating parties on the river and dancing at the Moulin de la Galette . . . an endless miracle.

I was still seventeen when I posed for his painting, *The Dance at Bougival*, in the arms of his brother in rue d'Orchampt. I felt a passion for him unlike anything I had ever felt for Puvis. And now I could feel the difference and it was a marvelous difference. I found myself in love with someone for the first time. Renoir would paint me in the nude in a shed he used as a studio. He was always tender, but it seemed like a dream, for in truth it was a fantasy. My moments on Renoir's arm, proudly watching the *midinettes* envying me with this charming, light hearted escort; our dancing at the Moulin de la Galette, and my mounting passion in his arms, were all part of that fantasy. Montmartre, to me was a home for lovers. I knew about Aline Charigot whom he had met the year before, a model for his painting "*Le Dejeu-*

nier des Chanotiers." I knew that he promised to marry her, but I held fast with a sinking feeling. I held fast. But it wasn't enough.

"I have always loved you," I said one afternoon in his studio, and I kissed his handsome face as he ran his hands over my full breasts and kissed them each in turn. "I have always loved you ever since I was a little girl when I saw you . . . and you don't even remember." But he avoided my eyes and I felt the inevitable approaching. And as if to confirm it *she* appeared that afternoon, there at the door and then in the room, a young woman whom I felt was quite plain looking. Of course this Aline was checking up on her prize, and her prize was Renoir. How could he love her? Certainly I was more beautiful and far more interesting and talented. Why she looked like a peasant with those almond eyes and snub nose and already quite plump. Couldn't he see it? *Dieu*, what self assurance she had! It was chilling.

"I don't want to disturb this pretty scene," she hissed out.

I put an arm possessively about him.

"*Mon Dieu*, so it's like that now, is it?" Aline said smiling. Her arms were folded smugly before her bosom. She thought a good deal of herself. I could see that. How annoying she was.

There were flickering scenes which now passed through my mind about what followed. There was Aline with a deadly calm manner, "I'm special, you know, because he's marrying *me*." There was Aline who turned to the painting, *The Dance at Bougival* still unfinished on the easel, and smeared the face on it. And I responded, "Why you bitch!" And to Renoir, who seemed utterly helpless, "Are you going to marry this witch? She'll never give you a moment's peace. She'll choose your models, ruin your paintings, and beat your children, and scream night and day!"

Frankly, it was all hopeless. She smiled, a confident, mocking smile and Renoir began to laugh. I forgave him.

Undoubtedly, I couldn't break his prearranged pact with her, and I drew myself to my full height, collected my things, and tasted ashes in my mouth, all the while blaming myself. I was disappointed in him and I felt used and betrayed. I promised myself I would never model for him again, a promise I broke, time and time again.

I turned to him and said quietly, "If you want me to pose, you know where to find me."

He half nodded. This witch held the door open for me.

"Whore!" I said low as I passed her.

But Aline continued to smile, the smile of complete victory.

There are some awful moments in one's life one never forgets. When I passed Aline Charigot standing so smugly in the doorway, I left with a feeling of indescribable emptiness. Renoir called me back several weeks later to complete a section of the *Dance at Bougival*. Aline stood by observing the whole modeling session suspiciously. My dislike for her grew in intensity and I knew it would last for a lifetime.

When Renoir finished the painting, I gathered my things and glanced at the *Dance at Bougival* for a brief moment before I left. Renoir had repainted the face Aline had not succeeded in destroying. The face was still mine and in this alone, I had won but the fantasy had dissolved. I arrived back at the tiny apartment sobbed for a few moments and then stopped myself. I finished a drawing and the terrible emptiness lingered.

If Miguel Utrillo was sent to erase the hurt that my affair with Renoir had caused, he possibly replaced the pain with something far more significant. It was to last my entire life.

And it happened at the Chat Noir, a cabaret with a huge open fireplace and blackened ceiling beams from which hung copper cooking utensils and all sorts of armor. In a room in the rear, personages like Guy de Maupassant read their stories aloud; and Miguel Utrillo gave a two hour lecture on the Bal del Ciri, dressed romantically in a velvet jacket and broad-brimmed hat of the Montmartrois.

I didn't want him. I decided that I would not give in to the temptation of loving him. The last thing I wanted was another love affair. Was this to be my life . . . a series of amours making their entrances and exits? I began to crave a permanent liaison. I certainly didn't want Miguel. But Miguel was the François Villon of my childhood. This time I felt that if I let myself love, I would be crushed. And of course, I gave in. Of course I loved. I concluded that this was to be my curse. How can one resist it? How can one resist that marvelous excitement which shimmers and swells between lovers? And being a free woman, as I called myself, I could not. And so I repeated my mistake in loving.

We danced at the Moulin de La Galette that spring. We dined together beneath the arbors of the Guingette and walked arm in arm as I had foolishly done with Renoir on the Boulevard Montmartre. And we played and fought like children, reconciling in lovemaking with a ferocity that shook me; he, with his dark curling hair and brilliant piercing eyes. Let the heavens descend. I didn't care. It was the *joi de vivre* as our bodies mingled and we rolled in the fields at the top of the Butte that unseasonably warm day in late March.

And to go from Renoir to Miguel Utrillo was madness itself. To have this succession of lovers was madness itself. To experience the whole gamut of passion from the love for Renoir which stemmed from my childhood a slow constant now hopeless flame which I knew could linger for a lifetime; to the erratic, intense bursts of passion which simmered and flashed with little constancy between Miguel and myself, seemed indeed a grand futility. It was all sown with the seeds of familiar pain which I would surely feel at the end of the affair.

And I paid. The affair never really ended.

It was in late April of 1883 that I told Adèle, "I think I'm pregnant."

"Perhaps you're wrong."

"No, I'm healthy and regular like a clock. I've definitely missed more than one monthly."

"*Merde*, how many?"

"I'm not sure. What should I do?"

"Perhaps you can lose it? Take a steaming bath . . . it helps. What will your mother say? He should have used a goatskin on his cock . . . they have that now. But it's too late, perhaps . . ."

"Adèle, you're no help. It's no use telling me now what he should have used . . . they only use that with prostitutes for disease. Men want their pleasures, *c'est ça!*"

"Who is the father?"

"I don't know . . . perhaps Renoir, perhaps Puvis, who knows?"

"Perhaps Guichet, the sailor, oh yes, he got into your culotte fast enough, or the waiter at the Nouvelle Athènes."

"Who cares, Adèle, who the father is. I don't want the baby anyway."

"What about Miguel?"

"Forget Miguel."

"Why should you forget him? Miguel should give you money. I thought he was rich. Make Miguel pay for his pleasure."

"I won't take a penny from him."

"You're *fou*, Marie. Why let him get off so easily? What happened between you two? He made you forget your affair with Renoir fast enough. Why did he leave? You're a fool with men, Marie, and think only with your heart. They use you, Puvis, Renoir and now Miguel. I thought you had more sense."

"I want nothing from him." But the fragrance of that early spring, our secret whispers warming the new grasses of the Butte, and the texture of his broad brimmed Montmartrois hat as I smoothed it would always remain a bitter sweet memory.

I skipped down the winding streets of Montmartre in an attempt to miscarry, much to the amazement of onlookers; and in the autumn, my belly was noticeably enlarged. Maman stared at me one afternoon, her eyes widening in horror, and she screamed, "Madame Pinchot told me you were having a baby, and I didn't see it . . . your Maman didn't see it. She said you slept with this Miguel in a room near the Moulin de la Galette, and now I'm ashamed to show my face."

"Did she tell you that I spotted her dear husband, Pinchot, there with a prostitute? By all means tell her, she'll love that."

"What difference does it make? Now she knows you're a slut. And I never even realized it . . . I don't understand."

"How could you notice anything when you're always drunk?"

"The whole Butte must be talking about it . . . and your affairs," she droned on, over and over again . . . and then, "Slut, *putain*, harlot, look at your belly! Everyone is laughing at me." Her tears made tracks through the grime on her neck.

"And who were you, the Virgin Mary?"

"God will forgive you. I've heard so much talk . . . these artists, Puvis de Chavannes and Renoir. Tell Puvis. He has money and can help us . . . he's not too old to have a child . . . please, Marie. God in heaven . . . then tell Miguel and he'll help us."

Her voice fell to a funny squeak. She dropped into a chair, wiped her eyes with the edge of her soiled apron, grabbed her flask from beneath her petticoat and wailed in her special brandy voice . . . and her breath sprayed the air of the small apartment, and the spray climbed its walls, and I wished Maman would drown in the amber liquid.

* * *

It seemed so long ago, and the present flooded the tiny room when my mother returned with tiny Maurice, and she strutted with a new pride. *"Mon petit pauvre,"* my mother cooed. "No one loves you but your Grand-mère, you're so beautiful, aren't you my little Maumau. Yes, I'm going to always call you Maumau. You know your mother is so cruel to you . . . all she does is draw her silly pictures." Maman bent down and kissed the tiny arms and legs.

"Well, just don't guzzle your brandy around him and I think that Maumau is such a silly name."

"You'll get used to it. Won't she, *mon petit*?" and Maman picked up the infant, cradled him in her arms, and softly sang a lullaby from her former Limousin countryside.

I was unaccustomed to seeing my mother in this maternal role. I remembered very little of being embraced by her, little of any affection at all. It was all so strange.

"And who is your papa, Maumau?" she cooed again.

"Let him be. Why do you bother him? It's absurd."

"Perhaps Maumau's real father will give him his name?"

"I told you that I don't much care who his father was. I wish he had never been born."

"Watch what you say for God will strike you down for not baptizing him."

"You fear God, I do not. I make my own life."

Maman crossed herself. "A model standing naked before a man, that's what you do. It's indecent and the work of the devil."

"Oh stop listening Maman to all that damn gossip about what goes on with artists, and of course coming from that hag Pinchot. Can't you see that with the money I can make as a model, perhaps we can move?" But talking to her was hopeless.

"A model becomes a prostitute, clear and simple."

"*Merde*, my money lets you stop scrubbing floors!" I shouted.

She didn't listen. "Well someone has to care for little Maumau, yes *mon petit*, you know already who loves you . . . I can see it in your eyes . . . such beautiful eyes, dark eyes, like . . . " she mumbled something and then looked up at me.

The infant began to cry, a low muffled sound.

"That's what comes from talking such gibberish to him. He has more sense than you have." I said sharply. And I took the infant to nurse. Afterward, I leaned back. Little Maurice lay content at my breast. I felt strangely at peace.

April had begun and a fresh fragrant new spring had painted Paris with the sun drenched green wash of the impressionists, and I watched little Maurice in the pram stare back at the budding sycamores, and I found myself laughing at how the infant drank in his passing world. Was I like that? What was he thinking? He really had such sad, soulful dark eyes. I bent down and kissed them and he looked up at me. Frankly, I felt a certain pride for the first time. He had survived. Certainly I thought that the infant would have died from it all, but he remained hardy from his winter airing, always returning with his grandmother, their faces whipped crimson from the biting winds.

I sketched the odd windows of the houses across the way with their dark green louvered shutters, the paint cracked and peeling, some shutters broken and gone completely. And slowly my hands craved to sketch little Maurice, his dark eyes glowing after his airing. It seemed so natural to render my child on paper in broad precise strokes of my pencil.

But he's really a pretty little thing . . . oh, no doubt his father would be proud to have such a handsome son, but then the father could have been anyone. I had modeled for Renoir even after our breakup, even after Aline had returned . . . and then the lovemaking . . . what a fool I was to give in to him after he used me so, but I loved him . . . and Puvis, modeling for his preliminary sketches for *St. Genevieve,* and on how many occasions did I . . . but Puvis is surely too old. Puvis? I would rather Guichet, the sailor, than Puvis. *Tant pis!* So much the worse. And of course, there's Miguel. I knew in my heart who the father was.

Maman returned with Maurice and resumed her cooing.

"Little Maumau, my beautiful little Maumau . . . *mon chéri,* you're hungry, aren't you . . . so your mother will feed you, yes, she will." She lifted the infant from the carriage. "Here, *mon vieux,* here's your dinner."

She handed the infant to me who was crying lustily for his meal and once again, I took a breast swollen with milk from my bodice and the infant grabbed for a nipple. "Oh how terribly he bites . . . my nipples are sore," and I looked at Maurice sucking happily, famished from his airing. He stared at me with huge dark eyes and continued to suck my nipple hungrily, and a glimmer, just a faint glimmer of some feeling for the infant passed over me. The little one was so dependent on me, it both frightened and irritated me. My life must be wholly mine without reservations to draw as I wanted, to take a thousand lovers if I wanted and not be burdened with this fruit of several moments of pleasure. The nipple slid from his tiny mouth, and he began to gurgle contentedly.

"He purrs like a kitten," I said and without thinking reached out and patted his full dark head of curls.

"You're beginning to like him a little, *hein?* " my mother said. "He's so beautiful. Look, Marie. His eyes are dark like . . ."

"Be still Maman. Oh, he'll do as babies go . . . all the same."

"Oh, I can see who the father is with half an eye . . . anyone can see it, Marie. Why do you deny it? Go to Miguel and get money from him. Why can't you let him help us?" My mother's voice drifted off into a gurgle as she reached under her apron and poured the amber liquid down her throat.

Go to Miguel . . . Miguel Utrillo. Miguel Utrillo, the Catalan. I repeated his name over and over again until the words grew meaningless, yet they still clamored for recognition. Miguel. The baby's eyes were Miguel's as though the fathers eyes were painted on the child. But even if I dismissed Miguel, the bitter aftermath would still be there.

The small amount that I earned modeling now provided for my small son and my mother. I sat still and reflected as I sketched. After the incident at Cormon's *Atelier* when I walked out to nurse little Maurice, I began to sit clothed for a Venetian Impressionist Zandomeneghi who told me of a large apartment on rue Tourlaque on the first floor. It was an exciting prospect, a building chock full of painters. Gauzi, from Toulouse, was on the third floor and was to be joined by a friend named Lautrec from the same province, and it was rumored that this Lautrec was a count. *Dieu*, wasn't he the midget I saw at Cormon's *Atelier*? And there were the other artists in the building . . . what a pity I was saddled with this miserable infant. Would I never be free? And as if in answer, my breasts ached with the fullness of the nursings. *Merde!*

The following day I visited Puvis' apartment in Place Pigalle. Puvis was more than receptive. I think he was afraid this was his own child, for he offered to pay the rent for the new place as long as was necessary. I offered to pose for him in return without payment and he refused. "This is a gift," he said in his matter-of-fact usual tone. "Get on your feet, child, for now." He pressed several hundred francs into my hand. I kissed him, a sweet innocent grateful kiss, that of a dutiful daughter. He seemed pleased but never questioned the paternity of the infant and never offered his name to the bastard.

When Maman, the baby and I were safely installed at No. 7 rue Tourlaque, I roamed through the three rooms, delighted. The new space for the family was a breath of freedom. My mother took one room with the cradle by her bed, I, another. The third room was used as a parlor and rudimentary studio.

I never thought I would take money from Puvis, no matter I had to live. I could be lofty minded if I were rich, but I'm too poor for great morality and I must do what I must. But I'll make the man wear an India-rubber next time. Adèle says it's the rage and I'll have a whole world of lovers to choose from and I have my drawing as well.

The year, 1884 swiftly drew to a close. With the new year, my Maurice, my pretty, plump infant began to take his first steps.

My nursings became fewer and he waddled through the rooms always followed and smothered by Maman. Was this really my Maman, with her missing teeth and gnarled hands, my Maman who never gave me one crumb of the love she poured on her Maumau?

In that early spring of 1885, in the kind of spring in which I met Miguel Utrillo, Adèle informed me that Miguel was about to leave Paris. How could the lover who helped me forget the hurt from the breakup of my love affair with Renoir cause me so much pain? It was two years since I first met him. He left knowing I was pregnant and when he returned, I refused to see him. And now, with the news of his leaving Paris for good, unexpectedly, I felt a sense of loss. It was as though my girlhood had ended. He persisted, through Adèle, in asking me to meet him one last time. Why not? I would show him I didn't care. We arranged to meet and returned to his room near the Moulin de la Galette where it all began. The room seemed smaller and cramped. But I caught my breath when I entered. The bittersweet memories came on strong, nostalgic and painful. I remembered my first glimpse of Miguel the only son of a prosperous Barcelona family, who had studied art at La Llonja. While painting, he changed to architecture, then to engineering. This brought him to Paris where he stayed in this room. But now his voice cut sharply through these memories.

"My studies are completed at the Institute and I'm going to Bulgaria." he said as we sat down on the bed and I tried very hard to show my indifference.

"Bulgaria? Where in the world is that?"

"It's not Paris, Maria. Won't you miss me a little?"

"Do you have to go?"

"I must, but I may return in a few years, who knows? I have the promise of a position as director of a mining construction company. So who knows when I'll be back to Paris. But I'll be back, Maria, wait for me."

"Wait for you? I assure you, Monsieur Miguel, I'm not waiting for anyone, least of all, *you*."

"You never forget or forgive. What I did I couldn't help, but now I would marry you if I thought the child was mine."

"How very generous of you. I never said Maurice was yours. How very magnanimous of you. Please don't give me charity. I don't need your help and can manage by myself very well."

"You're maddening with your impossible answers but I'll never forget you, my petite Maria . . . now about the baby."

"Why do you keep mentioning the baby?"

"You never speak of it as mine. Is it mine? Now it bothers me that Maurice could be my son, and you're so casual about it. Don't you care if it's mine? I just don't understand you but there's something you're hiding, isn't there? There's something else that's important to you, isn't there, isn't there . . . come tell me."

"Of course there is. It's my drawing."

"I don't understand. Drawing? What are you talking about? What the devil . . . why can't you be like other women?"

"Because I'm not. Good-bye, Miguel. Have a pleasant journey. And perhaps . . ."

"Perhaps, what?"

"Come back."

"Perhaps . . . frankly, Maria, I don't see that it matters . . ."

I didn't answer.

I regretted his leaving, but modeling and my drawing were now the important things in my life and the proceeds from my modeling, added to the sum which Puvis supplied monthly, kept us all together.

"You'll become a woman of thirty without a husband and with a small child." A thin amber stream dribbled from a corner of Maman's mouth." You should have married Miguel and he would have taken care of us. What happened between the two of you? How can anyone understand you? Why couldn't you have given Maumau a father? That's the least you could have done."

"I won't marry Miguel. He can't give me what I want."

"'You don't know what you want."

"Of course, I do. It's so simple, Maman. I'm becoming an artist. I want the freedom to do my art."

"You're *fou!* An artist . . . an unmarried woman artist . . . an unmarried slut. Why are we cursed? It's the scribbling that's ruined all our lives," It was her usual complaint.

But nothing she could say would shake me, nothing. Something drew me to the life of the artists and it seemed right for me. I felt it would be a life of excitement and enchantment. I just knew it. I heard the words *La vie Boheme* tossed about by the artists and they sent a marvelous shudder through me.

She just can't understand. Maman raves against women artists... particularly the unmarried ones and of course she has all of them condemned to hell fire. But I see it all as glorious. I don't care one fig about what she thinks. She is never going to change my mind, never. How odd that she was thrown into the life of the Montmartre Bohemians. How truly odd. So she lives as a stranger in their midst and drinks from her damn flask. If only Maman knew just one delicious moment of what I feel being among the artists, but she never did.

What is truly amazing to me is that I am her daughter. How can this be? And far more terrible is that I am to be that woman artist she rails against, a corrupted daughter of the wild Bohemians. How is this possible? I am truly to become my mother's nemesis. So much the worse.

My poor Maman.

2

[handwritten: Second Voice]

<u>Henri</u>

The Discovery

*B*eing crippled is just a fact of life I contend with. But I compensate for this affliction in other ways. I cultivate friends the way one garners flowers; and I deem myself an artist, a fledgling artist, but an artist nevertheless. Incidentally, I was born the son of a count. Although I shun using the title, I won't deny that being of nobility has come to my aid on more than one occasion. But, unfortunately in this life, one makes errors. I made a severe one. How could I have divined that fortuitous set of circumstances, our sharing the same house on rue Tourlaque would have brought me close to her? I never dreamed that Marie-Clémentine, the beautiful model who stood before Cormon's students so insolently that afternoon would cast her spell on my twisted body, stealing my innermost thoughts, and permeating my very being so that she held me in a kind of arcane limbo from which I was never freed, never finding resolution.

I only knew that evening late in 1884 as I sat with my group of friends from Cormon's *Atelier* sipping wine at La Nouvelle-Athènes that this Marie was all we spoke of.

"Did you never hear of a woman nursing, Monsieur?" piped Louis Anquetin in a high pitched voice. There was an accompanying roar of laughter.

"How was Marie in bed?" Émile Bernard asked.

"She was a taste of heaven on earth, a voluptuary," Louis answered with a studied casualness, always the ultimate authority on the conquest of women.

"That beauty moved into my building and it's anybody's guess who the father of her bastard is," said Gauzi.

"Take care you're not the father of one of her bastards," and Émile turned to Anquetin imitating Cormon's voice. "Why that bastard might be your finish, Louis!"

I was amused by the ruffle in the calm of Anquetin's equilibrium. "Not me," he protested. "That was years ago."

"I wouldn't go around bragging about my night in heaven with Marie, if I were you," and I adjusted my cane. "She'll make you support her and you'll be cutting meat with your father before long." Louis Anquetin was the son of a prosperous butcher who had a great desire to have Louis follow in his footsteps.

"I'll hang myself first," said Anquetin with characteristic calm.

"I'd pay a thousand francs to see Cormon take his pill again. I'd like to see it before he throws me out," said Émile.

"How much would you wager, Anquetin?" I dug the floor with my cane.

His cool eyes answered me. "I would pay two thousand."

"I would pay ten thousand," I boasted with supreme sophistication and they were duly impressed. They were all aware that I could back up my boast. As I said, there were occasions when I enjoyed my wealthy heritage.

At that moment, Maurice Joyant entered with my roommate, Rachou, and I called out, "Garçon, another round of cognac." A generous allowance bestowed upon me by my doting mother, Comtesse Adèle de Toulouse-Lautrec, conveniently eased the way.

"I wonder who is paying for all these drinks, Anquetin?" asked Émile.

"Not me, I assure you. My money is in tubes of Van Dyke brown," came an expected reply.

There was a hushed silence as all eyes riveted on me.

"Why is it I'm always the one to pay the bill?" I said.

"That's very true," babbled Gauzi, half drunk and slapped

me on the back. "It's very, very true. That's why I brought you to Paris, Count Henri de Toulouse-Lautrec-Monfa. Besides, you must earn that long title if you want to join us in rue Tourlaque."

"That's true," and Anquetin hiccuped.

"Watch out, all of you, that I don't return to Albi and join the hunt with my father who still waits for me there. My father delights in slaughtering foxes, deer and wild duck. He would be overjoyed by my surrender to his wishes. The poor deluded man still imagines me tall and handsome," I stated with bitterness.

My group of friends became very quiet and assessed me with a healthy dose of envy and probably pity. Of course they were aware of my stunted legs, but who among them would not have given his right arm for my heritage?

* * *

I did whimsical mocking drawings from the time I was a schoolboy at Albi in Languedoc, a descendant of the counts of Toulouse, a heritage that could be traced back to Charlemagne. It was a heritage I attempted to forget in Paris. And when I saw that model, Marie, on the staircase of my new studio, I marveled that I had so adjusted to my appearance. I knew of course what she initially saw was my grotesquerie; my absurd height of four and a half feet, my grossly thick lips, my coarse, oily skin, and the two stumps doctors facetiously called legs, upon which I ambulated with a cherry-wood cane. The only feature to commend me was a reasonable pair of eyes behind the pince-nez perched on my bulbous nose. What I saw as I dragged my easel and prepared to make the trek to the fourth floor studio was an incredibly beautiful young woman, more lovely than I remembered in Cormon's *atelier*, which belied her strident personality molded by the gutters of Montmartre.

"It's you," she said. "You were in Cormon's studio."

"Of course you are that marvelous model. I must commend you for standing up to him . . . we all enjoyed it immensely, and so far it's been the delight of my whole stay in Paris, but I've waited for you to come back."

"Your stay in Paris must be very dull. Cormon is a pig, a swine, a filthy swine, whose feet are planted in another century . . . please don't speak of him . . . I loathe him with his prissy manners!" Her face was flushed with anger and her vehemence amused me. "And you'll have a long wait for me to return. I refuse to model for him. I simply refuse." She flushed, a delicious passion crossing her features.

"He's a difficult master, I agree. But I would never want to be disliked by you. That would be quite dangerous."

"You're too kind to him, much too kind. But if I remember, I must say he didn't seem to frighten you, as he did all those poor chickens at their easels. When he's through badgering them there won't be a real artist left in the bunch." Her face altered suddenly into a look of total reproval. It was an amazingly malleable face which registered various emotions simultaneously. "I just hope he doesn't spoil that Bernard fellow."

"No. Unfortunately, I think that Émile's days with Cormon are numbered."

She stood with her hands on her hips, a totally striking figure with high coloring, glistening sapphire blue eyes, and a full voluptuous figure which I knew had been enhanced by the birth of a child. I remembered that lush nude figure standing for several moments at the *atelier*.

"Are you going to live here Monsieur?" Her voice was more melodious than her sharp rebukes to Cormon that day.

"Not live here, work here. I live with a friend at 9 Bis Fontaine."

"Oh, I'm impressed . . . you're so rich to live in two places."

"Yes, I must be rich," I smiled.

"And my friend Adèle who knows everything said you're a count."

I was displeased and didn't answer.

"You needn't make a face. I know what you are . . . and you have lots of money so I'll be good to you . . . Monsieur le Comte."

"What?" I began to laugh. "You're certainly direct, Mademoiselle and do me the favor of not using my title. My name is Henri."

"Henri, then and just call me Marie."

"Well, Marie, you're very beautiful and who knows that sometime you might pose for me . . . yes? I'm not as difficult as Cormon," I laughed.

I began hobbling up the stairs to the fourth floor.

She picked up one of my bundles. "Why did you choose a studio up there?"

"I'll manage. Don't concern yourself with it. I'm quite agile."

"I meant nothing by it, Henri."

"You meant that I'm a cripple, which I am. But I manage as well as anybody." We reached the top floor of the building.

"And this is your studio? How awful. You really must get someone to clean it. My mother knows a *bonne*." She threw open the windows of the hot dusty room.

"It'll be fine. I'm always impressed with a certain amount of disorder."

I cleared a small area in which to work and put down my easel and paints. Marie tried to assist me but when she picked up an object and placed it, I rearranged it. Then I looked upward at the high ceiling, a random act. I wished she would leave.

"You're impossible Henri," she laughed. I didn't answer. "I'm leaving which will probably relieve you. I have a modeling job, but if you need anything . . . anything at all . . . I live on the ground floor with my mother and baby . . . just call on me."

Cursing, several men hoisted up a pianoforte.

"A piano? *Mon Dieu*, do you know I never played on one? You must indeed be rich, Henri, to own one, but then you're a count."

"Mademoiselle . . . please . . ."

The movers stared at me, amused at my height. From repeated practice, I pretended not to notice.

"I'm an artist, Marie, nothing else," I said, my patience wearing thin. "Don't, just don't refer to my background again."

"*Tiens!* Au revoir, Henri. Oh, I forgot to tell you. I love the way you paint your figures."

"Only figures are important . . . nothing else exists . . . artists who paint only landscapes are idiots."

"*Vraiment!* I do only figures, as well."

"What?" My legs started to ache from the climb. What the devil is she talking about? What kind of fantasy does this handful of trouble entertain? Good God, I hope she's not one of those new women who deludes herself into doing everything men do. I rubbed the calf of my right leg. It felt no better. I must tell this one to Rouchou. I smiled at her indulging her maniacal whims and then instructed the men as to where to place the piano. The two laborers strained with the instrument, their bare biceps bulging and I ignored their sly ogling of my stumpy legs.

"Get on with it! Get on with it!" I banged the floor impatiently with my cane. *Dieu merci,* she finally left. This little one has too much to say. How odd. She has a curious equestrienne stride. Has she worked in the circus?

A wonderful idea crossed my mind. When the workmen left, I set up the canvas for a new painting, this one of the circus.

It was a hot July afternoon when we began and the twisted streets of Montmartre shimmered and blistered in the heat. The windows were flung open in my studio and I was finishing a painting. Marie was sprawled on a divan whose cover was patched and stuffing oozed from its seams.

"For the son of a count you have dreadful furniture, Henri."

"It's part of the atmosphere . . . and I told you not to refer to my background. I'll need patience to tolerate you, Marie."

"I'm sorry, Henri, but that's the way it is . . . you're a count, *c'est ça!* I'll say it again." She pouted and spoke without mercy.

"Are you always this maddening, Marie?"

"You'll have to bear it. Do you like the dust of the studio also? It's like the room of a maniac which you are not."

"It's the room of an artist. Degas won't let anyone touch his studio to clean, not even his *bonne,* and neither will I."

"Degas is *fou.* I've decided. I'm sending my mother to clean."

"So *you've* decided? Send nobody! I like it just the way it is." I spoke the last few words very deliberately as I signed my name to my painting of Maman, la Comtesse Adèle.

"Who is that?"

"My mother."

"I see you love your mother, *hein*?"

"You don't love yours?"

"Well, I don't hate her . . . she just drinks too much. She's good to her little Maumau, but not to me. I'm too difficult."

"Who the devil is Maumau?"

"My son, Maurice."

"Well, by that I deduce that it's her little Maumau, and not yours."

"You're far too clever for me, Henri."

I looked at her objectively. "Marie, how would you like to pose for my new circus painting? I could use you."

"It depends. What is it about?"

"The *Circus Fernando* . . . for the equestrienne on the horse."

"I'm posing for Renoir."

"You're posing for Renoir? Then I'm impressed, Marie. What is he working on now?"

"Something called *The Bathers*. I'm a nude figure."

"He probably added pounds to your figure and a big bosom."

"No, but I must admit that I look quite healthy. You certainly know when one is painted by Renoir . . . quite flattering."

"Well, when you're finished posing, find time for me but you'll find that I won't be quite that flattering."

"If I have time . . . I'll have to think about it," she said teasingly.

"I don't like to play games!" Her coyness began to irritate me.

"Why do you want to paint me?"

"Besides the fact that you're beautiful, I love all kinds of reddish hair. Most of the women I paint are redheads although yours is the color or sun-kissed cognac . . . yes, sun-kissed cognac."

She smiled for a moment and touched her hair, then she pouted, "I don't know. I don't like to pose for someone so fussy. I can see how exacting you are and so impatient."

"Do what you like. I'm not sure about *your* skill as a model."

"Why don't you consult Renoir about me? You may be a count but he's an artist."

"I assure you that at Renoir's age I'll be more renowned and a better artist. I won't be glorifying women ad nauseam."

"Well, I see nothing wrong with Renoir's women, dear count."

"They're so goddamn pretty and Degas thinks so too. A whore has more character . . . and I insist that you don't use my title."

"My women are not pretty either. I draw the truth."

What is she talking about? Why this about-face? If she thinks I'm going to dignify her artistic delusions, she's sadly mistaken. Why have women these peculiarities? Am I like Degas? No, I like the feel of women's soft bodies if I can stomach their idiosyncrasies with my mind intact. Is this little one trying to tease or torment me? I thought all this watching her expression.

"Let's make an end to this, Marie. We're not here to discuss Renoir and you can leave if you're displeased. I have painting to do. You'll either sit for me or you'll leave, one or the other. And frankly, you talk gibberish, always trying to be one of the artists, isn't that true?" I said abruptly.

She paused for a moment.

"I'll sit for you, Henri," she said in a voice suddenly dripping with honey. This sudden change of mood made my stomach churn. She had totally ignored what I said.

"But?" I asked suspiciously.

"But what?"

"There must be a condition. What? You must want something. I'll pay you handsomely, as well as Renoir, I assure you."

"I want you to be pleasant. I don't sit for unpleasant artists."

"Does Renoir go through this every time?"

She laughed, a delightful, girlish sweet laugh, her sapphire eyes glistening and she put her hand on my shoulder. Her touch felt like the fragile sweep of butterfly wings.

The months passed, possibly three, or six . . .I couldn't count the number of days or weeks or even months that I waited for her preparing my canvas over and over again for the anticipation of her arrival .Sometimes I thought I heard her knock at the studio door, a dainty knock but there was noone there. I began to look for another model for my circus painting. I still waited for her to appear as my model. She was nowhere in sight. I refused to go to her apartment. I saw her frankly as totally unreliable. That little one will not hoodwink me again. How exasperating. I'll have absolutely nothing more to do with her, when suddenly she made her appearance without much explanation.

"Well?" I asked.

"I await your instructions, Monsieur Henri. Renoir doesn't

need me right now." She stepped backward and curtseyed and her beauty sent a shaft of radiance into dark dusty corners. I rearranged my easel toward the light of dust laden misty windows, cleaned some brushes and selected the paints. She made no further explanation and I said nothing, but my stomach churned. Marie began posing within the hour and her professionalism became quickly apparent. Hours of modeling which fashioned her came to the fore, and she posed easily and skillfully. It was a difficult pose but she knew exactly what I wanted.

Undoubtedly, the woman was a witch! And undoubtedly I would be driven mad.

And I marveled again the following afternoon as she posed as the circus rider on the horse, preparing to jump through a paper hoop. While painting, the atmosphere relaxed and I found that I related all sorts of stories about Malromé. I told her how my father once kept an apartment in Paris, after my parents separated, where he did sculpting and kept bees, rode practically naked on his horse and exhibited other more eccentric behavior. I told her of my friendship with Gauzi from Toulouse who brought me here, of my boyhood schoolmate, Maurice Joyant and of my friend Henri Rouchou with whom I lived. She was a good listener and I was able to become comfortably outspoken and critical of art and various movements. We found that our ages were similar, I was a year older than she but our backgrounds could not have been further apart. And yet I found strange parallels. But her innuendos about drawing continued.

Why is it that everyone feels they can be an artist or writer? And if they have never executed a painting or book, they are sure that the seeds are within them. Everything in her background defied her drawing ability. When she was a child, she claimed a friendly coal-man gave her cinders and she would use these to draw on the pavement in the Place Vintimille. I didn't take any of this seriously and I hoped she would never force her scribbling on me. That equestrienne stride I noticed, came from her employment at the Cirque Moliere, and she related details of her fall. What amazed me, taking into consideration the coyness of women, was her freedom in the description of her liaisons, sexual and professional, as a model and mistress for Puvis de Chavannes, and Renoir. She obviously disliked Chavannes intensely and adored Renoir, but equally dismissed both sexual connections with little shame. She vaguely mentioned someone named Miguel Utrillo, a Catalan, who seemed to have disappeared completely.

Her insouciance baffled and disturbed me. What manner of creature was she? Yet her observations were quite astute.

"Oh, Henri, I love posing for you. Who taught you?"

"An old deaf gentleman named Princeteau, and a cold fish named Bonnat."

"I love the way you almost look through your models. Some artists hardly know the model's character at all. It is as though you're searching for the model's soul to transform into paint.

"Well put. I'm impressed with your insight."

"Perhaps you could . . . " and she caught herself.

"I could what?"

"It's nothing," she said.

"Say what you were going to say. I'll never understand women," I said. "They're always puzzles to figure out, always with deep dark secrets." I took out a bottle of cognac.

"You drink too much, Henri."

"It kills the pain in my legs."

But she never looked at my stumps. It wasn't that she deliberately avoided staring at them. She simply wasn't interested.

This amazed me most of all.

A stream of young artists came into my studio. Louis Anquetin was accompanied by François Gauzi and Émile Bernard.

I fetched a white apron, rolled up my sleeves, and with a felt hat pulled down over my eyes, I busied myself behind a low bar stocked with a variety of bottles. I prepared lemon peel and crushed ice, and juggled a variety of bottles as I made cocktails for my friends. I concocted the most heinous of mixtures and with each creation laughed gleefully and downed it like water. Making assorted concoctions was my love.

And of course, another love was in friendships. My friend Anquetin was about ten inches taller than myself, four years older and resembled Michelangelo. I felt an intense adulation of him, bordering on resentment, for he was all I would have hoped to be; he was handsome, healthy, an excellent athlete, a superb draughtsman, and extremely gifted. He fenced admirably and preferred women above all. He had conquests too numerous to count. And I knew he had slept with Marie.

I handed him a mixture. "My dear big man, drink this . . . it's marvelous." I always tried my concoctions on Anquetin first.

Anquetin sipped and coughed, "This would kill an army! What the devil did you put into it? Where's the absinthe?"

"You don't appreciate my special concoction that's simply superb. Here, Gauzi, have one." Gauzi took the drink, sipped and grimaced. "Your ignorance of wines is appalling, Gauzi. This is the most educated of mixtures."

We sat down on boxes, blew at piles of dust and generally marveled at this hodgepodge of assorted collections. It pleased me that everyone accepted the wild disorder. It was a huge room with paint peeling from the walls and crevices from which drafts blew the dust about the room. At the side was a huge coal stove. Marie escaped to an old divan, its tarnished nailheads half gone and its stuffing escaping from ripped seams. An old armchair was nearby, but its condition was so unsafe, it was left alone, and an empty chest of drawers stood near it. There was a general profusion of newspapers, plaster casts, books, oriental curios, a Japanese wig, a ballet slipper, a shoe with a fantastically high heel, jars with brushes and tubes of brightly colored pigments purchased in protest against Cormon. A nine foot stepladder stood precariously. There was a quantity of indescribable litter which surrounded everything, stools, chairs, a model's throne, pieces of Persian pottery, a model's platform, books with broken backs, a clown's hat, a pair of dumbbells, and netsukes. I delighted in this mass disorder, sometimes deliberately worsening it. I copied Degas' studio; Degas, my mentor, Degas my God!

The Circus Fernando, rested against the wall, its dimensions measuring over four feet by five feet. My skillful portrayal of horses impressed my friends, Bernard and Gauzi, and they noted how I had accentuated the thrust and speed of the horse, and the tension of the equestrienne, Marie, about to jump through a paper hoop. They whistled in admiration.

"Mix the absinthe," Anquetin said.

"I always knew you had a suicidal bent."

However, I opened a bottle of absinthe decorated with a blue foil. I served it to Anquetin by pouring it over a lump of sugar on a perforated spoon. I balanced that on the lip of a glass. Then I noticed Marie.

"Hello. What the devil are you doing!" I shouted, banging my cane. "Why are you wiping everything?"

"I'm going to serve your friends and I'm cleaning up. Must you always have your own way," Marie said sharply.

"I don't want you to clean it! I don't want you to do it!" I banged on the floor with gathering rage. "And the dust on the windows filters the light. Degas has dust on his windows . . . and every good artist has dust on his windows!"

"You're *fou* Henri!" Marie shouted back. "Who said anything about your windows, you stubborn mule!"

"I'll admit you're a lively pair," said Gauzi.

"Marie likes to battle," I said.

"You are the most finicky man alive. Nobody, just nobody can change your mind once it's made!" shouted Marie.

"Cormon is about to throw me out and my whole career is about to go down the sewer . . . and the two of you are arguing about God knows what," moaned Émile Bernard.

"Henri really adores me, can't you see that?" grimaced Marie.

"I can tell you that I wouldn't mind a cup of café au lait, Marie, and do you have any pastry?" said Gauzi poking around.

"I have Adèle's delicious croissants but take your hands off them," Marie scolded slapping Gauzi's inquisitive fingers. The artists pulled the boxes to the table which Marie had spread with a red and white checkered cloth. "Oh I charged everything to your account, Henri."

I breathed in the aroma of the coffee made on the coal stove with a new marvelous device Maman had brought from her kitchen in Malromé. It was called a percolator.

"I'm going to count on you, Marie as my hostess," I said in a conciliatory low voice.

"I'll have to think about it."

"What?"

"You're a madman, Henri," she shrugged dismissing me.

I knew she would acquiesce. Everyone seemed puzzled except Anquetin who drifted into a happy trance from the absinthe.

* * *

I don't remember exactly when the inevitable happened. Of course I was bound to stumble on it one way or another. Perhaps she was deliberately trying to lure me to the small room where she sometimes sketched and stored her drawings; perhaps she made too many innuendos about her art abilities which I dismissed as inconsequential and perhaps . . . but to conjecture how and why I found her drawing is really irrelevant. What transpired was astounding.

She stood in a corner of the room putting the finishing touches on a sketch of her son, Maurice, done in red chalk, and when I entered she looked up and put one hand to her breast.

"Why do you look so guilty? What the devil are you doing?"

"It's nothing." She walked away from the window.

"Well, let me look at it." I hobbled over to the drawing and my eyes widened. "*Sacrebleu,*" I whistled under my breath. "What is this?"

"It's a drawing . . . by me."

"I don't understand. Did you do it . . . is it yours?"

"Who else did it?"

"What?"

"Surprised? You don't think it's possible that I did it?"

"I'm not surprised. I'm astounded! I can't believe it. *Incroyable!* It's a miracle . . . truly a miracle!" I adjusted my pince-nez and my eyes traveled about the room. This was astonishing. I picked up my cane and pointed in the direction of another drawing lying across the table. "You did that? That drawing over there. Did you do that?"

"Yes."

I walked over to a wall where a drawing of Marie done in pastel chalk was tacked up. "And this one? Did you do it?"

"Yes."

"It's scarcely flattering, but amazing."

I circled the room. A drawing lay on the mantel . . . it was of an old woman and a baby. I picked it up.

"I did that one, also."

"And this?" I picked up a pastel lying on a small table. It was another drawing of an old woman and a child.

"Yes. It's all mine."

I sat down and wiped my pince-nez with a cloth and then set it atop my nose. I picked up the red chalk drawing of Maurice once again and examined it closely. It was a sweet delicate red chalk profile of her son. "There is something ethereal about the portrait and it's most odd . . . it is done with a tenderness which I've never seen you express toward your son. I've always suspected you felt more for your little Maumau than you let on. Now, tell me who really taught you."

"What?"

"Who taught you? Your lines are too pure and controlled not to have been tutored." I examined the various drawings closely as though attempting to spot some fraud, divine some explanation, find a key to the mystery as to why she should be doing these extraordinary drawings in secret and yet toss them off as though they were nothing. Why was it so difficult to believe that she could have talent? Were men all alike with their biases against women's abilities? Couldn't a woman be as talented in art as a man? Then why were there so few women artists? Was it the life they led? A woman such as Marie would be different, unfettered by society so why should she surprise me?

"I taught myself . . . Marie is the teacher, not Cormon, not Puvis, not any of your friends . . . not anybody at all."

She turned from another drawing she had begun and faced me flushed with passion and her hair ablaze with umber and russet tones all at once as though a light surrounded her; her old smock opened on a full bodice and in the faded blue pockets of her skirt, broken sticks of charcoal tipped their heads as they mingled with scrubby pencils. Chalk smudged her cheek.

I found that it was simple, so simple to spout the same old clichés about women. Did I really believe them?

"You're beautiful and talented, and a woman. I don't understand."

"Do you mean, Henri, that a woman cannot be beautiful, and talented as a man? What makes us so different?"

"Aren't you different?"

"It's only our lives that hold us back. But I'm never going to let that happen to me. What's there to understand?"

"I don't understand why you didn't tell me."

"You're a man."

"Ridiculous. What has being a man got to do with it? Degas helped the artists, Morisot and Mary Cassatt . . . and although he doesn't like women, he can recognize talent."

"I only know that men are like boys and they're fearful of women, at least they're threatened by them. I have known enough men to know that."

"It's a fantasy," I said wiping my pince-nez and watching her draw a scene from the window. "You're a fantasy, a figment of my imagination . . . not true."

"It's true, Henri. And tomorrow, I'll draw your picture."

"Positively not! Nobody draws this ugly face, no one but I, but we have to do something about you. You need a new name. Marie is too . . . plain, and there is a Mary Cassatt and Marie Laurencin. You need a name with more verve, more dash. Marie is too mundane for you. You need something more colorful."

"Don't be ridiculous, Henri. Marie is my name."

"What about Suzanne? It has flair . . . panache. Call yourself Suzanne. It has a ring to it. Yes, call yourself *Suzanne Valadon.*"

"I don't know. It's crazy to change it now."

"I like it. I say *yes*."

"I will probably say *no*. You can't rule me, Henri."

"Have it your own way." She was beginning to infuriate me. My voice rose to a shout. "I'm no longer interested. Forget it!"

"So you think it's such a small thing to change one's name? I'll wager the Counts of Toulouse wouldn't do it. And you think because you're a count, you have power over me?"

"That's absurd. That has nothing to do with it. And I don't want to speak of my title again."

"Of course you must have your own way, like a child. I will

be forever," and she signed her drawing, *Suzanne Valadon*.

"*Bien*, and I'll show your drawings to Bartholomé."

"Oh, thank you, Monsieur," and she curtseyed.

"I find your actions distasteful, Marie . . . Suzanne. I'm trying to help you, but I find it extremely difficult."

She said nothing but shrugged her shoulders. And then, with a sudden change of mood she smiled, a marvelous radiant smile directed at me, a smile of pregnant promise and it made the small room glow. Before I knew it she approached me. Her hand touched my shoulder and her lips grazed my face leaving the faint echo of a scent which hung on the air when she left. My heart suddenly raced and the whole incident was senseless.

When she came up to my room that afternoon, I hobbled about and blew the dust off a bottle of cognac tucked in the recesses of a cabinet. Why was my hand still trembling inanely? What she had given me earlier was an innocent little kiss which had thrown me into this turmoil. How ludicrous! "Come now let's celebrate a new light shining on the artistic scene, one Suzanne Valadon, that is if you can act rationally. *Salut*, my beautiful one." I quickly downed the drink with a huge thirst before she had a chance to lift her glass. "Come on, come on, drink up." I had finally mastered my emotions.

"Tell me, Henri, must I always pass a test with you?"

"You are incomprehensible! How many men have you driven insane with your idiotic antics? Behave. I have a surprise. How would you like a new hat as a gift for your new life?"

Her mood changed so quickly, I caught my breath. "Oh, Henri," she embraced me bending over my chair. I stiffened and half pushed her away. "I would love that. And I saw one I positively adore. I'm not ashamed to accept gifts from one so rich. Why shouldn't I take from life what I want?"

Her face was flushed and there was a childlike excitement in her startling sapphire blue eyes. I didn't realize her full beauty until that moment. "Then I will buy them often. You don't have to justify yourself to me."

"What a marvelous man you are. It's wonderful to know someone who can spend money freely when I have so little."

She amused me. "You are honest, Marie . . . no, Suzanne. You say what you think."

"And it will be very expensive, Henri. So be prepared."

"We'll go soon when you're free," I said, feeling protective.

"For that, yes. Oh, it will be a beautiful day," she said breathlessly. "Then I can buy my butterfly hat."

"What's that?"

"You'll see, Monsieur Henri, you lovely, lovely man," and she kissed me on my cheek. I held her to me for a moment and I could feel sudden desire pounding against my veins. My eyes behind the pince-nez must have shown it. And for a moment, her eyes widened with surprise. Then she laughed, a delightful little laugh, her petite frame pressing against my upper torso.

She watched my face as though she divined my innermost thoughts and it made me uneasy for within me an unfamiliar emotion, perhaps called love began to churn.

At La Nouvelle-Athènes, I hobbled over to the table where Bartholomé, Émile Bernard, Gauzi and Anquetin were sitting in their customary corner. I sat down next to Bartholomé.

"I want you to look at this." I removed Suzanne's red chalk drawing of her son from a portfolio, my finger over her signature. "Who do you think did this?"

"It's pretty good," said Anquetin. "It could belong to that fellow . . . you know, the fellow from Cormon's."

"Wrong," I said.

"It's yours," said Gauzi.

"Mine!" I exploded. "Are you mad?"

"Perhaps Morisot," said Anquetin.

"Why Morisot? It's not her style . . . too masculine," said Émile Bernard. "Look at the sureness of the pencil lines."

"Why do you think of a woman?" grunted Bartholomé. "This is not the work of a woman artist. The lines are too forceful. A woman could never draw like this."

"This is starting to irritate me. Who the devil does it belong to?" asked Émile.

"Alright, Henri, now tell us," Bartholomé insisted.

"You men are such misogynists you couldn't believe a woman

did it," I said. "It was Marie-Clémentine, now Suzanne Valadon, the artist."

"I don't believe it," said Bartholomé. "She never mentioned her drawing to me."

"I'll bet some lover did it," and Gauzi shrugged me off.

"I have seen her draw. It's hers," I said.

"You mean Marie, your Marie who put the croissants on the table in your studio and wiped everything, did that?" said Émile.

"She does it between lovers," said Anquetin.

"So do you!" retorted Bartholomé.

"I'm a man," asserted Anquetin.

"Frankly, I don't see the difference it makes," I said. "And your manhood has yet to be proven. It may be all talk."

"I still don't understand," said Bartholomé.

"She's drawn in secret since childhood... actually self taught." There was a silence. Disbelieving faces surrounded me.

"Surprising a woman is that good," said Anquetin weakly.

"What has being a woman to do with it? Cassatt is a woman." I said, "But she's not as beautiful and that makes it different to you. Of course that's absurd."

"Berthe Morisot is beautiful," ventured Anquetin.

"You men sound like an illogical pack of idiots!" I said. "Now here's another one," and I removed a nude from the folder.

Anquetin whistled. "She can certainly draw."

"I told you." I said. "You are all clods to doubt my judgment."

Bartholomé scrutinized both drawings for several moments. "She belongs to no school, that's for sure, a natural, Henri. Show these to Degas. Show him all her works if this is an indication."

"That's exactly what I planned on doing. I just wanted your opinion, Bartholomé. You're such a good friend of Degas, perhaps you could tell him about Suzanne?"

"But warn her in advance," said Émile Bernard. "Warn her about his tongue. He might hurt her and she'll never draw again."

"My dear Émile, you know Suzanne better than that. It wouldn't matter what he said to her. She would continue to draw. She's a confident, fearless one. Perhaps later on, I or Degas will show her how to paint."

"Oh, why does she call herself, Suzanne?" asked Bartholomé.

"I changed her name. You'll admit that the name, Suzanne has more panache."

"I thought all you two did was fight, Henri," said Émile.

I didn't answer but hoisted myself up on my cane and left.

Two evenings later I returned to La Nouvelle-Athènes with more of her drawings. All eyes rested upon me suspiciously.

"What the devil is wrong with all of you?"

"We've decided that you're fucking Marie, oh *pardonnez-moi*, Suzanne. Tell the truth, Henri, are you fucking her?" asked Gauzi.

"Go to hell. It's my affair. Am I not entitled to my privacy?"

"As a matter of fact, no. You're a babe in the woods when it comes to women, Henri. If you creep into bed with that little one, she'll eat you up and spit you out. We're your friends and we must protect you," Anquetin said now quite tipsy.

"What I do is my own concern so mind your own affairs. And I find your braggadocio exceedingly irritating."

"Did you speak with Degas yet?" asked Bartholomé.

"I'll speak with him tomorrow."

All eyes rested on me as I shuffled Suzanne's drawings back and forth holding each at arm's length. It was as though an inexplicable joy had touched me in exhibiting them.

"Look at your eyes, Henri . . . you're falling in love with that whore," said Émile. "Your eyes say you had Marie in bed."

"By God, no!" shouted Anquetin. "I warn you. All Paris has been between her legs. She'll cut out your heart before she's done with you. Henri, you're an innocent."

"You're all jumping to ridiculous conclusions. Must you speak salaciously of an innocent relationship? I'm leaving." I hoisted myself out of the seat. "You're a pack of wolves ready to tear her apart. I've shown you the amazing work of an untutored artist and you talk of mundane things," I shouted above the din and swayed perilously on a cane.

"Sit down!" half commanded Bartholomé, "and calm yourself. These drunken louts don't know what they're saying. Gauzi and Anquetin always drink too much."

"Yes, I say," said Anquetin. "Yes, I say, let's all marry Suzanne Valadon. Let's all toast her and her art and new name and lovely cunt . . . the greatest little cunt in the world which I was lucky enough to sample, Henri." He gulped down his drink.

"That does it!" I smashed my glass down on the table and the cognac splattered. Pains began searing through my legs as though to tear them off. I raised my cane menacingly.

"Calm yourself, Henri," protested Bartholomé.

"You animals! I'm leaving . . . and you . . . you will have to pay for all these damn drinks for a change, including mine." I stood up straight resting on my cane, adjusted my pince-nez, vest and coat and drew on my gloves as I prepared to leave with the bearing of a count at a height of four and a half feet.

Gauzi half rolled about the table laughing hysterically. "You should have come to me, Henri for advice before you did it. My closest friend, I must protect you. You did it, you did it and I know in my heart you committed that miserable fornication."

"No *she* did it, that miserable scheming one," babbled Anquetin. "I know her and she committed a crime, a heinous crime."

"Yes, a miserable female," laughed Gauzi hysterically. "She ruined you with her body, ruined you forever . . . a conniving dastardly act and we must do something, something to save you."

"My God, shut your mouths. You both sound ridiculous. Henri can certainly take care of himself," said Bartholomé.

Gauzi passed out and I took my cane and slammed it down on the table. He opened one eye and shut it again. My dear friend made me turn away feeling sick to the stomach. The pain in my legs intensified. As I left, from the corner of my eye I saw Bartholomé reach into his pocket to pay the bill. There was some justice, after all. I'll drown myself with cognac later on.

Somewhere in the back of my mind I began to plan the painting of Suzanne in the butterfly hat I had never seen. The scene in La Nouvelle-Athènes dismally crossed my mind with disturbing images of my new discovery, Suzanne, martyred by the drunken crew. I was suddenly overwhelmed by the humor of the situation and I laughed aloud. All the unpleasantness was dissipated by the deep visceral feeling I experienced that this portrait was the most important thing in my life right now, not Suzanne. Certainly not Suzanne. She meant nothing to me, nothing.

3

Suzanne

The Ogre and the Dream

On that spring morning Paris smelled sweet and green and a delicious expectation hung hushed on the air sweeping through the tortuous streets which lead up to the Butte Montmartre. I looked up at Henri's studio windows on the top floor of the building and was momentarily blinded by the glare of the sunlight striking the layers of dust. Henri stood before me leaning on his ivory handled cane warmed by the sun. His black and white checked trousers and flat brimmed bowler hat, made him look every inch an elegant man of the world, not the *artist-peintre*.

"What a glorious day!" I exclaimed hugging myself. I looked back at him and felt my skin prickle with anticipation.

"I love when you do that."

"What?"

"When you hug yourself. Nobody could do it in quite the same way." He looked at me with an embarrassing tenderness.

"Oh, I'm not aware of it." *Mon Dieu*, he's falling in love with me, I thought. Henri is falling in love with me.

How important I felt as the *cocher* helped me into the carriage. I had worn my best white smocked bodice. My skirt was gathered to a full bustle in back. Around my shoulders I wore a knitted shawl in carmine wool that my mother had made for me.

Atop my hair which fell into reddish curls sat a large deep blue bowler.

"Where to, *m'sieur?*" crackled from a hoarse throat.

"To the Boulevard Montmartre," Henri answered the *cocher* in an authoritative voice.

"How simply marvelous everything is!" I flashed a lingering smile at him . . . purposely coquettish . . . oh, Adèle, how deceitful we are, I thought.

"Your hat matches your eyes, *chérie*," Henri said in a low voice falling back in the plush seat crushing its softness.

I smiled. "Then I'll wear it often." I reached out and touched his hand. I felt it quiver but he didn't withdraw it. Oh, he is so very, very rich . . . he could take care of me and he'll teach me to paint and we'll be comrades in art."

"What are you thinking?" He held my hand more firmly.

"I'm thinking about my new hat. I can't wait . . . oh look at these shops, Henri."

"*Cocher*, take this way instead. Mademoiselle would like to see the shops."

The *cocher* grunted, an all knowing, partly mocking grunt. "*Oui, m'sieur*, and I will go slowly." He turned about and winked and I turned my head away with disdain.

My mind began to sort it out. What assurance Henri has, but then he *is* a count. How marvelous it must be to be a countess. How like a fairy tale that would be for he's a delightful little man and I feel myself drawn to him. How virile, how strong his personality is and I could love him, I know I could and his legs would bother Adèle but I wouldn't care a fig. Maumau needs a father and I could do my art in peace. He does have beautiful eyes, though and I could look into his eyes forever . . . now what is it? Why do I feel this way when he's merely going to buy me a hat but there's his mother, now there's a problem . . . now perhaps his mother wouldn't accept just a model for him . . . and perhaps the Comtesse wouldn't be so particular? She needn't worry. I would take good care of her son and love him.

The carriage made its way down the rue Montmartre which magically spilled into the much more impressive Boulevard Montmartre. Trees were budding everywhere. It was still early in the day and the smaller shopkeepers were getting ready to display their wares. But then there were the more expensive huge stores and posh shops. I felt as though a fever swept over me, the fever that luxury brought with it. Puvis had planted his seeds well ... unbelievable clothes and furnishings.

"See, there, right in the window ... my butterfly hat, Henri."

"Stop here, *cocher*," Henri called out and we alighted from the carriage, Henri hobbling on his cane. We entered the shoppe and greeted a short plump middle aged woman who rustled about in a plum colored taffeta dress with a huge bustle gathered in the back and she filled the room with her scent of roses and jasmine. Her ample bosom was covered with quantities of chains and pearls, and her glittering earrings seemed to catch the light of a thousand mirrors.

I had heard about this Madame Henriette whose clientele were the wives of important diplomats, and the general upper crust gentlemen of Parisian society and their mistresses. She employed *midinettes* who sewed the custom made hats in the rear of the store, young and older women from the *demi-monde* were paid very little. I learned about all this from the prostitute Céline, who was acquainted with various mistresses.

She looked with interest at us when we entered, a mismatched couple, and I could read in her eyes what she was thinking ... the beautiful young woman in a cheap blue bowler, and a grotesque midget, impeccably dressed. He must be important, else she wouldn't go with him. I saw Madame Henriette nod wisely.

"*Bonjour*, Madame, I am Monsieur Henri Toulouse-Lautrec, and this is Mademoiselle Suzanne Valadon."

"He is Count Lautrec," I corrected. "He's very modest."

Henri looked angry. "Don't do that, Suzanne. Don't correct me. You know that I don't want that title in Paris."

But I ignored him and said to the proprietress. "I would like you to remove the butterfly hat and ..."

Henri cut me off. "Remove the other hat in the window, that velvet hat. I would like to see it on her."

"That's not the one, Henri."

"I know."

Madame Henriette was impressed by his commanding tone.

He's a little man with a big ego. He wants his way so let him have it for the present, I thought and smiled sweetly. But I felt strangely helpless against the force of a will as strong as my own.

"I would like to see it on you," said Henri.

"It will look miserable," I pouted and sat before a glass on a plum velvet tufted seat. A huge crystal chandelier was reflected in a tall mirror on a walnut stand. She removed my cheap bowler turning her face away in disdain.

Henri grew impatient, hoisted himself onto his cane and hobbled about the establishment. Madame Henriette pretended not to notice his legs and placed the ribboned hat on my head.

I turned about impatiently. "What do you think, Henri?"

"I don't like it. Definitely not . . . perhaps the butterfly hat."

"Oh, Monsieur, the butterfly hat to be sure . . . and you have excellent taste . . . the most copied hat in Paris, created for Sarah Bernhardt for a play," the proprietress bragged excitedly.

"Sarah Bernhardt is at least twenty years older than Mademoiselle and I assure you that Mademoiselle will do it more justice," Lautrec said sharply.

"Let me assure you, the hat is not cheap, Monsieur le Comte," said Madame Henriette. "What I mean is . . ."

"I know exactly what you mean and the cost is of no concern to me," he cut her off impatiently.

"It looks beautiful on her." Oh, how she approved of this count.

"Beautiful, she is, *c'est vrai*," smiled Henri. He adjusted his pince-nez.

"Would you like to wear it Mademoiselle?"

"Should I, Henri?" I pretended indecision.

"By all means."

The buxom owner adjusted the bonnet on the curls I spent hours to fix.

"*Voilà*, Mademoiselle. All eyes in Paris will be on you."

After Henri paid the substantial bill, Madame Henriette looked at us leaving the establishment. How I disliked her smugness, her catering to wealth, but I held the box with my worn bowler packed safely inside. The ribbons on the butterfly hat perched atop my head, fluttered bravely in the breeze.

During the ride home I thought, poor, poor Henri. Should I

let him make love to me? No, not yet. Am I falling in love with him? I would be better for the pain in his legs than all the cognac he drinks. And I must learn how to control him. Before I'm finished he'll not be so pigheaded, *hein*?

Posing for Lautrec was a pleasure. He was undemanding, never insisting on not moving as Puvis did, let me talk incessantly, and after a half hour he allowed me to take a rest. And his friends streamed in at odd times. With each day, my admiration for him deepened. He knew exactly what he wanted and in which direction he was headed. His analysis of the artists who surrounded him was sufficient to separate those who were sincere in their artistic efforts and the braggarts who were superficial. He was never wrong. And in his art I felt a oneness because we had in common our dislike for "pretty" drawings; I knew that in the future I would most certainly disappoint any woman who wanted me to portray a pretty, untruthful portrait of her and Henri painted in the same harshly realistic manner. His paintings of me were barely flattering.

I modeled for Henri for several months after the purchase of the hat when he presented me with a necklace of tiny sapphires. "To match your eyes," he said. He slipped it around my throat and fastened the clasp as I sat on an old wooden chair in his studio. He kissed me lightly on my hair. I felt a stirring, a familiar rising emotion. Strangely, it was something I hadn't expected.

"Oh, Henri, how lovely this is."

"Like you are."

But his beautiful eyes looked troubled.

When I returned to his studio the following afternoon, his smock was off and the easel was pushed away. He hesitated for a moment and then drew me to the old divan and threw his cane across a table. He held me to him in a long embrace and kissed me on the nape of my neck, then on my cheeks, then my lips. He opened the bodice of my white muslin blouse and caressed and kissed my breasts, each in turn and whispered, "*Ma chérie,*" over and over again, as I slipped out of the skirt; and his mouth was everywhere on the body he had painted so often before.

"Your skin looks radiant in the sun's golden glow . . . has the texture of a Botticelli Venus. And your hair ... so radiant with amber lights, and I love how it's pulled back on the nape of your neck in a chignon," he murmured. His senses were inflamed but he held back, and I saw the fear in his eyes."

"Henri you speak poetry," I whispered kissing the eyes I loved.

"I don't repel you?" he said as he slowly revealed his stunted legs to me. "Can you make love to me, my precious Suzanne, my darling artist ... my gamine of Montmartre? Do I repel you?"

I answered by kissing him deeply, and our breaths mingled as we lay together, I only seeing the upper torso of his body which looked strong and virile. All else was feeling ... what was left I didn't look at and didn't care about. He made love to me, and for me he was whole. I felt his manhood thrusting into me deeper, his cock sure and seeking and whatever lack he had, whatever physical deformities he had were lost in a purple shadow. My eyes closed in the delight of the moment.

"How I have wanted you from the beginning, and I was afraid you would refuse me," he whispered.

He ran his hand slowly over the length of my leg, from the firmness of my rounded thigh, and followed the shape of the calf as it swelled and then curved into a delicate ankle. "It is so normal, so delightfully normal," he breathed. "Don't my legs repel you ... tell me that they don't, and that you want me."

"I don't even see them, Henri, you are whole to me," and I held onto his dark curly hair with both hands, arching my body, and straddling his body above the stunted legs drawing him into me. He came and fell limp in my arms, and then after awhile, leaned on one elbow and looked at my face.

"How beautiful you are," he said," how very beautiful. I always felt that a marvelous woman's body like yours was not for making love, it would be defiled somehow. Any ordinary woman can make love ... it doesn't matter but when I see a body, so lovely, so magnificent as yours, it was made to be caressed, to be loved, and I realize that I was wrong." And he murmured that this was the way a woman was meant to be, without guile, abandoning herself without false modesty and with an earthiness and zest for pleasure itself. That evening, we made love again; and his mouth slowly, hesitantly but then surely, and with greater certainty, found every secret part of my body; his tongue seeked, caressed, maddened, and he took me as *le orgasme* stiffened my body. Afterward he fell back and went to sleep in my arms. I felt the semen trickle down between my thighs and the worn divan became more stained. But I lay without moving, feeling my body pulsating and throbbing. The dawn came much too quickly.

When I returned to the apartment, Maman's eyes were wild and accusing through her drunken stupor.

I was late with my period that month and terribly fearful. *Merde*, not another baby! I should have made him wear those new India-rubbers but this time I would know who the father was. He with his money could well care for it and the child would be a count or countess. But no, I didn't really want another little one ... and so I took a steaming bath and deliberately carried a heavy basket of laundry down the cobblestone streets to a laundress to wash. Along the way, I slipped and sprawled out on the street. About ten minutes later, my monthly flow began. I breathed more easily. Back in the rue Tourlaque I tore a large cotton cloth into strips and fastened them into my chemise.

"*Dieu merci*," I said to Adèle. "That little Lautrec is in my bloomers."

That afternoon, I went up to see Henri who was painting at his giant easel. There was a kind of cataclysmic disorder which held one spellbound. A huge ladder stood against a wall, and the studio was littered with empty wine bottles, some rolls of canvas, a new velvet couch, and a glittering hurricane lamp which the countess had placed atop the pianoforte. The wine bottles came from his mother's wine cellar. The crystals hanging from the lamp were coated with a fine patina of dust.

He embraced me as I entered. He waved his hand showing me the new hurricane lamp. "As you can see my mother has bestowed upon me all the adornments of a nobler life. You can sit now on my plush green divan, and we can make love in style. Oh, this is for you *ma chérie*, and of course the color of your eyes." and he opened a small box. On a dark wine velvet cushion was a golden locket with a cluster of tiny sapphires on its cover with intricate filigree at its base from which hung a solitary sapphire. Inscribed on the back was, *"Love always, Henri Lautrec."*

"Oh, how beautiful it is. It's so charming. I'll wear it about my neck, always. You've been so good to me Henri," I whispered. "I'll put your picture in it."

"No, not my ugly face! Yours must go into it, so that someday someone will have it and see how beautiful you were."

"You're a good man, Henri." I kissed his cheek. "And you're a good lover," I said in a low intimate voice.

"I'm probably a fool but I want to buy several of your drawings, especially the red chalk of your son."

"You can have them for nothing, *mon chéri*," I embraced him.

"No, I want to buy them . . . then you'll feel what it's like to be an artist. One must sell one's work to be a success."

"*D'accord.* You may pay me but what else do you want?"

"I want to paint your picture in the butterfly hat I bought you so that someday your picture may hang in the Louvre."

"Everyone will think it silly."

"You will be immortal. You want to be immortal don't you?"

"I will be, Henri, through my art."

"*Touché.*"

"But I will let you paint me and then I'll buy my mother a new mauve silk."

"Somehow, I can't picture your mother in it. My little vixen, we'll start tomorrow, and Suzanne . . . please don't be late . . . you know how that upsets me."

"Why are you so goddamn exacting. There's nothing wrong with being a few moments late. Please don't spoil everything."

"Your few moments stretch to an hour. Anyway, I was brought up that way, Suzanne, punctual in all things. You'll have to accept it and not drive me mad with your antics."

"You exasperate me, Henri. I'll be on time tomorrow," I said crossly and then reconsidered, fingered the locket and kissed him on the cheek.

"Au revoir, *ma petite chatte* . . . you love me because of my gifts to you." He readjusted his pince-nez.

I didn't answer but walked quickly to the door. I turned back for a moment. "Oh, I have a favor to ask of you. Maman wants to know if Maumau can play on your piano in the future . . . of course he's still too young . . . perhaps next year?"

"Considering that Mozart played chords on the harpsichord at three and composed at five . . . I suppose it's all possible."

"Mozart? Who?"

"Don't fret about it, Marie. I'm planning to completely educate you and I'll instruct your son in the piano as well."

* * *

In February of 1886, we were tortured by bouts of unrelenting snowfalls. The roads were plagued with piles of slush and horse manure. Henri finished *Suzanne Valadon*, his painting of me in the butterfly hat and afterward took me to meet a Vincent Van Gogh, the brother of the manager of the Goupil Gallery. He had just arrived in Paris and fancied himself an artist.

Suddenly one afternoon, Henri's expression changed and he became very demanding. "Get your drawings together for my neighbor in rue Fontaine," he commanded.

"What? And who is your neighbor?

"You don't know?"

"Please don't play games, Henri." I had a sudden dread, "Not Degas . . . not he . . . I won't do it . . . I just won't do it!"

"But he's a Master, he's a God. You know nothing about him."

"He's a monster, a terrible man so forget it and don't tell me what to do!"

"You don't even know him, how interesting he is. As a matter of fact he comes from a wealthy French family, bankers and related by marriage to nobility in Italy."

"So that's your connection with him. He's nobility like you are. I'm surprised you even associate with the likes of me. I'm going home."

"You're going nowhere. You'll do as I say. First you come in late and then you threaten to go home." He held a cane across the door. "You'll not leave!"

"Don't you dare stop me, you arrogant fool! I won't meet him, and that's that. How dare you tell me what to do, how dare you try to control me . . . how dare you . . ."

But he paid small attention to my anger. In fact, I detected a smile playing about his lips. "Say whatever you please, Suzanne, but you can't erase the fact that he's a master artist, and if you're at all interested in your art, that's all that should concern you."

I thought for a moment and then tried a wheedling, gentler tone. "Oh Henri, I'm not afraid of anything, but I'm afraid of him . . . and I've heard him crucify the young artists at La Nouvelle-Athènes. I'd rather draw in secret. I just won't go. He has no heart, always grumpy and complaining and always, always with a sour face, hating women."

"How are you so sure he hates women?"

"The ballerinas in his drawings always have ugly faces."

"Now that you've said your piece, I'll say mine. You'll get nowhere and be nobody, nobody at all. And when you get too old to model and become fat and useless, don't come running to me . . . and at the end they'll put you in a pauper's grave."

"Oh you're a wicked one alright. You talk so importantly and we're the same age . . . so you're a count, and that doesn't impress me one bit."

"But of course it does or you wouldn't keep mentioning it. And I have money, Suzanne, and you have none."

"I'll manage pretty well without you. I'm leaving."

"If you leave I'll call the whole thing off and you'll get nowhere. You must have a patron, Suzanne, or you'll be no one."

"You be my patron. You brag but do nothing for me."

"Degas is a great artist. He can help you get established in art and instruct you. I am an unknown artist and can't help you. Anyway, I need his opinion."

"You're very cruel, Henri. I don't care one fig for his opinion. He's a mean, terrible old man."

"I owe a great deal to him. There are compositional devices I use which he's invented but you wouldn't understand. He made me aware of a whole range of subjects, scenes in cafés, women at their toilette, dancers, music hall scenes, and laundresses. Never speak against Degas to me because he's a master." Henri began pacing the floor in agitation, hobbling on his cane.

"He's a monster, you mean, an ogre . . . you can ask anyone."

"I don't care what anyone thinks. Degas is a genius. And don't pretend with me. Nothing frightens you, Suzanne. I know you better than that. I'll set up an appointment, so put your drawings into a portfolio, dress demurely, be soft spoken and smile sweetly and don't chatter inanities . . . if there's anything he hates it's brainless women who chatter endlessly. Be clever and say only what's utterly important."

"I hate him and I would die before I set one foot in his house."

"You lie, Suzanne. You will go. You have the courage of a lion and please get on the good side of Zoë, his housekeeper."

"Do I have to worry about someone's *bonne*?"

"You have to worry about this one. Just do what I ask."

"And why should he want to see *me* . . . I, an unknown?"

"I told Degas I was sending him a born artist, one without instruction and a woman of fire. And Bartholomé is a good friend of his and spoke up for you. You're a lucky one, Marie."

"Marie? You say Marie, when you're angry with me."

He thought for a moment. "Suzanne, oh, goddamn!" He put his tubes of paint away. "Just leave me in peace. Leave me a shred of what's left of my sanity. Let me recover my composure. First you're late, and you deliberately do it, and then you're exasperating!" he shouted. "We'll continue the painting later." He poured some cognac down his throat, complained of his legs and sat still looking at me sadly. My heart went out to him.

"And when do I have to present myself to this ogre?"

"Tomorrow, and be on time. I wouldn't trifle with Degas if I were you." His voice was demanding once again and he banged on the floor with his cane and I tried to restrain myself.

I was quite subdued when I rapped the door knocker at the Edgar Degas home in the rue Fontaine that afternoon with a portfolio under my arm.

Will he like my appearance? I thought, and I came to him demurely in a navy blue muslin frock. Around my neck I wore Henri's locket and at my ears were tiny pearls. A meticulously clad housekeeper came to the door. She was pleasant looking with an efficient manner. "You are Zoë," I smiled.

Zoë apprised me from head to foot, half-acknowledged me

and coolly asked, "And who should I say is calling?"

"Marie . . . Marie-Clémentine Valadon." I bit my lip and held the huge portfolio closer to my body.

Zoë took my cloak and disappeared, and then voices were raised in some sort of dispute. I had a desperate desire to run out. It's not too late . . . I don't care what Henri thinks. He isn't going to run me, and I'll call myself whatever name I please.

A thin wiry man of average height appeared wearing tweeds, and his eyes were piercing and impatient, his manner aloof and his lips pressed firmly together as he furtively noted my face and figure. He was very much as I remembered him at La Nouvelle-Athènes but far older than the gentleman who had given a twelve year old Marie-Clémentine ten francs for her starving family. Of course he wouldn't remember me. It was so long ago.

"Come on, come on child," he said impatiently as he closed the vest on his salt and pepper tweeds.

"I have . . . " but he never let me finish.

"What have we here?" He muttered something under his breath and then *"Merci."* He hadn't forgotten his manners. He took out a handkerchief and rubbed his eyes as he went over to the light of the window. I had heard talk of his poor eyesight.

Will he never open the portfolio?

Degas opened the folder, removed the drawings and looked at the first one of Maman and Maurice.

"Suzanne Valadon . . . not Marie?"

"I . . . Henri said I should sign it so. It had more panache."

He half smiled for the first time. It was an odd forced smile never fully blossoming. Then he took a magnifying glass and looked at it, examining the drawing minutely. I was afraid of what he would find. He put the drawing down on a small table and took another to the window. His silence drove me mad. If he would only say something, anything, but he went on to the next and then the next. His face drew to an immense frown. In a few moments I'll leave. *Mon Dieu,* how he hates my art. Why should I stay? I'll leave, that's all, I'll leave.

He looked up at me from time to time and his facial expression worsened.

Merde, what a terrible little man. But then it's no surprise. I knew he would be. I'll grab my pictures and run out, *c'est ça!*

Degas finished viewing the drawings and returned to the beginning ones. The suspense was unbearable; the wait for him to utter an opinion, any opinion was interminable. But he said nothing. There were no compliments, not even for the one Henri loved, the chalk drawing of my son which he lingered on, holding it away from him. If only he would insult me. Oh, he's a monster, alright. Why doesn't he say something?

I watched Degas wipe his nose and eyes as he turned away from the light; for the first time my eyes wandered and I noted a pastel drawing of dancers unfinished on the mantel.

"Who taught you?" the ogre said breaking the stillness.

"What?"

"You heard me, young lady. Who taught you?"

"Nobody. I taught myself." I tossed my head. Let him go to the devil along with his friend Henri!

He didn't answer. A look of suspicion narrowed his eyes, "Is that the truth?"

"You will have to believe me, Monsieur. I'm self taught."

He stared at my face and hair for a moment. I watched his expression which was exceedingly glum. I sat down in a chair and played with my hands. The whole experience was proving to be a nightmare and it was surely my own fault for coming.

Slowly he placed the drawings back into the portfolio. I looked up and Degas said in a strange far away voice, "Yes, it *is* true. You are indeed one of us."

"What did you say?"

His eyes softened and an unaccustomed smile played about his lips. His face seemed strangely altered.

"You are indeed one of us."

His words took wings and soared.

The moment was filled with magic.

I took up the portfolio and began to carry it out as in a dream.

"Wait, Marie, where are you going?"

"I was leaving."

"Please stay Mademoiselle, I want to speak with you about your art. You don't paint?"

"No."

"Why not?"

"I'm afraid. Perhaps Henri will teach me."

Degas didn't answer and then said, "I want one of your drawings. I'll take this one in red chalk." He hung it on a wall in his dining room. "There, you will hang next to Cassatt."

"Cassatt?"

"A woman painter, Mary Cassatt."

"Thank you, Monsieur," I murmured.

"And I will call you Maria, not Suzanne . . . no matter what Henri thinks. You'll be my *terrible Maria* because you draw without instruction and your lines are sure and without fear. You will come and visit me when you do your drawings, and then soon you'll be painting . . . and we will be friends."

Friends? He must be mad. I could be friends with Degas? I thought, and I nodded weakly. Suddenly I felt faint, but a curious thing happened. I stared at the forbidding face as slowly my fear of him vanished; the artist began to intrigue me.

"Monsieur, I will indeed be your friend and I would love you to guide me." The monster looked at me and his sneer dissolved, and he became almost human.

"The pleasure is mine," he said and kissed my hand. I was astounded at this graciousness. I felt very important.

I left gliding through a delicious vapor with the huge portfolio under my arm and I felt the eyes of the middle aged man in the salt and pepper tweeds watching me . . . watching me . . . trying to come to some conclusion about me. Undoubtedly, he finally accepted my talent as he followed my movements out of his home, accepted what I was and what I came from. He knew that I was self-taught and suspected that I was some kind of free spirit. I liked to believe that the Montmartre streets where I learned my craft was where I drew my strength. I felt, somehow that he understood all of this. . . . the Master of painters, the great Degas.

It seemed a fantasy.

4

Degas

My Terrible Maria

Very talented . . . no, unbelievably talented, this elfin creature, my terrible Maria with the bright piercing eyes entered my life clutching a portfolio under her arm. And she drew me to her like a magnet. I thought about her a great deal since that afternoon and only Zoë dislodged me from those thoughts.

"Monsieur Degas, what do you want for dinner? It seems to me that you are losing your hearing as well as your eyesight . . . and take care," she warned as she watched my Maria striding down the Rue Fontaine with the springy pelvic stride of the circus, "Watch that little one. She still looks like a bundle of trouble to me." Her eyes narrowed suspiciously. "She has a bastard, that one. I've heard stories from Madame Pinchot, wife of the baker."

"And who the devil is Madame Pinchot?"

"You men know nothing of the gossip of the Butte."

"Oh, go back to your cooking, woman!"

"You'd better not bother me while I make my orange marmalade this afternoon. Of course, you enjoy being so sharp tongued."

"I do!" I said grimly working on a pastel drawing. I turned to pastels when I was totally convinced I was going blind. My faithful servant Zoë now reads the newspapers to me to spare my eyes. But would you think the doctors agree with me? No, they see little wrong with my eyesight. When I'm totally blind they might admit I was right in my fears.

Now for my terrible Maria. Some pattern of divinity brought her into my life, for she's a female in the untutored, unrefined state without the coyness and artificiality I detest. Even my Zoë, is slowly being won over. Poor woman, my *bonne* grasps at anyone to alter what she states are my terrible moods. And my Maria, in truth, tranquilizes my poor sick body, softening my impatience, and delighting me with her earthiness. She visits me at my studio almost every afternoon, always bringing some drawing, and chats incessantly about the gossip in the Montmartre. And I love it. How I love it. My outgoing, passionate "terrible Maria" is a perfect foil for my neurasthenia.

Women! I'll never understand nor tolerate most of them. Frankly, for all my drawings of women, for all my renderings in paint and gouache and pastel, I deliberately make them quite plain looking, for women in general are in this mode. I'm certainly not going to pretty them up like Renoir. Frankly I'm suspicious of the whole lot of females, have little patience for my models, am annoyed by their coquetries and very obvious wiles and moods. The entire female gender is susceptible to the most fraudulent modes of conduct and subterfuges. Yet, I suppose it's a quirk of mine but the female anatomy holds some artistic attraction for me in its design and movement.

"Women are a damned nuisance with their coy ways." My usual complaints about my models and women in general were made to my friend Bartholomé as we sat having an *apéritif* at La Nouvelle-Athènes. "And what a feat it was to do my drawing with my last finicky model. She refused to pose in the position more than a few minutes at a time. She was much too old and she complained incessantly about her back."

"You can't tolerate them because you haven't loved any."

"What kind of logic is that?"

"Don't you ever have the desire for a woman?"

"All I need concern myself with are the size of their buttocks and breasts for my painting. I had one model with pear shaped buttocks and another who stank. And I can't endure their whims.

And some get crazy with their menstruation each month, a biological malfunction. They are certainly an illogical crew and anatomically inferior because of nature."

"I have a beautiful model for you, Edgar. She's modeling for Zandomeneghi but she was made to order for your ballet scenes."

"Send her to me in several weeks."

"She's a Jewess."

"I won't employ a Protestant, so why a Jewess? You're deliberately bating me, Bartholomé. I can always see through you."

"How can you be so bigoted? Your friends Ludvig Halévy and Camille Pissarro are Jewish."

"There are always exceptions."

"*Tiens!* And speaking of models, how is that little vixen, Marie or Suzanne, or whatever she calls herself."

"My wild Maria has no counterpart in Paris, and is the most unusual occurrence that has come into my poor sickly life. She is completely untutored, a wild gamine of the streets who has an amazing inner discipline in her art. Of course, she will have to be shown how to paint. It will be difficult because you can neither change, modify nor correct her. She is a maverick, beholden to no one . . . an unschooled maverick, but I will supervise her and it will be difficult. I try to teach without trying to influence. It's strange how she has a fear of painting, but for her drawings, she shows great strength. The lines of her work are supple and forceful. How could all this have come about? It's an enigma. Berthe Morisot had lessons but not this one. She's a natural in every sense of the word."

"And she's a beauty, *n'est-ce pas?*" Bartholomé smiled.

"I'm not interested in her appearance," I said. "For me she lives solely as an artist and not even as a model." But I sat deep in thought.

"What are you thinking?" Bartholomé asked.

"She is a phenomenon, my wild Maria. You know, I have racked my brains and I have searched for some reason, some school, some trick to her drawings and it eludes me. How this phenomenon happened, this illegitimate daughter of a peasant, an ignorant peasant, a charwoman who doesn't even want her daughter to draw but would rather have her do the laundry. A phenomenon! Such a miracle comes once in a lifetime."

"It comes from somewhere . . . perhaps the father?"

"What? Who? Who was he? There was no one but a thief."

"She is not the first . . . Anquetin is the son of a butcher . . . and Cézanne despises his father, a banker who is a true bourgeois and wants a lawyer for a son, not an artist. And if Pissarro, Renoir, Monet and you hadn't encouraged Cézanne, he would have gone into the family business long ago . . . and Lautrec . . ."

"What about Lautrec? Lautrec's family all drew and Henri's father, the Count Alpohonse modeled little statuettes of horses and hounds as eccentric as he is, and Lautrec's uncles showed talent in art so there are exceptions, but you forget one fact, my dear Bartholomé . . ."

"And what is that?"

"That she is a woman, and women have their lives circumscribed for them, miserable as it seems."

"Not this one . . . she's different . . . in fact I'm thinking of collecting her work."

"She is indeed different. She is an upstart raised in the streets. Her mother supposedly was raped by some derelict and forced to leave a position and come to Paris . . . wandered with my Maria in a basket and quite by accident, mind you, arrived in Montmartre . . . became a charwoman and an alcoholic I might add. She has a contempt for women artists and has done everything to discourage my Maria."

"But there are other women who are artists."

"Who? Cassatt and Berthe Morisot? They both come from solid upper class families and have artistic training. The financial end is of no concern to them . . . they have money for their needs but this one has an alcoholic as a mother who looks to Maria to support her. Marie-Clémentine is an unbridled animal without restraints who dropped out of school early, a female totally of her own making, and I insist again, she has no counterpart in Paris. I ask you, where does her talent come from?"

Bartholomé gulped down the remainder of his *apéritif*. "*Garçon*, another Benedictine, and what will you drink, Edgar?"

"Some Perrier water . . . my digestion is very bad."

"As usual, Edgar. Try one night with a woman and she'll cure what ails you."

"*Dieu merci*, I don't have some female torturing me." Then I became lost in thought. "She's a discovery, Bartholomé, a discovery, that petite deviltress, Maria."

And how is Mademoiselle Cassatt, your other protégée?"

"I expect her tomorrow. Hopefully she won't bring her damn family along. They are a well meaning group but I don't have the patience for them. One American is enough for an afternoon."

Mary Cassatt was seated on a cane back damask gold chair watching patiently as I nailed up a painting on my dining room wall. My protégée looked her customary pleasant and elegant self that afternoon with her straight small features. I have never really been attracted by the costumes of women except to paint them if need be, but I must say she wore a marvelous outfit, *très chic*, a very fashionable celery green walking suit with black braiding down the front of the bodice, sleeves and under-skirt and bustle. Atop her head was a celery green toque and a matching muff of gull feathers. Her white kid gloves lay on a table. My Maria stared in admiration when she entered unexpectedly, and I saw her eyes widen as she scanned Cassatt's outfit. That's the way the upper classes were, all breeding and refinement. My Maria was certainly not of their world . . . in her simple gray muslin dress . . . the black weskit over some sort of white bodice and the carmine shawl supposedly knitted by Maman Madeleine so carelessly tossed over her shoulders.

"Ah, my Maria, this is my good friend, the artist, Mary Cassatt, and I hoped you would meet someday, and now look at this painting by Cassatt. What do you think? Do you think you will do as well, eh?"

"I don't know . . . I don't paint, Monsieur." Her eyes betrayed her. Perhaps it was envy? Maria was completely transparent.

"Eh . . . that will change . . . isn't that so, Maria?" She didn't answer but murmured something in praise and then faced the artist.

Beside the fresh beauty of *ma petite* Maria, Mary Cassatt looked very much a woman in her forties; her face registered a proper expression but I was surprised that her eyes grew cold as she looked back at Maria so objectively.

"Mary Cassatt is an American," I interjected.

Maria's eyes betrayed her again. I divined that she saw this spinster as having devoted herself solely to her *métier*; that this was her life to the exclusion of everything else, love, marriage, children. It was something that she, my Maria, would never do. She wanted everything, the *love and the art*. These were her rules. To have a man's body, to love him, was too precious to relinquish. For Maria, one could do both.

I met Cassatt in Paris in the late 1870's and we were seen everywhere together. We worked side by side on prints, she as my protégée. It was all innocent enough. At one point there was talk that we were romantically allied. Of course it was absurd, for Cassatt was thoroughly chaste and I'm sure remained a virgin now at 43. Her chastity would never allow for any romantic liaison I can assure you. And I certainly didn't want any.

But my wild Maria could consort sexually with all of Paris if it so pleased her. She, the Bohemian, the child of the streets, was Cassatt's opposite in all ways save her art, and with the cool detached and critical gaze of Mary Cassatt, I felt that Maria instantly disliked her. "Why does a virgin paint children? What does she really know about life, she who has never held a man in her arms? Why does she never paint men?" Maria asked me repeatedly afterward.

"I see you're busy with your guest, Monsieur Degas. I'll leave."

"No, please stay, Maria . . . we're only discussing some business matters and Zoë will serve some café au lait and pastries. You've tasted Zoë's pastries and thought them superb."

"I must go. My little Maumau has had some problem," she lied. How I knew when she lied. She was so transparent, my Maria. Her Maumau had his Grand-mère to fuss over him.

"As usual, children, God spare me from them and *Dieu merci*, I haven't had any. I have all I can handle with my failing eyes."

"Children can be comforting in one's old age," said Mary Cassatt, looking wistful for the moment. "I regret sometimes . . ."

"In one's old age, children should be on their own and out of sight, otherwise they're a damn nuisance, extracting money for their empty brained mistresses."

"Oh, you *are* the cynical one," said Cassatt. "You would have made a marvelous father and had a family of artists like Pissarro."

"Me? Never! And certainly not with some feather brained mincing woman. Never . . . with her scheming ways!"

"Don't mind his talk," said Mary Cassatt, her eyes softening into a myriad of lines. "I never pay attention." They both began to laugh.

"I'd die than have some scheming shrew carping at me all day long."

The two women laughed louder, now more heartily. I knew I could be droll in my adamancy and I didn't mind being made the butt of the humor. It was a change of pace.

"Do you know why I won't marry? It's quite simple. I would be in mortal misery all my life for fear my wife might say, *That's a pretty little thing,* after I had finished a painting."

"Nevertheless, I think I'll introduce you to my American cousin," said Mary Cassatt, wiping her eyes. "She's already set a trap for you."

"What me? She won't catch me here, I assure you. I'll run out," I said. "And furthermore, she will probably drive me mad with fashion. Did you ever ask yourselves what women would talk about if there were no fashions? Life would become unbearable for men. Why if women were to break away from the rules of fashion, the government would have to step in and take a hand."

The women convulsed with laughter. I was enjoying every moment of this exchange. I exaggerated my disdain for women with my histrionic ability.

"Oh, Edgar, you don't mean a word you say."

"Never mind, never mind. Look at this wild one's drawings."

My American Impressionist began to examine Maria's work on the wall. Then she approached *ma petite* and graciously took her hand.

"You have talent, Marie . . . and you were never taught? It's astounding. I hope someday to see your paintings . . . and what school do you think you'll be a part of?"

"No school," said Maria. "I am my own school . . . always."

Cassatt stared at this young beautiful Bohemian and dropped her hand. "Really? That's interesting. But then you'll have difficulty being accepted."

"I will be recognized for myself, Mademoiselle Cassatt, you'll see." Maria asserted.

Mary Cassatt's eyes widened as she again examined my wild one's work.

"My Maria doesn't lack confidence in her abilities, as you can see," I affirmed.

I stood still reflecting long after the two women left, for they were so completely opposite to one another. What wild untamed force fascinated me about Maria until the obsession grew and flooded my very being, infiltrated my daily life? When she failed to come to see me, I became despondent and sent Zoë to fetch her. Only Maria and her visits, her new drawings executed under my scrutiny as she unfolded before me, and her perpetual gossip about the happenings in the Bohemian circles of Montmartre, could soothe my terrible moods and give me the impetus to continue. Only *she* could quell my despondency. Only *she*!

"Have you no ears, Monsieur Degas?" Zoë, broke my reverie. "I've been calling you for ten minutes, and if your dinner grows cold you'll just complain and complain."

"Enough!" I shouted. "Alright, alright, I'm coming," and I placed my wild Maria's drawing back on the wall.

Two evenings later, Zoë went to rue Tourlaque to fetch her. She found my Maria, quite nude, in Lautrec's studio. Was she posing for him? What the devil were they doing? I didn't know. I only knew that she was unable to come to me. Somehow it sent me into a terrible rage.

Grand-mère
The Hag

My little Maumau, my own little Maumau . . . I take care of him every day, but no one knows anything about me. I'm just an old hag in my daughter's drawings . . . but my Maumau, my little Maumau, he makes me whole. It was God's miracle that he was born. The funny mist, the fog from the brandy which I walked in each day from the time I became a charwoman here in Paris and washed the stinking chamber pots and the filthy floors, the fog disappeared, pouf, vanished like a puff of smoke, and for awhile, I became like the other young matrons, like the one I never was . . . tending my child, my little Maumau, the precious bundle that devil Marie gave me. And do you think she cares about him? Never! Perhaps someday she'll feel what I feel, what I have never felt for her, my Marie. But she's selfish, that one, only concerned with her scribbling and her lovers . . . never Maumau, except to draw him. But when she takes a crayon and draws his picture, a miracle comes over her, for what I see in her eyes might be love for the child.

But she's a cruel one, that Marie, she's such a cruel one. Do you know why? She's torturing that *petit monsieur*, of course. Oh, I know what she's about. She can't fool me.

"It's a pity what you're doing to that *petit monsieur*, a pity. It's not all modeling that makes you run up and down the stairs."

"He's teaching me to paint, old woman."

"Old woman? This old woman is bringing up your son while you sleep with every artist in Montmartre. What a mother you are. And you, torturing that poor cripple so that he comes to our door when you're late. How can you do that to him? He can barely walk on those stumps, let alone hobble down the steps looking for you."

"Mind your own affairs!"

"I can't believe you would accept that freak for a husband. Well, he's too smart for you and you're not going to fool him. He'll catch on soon enough that you don't love him . . . that all you want is his title."

"What's wrong with a title?"

"He's a freak."

"It doesn't bother me what he looks like."

"And would the *petit Comte* want Maumau as a son? Tell me that, Marie."

"Henri is good to Maurice. He would take care of him."

"I don't think he'll marry you."

"I have a trump card, Maman. Be clever . . . you can be wearing silks and satins and I can be a countess and stop modeling and work on my art. He's a very fine artist, Maman. I respect his art and he's a fine man."

"But do you love him? You can't tell me you love him and don't notice his stumpy legs. Ugh! My flesh would crawl if I had to sleep with *that!*"

"It doesn't bother me. He'll give me what I want."

I thought about it again. Perhaps . . . and I downed some brandy. After all, what was I? I had only wound up a charwoman. My daughter, a countess? But the thought of Marie making love to a freak sent a shudder through my body.

"*Mon Dieu*, it's not possible," I crossed myself in fear.

But how my little Maumau loved the *petit monsieur*, and how he ran to the piano in the midget's apartment and banged on the keys. Oh, what a good man he was to give such lessons to such a child so young. The poor Monsieur hobbled about, waving his arms to the music, and patted my Maumau on the back to encourage him. And this poor, poor man is a Count. I would wait for Maumau's terrible playing to end and tried to straighten out this filthy studio. Of course the Monsieur didn't want me to touch anything. After the lesson I would take my little Maumau by the hand and the poor *Comte* smiled at him and we would climb down the four floors to our apartment.

"I love the *petit monsieur*, Grand-mère," little Maumau would say after his piano lesson. "How I love Monsieur Henri. Don't you love him Grand-mère even if he is so small? Love him a little bit, please love him. I hope Maman loves him too."

"Oh, Maumau you're a wise one," I murmured to him, my Maumau.

I wanted to know the truth of the whole thing. What was she doing to him that the poor Monsieur looked so desperate? The poor midget was in agony. My daughter was a devil. Perhaps I'll bake him some pastries. It was small payment for his lessons to Maumau . . . the poor little man. I cry for him.

Mon Dieu, I'll climb the four flights of stairs to *Monsieur Le Comte's* studio. I would simply make a friendly visit to the midget, greet my daughter who was probably modeling, and leave. There was nothing wrong with that.

I trudged up the stairs the following day with little Maumau following closely behind me, munching on one of the sweets. The door to the midget's studio was partly open when I peered in. Did my daughter think I'd be afraid to come? I slowly opened the door wider pulling Maumau behind me and then, *sacrebleu!* I felt like I was choking on what I saw. I rubbed my eyes. It wasn't possible. My Marie was lying completely naked on a green velvet divan like some *putain* in a *maison close*, amidst that filthy hodge podge. Wasn't she ashamed to show off her nakedness this way? Was she modeling? I looked about. That mess got worse each day. And the windows, *Mon Dieu*, I had never seen such filth on windows. How does his Maman, the Countess, visit him? What a disgrace. I covered Maumau's body with my own, first turning him about so that he couldn't see her.

But it was the *petit monsieur* who amazed me; my mouth fell open in horror and I crossed myself and looked heavenward.

What did I do to deserve this monster for my daughter? Of course she must be mad to . . . I cannot even think the words . . . Monsieur Henri was sitting on the divan, half naked, kissing and caressing Marie's neck and shoulder and breasts and was breathing heavily. Such a sight to behold for a respectable woman like myself. I had never seen him without his pince-nez, and I was surprised that his eyes looked fine and expressive, but his huge nose and fat lips, ugh! I pushed little Maumau behind me again to block his view, but *Mon Dieu*, such a terrible sight this body of Monsieur Henri . . . such little midget legs now exposed for everyone to see. I crossed myself again as I stared at his poor, poor body. Such a horror, this midget. How could she stand such a horror? I wondered at that moment about the poor, poor Countess and what she must feel to have given birth to *that*. I saw that his pince-nez lay on a table and his cane had dropped on the floor. How can my daughter stand him, even bear to touch him . . . how can she look at him? Ugh! He makes my skin crawl!

"I want to play on the piano," whined Maumau behind me. "Let me play the piano, let me play it . . . please, please . . ."

They both heard my Maumau's voice coming from the door, and this Henri quickly pulled a cover over his midget legs, and Marie sat up and pulled a smock about her shoulders. "Don't come when I'm modeling . . . just leave, Maman," she said lowering her voice as she stared at Maumau. I shuddered cursing, and I crossed myself again and put the small cakes outside the door. Little Maumau peeked from behind me at the scene. "Come, *mon cher*," and I grabbed his hand.

"I saw Maman in there. Wasn't that Maman?" he began to wail. "That man is hurting her," he cried louder. "Why hasn't she got her clothes on? That man is going to kill her!" He began to scream.

"Be still, Maumau and come, *mon petit-fils*. She's modeling."

"Oh . . . but Monsieur Henri had no clothes on too."

I pulled my Maumau down the stairs with one hand, my body shaking and held onto the railing with my other hand . . . made for the bottle as soon as I entered the ground floor apartment. *Mon Dieu*, I have to forget that terrible sight.

"Why are you shivering Grand-mère? It's true that Monsieur

Henri is killing her. Maybe he'll turn her into a midget like him . . . I heard it once in a fairy tale."

"Stop talking, Maumau."

"Why hasn't that man any clothes on? I saw him. I saw him, and his legs look funny. I want my Maman . . . I want my Maman . . . I want her," and he began to wail. "Something terrible will happen to her . . . he looks like a monster and he'll put a spell on her; I want Maman!" He threw a chair down and looked up to Monsieur Henri's studio. "I want to go back up there! That little man is killing Maman," he wailed terribly.

"She'll be alright, be calm Maumau, and she'll come down soon, you'll see."

"I want to go up again," he cried louder and screwed up his face. "I want to see her," he screamed and then threw himself on the floor and kicked his arms and legs. I felt like hitting him but I never did.

"Oh, not again, Maumau. Don't throw a fit again or I won't love you . . . wait," and I bustled about the kitchen and dished out a bowl of soup into which I had poured some wine. "Here, drink it and you'll feel better."

"What is this wine soup called again, Grand-mère?"

"It's called a *chabrol* and the peasants from the Limousin countryside drink it. They give it to the children and it's good for them. Don't you like it, Maumau?"

"I love it, Grand-mère. It warms me up when it goes down and it makes me feel like I'm somebody else . . . give me some more." I spooned some more hot soup into the bowl with a huge ladle I had brought from Bessines and added the red wine.

"Here *mon cher* Maumau . . . soon you'll relax and feel better."

Maumau finished the soup in noisy slurps. "I love the taste, Grand-mère. Tomorrow you'll give me more."

How I loved this child. I smoothed the lock of hair which fell into his eyes and patted his cheeks.

"It makes me sleepy, Grand-mère."

"Good. Now lie down." But my little boy sat staring upward, such a little boy with a pale face and such sad blue eyes, the sad eyes of one of my Marie's lovers, the very same . . . of course I had seen those eyes in another, the eyes of Miguel Utrillo . . . I crossed myself. Then I leaned over and kissed him on his dark hair.

He is mine, not my daughter's and I am his beloved Grand-mère, and he watches me wash the soup bowl he eats from, watches me bustling about the kitchen and loves everything about me, yes, about *me*, not my daughter. Not *her*. He even loves the way my voice gets thick with brandy, and he isn't ashamed of me the way my daughter was as a child. I can drink as much as I like and he loves me just the same. What he loves most is sitting on my lap listening to my stories of the Limousin countryside. I am his dearest Grand-mère, and he sleeps with me and eats with me and sometimes at night I sing him to sleep with my old lullabies from Limousin. I am his whole world.

6

Henri
Love and Torment

*M*y beauteous Suzanne, my petite artiste, my free spirited one, my talented one and my very treacherous one. I can't trust her, believe her, accept her for an instant, and I know she'll destroy my life and my soul if I let her. Yet, I'm still helpless to fight what I continue to feel for her.

And so she continued a part of my life and the artistic and bohemian community as well. I used her as my hostess to elegant restaurants, lively boating parties or more intimate affairs in Père Lathuile's latticed garden on the Avenue de Clichy. She was the sole woman artist in the group. She, with her lively wit and biting tongue, vivaciousness, earthiness, radiant spirit, occasional histrionics, directness of her opinions voiced in an open unabashed manner, and her striking beauty, made a perfect foil for me. Her very petiteness made me appear taller. But she was no fool. She saw that they were versed in art and movements and she was untaught, save for myself and Degas. But I will continue to teach her and she will learn . . . how she will learn.

And it was at the informal gatherings in my studio where artists sat on boxes, that Suzanne wiped the dust from a table and set out bottles of cognac and absinthe. I had an innate skill in making cocktails, and the drinks flowed abundantly accompanied by our usual diatribes against the Cormon studio.

I invited Theo Van Gogh's redheaded, red bearded brother, Vincent to my studio and he came in a pair of worn workman overalls with knees smeared with paint. He had become a lay preacher, did missionary work among the miners, and then at thirty-three, surprisingly turned to art as a salvation. Without a word, he stood several canvases against the wall. The group looked awkwardly at one another and then ignored him.

"What do you call this work again, Vincent?" I asked.

"The Potato Eaters," Van Gogh murmured, and nothing more.

"It looks even better now than it did this afternoon," I said, trying to be complimentary while looking at Anquetin dozing.

Gauzi stifled a laugh, "Aren't the colors a bit dark?"

It took several minutes for Vincent to collect his paintings and storm out. He never said a word in reply.

"Animals! You're a miserable and unfeeling bunch of swine!" Suzanne burst out her eyes flashing.

There was low laughter in the room and then I tried to change the subject, "Thank God I finish with Cormon this year. I painted the model with pubic hair. He won't tolerate my vulgar displays. He wants me to paint a woman like a shaven chicken."

"Look at that Vincent and you see that all painters are lunatics. One must be slightly mad to devote one's life to a piece of canvas smeared with color," said Joyant, and everyone but Suzanne laughed. But the laugh didn't fool me. It had a bitter edge.

In the next few months Suzanne and I went to the countryside where she drew and I painted. Sometimes, we would set up our easels at the fountain in the Place Pigalle where I would pay one of the models for posing. We looked at one another's work, criticizing, suggesting, exchanging views and I showed her a simple palette she could use to begin her painting. There were two chrome yellows, vermilion, zinc white and turkey red.

She began to paint, unsure and without the boldness of line which characterized her drawings. I corrected her, encouraged her but she shook her head and returned to her pastel chalk. Painting was not yet her medium. After a while, she developed a new determination, thinned the colors on a palette with some turpentine, and sketched the outlines of a child of the streets on a cardboard. If the beginnings of color were but feeble attempts, they were her own and I saw the incipient evidence of her unique style. At this point I put her in the hands of Degas.

But I wanted more. I would refine her. I advised her on clothes she should wear, and educated her on places to dine and cultural events of the day. I wanted an intellectual equal and so I gave her difficult books to complete an education which she lacked. I presented her with Nietzche and Baudelaire.

Gradually, her vocabulary broadened, and the coarseness of the gutter which crept into her speech, softened. But when she was angry, she lapsed and peppered her speech with the streets of her childhood. As she read, she explored the meaning of words and endlessly questioned me about their usage and she began to express herself with increasing polish. Slowly she began to write short notes, then brief essays, essays of style and wit about what she felt. It was surprisingly good writing, and remarkable insights both about painting and of life unfolded before me. "I have been drawing madly," she wrote, "so that when I no longer have any eyes, I shall have them in my fingertips."

But Suzanne was undoubtedly Suzanne, the unpredictable, the beautiful young model and artist who could flaunt all convention, indifferent to others' opinions. And unfortunately, ultimately, our natures got in the way. Suzanne's erratic nature grated on my nerves, and added to my annoyance with her insouciance and unwillingness to be tied down to anything definite.. But I continued to pose her, this time for an ink drawing of a laundress with a basket on her arm hurrying through the streets.

Dealing with her free spirit was like dealing with the wind, and she drove me wild.

* * *

When she came into my studio one afternoon, I was hobbling back and forth. Finally I threw my cane across a table in agitation. "When do you expect me to finish this drawing? When, may I ask?"

"Don't be so impatient," she said pouting.

"Impatient? Impatient? I want you on the street of rue Tourlaque immediately! Certainly you know where the rue Tourlaque is don't you? It's not so far, do you understand?"

"Lower your voice. You're shouting."

"I'll shout as much as I want. How dare you keep me waiting! You're to model for me so that I can finish my work. Let me enlighten you in the event you've forgotten what I'm working on. It's called, *The Laundress*. Do you understand? Do you remember now what I was working on? And if you look, you will notice that *Le Cirque Fernando* is still standing unfinished against the wall. Can you possibly guess why? You are not to keep me waiting one extra moment. And another thing . . . why didn't you sell me your drawing . . . the one on his wall?" I shouted.

"I'll get it back for you."

"He'll never give it back. Degas will never give it back. Don't you know that? Why didn't you sell it to me?" I shouted in exasperation. "Degas parts with no art. It's a mania of his. He just took back a painting he sold me with his old excuse again that it is unfinished and I gave it to him. How could I have been so stupid! What a hoax. He never returned it and it's infuriating. He keeps retouching it and wants an impossible perfection."

"I really don't care. It's amazing that you criticize Degas."

"He's a damn hypochondriac."

"His complaints run off my back, Henri. Did I tell you that Bartholomé went crazy over my new drawings and he's now collecting my art? Can you believe it?" Then Suzanne's expression softened. She moved over to me and embraced me, bending over me as I painted and ran a finger down my cheek.

"You're exasperating. Leave me alone."

"Henri, *chéri*, please forgive me for being late the other day. You're much too demanding. Please say you forgive me. You must humor women you know. We're quite unpredictable," she said coyly and kissed my wiry beard, and removed my pincenez. "Don't hide your beautiful eyes, Henri." I looked up and a depth of tenderness welled up inside me. Oh, how I wanted to believe in her. My hands moved over her bodice and into the deep cleavage of her breasts. I unlaced the black weskit and opened the tiny pearl buttons of her white muslin blouse and held a breast to my lips and encircled the nipple with my tongue. Her eyes grew misty with desire. "Wait, Henri," she whispered as she quickly stepped out of her skirt and chemise, and we lay on my mother's plush divan entwined in one another.

"You are my madness, Suzanne," I breathed, as she kissed my eyes, my only good feature. "You drive me wild while I paint, while I sleep, in everything I do and you are the most exasperating unreliable, unpredictable, woman, and I think I love you. Suzanne, tell me, what am I to do . . . you will drive me insane!"

"Don't think, *chéri*," she whispered. "Don't think."

But by the start of December my friends' remarks about Suzanne's sexual proclivities finally left their mark on me. Their implications tortured me, tormented me so that every late moment, every mention of a former lover's name, every excuse she used loomed suspiciously. I found myself unable to work. And the musky fragrance of her body, a woman's body, lingered with me, and in my thoughts my tongue probed the sweet body I had painted that afternoon. I remembered how her skin came alive in the winter sun's mellow glow with a luminosity which seemed burnished by the light.

Christmas found me hobbling to and fro in my studio impatiently. "Where have you been? I've been waiting here for an hour, and I'm never going to finish that drawing, never."

"Poor Degas, I've just come from him poor man. He sends Zoë to me if I don't come to him."

"You're a liar . . . a goddamn liar! I've just seen Bartholomé and you weren't there."

"I met Adèle by accident."

"Adèle! Another lie . . . another miserable lie." My voice dropped. "Lies cost you nothing. Oh, how you excel at inventing the most amazing fabrications. But everyone sees through you, make no mistake. My friend Gauzi saw you with some Breton waiter from the Chat Noir. Is he your lover now? I'm not enough. Of course, I'm only half a man . . . you need the other half. I won't put up with it, Suzanne. You won't cuckold me."

"I don't know what you're talking about."

"You know very well what I mean. You sleep with all Paris!"

"You're *fou*, Henri! Am I not allowed to speak to anyone but you? Why have you grown so suspicious, why?"

"Suzanne, everyone knows you're a liar," I said quietly.

"Oh, so everyone knows it. So your precious friends have been feeding you garbage, have they?"

There was a change of venue as she softened and approached me. "Oh, Henri, please don't scold me. Just teach me to paint, and I'll always love you, Henri."

"You love yourself, Suzanne, none other."

"You never believe me. Alright, I'll pose for you and not say another word and suffer your cruelty." She dropped her skirt.

"Why should I believe you? Put your skirt back on! Do you take me for a dunce? There's no sitting today."

"Oh Henri," and she sat down next to me on the divan. "Henri, please don't treat me so when I love you." She embraced me. I stiffened up. "Henri, I love you. Can't you feel it when we make love, when you hold me in your arms?" Her voice became low in intimacy. "No other man has made love to me the way you have . . . none . . . and I've never felt the rapture I've felt with you when you have me in your arms." I realized that she was being truthful but was also battling for an easier life with every fiber of her being. "Marry me." she whispered. "We'll celebrate the new year with our marriage." It was a seductive whisper but her proposal of marriage was badly timed.

"You don't really want me. You still sleep with others. I know that for sure," I said slowly, reflectively.

"Well then, I'm leaving. I won't be insulted. Do you realize what you've done, Henri? I've proposed marriage, a demeaning thing for a woman to do. I've humiliated myself, and all you do is insult me," and very dramatically wiped her eyes.

Did I believe her? It was so much easier to believe her. I questioned what it was that she really felt for me. "False tears, Suzanne. Your eyes are as dry as mine. You annoy me. Don't try these women's wiles on me. Sometimes I think that Degas is right about women. All they give is misery. Just go."

"So *I* annoy *you*? You think that *you* don't annoy *me*? You're forever dictating to me . . . you tell me what to wear, what to paint, what to read, what I should have said to your goddamn friends, and even what to eat. I'm thoroughly sick of your arrogant ways. You think you own me, but I assure you, my dear count, no one owns me. And if I annoy you, you don't *have* to see me again. You certainly don't have to suffer on my account!" she shouted and slammed the door. I waited for a few moments hobbled to the door and opened it. Then I took her in my arms.

The following afternoon I became extremely agitated and downed one cognac after another. How I wanted to believe her. Then I searched Suzanne's face intensely. "I want to speak to you. This whole matter is driving me mad and I'm unable to paint. I want the truth from you, only the truth. Are you able to give me that? If you don't love me I can accept it, but just don't deceive me. I can't stand deception. Suzanne; are you in love with me, really in love with me, or is it another trick?"

She looked away from my searching eyes.

"No, look at me, Suzanne," I insisted. "Do you love me?"

"Of course, Henri."

She rose and embraced me, and I fought being drawn down again into a carnal maelstrom. What was it that she projected?

"No, sit still. I don't think you're talking of love. You're talking of our sexual relationship. Love is a different matter and doesn't consist only of desire, love making and jealousy. And it's reached me that there are others, and that hurts me deeply."

"Why do you speak of jealousy when you're the only one who is so insanely jealous? I told you yesterday. There is no one, I swear. What must I say to convince you?"

"And of course you know that your former lover, Miguel Utrillo is in Paris."

"I haven't seen him. He means nothing to me."

"Really? Isn't he the father of your child? You suffer from no lack of imagination and lies cost you nothing. You disappear whenever it suits you and then you reappear when you so choose with goddamn excuses . . . all lies. And I've been foolish enough to believe the most improbable reasons for your absences. Do you take me for an idiot?"

"Miguel has nothing to do with me."

"I'm an artist, Suzanne, and I cannot help but see similarities, and your little Maurice is a young version of Miguel."

"I haven't even noticed. Anyway, it's all in the past. You can't hold my past against me, Henri, or we can't go on."

"I sincerely want to trust you. Even Degas calls you a she-devil. He may be right. You disappear and lie about where you've gone, and you skip modeling appointments and make up impossible stories, and now you say you're in love with me. How can I believe you? I think that love is as big as the person behind it. How much can you really love? Perhaps you've never loved anyone but yourself. I don't think you even love your own son."

Suzanne mouthed a silent protest.

"Don't refute this. Don't try. I've seen no evidence of your loving anyone, not your son, your mother and certainly not me."

"Why must I have to pass a test? Haven't I proven myself to you? I love only you." She stroked my hair.

"It's not . . . not enough. I still have reservations." But I became more tender. "If you really love me, you'll have to think about it carefully." I sat down and poked randomly with a brush at an unfinished canvas, and blew layers of dust from the table. "Suzanne, you have to think that you are young and beautiful and . . . healthy, and I'm a hopeless cripple . . . always in pain."

"It doesn't matter, Henri. You're a good man, a fine artist and a wonderful lover."

"And rich," I added.

"Well, I won't refuse wealth, but it means nothing to me."

"Of course that's another lie, Suzanne. My money could give you the life you want. Even a fool could figure that one out."

I must have touched the truth because she flushed and said passionately, "The trouble with you, Henri, is that you're much too demanding a lover and I will never forget how cruel you are and will never forgive you."

She wiped her eyes and stormed out.

This time I didn't go after her.

Several days later, Gauzi and little Maurice burst into my studio. Maurice cried. "Maman is going to kill herself because of you! You've got to stop it! She's got a knife in her hand and she's going to stick it into her heart." He was sobbing furiously.

"What!"

"Henri, it's true. You've got to stop her!" Gauzi said.

"Pl . . . pl . . . please . . . Monsieur," Maurice sobbed hysterically, "do something before she's dead . . . please . . . please . . ."

I hobbled out of my studio and down the staircase one step at a time, holding tightly to the banister, forgetting my cane. Once outside Suzanne's apartment, I heard Maman Madeleine screaming, "That's a fine mess you made . . . to pick up a knife like that! You frightened poor little Maumau out of his wits. What good do you think it will do you?"

I stared through the door which was partly ajar, my throat closing up and my legs sending shooting pains through my body.

"Henri won't marry me. I had to do something. Even Gauzi was impressed . . . perhaps Henri will be."

"So that's what comes from all this scribbling . . . and he'll never believe it . . . oh, he knows, he knows you wouldn't kill yourself. He knows. He's a fine, smart man, and it's a real pity."

"You're wrong, I'm very fond of him, and . . ."

"But you don't love him."

"If he's good to us, I could learn to love him. I'll be a good wife to him. I would love to be a countess, Maman, and have the freedom to paint and have beautiful clothes. Most women look for money in marriage. Why should I be different?"

"It's wrong to fool a midget. And he believes that you love him, the poor, poor cripple."

"Of course he believes me, even with his clever ways. He believes me because he's a fool like other men. Didn't I ever tell you, Maman that men are no match for the cleverness of women? Deceit was mixed in with our mother's milk from the time we were infants. Look about you, Maman. The women who trade their bodies in marriage for respectability and convenience are no better than the whores you ridicule. But at least as a countess, I'll paint and contribute something to this life besides spawning little babies."

I heard Maman Madeleine grunt, and saw her take a long slurp of brandy, wipe her mouth and fall into a chair.

I began to shake and struggled up the stairs to the studio stopping at each step while clutching the banister. I sat on the divan on which we made love and then cried with my head in my hands. I wanted so much to believe that she loved me. I could even excuse her attempt at feigned suicide if she loved me, for I could ascribe it all to the wiles of women but there was nothing, nothing. I looked up at one of her drawings on the wall and wiped my eyes. It was all a hoax, no love, all false . . . all false.

I sat awhile, and then hobbled over to the cabinet and took a bottle of cognac and poured out glass after glass, downing each quickly. Then I lay down on the divan, took off my pince-nez, wiped my eyes, and stared at the painting of Suzanne in the butterfly hat which hung on my wall.

It was spring of 1887 when Suzanne started modeling for my *La Buveuse*, The Drinker. As time went on, our relationship grew more strained. I painted her seated before a bottle of red wine at a table at La Nouvelle-Athènes, her disgruntled, nauseated, tired face resting on her left hand and her eyes staring vacantly in the distance. It was a picture of an older woman, not one in her early twenties. Perhaps the painting reflected the dissolution of our romantic interlude. It was a far cry from the fresh faced Suzanne of Renoir's *Dance at Bougival* or my *Suzanne Valadon* of the butterfly hat.

Now that my major work with her was finished, I became even more distant as though I detached myself completely from any emotion I once felt. She made overtures of affection to me and tried to rekindle some of the voluptuousness which had marked our lovemaking, but I remained unresponsive.

"Don't try your little tricks on me. I've had enough of them. I'm not interested." I sat still on the green plush divan on which we had once made love.

"I love you, Henri . . . and you won't believe it."

"Don't sicken me with your lies. Just come in tomorrow for your session and don't keep me waiting. Your lover, Miguel will have to be patient," I said bitterly.

"*Merde*, Henri, you won't drop it, will you?"

"And you, Suzanne, are a liar, as usual."

When she left I felt the terrible chill of loss and wanted to call her back and hold her in my arms again, kissing her sweet body. Oh, my Suzanne, why couldn't you be honest with me? I love you ... oh, my God, I do love you. And of course you know that, you improbable, exasperating, deceitful, vixen. You do know it. And of course you count on that

* * *

There are moments in my life that I feel I'm watching the enacting of a play, and aside from its direction, I'm not part of it. I'm not one of its actors. It's always done at a distance and it's always unreal. That aspect of unreality is the main ingredient.

The play unfolds this afternoon and its characters are a banker and a model. And it plays to the bitter end.

I have a friend, Paul Mousis, who has a talent. It's not in art but in making money. He's a banker, a bourgeois in strange surroundings, for he is a nightly habitué of the Auberge du Clou and the Chat Noir cabarets. He buys drinks for scores of artists and generally becomes a part of Bohemia, a fish out of water.

He visits me this afternoon at my studio, and watches my Suzanne posing with an interest bordering on salaciousness.

"Paul, I want you to meet my model, Suzanne Valadon. Suzanne, this is a gentleman of great means. I know you'll be interested." My voice is insinuating and Mousis is puzzled.

Her eyes flicker as she continues her pose.

"He's a wealthy banker," I continue bitterly, "someone like myself who can keep a woman and her family in style."

"Henri!" Mousis says sharply. "There's really no need to . . ."

"Oh, yes, there's a need." I say insistently. "*She* has a need." Oh how sweet and coy she is when she wants to be . . . deceitful like women . . . my God, Degas is right, I scream to myself.

"Have no fear because his words don't bother me," she smiles sweetly.

"Don't speak because you're ruining your pose." I feel myself becoming agitated. Why am I becoming so excited? I'm only the director of this scene. After all, it is I who invited Paul Mousis here. I must become more detached.

Mousis reddens. "It appears that I've arrived in the midst of some, some difficulty between you?"

"Not at all, Paul," says Suzanne breaking her pose and sitting up. "Don't give this a second thought . . . too much cognac."

"The sitting is over!" I shout. "I will call you to complete it when I need you, Marie." I say her former name deliberately, pronouncing it very clearly, but her face shows no expression.

Paul stands still, his eyes drinking in Suzanne's beauty and is uneasy. "I think I'll be going, Henri," and he takes his coat.

"Oh, wait for me, Paul, I'll go with you." She smiles fetchingly for my benefit. I take a bottle of cognac from the shelf.

Suzanne changes her clothes swiftly behind a screen, slips out of the drab dress she has worn for the sitting, and unties her hair. She steps out and stands for a few moments in her chemise, deliberately dropping one strap to expose one breast . . . its pink nipple appears like a delicate shining rosebud. Mousis glances at her furtively, is hypnotized, flushes and looks away. She stares at me flaring her nostrils in defiance and I murmur, "Whore," beneath my breath. Mousis pretends not to hear.

She dresses quickly and comes forward, radiant. "Come Paul," she says, tucking her arm into his. I hate her intensely for it! Mousis looks flustered as they leave the studio.

I take a drink from the bottle of cognac and then hobble over to the canvas I'm working on. I pick up a brush and then throw it down. I sit still by the window and watch Suzanne and Mousis leave the building. They seem to dissolve into the atmosphere.

I'm charged with an emotion I can't handle and even the cognac can't stifle it. Its force had been building up for weeks and I attempt to stem it but I'm helpless. I keep adjusting and readjusting my pince-nez until the huge tidal wave of frustration and grief overwhelm me. It's sorrow for what I have lost, for the moments of joy I have felt with her, for the love I have for her, and for the normalcy which has been denied my stunted body, something I had learned to deal with over and over again; all this sweeps over me in a giant deluge, pressing for final release.

Then I begin to sob.

The play is over.

7

Suzanne
The Gay Nineties

*D*ear Paul Mousis, so dull, so painfully dull. It was all quite amusing, a veritable exercise in womanly guile. How my dear Degas would detest me. *Grâce à Dieu* he never saw it. Everything I did amused this Paul Mousis, and I flaunted every womanly wile, every asset, dangling all the voluptuousness I possessed in front of him in promise. I was intent to compensate for what occurred with Henri with a vengeance. Before the evening was over, Paul's hands glided over my silk taffeta in the darkness of the coach, with the *cocher* given repeated orders to travel about the boulevards. He unlaced my black velvet bodice and uncovered my full breasts. I heard him moan as we clung together, his breath coming faster and his kisses deepening, awkward, and he ventured unsure with his tongue; his hands moved beneath my petticoats fumbling, searching. *Merde*, he was like a schoolboy. It amused me that our match was so uneven. His very inexperience lessened any desire I could have. Of course he was in love with me but it didn't matter. I wasn't sure if I wanted him. He tried to take me home with him to make love to me, but I held back much against his insistence, and within a few weeks he proposed marriage.

Frankly, I felt dizzy at the rapidity of the courtship. I hadn't really expected his offer of marriage and promptly turned it down. He pursued me all through the remainder of my sittings for Lautrec, and if I didn't feel passion for Paul, I felt affection. He was kindly, always bringing a gift for Maumau when he called on me, joked with Maman, flattered her and admired my art, being something of a dilettante. But it was the promise of security and respectability which drew me to him. It was the respectability which Henri wouldn't give me. I craved the release to do my art and Maumau desperately needed a father, but try as I would to convince myself, I couldn't come to a decision.

The Paris Exposition burst upon us in 1889, a frenzied fever.

Degas sent a hastily written note through his servant asking me to accompany him to the Exposition. "I'll call for you early tomorrow morning with my carriage, and wear stout shoes," he instructed me.

I approached the solemn faced Zoë who was practically out the door.

"Tell Monsieur Degas I should be delighted and honored to accompany him. How is he?"

"Oh, Mademoiselle, you know how he is . . . always complaining about his eyes, always complaining about something. After you visit us, he's always cheerful. What kind of news do you bring for him to change so, not like those silly models with their idle chatter. But with me, he's always acting the invalid, always grumbling about something or other. He says that you are balm for his soul. Even his eyes improve when you come, so you must come more often, Mademoiselle."

The following morning the landau arrived and I kissed Degas with affection on the cheek as he gave the *cocher* directions to proceed to the Exposition. I felt a tremor of excitement and intense feeling of pride of having been selected as his escort.

He carried himself well, was wiry, of medium height, well proportioned, imparting an air of distinction. He dressed conservatively with a refined elegance, and wore a top hat. He wore tinted glasses to protect his bad eyes from the glare of the sun, had a closely cropped beard and closely trimmed hair. I felt vastly important by virtue of his importance. He was the Master the other artists looked up to, and because of his biting criticism, feared him and cowered before him. But not I. I seemed to dull his sharp tongue and soften his caustic remarks. His barbs rolled off my back like water, but he made them infrequently. I always spoke my piece with him, and I knew he admired my honesty.

"You and Mary Cassatt are the only women I can tolerate," he often said in a grumbling voice, "but I hardly see her . . . must be her damned family." And I would always answer with some playful affront against Cassatt, saying, "Of course I'm the better artist." But Degas said nothing. He revered Cassatt and was her mentor in art as he was mine.

The day was a brilliant one, full of the light and sunshine of a late spring morning as though it stood as a monument to the light filled canvases of the Impressionists in Volpini's. The Exposition had opened May 1, and there was a kind of muted hysteria in this celebration of the centennial of the French Revolution. I felt the mounting excitement surrounding the Exposition. There was the new Eiffel Tower built for the occasion which for weeks had been blasted by critics for its cost of fifteen million franks, the refusal of the royalists to display any flags on the day of the opening and the boycotting of the exhibition by the nobility. What a mad influx of foreigners buying up cheap little replicas of the Eiffel Tower. It was all a delirium pervading Paris. My God, how this frenzy surrounded us.

Degas and I stepped down from the carriage and saw Henri Lautrec sitting at a sideshow in the rue du Caire, drawing feverishly. Near him stood a young composer he introduced as Claude Debussy, who in turn introduced an odd looking friend as Erik Satie, a struggling piano player. This strange individual wore a rumpled gray velvet suit and promptly stared fiercely at me. Henri continued drawing with his thick squat neck, muscular shoulders, and rolled up shirt sleeves exposing his sinewy arms. I chatted briefly with him attempting to thaw him out but I should not have bothered. How dead our romantic interlude was. My coyness had no effect on him and he ignored me completely.

Degas stood by making caustic comments about the Eiffel Tower, and paused for a moment to introduce me to James Whistler, the American painter. He was a mass of complaints, "The government would do better to foster the talent of some of the starving artists. We have talent falling by the wayside and this structure is a veritable abomination and a thorough squandering of public funds. I hope this doesn't happen in America," he said to Whistler. "I have no fear Jimmy, that the whole business will be investigated including George Eiffel himself. What d'you say, eh?" Degas said using his favorite expression. He pointed his cane in the direction of the Eiffel Tower as though his gesture would demolish it.

James Whistler listened and smiled impishly.

"I'll see you at Halevy's tomorrow night, Jimmy. Otherwise visit me at my new address, rue Victor-Massé, and taste Zoë's pastries and marvelous marmalade.

"I'd rather see some of the Daumiers you collected, Edgar." I tugged at his arm and we turned toward Volpini's.

"I hope we meet again, Mademoiselle," Whistler tipped his tall silk hat, flashed a practiced charismatic smile and took off. He looked back. "Oh, come to my studio next weekend Edgar, and bring your lovely protégée. I've done it all in blue and white, quite a feast for the eyes."

"Terribly histrionic personality, that fellow," reflected Degas, "although I do admire him . . . good artist, but he looks so goddamn middle aged."

"I rather liked him," I said.

"Be careful with these Americans, an interesting lot but still a bit uncivilized, a bit unbridled . . . stems from their revolution, a peculiar form of government formulated by an undisciplined pack of hotheads. The country is barbaric with an abhorrent group of savages called Indians with feather headdresses and red skin and cannibalistic, I've heard . . . perilous country where one cannot go west for fear of being slaughtered. How does anyone survive, I ask you? Mary Cassatt escaped from them, but none too soon. She came from a hedonistic place called Philadelphia, a bunch of barbarians who ignored her art, provincial pigs, cultural misfits! In America they care little about art, a country completely without culture, but enough of this, walk faster."

I tucked my arm into his. Degas walked briskly, taking long strides so that I half skipped in an attempt to keep up with him.

"It's bad enough here where monstrosities are built like that

Eiffel Tower for which mad architects are thoroughly responsible, mad architects! Can't you walk more quickly? *Sacrebleu,* don't take mincing steps like a damn female! I would like to witness this atrocity which passes for an artists' exhibition."

"You're not going to get me to move one whit faster, Monsieur Degas."

"Women." Degas grumbled.

But I walked with quickened pulse, and what I saw on Volpini's walls was dazzling.

The paintings were framed in white against deep pomegranate walls. Degas stared and his lips muttered something, and his eyes widened in amazement. In the cheap restaurant, among the cheap smells, scrambling about the tables in the dining room, between waiters carrying trays and patrons milling about, were the artists in a frenzy to hang their pictures suitably, to be noticed by the patrons slurping their soup.

"The idea of putting the paintings in white frames was an innovation of Gauguin," Émile Bernard confessed to Degas. "He is mad to have us against red walls and exhibit in this place."

"Who will observe any of this?" said Degas. "Absurd."

"Who is that?" I motioned to a figure directing the exhibit.

"That is Paul Gauguin," Degas replied.

"Ma fois! He cuts quite a figure." I stared in admiration.

"Interesting fellow, this Gauguin. He was a stockbroker and the damn fool left his wife and family . . . gave up all that money and ran to painting and sculpting. He spent some time with Bernard in Pont-Aven . . . developed a style called Symbolism . . . and poor fellow, got himself involved with that madman, Van Gogh in Arles, who himself landed in the hospital."

"Where is Gauguin's wife?" I asked.

"Somewhere, crying her eyes out, depending on the little money he sends."

"What courage it took for him to do that."

"As a woman, I should think you would condemn it as irresponsible."

"As an artist, I see it differently."

"I see by your eyes that the paintings fascinate you."

"How marvelous it all is."

I felt the excitement as I flitted from one painting to another, but I saw the work of only one, Gauguin. He mystified me with the brilliance of his tropical color, with the primitiveness of his art combined with the luminosity of Oriental cloisonné. I didn't understand the theory behind what he accomplished. But I understood the emotion, for it was akin to my own, in the firmness of the dark sure lines and clarity of my own work. It seemed as though his perceptions melded with my own, and he had a strong impact on my own artistic striving. Here was a fresh view of life which I had not yet thought about. I lost myself in the clear, flat colors of his canvases, and Degas watched me as I tried to drink in everything Gauguin had done. I marveled at his artistic rhythms and could identify with his alienation. I thought of the drawings I had made alone in my room, so secretive and so individual.

When I left the exhibit with Degas, I felt that something very significant had occurred.

"I think this exhibit will have an effect on your art, Maria, what d'you say, eh?"

"I don't copy any artist." I said bravely.

"We'll see, my Maria, we'll see."

In 1890, a new decade began.

Henri went to Brussels for an art exhibit and challenged a Belgian artist to a duel because he insulted Van Gogh. All Montmartre was entranced with the incident, with visions of Lautrec hobbling about a dueling field. Roars of laughter filled La Nouvelle-Athènes.

"Ridiculous and ludicrous," grumbled Degas. "The audacity of him! Only a count's son would have such audacity, and a cripple at that, poor devil."

I watched Henri grow in importance with a mixture of pride, envy and frustration. This is the artist I had held in my arms, my body entwined about his poor misshapen limbs and had wholly received his passionate advances with an acceptance which precluded his grotesqueness.

I continued seeing Paul Mousis whose relationship with me remained status quo. Upon my insistence he took me to the Moulin Rouge where Lautrec's new painting, *Au Moulin Rouge*, was unveiled. I had watched Henri do this painting from prior sketches, with his customary hat on his head in the tranquillity of his studio. At the Moulin Rouge, which opened in 1889 on the Boulevard De Clichy, I saw Henri accompanied by his friends, Gauzi, Anquetin, Henri Rachou and Joyant. Friends continually flocked to him. But when I saw him I felt like embracing him. Was that love or some absurdity of regret?

News reached the Montmartre of Vincent Van Gogh's confinement in an asylum, of his shooting himself on July 27th and dying soon thereafter. Several months after, his brother Theo went mad, was committed and died, stirring up much commotion among the artists in Montmartre. The deaths of Vincent and Theo seemed to shake the very foundations of La Nouvelle-Athènes.

"Why the devil did he do it? How does a man have the guts to shoot himself? The sun got to his head, that madman," said Gauzi. "It scares the hell out of me . . . I think I'll leave art altogether." He sipped some absinthe.

"I know why he did it," said Anquetin. "He painted as a patient in an asylum at St. Remy. It's the ravings of a lunatic. One has only to look at his *Starry Night*, and the twisted writhing, mad brush strokes to know his lunacy."

"Yet, one can feel the intensity of what he was trying to say, *n'est-ce pas?*" I interjected. "I can understand that."

"Well put," said Joyant.

"You just have no heart, Louis," said Lautrec. "Women have gone to your head."

"Pigs!" I said. "I'm ashamed of you all. Poor Vincent never earned a sou with his art. He was a genius, Anquetin."

"I only feel sorry for the fool . . . the world will soon forget he was ever here. That's the tragedy," said Anquetin.

"That fate awaits all of us," murmured Joyant.

"I refuse to believe that I won't matter and I owe it all to Henri. I would be nothing without him." I said.

"Don't try to patronize me, Suzanne," said Henri, but he smiled at me, an unaccustomed smile, a smile of pride at his discovery of my talent. The wound was beginning to heal.

Several weeks later he called on me. "We'll all be there again at the Auberge du Clou including Henri Rachou and I want you to meet my cousin, Dr. Tapié de Céleyran."

I nodded, pleased.

"*Bien*, so you'll be my hostess once again."

"I wondered when you'd ask me." I bent over him as he sat still, impeccably dressed, holding his cane and drawing imaginary lines of a painting with its tip.

"Oh Henri, can't it be as it once was?" I ran my finger down his cheek. I felt a strong feeling of affection and desire at that moment. Was it love?

He flushed for a moment, his eyes troubled and they reflected an awful turmoil. He stiffened and jerked his body to one side.

"How was it? I don't remember now."

"You know how it was. Why do you torture me?"

"I torture *you*? *Incroyable!* How many lovers have you had since leaving me? Of course, Mousis. There must have been a dozen more . . . Miguel Utrillo is back in town . . . now you can go back to him. He must have quite a cock on him!"

"I love only you Henri . . . and you know that's the truth."

"*Vraiment!* You would love half a man when you can have so many whole ones? But Marie, it's known that you love no one but yourself. Even Miguel and Paul Mousis must see through you and your fabrications. Well this discussion bores me. It's a familiar one and nothing has changed between us, nothing. If you want to be my hostess, we'll resume our friendship on a casual basis."

He stood up to leave, stood an erect four and a half feet, avoided my eyes and hobbled out on his cane.

I painted, but my brush felt curiously empty afterward; and for the first time in my relationship with Henri Lautrec, my eyes welled with tears.

Henri's cousin, Dr. Tapié de Céleyran, came to Paris and they became inseparable. Céleyran was an odd looking man, attenuated with gold rimmed glasses on a beak-like florid nose, black and glossy hair parted in the center, a slight stoop, a long mustache, and a long coat exposing a heavy watch chain which crossed his stomach. Henri, poor stunted Henri, his head crowned with a bowler, stood beside him, comically beside him, completely dominating him, never allowing him to express any opinion about art or deal with anyone Henri didn't like. If Tapié adored Henri, he didn't show it but was with him constantly, virtually Henri's slave. I couldn't understand the relationship except that this doctor almost enjoyed being the butt of Henri's jibes. Because of his cousin's attachment to the Hospital International, Henri attended operations and made studies of the surgeon Pean.

It was an evening shortly before the new year when we met at the Auberge du Clou. Joyant spoke of his position at the Goupil's Gallery, Émile Bernard spoke of Pont-Aven and the arrogance of Gauguin and Henri spoke of a commission to design a poster for the Moulin Rouge.

"How do you think you'll do it?" asked Anquetin.

"What about the concept of the *Gay Nineties?*" Henri said.

"I love it, Henri," I smiled sweetly. "It has a decided ring to it. *The Gay Nineties.* Don't you think it has a ring to it, Dr. Céleyran?" I deliberately questioned him, amazed at the doctor's lack of emotion.

The doctor half nodded his approval and opened his mouth as though to speak.

"Don't overdo it, Tapié," Henri said sharply. "You know nothing about art." His cousin quickly became mute.

"Why can't he speak, Henri?" I protested.

"It's none of your affair, Suzanne!" Henri's eyes flashed angrily and he stamped his foot.

"You're still impossible." I forgot that when Henri didn't get his way he could be difficult and a bit childish. I felt myself take a step backwards in our relationship.

There was an embarrassed lull.

"What will you paint, Henri?" asked Rachou breaking the silence.

"Probably a dancer. I might do this La Goulue, the glutton, kicking up her skirts. Here's a sketch of what I have in mind." He pulled out a wrinkled paper from his pocket.

"I can barely make it out," said Joyant. "Who is this behind her?"

"That's her partner, Valentin le Désossé."

"I think it's marvelous, Henri," I said.

"I don't appreciate your compliments, Suzanne," said Henri irritably.

"Did you hear about it? La Goulou was found in bed with La Môme Fromage, her lady dancer friend. She goes both ways, that pig," said Gauzi. "She denied it, but La Môme Fromage said they were in love with each other. Yvette Guilbert said that La Môme Fromage is a dachshund turned into a woman, short legs, long body and plumpish."

"Where do you get your information, Gauzi?" said Henri grimly.

"Did you know that the girls dance there without their culotte," said Anquetin. "When they cancan, there are no secrets."

The drinks flowed freely; absinthe, cognac, Bordeaux, Beaujolais and Pommard were passed about, along with a host of others. I was in a mood for the *Green Muse,* absinthe.

I usually didn't drink. It didn't take long after I tasted it for a peculiar pleasant warmth to settle on me and everything bathed in a mellow golden glow.

"I hear that white absinthe is more powerful than the green," I blurted out to the group.

"Keep away from absinthe, Suzanne." Henri ordered.

"Why?"

"Simply because I said so. Did you know that Victor Hugo saturated himself in it and it killed him and he's not alone. I order it because of these idiots."

There was a general murmur from the group at the table.

"I don't believe you. It's harmless."

"Believe anything you want, Suzanne. You're too delicate. Of course, you'll do as you please as you usually do."

"Of course."

The talk at the table became more animated and I felt marvelous. The Green Muse had done its work as I hugged each artist in turn. I loved them all. I left Henri for the last and he held me for a surprising moment when I embraced him. The group stared.

"Did you hear the good fortune of my friend, Paul Cézanne?" laughed Émile Bernard. "His father died and left him an income of twenty-five thousand francs, and now he can paint in peace and take care of that witch Hortense . . . never earned a sou in his life from his paintings . . . finally found a use for his father."

"Do you still admire his paintings, Émile?" asked Bartholomé.

"I think he's a genius . . . see Cézanne's paintings while Tanguy still has them. They're like his children."

"Who else would have them . . . they're an atrocity," said Gauzi. "Frankly, I'm thinking of leaving art altogether to design furniture . . . had enough of the *midinettes* here, and thinking of returning to Toulouse. I can marry, have a fat dowry, and her father will set me up in business. *La vie de Bohème* is not for me."

"Every man to his own taste, but I remember your betrothed in Toulouse, and besides her mustache, she resembles a cow. What has she to recommend her?" said Henri.

"Money!" I answered wryly, "of course, money."

"You certainly know a great deal about that Suzanne, don't you? You know what it takes to keep a woman in style," said Henri.

"Oh, you dear man. You know you long to keep me in style," I said without smiling.

"Really? It's taking a bit of doing on your part, isn't it?"

His bitter tone caused another awkward lapse in the conversation. Even through the drink, I felt an awful frustration and that sadness of loss coming over me.

"By the way, I heard that Renoir got married, and he can't cough up the rent. It's a case in point," said Gauzi breaking the silence.

"*Aline*? To Aline Charigot . . . did he marry Aline?" I blurted out. Henri looked sharply at me. His face looked odd and his features fractured as though they were disassociated from each other. I had heard that absinthe did this.

"Was that her name, Charigot? He married his model," said Bernard. "Already had a five year old son with him . . . must be the style. Monet did the same."

Henri continued to watch my face with interest; I forced a blank expression, but my cheeks burned hotly. I didn't feel well at all when Miguel Utrillo swaggered over to the group, his pipe in hand. Was I going to throw this stuff up?

"Well, welcome my old friend, Miguel," said Henri Lautrec in a loud voice. "Now when did you come back to Paris? I thought you were here," he said glancing at me. "*Garçon*, bring over a chair for my friend, Miguel, and some cognac, or would you prefer another drink?" His voice was husky with emotion. He now ignored me, his bulbous nose a startling crimson.

"No, cognac is fine."

Miguel sat down on the chair brought by the waiter.

"What brings you to Paris, Miguel?" Bernard asked.

"I'm the art critic for the Barcelona paper *La Vanguardia*."

Then Miguel's eyes swept over me and I felt my body come alive. I looked up at Miguel and felt an old flush of excitement creep over me. I convinced myself that my trembling was sheer madness brought about by the wine. His dark presence soothed me like a balm for Henri's sarcasm. "Where are you staying?" I asked dispassionately.

"In my old room at the Moulin de la Galette . . . it has memories" He looked significantly at me.

"Of course it does," said Henri hoarsely. "And Suzanne remembers every one of them, don't you Suzanne?"

"Shut up, Henri!" I said in a voice husky with drink and the room whirled crazily.

Dr. Tapié suddenly cleared his throat and broke the stillness. He sensed Henri's agitation and ordered cognac both for himself and Henri. I was amazed that Henri allowed him to call the garçon. The doctor downed his drink, sat as sanguine as before, with hardly a ripple in his phlegmatic facade.

Everyone stopped talking and looked at one another. The atmosphere was charged, yet no one knew why. An uncomfortable silence was replaced by a shimmering expectation of something suffused with emotion and building like an impending orgasm. I felt it, one of my crystal moments; it happened once when I entered Degas' studio with the portfolio under my arm; and once when I first modeled, an exquisite sense of belonging.

I found that I lost control over my words. "I have a boy . . . you know . . . I have a son . . . who has a mother . . . but the papa . . . who is he?"

"Be careful, you're drunk, Suzanne," said Henri. "You never

could drink anything."

"That's not true, Henri, not true. And you're not my keeper, so shut up! And I'm not drunk. I'm sober, very, very sober," I hiccuped, but the talk at the table sounded jangled, and Miguel's face altered . . . he was as he had once been, younger and more passionate. "And who would like to guess who the papa is?" I continued laughing.

There was a nervous laugh from Anquetin as everyone looked at him.

"Shut up, Suzanne!" said Henri. "You've had far too much. Oh, Anquetin, don't look so frightened. She's not pointing to you as the father, yet."

"Who *is* the father of your boy?" asked a matter-of-fact Gauzi.

"I'll have to think about it. It might be Renoir or Chavannes or . . . perhaps . . . ?" And I looked at Miguel.

Miguel flushed and everyone grew quiet. There was an uncomfortable silence and then Miguel spoke with a tremor in his voice.

"Well, if it's Renoir or Chavannes, I would be happy to sign my name to the work of either of these two artists. Call him a *Utrillo*, and I'll become Maurice's father. I'll be glad to sign a declaration of paternity, Maria."

The silence was deafening and then a surprised murmur.

"Are you joking, Miguel?" asked Henri.

"I'm dead serious."

"Are you sure you know what you're doing?" asked Rachou.

"Yes," responded Miguel.

Then I said in a low voice, "Agreed." My heart beat furiously.

"Fine. We'll go to the *mairie* next week," Miguel said unsmiling.

"*Bien*, I'll hold . . . hold you to it." I stumbled over my words.

There was an awkward silence when Henri ordered a new round of drinks to celebrate the occasion. Henri's cousin shook his head, and attempted to say something. "It's none of your affair, Tapié!" shouted Henri and Dr. Tapié quickly shut his mouth. He didn't speak for the rest of the evening.

A bitter cold gripped Paris the following week and when Maman dressed her Maumau in a little suit, a white starched shirt and high laced up boots, she despaired of Miguel's coming at all. But Maumau waited expectantly and I slicked down his hair for the occasion but he fidgeted so. The prospect of a new father was no small thing. It was something I never had.

When Miguel arrived, his coat was dusted with snow and he blew on his fingers as he warmed himself before the ancient stove.

"You're going to have a real papa now. Miguel Utrillo is going to be your papa," I said to a confused Maurice who continued fidgeting and slipped on and off his chair.

The deed was executed while Maman Madeleine clutched an overwhelmed Maumau tightly by the hand. Maumau was legally adopted and was to be known as Maurice Utrillo from then on. Maman continually muttered through the proceedings but it quelled some of my own nagging torment of having been born a bastard.

The edict of paternity read:

"On this day, January 27, 1891, I hereby recognize as my son Maurice, born December 26, 1883, whose birth was recorded on December 26, at the town hall of the 18th Arrondissement as the son of Marie Valadon and an unknown father . . . on the declaration by Miguel Utrillo, 28, journalist, residing at 57 Boulevard de Clichy, who recognizes as his son, Maurice."

Maurice, now, legitimately had a father.

There was only one trouble with the new surname *Utrillo*. Maurice refused to accept it.

In the winter of 1892, I decided to do a drawing of Miguel. It was as though I sensed that he would leave forever. He posed for me in the stillness of the small room near the bar in the Moulin de la Galette. I drew the Catalan in profile *Miguel Smoking a Pipe* with his aristocratic features, downcast eyes and air of pensive sadness about him; and when I finished he looked at it and remarked about his likeness to Maumau. I said nothing.

"Maurice is now my son. You have only to look at this drawing," he said.

"When are you returning to Barcelona?" was all I answered.

"Not for a while yet. Oh, Maria why do we fight? I loved you once. Why do we always quarrel? I have asked myself this question a hundred times and can't find the answer. I probably still love you."

"I love you Miguel for what you have done for Maumau," I answered.

"Not for myself? Nothing more? What's wrong? Let it be as it used to be . . . let it be, my delicious one . . . let it be. I've thought about it often, and if you would come back with me . . ."

"And do you think for one moment that I would leave Montmartre?"

"Yes."

"My dear Miguel. Certainly, you don't know me. I would never be far from here."

"Do you remember that we once ate beneath the arbors of the Guinguette and made love in this little room? Tell me how much will you remember, Maria, tell me."

I remembered that we once met naturally, a kind of magic enmeshing us. Oh, how utterly helpless men were and yet how wonderful. How I could kindle in them that spark of pure longing by just pressing my body close to his at the Chat Noir; it was quite by accident of course and *voilà*, his cock pierced a hole right through me. Men were absurd in their needs . . .

I remembered that he once murmured, "Oh my beautiful little one . . . in Spain you would be my little Maria." He had said this over and over again the first time he took me. He pushed my skirts high then and his hand caressed my body wet with longing, and I surrendered to him eagerly, again and again as the grasses grew tall; and we lay in a clearing behind the shade of two budding poplars. And everything smelled fragrant that spring at the top of the Butte . . . so that Miguel lay, his bare chest exposed, covered with a mat of dark curly hair, and I was in his arms. We lay, our bodies caught in the dappled sunlight the Impressionists used. And it was all a dream and a kind of poetry.

And I looked up now at a very sedate Miguel Utrillo. Gone were the velvet jacket and romantic broad brimmed hat. He was now very soberly dressed in gray tweeds, it seemed years from the time we had met and we both had changed. Somehow, Miguel seemed much older to me and less Bohemian, less debonair in his ways. He was now a bourgeois writer on *La Vanguardia*. And to Miguel, I probably appeared more thoughtful and less headstrong. The Miguel who had lain bare chested with me on the Butte Montmartre had vanished with the passing seasons.

His eyes widened, but he embraced me and I finally surrendered to him, and we made love in the cramped room with the voices from the bar at the Moulin de la Galette coming through the walls. It was the way it once had been; it was the lovemaking which may have produced little Maumau. And yet I knew it all would end, it somehow had to end.

"You will always be my Maria, my wild beautiful Maria," he whispered afterward. "Why can't there be more for us? Tell me if I'm wrong before I finally leave . . . perhaps forever. Tell me."

"You have a position in Barcelona and of course you have your mistress. What *is* her name, Miguel? It's funny but you never told me her name. Why didn't you marry her a long time ago? How much simpler and less painful it would have been."

"What? Never mind all that. If I knew you loved me I would be forced to give it all up and stay here with you and Maurice."

"I don't want to force you, my dearest Miguel and you don't fool me for an instant. Your heart is in Spain, probably with her. It didn't matter that I loved you then. With all your talk of love, when I told you I might be pregnant, you couldn't face it and escaped to Spain, back to your mistress when you should have been here for me in my arms. Oh yes, the news reached me from one of the Spanish artists who came from Barcelona. I had to accept that you weren't really in love with me. Why did you leave me, why? Our lives might have been different. And would you leave your new position in Spain? I think not. And as far as your offer to stay with me, I think you're afraid I might accept."

"I marvel that you can be so independent. Don't you care at least about Maurice?"

"I care about my art, Miguel."

"You don't love me, Maria. If I leave, I warn you that it may be forever. I want to marry and have children."

"Then marry her and have hundreds of little ones!" I said in a controlled voice. "I don't want to tear you away from her."

"Then I will!" he answered. "I certainly will! You're exasperating. I never know what you want. I don't think you know what you want. But I'm glad of the Act of Recognition. I'm happy I gave Maurice my name. I'll never regret it. I know he's my son and he'll make me proud of him someday. Wait and see. You feel nothing for the child. I can see that."

"Nothing. Does it shock you? I'm not the good little mother you expected?"

"You're a heartless bitch! Nothing can change you."

"If you're so concerned . . . take Maurice back with you. I'm sure your mistress would love it." I said with a studied restraint.

He stood, his face flushed, attempting to decide something.

"Don't worry about it, Miguel. Marry your good little woman and go on with your life and have little ones . . . perhaps they'll even resemble Maurice. I'm going," and I took my drawing of Miguel and left. But when we parted, it was with a feeling of sadness and emptiness. Somehow, we both knew there was a finality about it. We knew it was for the last time. Before I left I memorized his dark curls now prematurely gray, and deep flashing eyes, eyes so like those of Maurice.

And during that January frost of 1892 which thawed and melted into the spring, Miguel remained in Paris for a while during which time he hardly saw my son or me.

He finally left and returned to Barcelona to continue to work as an art critic. I couldn't understand my own actions. Why didn't I do more to hold him? This time he would have married me had I so wanted it. Then what was wrong? I knew that ultimately he belonged in Spain where he would marry and have sons like Maurice, and I belonged in Montmartre. Time proved me right.

The rest I grappled with for years to come.

I never saw Miguel again, but by virtue of the adoption, he left my son a part of himself, his name.

But when I drew my son several months later, I marvelled at the growing resemblance to Miguel Utrillo; how much alike they were, the set of the head, the way Maurice shrugged his shoulders and the rolling pattern of his speech. And I wondered if my son would ever achieve anything of any importance. If I wasn't ordinary, why the devil should he be? I bent over and kissed his sleeping figure realizing that he was still part stranger to me. I titled my drawing, *My Utrillo*, using the name without thinking. *Maurice Utrillo*. The name merged with a consciousness that was always inevitable.

* * *

I didn't care that the art of Paris changed daily like a kaleidoscope. I lived through patterns of new art and new movements which translated into fresh precepts, the very changes taking altered forms. It all touched me little. I painted as I chose. And all the while I painted Paul Mousis pressed me to leave Montmartre, pressed me for a commitment, but I was still unsure.

In the ensuing months whatever feeling I had for Mousis at the beginning had cooled but this didn't diminish his desire for me. I was to become the dutiful accomplished wife of a banker, and to placate me he offered to rent a studio for me in Montmartre so that I could divide my time. But still lurking behind it all in the shadows, was Henri Lautrec who had loved me once and had the greatest impact on my life. This grotesque dwarf who stood four and a half feet high with his large head, heavy brows, large nose and thick, flabby lips was standing in the wings and still holding me with a magnetic force. I was sure it was inevitable and ironic that I, a bastard, a daughter of an alcoholic charwoman and an unknown father would be made a countess. And I would paint, and he would paint at my side, instructing and supporting my artistic endeavors. And for all this I would love him for bestowing on me this fantastic life. Marriages were built on far less.

But something intervened in the form of a musical genius.

"My friend, Erik Satie, the great composer," said Paul. "Meet Suzanne Valadon, a great artist."

"Of course you recognize me, Mademoiselle Suzanne." His legs straddled the back of the chair as he leaned forward and looked intently at me that evening at Auberge du Clou.

"What's new besides your being a piano player here?"

"Oh, just a prelude or two, Paul. What a lovely friend you have, and such a beauty and an artist, all quite commendable." He looked intently at me again.

"I recognize the same velvet suit. You were with Debussy at the Exposition," I said.

"I have twelve identical suits . . . and Debussy was with me."

"How extraordinary."

"That Debussy was with me, Mademoiselle, or that I have precisely forty gray lavallières and fifteen pairs of gray shoes?"

"You have no suits in blue? How sad."

"Of course not, Mademoiselle. Why should I wear blue, or brown or any other color, when I'm so fond of gray. Have you an answer, beauteous one?" Behind his pince-nez and flowing hair, his eyes gleamed with a puckish look, half humorous, half sensitive. At that moment I wanted to paint him.

"This conversation is idiotic." Paul muttered.

"Idiotic? You just don't understand subtleties," answered Erik, wryly.

"I understand inanities. Oh, come, Erik, what have you been doing besides buying gray clothes?" said Paul impatiently.

"You know what the devil I've been doing, why do you ask? You see I'm here in this goddamn place. That bastard Salis gave me the sack at the Chat Noir. Then I tried to get into the Institute several times, once when Gounod died and that miserable scum of the earth, Saint-Saëns, wouldn't let me in. I wrote him a letter telling him that he is in danger of hell-fire, the bastard. Nobody takes me seriously. They think me a buffoon."

"I told you to be more serious," said Mousis.

"*You* take me seriously, Mademoiselle. Come to my room, I'll play *Gymnopodie* for you and you'll die of it. You'll swoon in my arms and fling yourself into my bed, *voilà*. I'm already madly in love with you. I have been so since I saw you at the Chat Noir." He turned to Paul. "By the way, Claude Debussy copies my style. In spite of what you've heard to the contrary, *I'm* the father of modern music, the only one."

"You're the father of lunacy," muttered Paul.

"Don't concern yourself, Paul. It doesn't matter. If she cannot make my white meals, she'll not do for me anyway."

"I don't know what you're talking about," groaned Paul.

"What are your white meals?" I asked.

"You shouldn't have asked . . . he's *fou*," said Paul disgustedly.

"No, I want to know," I insisted.

"To answer your question, my precious little Suzanne, my food is white, all white. I only eat eggs, sugar, fat of dead animals, shredded bones, veal, salt, chicken cooked in white water, coconuts, moldy fruit, turnips, white varieties of cheese, certain kinds of fish without skin. I never talk when eating for fear of strangling myself. Can you make these meals Suzanne?"

"I'll have to think about it."

"Well, while you're thinking, I must add, I breathe carefully a little at a time and dance very rarely. When walking, I hold my ribs and look steadily behind me. My expression is very serious; when I laugh, it is unintentional, and I always apologize very politely. And when I finally break with you, I call the police."

"What?"

"The police stands guard at my home so you'll never be able to break in. I'm giving you fair warning."

"You are crazy, Erik, stark raving mad. You should really see a doctor," and Paul managed a twisted smile.

"And another thing, petite Suzanne, I sleep with one eye closed in a round bed with a hole in it for my head to go through."

"I would like to paint you, Erik," I said wiping my eyes.

"A most noble aspiration. Do you know that I have learned more about music from painters than I ever did from musicians? I'll have to give it some thought, but are you ready to be my love, because I have to return to the piano. If you like we can be married soon . . . but it's late now, about three in the morning and the *mairie* is closed. Perhaps another time, Mademoiselle."

"As you can see, he's insane," said Paul as Satie flowed over to the piano in his gray velvets.

"I enjoyed him," I laughed. "Is he talented? I want him to sit for me in his lavaliere and gray velvet and fantastic hat. Monsieur Degas wants me to do a portrait."

"Don't waste your time, he's a clown, Suzanne, pay no attention, a veritable clown. That's why he's a failure. He has talent, I suppose, but nobody takes him seriously. You would be wise to stay away from him."

"What a pity, I feel sorry for him. He's like a little boy."

Satie subsequently invited Maurice, Maman and myself to the theater and announced our arrival with a brass band.

I doubled with laughter, and Maurice jumped up and down in glee fascinated by the attention, while Maman shook her head and glared at him with instant hatred.

"Madame Pinchot will tell the whole of Montmartre about this crazy one you're with, mark my words," and her eyes darted furtively up and down the street for familiar prying eyes.

If Maurice enjoyed him immensely and waited for him to arrive at the apartment in expectation of another strange caper, Maman bemoaned my fate.

"My daughter consorts with a lunatic, a starving piano player when she can have that banker, Mousis. You can laugh all you want but we are cursed, clear and simple. A model becomes a whore and a woman artist is even worse," came the expected monotonous drone. She ran over to a shelf, rummaged through some canvas bags and found a bottle of brandy. She put the bottle to her lips, guzzled it greedily to drown her despair, and then wiped her chin with her sleeve.

When Satie and I entered his bare attic room at No.6 rue Cortot, I saw two wooden benches, a table and a wooden chest. There was no bed. An old pianoforte was squeezed into the room, its keys chipped as though bitten into. Then something in the corner caught my attention. Twenty umbrellas in different colors stood in a tall barrel, and various suits of gray velvet hung about. There also appeared countless stiff collars, piles of shirts and waistcoats.

"What in the world are all these for?" I said poking into the umbrellas.

"Small idiosyncrasies of mine."

"Besides your white meals and your velvet suits, you have others?"

"Suzanne, listen, I have written another composition just for you. It's called *Bonjour little Biqui, Bonjour*. Of course you know I adore you."

"Why do you call me, Biqui?"

"Can you think of why I shouldn't call you Biqui?"

"*Zut alors!* Is that an answer? And I thought you had a round bed with a hole in it for your head."

"Don't trouble yourself my dear, a mere delusion."

"I don't know why I came here."

"You love me, my Biqui." He laughed and sat down at the piano and began playing the piece. I didn't understand it. The music sounded discordant.

He read my mind. "Well don't worry. I'll have to teach you dissonance. Don't trouble yourself my Biqui. I'll play something else."

"What's it called?"

"Dried Embryos."

"How horrible!"

"Beloved Biqui . . . you must not trouble yourself, my little elf. Would you like to hear a timetable for my activities?" He drew a paper from his velvets. "I rise at 7:18 and am inspired from 10:23 to 11:47. I lunch at 12:11 and leave the table at 12:14."

"Please, Erik, enough!"

He rose from the piano and embraced me, and in half humorous reactions to his fierce advances, I found myself surrendering to the intensity of his passion, so different from the phlegmatic lovemaking of Mousis. But the whole affair was absurd. It wasn't possible that this man was in love with me.

"Erik," I said afterward, "I'm only here to paint you and you're involving me in all kinds of things. I don't want to make love to you. Do you understand? I just want you to be my first portrait. That's all I want . . . to begin my painting."

It took several days to finally sit in his bare attic and sketch the *Portrait of Erik Satie* on a canvas. He wore his gray velvet lavallière, suit and battered hat. I worked swiftly, first in charcoal and then in color. At first I was unsure in this new adventure for me for the subtlety of pigment wasn't like drawing . . . and I struggled with the rendering of light and shadow. But then

I could see some style emerging and I wanted to finish Satie, who sat with his emaciated face, pince-nez, twirling mustache and odd looking beard.

Several weeks later, I was in the final throes of my painting. "Erik, you must learn not to move so, I'll never get you right. I want to have something to remember you by."

"Remember me? Remember me?" He turned white. "You're not leaving me," he said in a tremulous voice.

"Hold still, Erik, and don't speak." I wanted to finish as quickly as possible and disappear.

"How can I hold still?" He grabbed my arm, "Say you'll never leave me, say it. If you leave me I'll stop composing and stop eating . . . even my white food."

"Alright, alright. Just sit still." There was no sense fighting with him. "Just shut up. Pose and let me finish. You're mad."

"If I'm mad, you keep me sane. Without you, I'm lost. Remember that, my Biqui."

"Nobody can keep you sane, Erik . . . and if you don't stop moving, I'll have to leave."

"I'm madly in love." He held onto me while I struggled to put away the tubes of paint. "I'm the most fortunate and most miserable of men. He flung himself on me and held me close to him dragging us to a pile of blankets on the floor. "Make love to me again and let's climb to the highest plateaus of delight."

"Go to the devil!"

But his hands caressed me, unbuttoning my dress and tearing off my chemise, and his breath came quickly. It was madness to make love to him for his wild possessiveness and melodramatics half frightened me, half amused me. His declarations of love I saw as absurd, yet in his lovemaking, his humor left and the seriousness of passion transmuted his face. What I did fear was that I could possibly become pregnant again.

"Oh my Biqui," he murmured breathlessly, "oh my beautiful petite one," and we rolled on the dusty floor.

"It would be nice to make love on a bed for a change, Erik."

"It would be so bourgeois."

I suddenly sat up. "I want you to do something for me, Erik."

"Anything, my love."

"I want you to wear an India rubber next time."

"A sheath? Never! I don't spoil my pleasure with a sheath . . . would you deny me the pleasure of entering your moist warm cocoon, unsheathed?"

"Be damned, Erik!"

"I never heard a woman demand such a thing. As a woman it's part of her risk to take chances, part of her destiny . . . that's nature." He put his head in his hands. "It's an affront to my masculinity to wear something on my private organ."

"Erik, you can sit looking at your precious cock for the rest of the evening. I'll be back tomorrow to finish your portrait."

"I know you'll leave me when it's finished," he protested. "Please stay tonight, I implore you. I know you're going to sleep now with Paul Mousis. Haven't you any morals, woman?"

"I can't afford them and I'm sore from sleeping on your floor, and I'm tired of eating shredded coconut. And damn your white meals. Get someone else to make them. I'm not your servant."

After the Easter holiday, Erik bought a cot but it didn't help. I lay on it and decided this would be my last visit to his absurd little room. My painting was finished so why in the world was I here with this composer? He really meant nothing to me. And I grew tired of his endless protestations of love, his absurd humor and even his lovemaking was losing its intensity. Erik sensed something, stopped playing and jumped off the piano stool, knelt at my feet and kissed my hand, and then his lips glided up my arm until they rested on a bare breast poking from my peignoir. "I'm a lovesick lunatic, and my compositions are all for you, my sparrow, and I have something else for you. I bought a box of rubber sheaths for the penis . . . someone called them condoms, a strange word, and they cost me fifteen francs a dozen. Would you believe it . . . fifteen francs and the quack wanted twenty francs. Now, I won't be able to eat for a week just for a few moments of pleasure."

"*Merde!*"

"You use such an epithet when I compose new chords of passion to play upon your quivering flesh and pluck your strings so deliciously."

I smiled at first, "Did you say my quivering flesh?" And then I convulsed into gales of laughter. I pushed him away.

"I can't stop," and his mouth kissed my bosom and went onto my belly which still shook with laughter.

"I have something to tell you, Erik."

"What?"

"It's got to end. I'm thinking of getting married."

"Marriage! A woman like you is thinking of marriage? You are not a bourgeois piece of shit. You're marrying that pompous ass, Mousis, I knew it. *I'll* marry you."

"We'll starve. You own three pieces of dilapidated furniture, forty umbrellas, twenty velvet suits, a piano, and something peculiar you call a bed."

"My Biqui, my sparrow, I'll go mad if you leave me. You're my sanity, and I wont be able to write another thing."

"I'm sorry, Erik, but I'm leaving." I dressed quickly and gathered up my paints in a leather pouch. "You can send my easel to the apartment. *Au revoir,* my dear composer."

He held my leg in a tight grasp as he fell to the floor.

I looked down. "Please, Erik, act like a man if that's possible."

"I'm just your puppy dog, your lackey." He jumped up and blocked the door.

"You're a madman. Let me out!" I beat on his chest.

"Never!"

"Lunatic! Let me out! Let me out!" I pounded again on his chest, my lips set in determination. A feeling of fear swept over me. Suppose he became violent? "I'll scream, Erik, and the gendarmes will come and lock you up in a madhouse."

"Go ahead. My life is over, anyway. I'm through composing. I'll tell my friend Debussy that my work is over. I'm throwing out all my music and Claude will certainly blame you and so will the whole music world."

"Well you should throw out your *Dried Embryos* you lunatic."

"Oh, how cruel you are," he yelled out. "Now I see how cruel you are. You can go. Yes, you can go and I'll kill myself and you'll laugh . . . you and your drunken mother. And that pompous ass, that Mousis, that boring bourgeois, who can't even get it up to put your India rubbers on . . . that fat materialist . . . and he can't even fuck . . . that impotent tub of lard."

He picked up a table and threw it against the wall. The leg of the table shattered and the table lay on its side. At that juncture, I saw my chance for escape and dashed out of the room and slammed the door, opened it again and threw in a bundle of socks Maman had darned for him. "And another thing. Do you hear me, Erik? Stop posting those lies about my virtue in your windows. Must all of Paris know about me? How did I get involved with the likes of you, you . . . you monster."

Several moments later, he opened the door and yelled down the stairwell, "Take this," and flung my easel down the steps. "You don't understand me, don't understand . . . like all women, like all women. Why am I in love I ask you . . . why? Love is a sickness of the nerves. It's serious, yes, very serious . . . myself, I'm afraid of it, I avoid it. My problem was that I forgot to avoid *you*. So wait until you see what I post about you in my window, my only love. The whole world will know what you are . . . the whole world. They will all know how you've used and abused me, you slut. You are a miserable whining scheming whore who sleeps with all of Paris; whose cunt has been sampled by every miserable bum on the street, you vile excuse for a woman. Don't think I would ever marry you, or any other damn female. I won't be made an ass by any of them. You think you can cuckold me? Think again you miserable scheming female. You can't even make my white meals properly . . . worse than a *putain* of the streets of Montmartre." He wiped his eyes. "Your name will be reduced to a pile of shit when I'm through with you. Even your precious Mousis won't want you, that impotent excuse for a lover."

"*Merde!*" I swore and picked up the easel. "Go wash your socks and you know where to stuff them! And incidentally, I think the rats are eating your piles of velvet suits."

" . . . vicious, vicious woman . . . you're so ignorant you don't even know what a genius I am," he shouted back and slammed the door.

SUZANNE

I received a letter two days later—

Paris, the 11th of the month of March 93*
Dear little Biqui,
*   Impossible*
to stop thinking about your whole
* being; you are in Me complete; everywhere,*
*   I see nothing but your exquisite*
*   eyes, your gentle hands*
*   and your little childish feet.*
* You, you are happy; My poor thoughts*
are not going to wrinkle your transparent forehead;
any more than worry at not seeing Me.
* For Me there is only the icy*
solitude that creates an emptiness in my head
*   and fills my heart with sorrow.*
* Don't forget that your poor friend*
hopes to see you at least at one of these three rendezvous:
*   1. This evening at 8:45 at my place*
*   2. Tomorrow morning again at my*
*   place*
*   3. Tomorrow evening at Dédé's*
*   [Maison Olivier]*
* Let me add, Biqui chérie, that I shall on no account get*
angry if you can't come to any of these rendezvous;
I have now become terribly reasonable; and
*   in spite of the great happiness it gives*
*   me to see you*
I am beginning to understand that you can't always do
*   what you want.*
* You see, little Biqui, there is a beginning to everything.*
*   I kiss you on the heart*
*   Erik Satie*

* See Acknowledgements in Bibliography

The note bore the blue embossed stamp for the Society of Old Hens founded in 1881 by Satie, complete with the motto, "Eagle I cannot be, Turkey I scorn to be, Hen I am."

On a quiet afternoon, I uncovered *The Portrait of Erik Satie*, my first adventure into painting, and stood back looking at it objectively and that delicious shudder of the excitement of creation rippled through me.

But did the painting portray the essence of Erik Satie, my recent lover? Did it capture his puckishness, his dry humor, his excessive idiosyncrasies? How many would guess at the eccentricities of this twenty-six year old Bohemian who owned countless velvet suits and umbrellas, wrote dissonant music and posted protestations about my virtue in his window for all to see? The portrait looked out with a gauntness, bearded and mustached, a pince-nez and worn hat, painted with glowing colors and bold brush strokes I observed from Lautrec and perhaps Van Gogh, but the strokes were from a firm hand, solely my style. Had these two artists influenced me? Perhaps. But my own style was developing. This much I keenly felt.

The unpleasantness which preceded the letter evaporated. Erik Satie told me that I was the only woman in his life he ever loved. I believed him. And I believed something else. If I had a talent at all it was for attracting genius. Satie was undoubtedly a musical genius who, with his dry humor would never fully be acknowledged in the music world. I wasn't wrong.

* * *

The seasons passed swiftly and by the spring of 1894, I heard that the little colour dealer, Père Tanguy died of cancer at the Hôtel de la Pité. He, from whom I had purchased my first pastels seemed like a perennial fixture on the rue Clauzel.

In October of 1894, *L'Affaire Dreyfus* began and anti-Semitism reared its head. A Colonel Henry informed Edouard Drumont, editor of *La Libre Parole,* that a Jew, Captain Dreyfus, was imprisoned for giving secrets to a foreign power. Drumont published the information, that Dreyfus confessed everything. There was a public anti-Semitic outcry. After a swift prosecution, Captain Dreyfus was condemned to life on Devil's Island.

And suddenly, Degas came to life with anti-Semitic slurs, and it was as though he couldn't pin enough of his ills and general dissatisfaction with his fellow man on the Jews. I was surprised and dismayed. In a short time, his long relationship with his Jewish friends the Halèvys and his fellow artist, Pissarro, ended. There were now Dreyfusards and Anti-Dreyfusards in Paris. Along with Degas, the anti-Dreyfusards were Renoir, Cézanne, Forain, and Gerôme. And among those who were pro-Dreyfus, were Pissarro, Lautrec, Monet, Valloton, Sisley, Cassatt, and Zola. Monet's friendship with Degas was severed. The paintings of Pissarro and Monet which Degas had purchased, were removed from Degas' dining room wall. Most of the young artists and intellectuals of Paris such as Zola, were pro-Dreyfus. Degas ignored them all.

Having little religious identification, the fact that one was a Jew or Gentile was of no concern to me. The fact that one was an artist was far more important. But as to Degas, his anti-Jewish sentiments seemed to me part of his usual misanthropic attitude.

In the cafés of Montmartre, the habitués were joined by two new faces, Matisse and Oscar Wilde, and discussed *J'accuse* by Zola. *J'Accuse* claimed that there was proof of the innocence of Dreyfus which was suppressed. As a result of the assertion, Zola was tried for libel, fined and given four months imprisonment. He appealed the verdict and fled to England. The antisemites began rioting all over France. Soon after, Colonel Henry confessed to his forgery of a letter that helped convict Dreyfus. The Colonel was tried, convicted and sent to prison. There he shot himself. And Degas' antisemitism flared up again worse than ever. He was one of the most vocal of all. Again, I hardly shared his sentiments about Jews. His refrain was all too familiar.

"I want you to know, my Maria, that unfortunately, Mary Cassatt is a Dreyfusard and sees me infrequently. What a pity. I would forgive her for defending that Jew."

"Pissarro is a Dreyfusard. Why won't you forgive him?"

"Pissarro is a Jew, himself, like the Halèvys. It makes a difference. Cassatt and Monet are just misled. They have been duped like most of the young artists and intelligentsia."

"I think that Pissarro is a marvelous artist."

He ignored my remark. "Someday Mary Cassatt will change her opinions, damn Dreyfusard. Now what have you been doing with your art?" He abruptly changed the subject. I said nothing in response but watched him reworking his pastel of a dancer.

But after leaving him, I suddenly felt uneasy . . . that everything was passing too rapidly. I saw myself at a significant milestone in my craft. I climbed to the top of the Butte and attempted to reassess my life. Certain things were immediately apparent. Undoubtedly, whatever reservations I entertained about Degas' prejudices, he had left his mark on my future. He was my glorious mentor. How fortunate I was. He had helped and guided me as he had done with Mary Cassatt, and changed my perception of myself as an artist. I had already become Madame Valadon, the painter, making a small stir in the community. To be recognized for one's abilities was still tremendously gratifying.

My ludicrous affair with Satie left me empty, but for some reason it provided the impetus for accepting Paul Mousis. Perhaps it was to fill a void. And yet, to submit to Paul's wishes would be virtual imprisonment in an endless vacuum, a tedium which would prove barren to my art. This was an eternal damnation for being so cruel to Henri. *Mais non, mais non, mais non!* I just won't do it! I won't ruin my art in a loveless marriage!

But when I saw Paul again I told him that I had relented. We would all join him at the big luxurious home at Pierrefitte, but on my terms. I wouldn't marry him but would remain as his mistress.

"Impossible! It will never work." Adèle said. "You? Never!"

"I will make it work . . . in this way I can paint without interruption. I'll have a cook, a butler and several housemaids and even a personal *bonne* named Catherine from Brittany. Can you imagine such luxury?"

"Are you trying to convince yourself, Marie?"

I shrugged my shoulders, attempting to push away my doubts. But I knew that Adèle was probably right. Even as a mistress, Paul would expect wifely duties and the social amenities including lavish entertaining of his dull business acquaintances. I would indeed earn such luxury with false passion and mindless chatter with dreary matrons. He frowned but accepted my terms. He promised me servants, couture clothes and whatever furnishings pleased me. He promised me nights of dancing, and theatre and opera. He promised that he would be a father to Maurice and send him to school, paying for his tuition at Pierrefitte. Above all he promised me the studio in Montmartre and time to do my drawings and paintings.

He promised me the world.

Maman smiled for the first time in years when we left the dreary apartment on rue Tourlaque and moved into the Château of the Four Winds, the name Paul gave his home. I divided my time between the home at Pierrefitte and the studio he rented for me at No. 12 rue Cortot. At his sumptuous home although still his mistress, I became a proper matron.

But it was at the studio in Montmartre that I became alive. The old familiar passions came to the fore. No. 12 rue Cortot was replete with history, many artists having lived in the building. Émile Bernard occupied one of the apartments. And it was at this studio that I continued with my art. I would stay at the studio sometimes for several days, and would leave my mother alone with Maurice, the servants and Paul. I drove into Montmartre from Pierrefitte in a mule drawn dogcart accompanied by two giant wolfhounds. The drive took me forty minutes and as I passed along I created a stir. As I rattled down the cobblestones of rue Cortot, neighbors peered at me from windows and once in the studio, I flung off my expensive blue silk dress.

Paul didn't take too kindly to my overnight visits at my studio being deprived of his bed companion, but said nothing. He understood that art was my life's blood. But at Pierrefitte, I became a gracious hostess. It was what I had expected and filled the role with surprising ease. But I became more tactful, more restrained. I realized that this was not Bohemia. Bankers were undoubtedly not artists. The talk was not of Impressionism or Symbolism, but of servants, their foibles, menus for the ménage, and fashions of the day. The mansion was lavish and endless bric-a-brac floated through the house without a place to put them. And then I discovered flowers and tended to them with a passion. I examined each bud and nursed bunches of blooms at each stage as though they were my children. I spent countless hours in my garden, pruning and planting and became an expert on the various varieties and their annual idiosyncrasies. And besides gardening, I also found couture.

I read *La Vie Parisienne, Modes Parisiennes* and the *Journal des Modes*. My knowledge of the latest in women's couture enabled me to inform the other wives of bankers about the ultimate in chic. My scanning the fashion magazines did nothing to slake my thirst for new gowns. Names of designers were tossed about on my lips and Paul fawned over me, seeing me as a lively, talented, beautiful woman meant to be coddled, and I basked in the knowledge that he would deny me nothing. I became his pampered doll and emulated women of taste and refinement like Cassatt. To the opening night of the theatre I wore a daring new one shoulder décolletage, with woven ribbon florals cascading down the skirt to the floor glittering with paillette encrusted stems and a hand painted fan of sapphire blue roses. It was purchased by a beaming Paul in the sumptuous establishment of Charles Frederick Worth, and the bill was staggering.

And when the evening passed, still wearing the creation, I finished a painting of the scenery about the Château, the pigments thick on my palette; when I was done there was a long smear of turkey red pigment across the glittering paillette butterflies which cascaded down the skirt. The red slash cried out in angry contrast against the sapphire satin.

I had everything and yet a curious emptiness remained. I thought of Henri, that stunted Henri, and our painting together, instructing together in our trips to the countryside and our loving afterward in his chaotic studio. I thought of Henri and the very frustration that thought engendered angered me. I should have been superbly happy, at least content with my life. But my comradery in art with Henri lingered. The memory didn't fade, sharpened all the more by my life with Paul.

* * *

But a new period in our lives was to begin; a period fraught with worry, frustration, fear and general chaos. In one word it was in the person of my son, my beautiful son, Maurice! Maman's little precious Maumau was a child who would ultimately turn our lives upside down. Maurice, the child I was just beginning to reach out for, just beginning to accept into my life created a peculiar pattern filled with unknowns. The child who was taught by Henri as he struggled on the piano keys was worsening every day. At times I even blamed myself for not accepting the intricacies of his nature. Rubbish! The dismal fact was that I simply couldn't understand him.

I couldn't understand this product of my womb. I couldn't understand this child who from the age of five made a daily climb from the sanctity of the rue Tourlaque up to the Pension La Flaiselle in the rue Labat where I had enrolled him. He was mortally afraid of school and held onto his Grand-mère's hand for dear life as he made his daily trek. But in spite of all her affection for him, Maman couldn't stem the tide which swelled daily. Maurice was already exhibiting the depressions and tantrums which worsened each day. When he was thwarted, he would throw china cups, rip up anything in sight, and throw himself on the floor kicking his arms and legs, sobbing uncontrollably.

It amazed me how rapidly he grew, now awkward and lanky, all elbows and knees, once a past intrusion in my life, now something more. And when I drew his picture a warm kinship guided my hand; the red chalk outlined his face and body with sure loving strokes and he was mine, mine alone. But when the picture was completed, the feeling evaporated. Why? And then what difference did it make? My motherhood was an accident, so why be concerned about him? I felt a burgeoning inside of me. Was it tenderness? What was it?

I caught him looking at me at odd times with Miguel's eyes,

and an anxious adoration, a worshiping complex child. And I saw my own deification mirrored in Maurice's eyes. My very presence filled him with inexorable joy. He hung onto my arms when I entered the room and sat watching every expression on my face, any response I could make, and reflected any feeling which I was experiencing in an empathic frenzy. He reached for my hand, looked beseechingly at me, and when I appeared in good spirits, he sidled up close to me, leaning his little head on my breast. I just didn't understand. I had never demonstrated this affection for Maman.

Doctor Ettlinger, my neighbor at Pierrefitte, was a follower of the theories of a certain Dr. Freud, a feeling of unnatural love toward one's parent, particularly of the opposite sex. Certainly, this Dr. Freud was *fou*. But as Maurice grew his pleas never changed. I heard the same refrain each year so that I could repeat it by heart. "Oh Maman, if you stand still like that, you are beautiful like a statue. I love you, Maman. Do you love me? Love me, Maman and don't change like you do . . . don't get angry, please don't get angry."

"You get angry too, Maumau."

"But I get frightened when you get angry. I get frightened because you're not always the same and I want you the same."

"Nobody can always be the same all the time. But I love you too, Maumau." I embraced him and the child clung to me, his large eyes limpid like deep pools of water.

"See how good you are now, but tomorrow you'll change and be different, and then I won't even see you, Maman. Do you really want a little boy? I'm not sure. Do you really want me?"

"Of course. Don't you believe me?"

"Yes . . . I guess you do . . . I know you do because you always draw my picture. You're an artist, Maman, and an artist draws something she loves."

"That's a wonderful thought, Maumau. You're quite intelligent."

He beamed, his eyes bright with a mixture of pride and adulation.

"Maman loves me, she loves me . . . so I'm lucky, I'm lucky," he sang over and over again to Maman Madeleine. He clung to me and a look of intense idolatry passed over his face. "You're so beautiful, Maman. Even the boys at school say you're beautiful. I hope you never get old with lines on your face."

"Everyone gets old," said Maman Madeleine, wearily. "Look at me." She closed her eyes as though she was to be scrutinized.

"No! No! Maman will always, always be young, you'll see." His voice rose in pitch until its shrill timbre pierced the very core of the old woman's dazed reverie. Her eyes snapped open.

"Be calm, Maumau, be calm," she murmured in a droning monotone, automatically, repeatedly, an instinctive response learned from the years of Maurice's tantrums. They were meaningless words and after she uttered them, Maman would lapse back into her vacant stare.

If the complexities of Maurice's nature created impossible waves for me to wade through, that tide was lashing chaotically at the shore and threatened to engulf me.

A new era for Maurice was now being ushered in and it was menacing. He was becoming a possible bona fide alcoholic. And he added a nuance to the brew. He ran away.

Maman Madeleine was beside herself and wailed continually, "I knew he would run away. He was so unhappy at school. He said they called him blockhead. Why do they call him that when he's so smart? And he's so clever in mathematics."

"Shut up! Stop your infernal wailing and fetch the police. He's probably not far."

But Maman seemed immobilized and she rocked furiously, drinking a full bottle of brandy. After she finished guzzling it down, she sat in a stupor, the tears streaming down her withered cheeks, clasping and unclasping her hands, the drained bottle falling to the floor. "Oh my Maumau, my poor, poor Maumau. Nobody loves you but me," she droned on.

"Your poor, poor Maumau. You did it yourself. You did it with every glass of wine you poured down his throat, goddamn you! You've ruined him!"

"I've ruined Maumau? I've ruined him? Then manage him yourself," she babbled, waved me away and moaned, "Maumau's disappearance is God's retribution for our sins."

"Oh, damn!" and I slammed the door.

The following morning, a gendarme found Maurice dead drunk in St. Vincent's cemetery leaning against a tombstone surrounded by empty bottles of wine.

I turned to the gendarme whose eyes swept the home in admiration. "Perhaps you can help me move him into the drawing room?"

He nodded, crouched down and lifted the boy easily; he carried him to a shining silk sofa which Catherine had spread with towels. As Catherine pulled off Maurice's boots, giant globs of mud fell onto the Aubusson carpet. The mud and other assorted filth had made its trail on the marble floor from the entrance and through the thick lush carpets.

The gendarme turned to me. "But why was he so drunk, Madame?"

"A childish prank, I assure you. School friends have put him up to it."

"A prank," echoed Maman who had waddled into the room.

The policeman stiffened as he breathed the smell of brandy which surrounded her like an aura, and backed off. "I understand, Madame. I'm sorry." His eyes were wise as he made a motion to leave.

"Well *merci*, Monsieur," I said.

"Ah! Madame Mousis, if you have further trouble of a similar nature, don't hesitate to call upon me. My name is César Gay. Come to the prefect in Montmartre and ask for me. A mother so beautiful should not have such trouble with her son."

"I'll certainly call upon you but this is the end of it."

"It is certainly the end of it," echoed Maman.

"I think not," he wrote his name on a slip of paper, *César Gay*. I mouthed the name aloud, "*César Gay.*"

I tried to ignore it with the warmth of a new spring as I sat on a hill outside our palatial home and painted. I tried to ignore it even as Maurice lay in a drunken stupor on my sumptuous sofa, puking, groaning, filthy, and muttering incoherently. I thought of his drinking but then submerged my fears. The morning was too beautiful to fret about unpleasantness.

But Maurice worsened and so did the awfulness of it.

"Madame?" The door to the lavish house at Pierrefitte opened and the gendarme, César Gay reappeared. "Madame, here is your son." Maurice was limp as Catherine rushed in and pulled off his boots and shook them outside. The spring rains had done their job well, and the gardens of Paris had the consistency of thickened pudding. The gendarme made a motion to carry him upstairs.

"If you would . . . thank you for coming," I said.

"No problem here." He easily flung Maurice over his shoulder like a sack of potatoes and his boots made deep imprints in the lush carpeting. I followed closely.

"Can we call on you again, Monsieur?"

"I'd like to retire soon and buy a small bistro with money I have from my pension, but not for awhile . . . yes, call on me."

The same scene was to be repeatedly etched in my mind as the pattern of the marble was slowly infused with a patina of vomit. The sickness of his alcoholism began to churn inside of me coupled with a now familiar panic. My son was eleven years old.

The problems I was having with Maurice's drinking began to invade my very soul. Dr. Ettlinger gave Maurice some medication to sedate him. The powders mysteriously disappeared. For a while, I stopped drawing and painting. Then something took hold, a slow anger which made me reassess my present life and where I was heading. Where was Marie-Clémentine, the wild child who once existed, drawing her pictures on the Butte? Had she really become the artist, Suzanne Valadon? Henri Lautrec had such faith in my talent. Was I now to drop everything and be the good little housemistress and become immobilized as the troubled mother of a troubled son? Henri made the discovery and opened new horizons for me. Was I to close up those horizons? I rebelled against the distraction of a frankly alcoholic son. Was I so self absorbed? Yes, I *am* an artist; this is what I *am* and it is part of my being. And I will be a fine one in spite of my background, my lack of training, my mother's wailing and drinking, and Maurice's problems. If I am a selfish one, and not a good mother, *so be it* but can one be all things? The evils can all crash about me but I *will* do my art. I will do it and on my own terms, not one of the pack. I was called a maverick. I suppose that's what I am.

I caressed Henri's gold locket lovingly with my fingers. I still wore it around my neck and it was still empty.

8

Degas

The Mentor

I laughed all the while I submitted my Maria's entire group of drawings of her son for an exhibit called Impressionists and Symbolists. It was such wicked, such marvelous fun to put her in their midst, those damn incompetents. They claim that a picture before being a horse, a nude, a woman, or any subject at all is essentially a flat surface covered with colors assembled in a certain order. My eyes are bad enough without having to be concerned about this trivia.

"I don't understand all this. I just draw what I feel."

"Don't concern yourself, Maria. They're all idiots, anyway."

But during the course of the exhibition, one of the young art critics, Francis Jourdain, was struck by her drawings and praised them highly; her first written acknowledgment stressed her search for truth in her craft. The child suckled by the crude reality of her life and the Montmartre streets came through in her art. I felt fulfilled that a critic such as Jourdain should have recognized her ability. All her drawings were sold, *voilà*.

During that spring, my mad friend, Gauguin, returned from Tahiti to exhibit, and visited me in my studio dressed in a long blue coat with mother-of-pearl fastenings, a blue waistcoat topped with a yellow and green collar, an astrakhan cap, white kid gloves and a carved cane; and he gesticulated wildly leaving a trail of denunciations of his friend, Émile Bernard and the Symbolists, "They are followers, and I the leader, *c'est ça!* I'll be remembered, the *only* one. Now, I hope you're coming to my exhibit, Edgar. Don't desert me like the others."

He scarcely took notice of Maria who was quietly listening, but when Gauguin stormed out I muttered to her, "A madman. A bona fide lunatic. It will take me a day to recover from him. It's his syphilis that makes him mad, poor chap."

"How marvelous he is, Monsieur Degas. How much I would like to paint like him."

"You will paint like Maria, no one else . . . but you appear to have stopped painting."

"It's far too complicated," she told me. "And the pigments are a nuisance, and I'm forever cleaning up the brushes. My painting of *Erik Satie,* was a bother. I've decided to stick to . . ."

"Please, I don't want to hear it. You must paint," I said, "or you'll never progress in your art. You must paint, Maria. Your Erik Satie is quite good. Why shouldn't you develop further? Borrow my turpentine and empty canvases my Maria."

And she drew now on what she had observed in others. She had watched Lautrec at his painting, observed his meager palette which he rarely cleaned, and used his technique of first blocking out the canvas with colors thinned with turpentine. She ingested something of the paintings she had seen in the various exhibits, and at first her paintings seemed to be a synthesis of artists which she infused into her own expression. Undoubtedly, they were a groping, an early experiment in color, and the colors were like those of the Fauves, with brush strokes which were the broad streaks and hachures of Lautrec and Van Gogh. Her choice of women models didn't surprise me. She chose her women as plain and ordinary from the working class. They were usually heavily built, squat, dumpy women who neither smiled nor tried to look pleased with life.

I offered suggestions. "This could be clearer . . . or . . . this is too much in shadow, or the pigment is muddy here . . . or you would bathe in turkey red if I let you," and then I corrected with a light sketch on a pad. I never touched her drawings or paintings. But essentially, I left her alone to develop, and saw the struggle she was having adjusting to this strange new adventure into pigment. She explored her new adventure into color, her brush lovingly stroking or bravely assaulting her canvases with increasing assurance. I felt painting would convey her passionate temperament, her forcefulness and her unrelenting, uncompromising eye. I knew I wasn't mistaken.

I attended Gauguin's exhibit with my Maria and stayed a short time. My artist friend, Berthe Morisot, stood before a painting, and I had almost forgotten how striking her appearance was. She was delicate looking with a kind of luminous yet classic beauty of regular features and finely textured skin. I calculated that she was already in her fifties, her figure still slim and graceful. She was fashionably dressed in a walking suit, I suppose done up by some couturier like Patou, of light gray wool crepe and I liked the way her gray hair was pulled back and twisted into a chignon under the velvet bonnet, and made a note to incorporate this into a pastel. She held an umbrella and pointed to two paintings while chatting with Gauguin. Her daughter, Julie, a pleasant enough girl of fifteen stood by patiently.

I looked toward Maria. How my Maria had envied Morisot whose parents encouraged her to paint. How she would have loved to have been in that upper strata of society like Cassatt and Morisot. "What a marvelous thing to do, to encourage her to paint," my Maria said. How Morisot would have been appalled by the drinking of Maman Madeleine. And Julie was the soul of propriety . . . no hedonist, this child, wild and unschooled like Maria. The talk was that Berthe Morisot had been in love with Edouard Manet, but finally married his brother, Eugène. She had this daughter at 37 years of age, too late to have a child if you ask me. No matter, the poor woman was now widowed.

Gauguin paced back and forth, "Damn the Beaux Arts! Damn them all! I'll be glad to get out of Paris and back to my *vahine* Tehora, a savage who understands my paintings more than these simpering idiots. And when I leave Paris, I assure you it will be forever. Damn them all . . . damn them and their damn morality! I trust you're buying something, Edgar."

I wondered what Paul expected of me. *Sacrebleu*, I already bought several paintings; now what more did he want from me? I'll help the poor fellow out and buy his *Fatata* but I'm not sure I'd pay him what he wants. I don't even want the painting. But I seem to be his only salvation.

"Oh, calm yourself, Paul. Come, meet my Maria who calls herself Suzanne Valadon, the artist, and she adores you." I said.

"Are you one of those simpering pseudo-admirers of my art, obnoxious dilettantes, who won't give a frank for a painting?"

"Why are you insulting her? She's a remarkable talent," I said.

"I still ask, what are you?" repeated Gauguin. He was mad.

"I'm a free woman."

"Is that what you are, a free woman? You are a free woman? *Alors*. You should have met my astonishing grandmother, Flora Tristan; there was a free woman, and beautiful. I thank God for every drop of her non-French blood which gave her courage and made me a pariah the way she was. She died fighting for the poor all over France. She was branded as a mad socialist. As far as being free, my dear Maria, the day that a woman's honor is no longer located below the navel, she will be free."

"It makes no difference where my honor is located I assure you. I live as I want," Maria said bravely.

"Well put. You have a little spirit in you, *ma petite*, I'll give you that," he said. "And of course you're aware of your beauty, or are you? It doesn't go to your head, does it?"

Maria smiled and just stared at his fantastic crooked nose.

"Come on, come on!" I took out my pocket watch and felt a twitch in my cheek. "Let's face it Paul. You have to go to your island. You have to have people around you with flowers on their heads and rings in their noses before you can feel at home. And now the critics have you in an uproar."

"Damn the critics and sit down, Edgar!" growled Gauguin. "I can tell you that I'm leaving Paris in order to have peace and quiet, to be rid of the influence of civilization. It's their goddamn morality. Are you moral, little one?" he said dryly to Maria.

"I doubt it," she answered.

"That's encouraging. Morality is the source of all hypocrisy and of many physical evils; it engenders the great traffic in flesh, the prostitution of the soul; it seems to be a virus born of civilization, for among the savage races of Oceana and the black peoples of Africa there is no such thing, and . . ."

"I have to piss!" I complained cutting off his diatribe.

"Why can't you sit down, Edgar?"

"Because I've had enough of your ravings. The fact of the matter remains that I still have to piss somewhere . . . so that's the state of the art. *Au revoir.*" I walked quickly into the fresh air with Maria close at my heels.

"Pay no attention to Gauguin, Maria. He is a genius but a study in sheer lunacy."

"I adore that man and his art of course," Maria said earnestly.

"You'll never cease to amaze me, my Maria, never. And now I've arranged for a public exhibition of your drawings at the Salon de la Nationale, an important annual exhibition." That damn Puvis de Chavannes, the founder of the Salon, of course discouraged Maria and thought I was losing my judgment.

I called on my friend, Bartholomé, who wrote a letter to Paul Helleu, the president of the Salon, to look at her drawings and see their unusual qualities. And the selection committee chose several studies she did of her son and mother. She had now in truth become Mademoiselle Valadon, the artist, who was developing her own style, clear, realistic and strong.

Of course, several weeks passed before I heard from her again. Oh, she was such an ungrateful one, such a trial. Do you think she cared that I stayed in my studio afflicted with all kinds of ravages to my poor aching body? Do you really think she cared? I sent a note. How else would I get my Maria to come?

"Oh, my wild Maria, I'm glad you're here." I said to her as she entered breathlessly. "Where have you been? Here I am getting old and blind, *la vue, la vue.* But then, I could never expect any sympathy from you."

"Monsieur Degas, your eyes are not nearly as bad as you think." She never believed me, that little one, not for an instant.

"Have it your own way, Maria, but I have a project for you. I'm going to teach you to make zinc engravings."

"No, painting is enough of a chore."

"You can handle it. Now listen carefully to what I say, and I'll expect you to become a master at printmaking and make a million francs with your first group of etchings. What d'you say, eh? No matter, come, we're wasting time, deadly at my age. Now be quiet, Maria and watch, for your whole future depends on this."

* * *

In 1889, I moved to an old-fashioned building at 37 rue Victor Massé in Montmartre which my Maria helped me find. I occupied all three floors of the building; and on the third floor was my studio where a thick layer of dust on the bay window refracted the light. Here is where I kept my printing press.

The following afternoon she returned, and I smiled as I saw her put on a coarse cotton muslin skirt and shirt which she covered with a long white smock which fell from her shoulders to the floor. She tied up her hair in such a fashion . . .

The press was at the back of the studio. There were shelves surrounding the press, which held pots of grounding material; and she was fascinated by the red spindles which I began turning. I had sectioned off a small area of the acid bath into which I dipped the plates to be etched. Formerly Zoë had carried up three gallons of water a day and a pipe carried the dirty water to the outside courtyard. But now plumbing was installed so that water came up into a sink. A small coal stove warmed the room.

I gave her copper plates from the metal monger and showed her how to polish them with emery and pumice; and then we coated the backside of the plate with a resin that would protect it from the acid bath. *Alors,* now we were ready for her drawing. I covered certain areas with acid-resistant liquid resin which was left to dry. A portion was lightly coated with aquatint powder. How she watched me with growing excitement as I took the plate and held it over the brazier causing the aquatint to melt and adhere to it. Then I turned the red spindles until the plate was squeezed through the press, the pressure of the top roller pushing the soft wet paper into the inky recesses of the plate transferred the image.

Maria's eyes widened as the tones developed in her drawing. The engraving process of scratching the lines through the resin was a revelation to her. She was anxious to attempt it. I hovered over her engravings, going over the plates repeatedly using a magnifying glass. "*Eh*, bien," and then one afternoon, I gathered up a series of her etchings, "Now you are ready to exhibit," I said. "We will contact the new art dealer, Ambroise Vollard, and arrange to have a show of your engravings. He has already invited me to dinner."

"Have you accepted?"

"I told him to hide his cat and tell his female guests not to put those perfumes on themselves. I can't stand it. There is nothing better than the smell of warm toast. What do you think, eh?"

"I think you try to appear to dislike women and yet you paint them so marvelously. You're becoming far too fussy."

"What a tongue you have in your head. I would only take a criticism like that from you, my wild Maria. You can't help it."

"Monsieur, have him invite me to dinner as well."

"We shall see if you deserve it, that is, if your prints are well received."

My Maria pouted.

Her twelve etchings made a small stir in the artistic community. The critic Roger Marx described her work, in particular the nudes as "having the gloss and hardness of marble."

I found myself repeating over and over again. "You are a marvel, my wild Maria, a veritable marvel."

I still had to repeatedly send letters for her to come. Nothing had changed. My maverick artist could make the most normal man relinquish his sanity.

Tuesday

My terrible Maria,
Where are you? I have not heard from you for over a month. You must go on with your drawing and painting and make the most of your talent. I look forward to seeing some of your work. Why do you ignore me?
Degas

She brought me a nude, almost condescendingly, and I examined it for an engraving, the imperfect body showing the flaws created by living. I thought of Renoir and his pretty paintings of his damn women. His females bothered me with their pure, virginal faces and sumptuous bodies. Rubbish, Paris is composed of sluts and women of little beauty.

"Your nudes are honest, showing flawed bodies. You've progressed in your art, Maria. The public might say that I helped you. Oh, how the world distrusts a woman painter, especially one guided by a man. Everyone sees the hand of a man in her craft."

"The public can be damned, Monsieur. I paint and draw as I like. My women are often not pretty but they tell the truth with their bodies; some of my models are fat and flabby. It doesn't matter to me. This is the way life is, women are. The body of a woman of fifty is not like that of a girl and bearing children has surely changed it. How can one paint the body of a woman without wrinkles, without sagging flesh, if that's what one sees? It's truly dishonest. Perhaps I have been influenced by you, but the interpretation is wholly my own, *c'est ça*"

"My terrible Maria, you use a hard and pliant line in your work that's truly your own. I would recognize it anywhere. I would say, *voilà*, there's a Valadon, when your work hangs in the Louvre."

"And I will hang there, have no fear."

"You have enough confidence in your art, my Maria, for all the artists in Paris."

She smiled in agreement.

It was a month later when she visited my studio again. I was busy doing endless retouching of two bath scenes which I had painted years before. I scandalized all Paris by my nudes. I threw their damn respectability about women in their faces.

"That painting, *Mon Dieu* . . . it's remarkable."

The crimson painting of *Miss La La at the Cirque Fernando* as I called it, literally jumped off my dining room wall.

"Notice the perspective, wild Maria. I retrieved this one from Renoir, the fool. I told him that it was unfinished. If he thinks he'll ever get it back he's sadly mistaken. I don't know why I let him have it in the first place."

"*Incroyable!* Miss La La hangs from the ceiling with her teeth like a gigantic fly."

"You should appreciate a circus acrobat, Maria. Every museum in France wants this painting and it stays here. They'll all ruin it. Someday everyone will copy the angles of my painting. But I must tell you something else, Henri's health is worsening. I heard this wretched news from Bartholomé. Lautrec has a rowing machine, poor chap, to strengthen his muscles. He puts on a yachtsman's cap and a shirt of red flannel, and rows with all kinds of straps for hours in the middle of his studio . . . but then, what good will it do him? The idiot should stop drinking."

"Poor, poor Henri, but how he can paint, and his posters are a marvel. My poor, poor Henri." Her eyes filled. Frankly, her reaction didn't surprise me. What the devil had gone on between them? Of course, I knew. I really never thought otherwise.

"So your irritation with him has gone for . . . ?"

"My irritation?"

"Don't play games with me, Maria. Since when have you become a respectable bourgeois to put on all these subterfuges? How I hate this quality in women. I liked you because you were honest, Maria."

"*Touché.*"

"I never understood your relationship with Henri, but I'm too old to be concerned with such matters."

"Henri and I were lovers, Monsieur. I wanted to marry him."

Lovers? My God, I thought, how, and why? "You don't have to tell me . . . but lovers with that cripple? That's a wonder. And tell me, were you really in love with him? Now, the truth. I've been very close to Henri and I want the truth from you."

"I'm not sure. I did have affection for him and in some way it was tied in with my art, and he helped me."

"And what else did you want from him . . . a title perhaps? Don't deceive me, Maria." I wondered why this mattered so much to me? Why?

"I would love to have been a countess. Why should I refuse a title? It was a chance to do my art in peace and have my son and my mother taken care of. Oh, there were those who thought that I was a scheming one but I think now it was more."

"Do you know what I think?"

"You think I'm a selfish one and I know I am."

"That's true but you're developing a soul, Maria. I think that you love Henri as much as you can love anyone."

"It's amazing but that's what Maman said. Yes, I'm drawn to him but is that love? Sometimes it frightens me."

"Don't you see that you love Henri? Don't you realize that? I hear it in your voice and have seen it in your eyes. And it's indeed a wonder . . . for a person such as yourself to be in love with him is a wonder."

"I never saw his infirmity, I told you that."

"I could believe it about you, but to still be in love with that monstrous looking cripple is a wonder nevertheless."

She didn't answer but her face became oddly flushed.

I stood still reflecting long after she left. Lautrec? Why was I so concerned? I was only concerned with her craft. Why did she cast such a spell over me? What was there about her that was so different from the others, the countless models I had drawn, the myriad of women I had recoiled from? My wild, untamed, precious Maria was a veritable miracle both in her earthy craft which was so startling in its execution, so unique, and in her very appearance which had a depravity which fused with her beauty. It was a depravity born of the streets of Montmartre. And I accepted it, but what was it? What did she hold for me? I fought something within me that was stirring so insidiously. Was it jealousy or was it a desire to possess her? *Incroyable!* For among the countless women who stood naked for me to paint, my Maria was a woman who had never undressed for me, whom I had only seen unclothed in the work of Renoir. Bartholomé once asked if she were my mistress. Ridiculous! I certainly wasn't in love with her . . . Maria. My wild Maria. My she-devil.

9

Sixth Voice

Maurice

The Magic Soup

Oh, how I loved to torment Grand-mère. How I loved to torment her. It was so simple and it gave me all the attention I wanted. And she wasn't a bit like Maman for she would forgive me whatever my behavior, and it was so easy for me to throw a tantrum. But when I threw a tantrum my poor Grand-mère thought the *chabrol* always worked but it didn't, and sometimes it made me want to break the china cups that remained. I stared at the flowered china cups she brought from rue Tourlaque sitting on a blue and white checked table cloth.

"I don't like the name of Utrillo . . . it's not my name and I'm not using it! My name is Maurice Valadon."

"My grief will never be over." I watched her wring her hands. Her hands moved about like magic doing scrubbing tricks at her washboard and in her pots. How red they became with the lye soap which seemed to burn them up. All peasants seemed to have hands like hers, bony and creased like fallen leaves which withered in the sun. Large veins stood out, veins which fascinated me as I stared at them. The veins stood out in her neck, one running down the side of her face, mixing with the wrinkles which puffed in and out like whiffs of smoke. My eyes traced a vein . . . it really came from her forehead and trailed down her cheekbone until it fell into her neck and sagging breast. Where did the vein go? Did it really come out of her toes? I stared so long at its winding route that it hypnotized me.

"My name is Maurice Valadon," I began again, noticing that the vein joined another vein at the base of her neck.

"Your name is Maurice Utrillo!" my Grand-mère shouted and the vein grew bigger and bluer and stood out at her temple when she grew angry.

I looked away from her neck. "My name is Maurice Valadon, my name is Maurice Valadon . . . my name is . . ."

" You're driving me crazy. Do you think Miguel would give you his name if he wasn't your father, Maumau?"

"He's a fake so he's not my father."

"Why not?"

"If he was my father he would be here with us. He went away so he's a fake."

"Don't bother me."

"So who is my father?"

"Miguel Utrillo of course."

I screamed and threw a chair against a wall. "My papa is not Miguel, don't you see that? Maybe Miguel is someone else's papa? He's the wrong one. Grand-mère stood, her eyes wide with grief and said nothing. Her silence irritated me. I pulled off the checkered tablecloth and the china and silver went flying.

She wailed, "Maumau, I'll give you some soup. Sit down, sit down, *mon cher* Maumau . . . it doesn't matter what you call yourself . . . just sit down." Her eyes pleaded with me. Maman would never do that. She would have slapped me. Then Grand-mère bent, picked up the cloth and swept up the broken china.

"See what you did, you wicked boy?" But she said this gently in a soft voice. I could do and say anything and she wouldn't be angry . . . not like Maman.

She poured some hot soup into a bowl and reached for the wine. I enjoyed watching her as she stirred her magic soup like a witch, her lips moving the whole while. Perhaps she's becoming *fou*? That's what happens to old ladies . . . they don't know what they're doing. Perhaps I'll torture her again.

"I don't want that name . . . I want a new name," I said hoarsely.

"Call yourself anything you like. Just don't bother me."
"So where is he?"
"Who?" Some soup dribbled from the corner of her mouth.
"This Miguel . . . the one supposed to be my father."
"He left. He went away."
"You see? I was right. He's bad. He's very bad, or else he would stay with me. It shows that Miguel Utrillo is really not my father. My father is somebody else."

Grand-mère pushed the soup away and rose. She went over to the pantry and gulped her favorite brandy from the bottle. How she drank. I never thought ladies drank like that.

"Maumau, calm yourself. I want to ask you . . ."
"I want some wine first."

She breathed a sigh of relief and poured some wine into a glass. I became so thirsty for it that I seized it and gulped it down like the way she did. "I just love it, Grand-mère. I just love it. It feels so warm when it slides down and makes me feel like somebody else . . . that's why I love it."

Grand-mère looked guilty. "It's not good for you, *mon petit*."

"It must be good for me. It makes me feel so good, Grand-mère. You drink it also and you like it."

She turned her face away. "It's not good," and her lips began to move again. I could tell she was ashamed.

"What do you want to ask me, Grand-mère? It sounds like a big secret. Tell me."

"I just wanted to know how you like living in this big house with Monsieur Paul and Maman."

"I hate it, Grand-mère."

"Of course you would say that."

"No, I like living where we lived before. Did Maman marry Monsieur Paul yet? She didn't even marry him."

"I'm trying to make her do it."

I felt a desperate panic. "Don't make her do it. I don't want it. He's not my papa. I hate him. I hate him. Please make him go away. Please let's go back to Montmartre, Grand-mère, please let's go back. I don't like my school here. Please let's go back. Make Maman go back. She doesn't like that fat Paul anyway."

Grand-mère gave me a funny look. "How do you know she

doesn't like him?"

"'She liked the *petit monsieur* much better, I know it!"

"You shouldn't say that about Monsieur Paul."

"I hate him. And anyway, I'm not able to do mathematics at the new school. I like mathematics and they don't listen to me."

"Be calm," said Grand-mère wearily.

The terrible fear came back. "I don't want to stay here. I don't want to. I don't want to live with that man, Mousis. I want my own papa. Give me my real papa!" I began to shriek.

"Be quiet, little one, be quiet."

"Grand-mère, if I write to Miguel, will he come back?"

Grand-mère looked at me with a strange light in her eyes. I had given her an idea. "Maybe, Maumau you'll send him a nice letter telling him about everything." Her eyes scrunched up.

"What will we tell him, Grand-mère?"

"We'll tell him how lonely you are and how alone we are and how old and sick your mother is . . . and how your mother is working herself to the bone and how we all cry ourselves to sleep every night. We'll tell him that he shouldn't stay away."

I put my head in my hands and cried. Then I kicked a chair and screamed out, "I have no papa! He's a fake! I have only his name and I'll never, never use it. I will be Maurice Valadon, always. Miguel just doesn't care."

"And what about Monsieur Paul?"

'He's not my papa either. He's not even married to my mother. They're all fakes. And people say bad things about them . . . about us because they're not married. They found out, Grand-mère. They say Maman is a whore. I hear them."

Grand-mère said nothing, but she leaned back in her rocker. I suppose I made her very tired because she dozed off. I crept to the china closet and took an unopened bottle of nice red wine from the shelf. I tiptoed out of the kitchen, hid it in my schoolbag and then I returned. Her head had fallen back in her chair and I counted her missing teeth. *Mon Dieu*, she had only three left on top, and two on the bottom. The bottom ones were rotted out and made my flesh crawl. But in spite of the terrible sight I had just seen, I still loved my Grand-mère and would still sleep with her, cradled against her breast as she snored. I bent over and kissed her on the tip of her nose. She opened one eye and snorted.

* * *

"Maman," I said, as we sat on the grassy slope where she set up her easel, "I don't want to go to that school." She looked so beautiful with her hair tied up in a kerchief and blowing in wisps in the breeze. No one in that school had a Maman so beautiful.

"I want to go to school in Montmartre like I used to go . . . where the boys are like me, and they won't laugh at me and call me names . . . please, Maman, please let me go."

"Alright, I'll speak to Monsieur Paul about it. *Chéri,* wait a bit longer. You almost have your diploma, and soon you'll be out." I leaned on her shoulder and she patted my cheek. "Sit with me, *mon vieux,* and look at the beautiful scene. Don't you think I'm lucky to be able to paint like this?"

"I would hate to paint. I would hate it."

"Then what will you be?"

"Oh, Maman, I want to be a scientist when I grow up."

"*Vraiment?* A scientist. I know very little about science, but perhaps Monsieur Paul can help you. A scientist? You do like mathematics. But of course, Maurice, you have time yet to think of it. Who knows, perhaps you'll be a famous statesman?"

"No, I really want to be a scientist."

My eyes devoured her. She looked like a fairy princess to me. She stopped to brush her hair and twisted it round and round. I loved the way it shown in the late afternoon sun. Yes, she was a fairy princess, perhaps even a goddess, a *Goddess of Art.* I had heard of goddesses in school. She was mine now, this instant, this divine moment . . . my beautiful mother whom I could have all to myself and not share her with fat old Mousis who always took her time up. I hated him for that. I hated him for taking my mother away. And what did he do in the bedroom to her? I had heard things from other boys as to what grownups did. Is that why that Mousis lived with her so he could do those nasty things to her? I imagined him with his pants down. I saw him once going to his bath. How ugly he looked worse than the *petit monsieur*. How could my mother do such things with him? And once I heard them quarreling in their bedroom. Was it because she didn't want him to put his awful thing into her? That's the terrible thing the grownups all did. How could she let him, she a goddess and so beautiful? How terribly awful. I shivered at the thought of them in bed. I would like to kill him when he's going to do this terrible thing to my mother, I'll pour boiling water on it; I could even cut it off. Then he could never put it in her again. What fun!

"I'm glad to see you smiling, *chéri* . . . things aren't as bad as you make them."

But I smiled with my secret thoughts about the awful things that this Mousis did and felt the warm sun on my skin.

Maman looked up and suddenly sniffed the alcohol which blew across to her on the wind. I knew it because she stared accusingly at me. But I sat innocently looking all the world like her little contented school boy whose bag of books were bound up with a leather strap. I felt the bottle of wine hiding safely in my bookbag and I would go to my hideout this afternoon and drink it there. The thought made me feel excited. I would drink it ever so slowly to make it last.

This Mousis tried to make me like him later on by buying me a piano for my birthday. Frankly, I just wasn't interested but they wouldn't let me alone.

"But, *chéri*, you played on Henri's piano," Maman insisted.

"I loved to play on it because it was his and I loved watching him hobbling around on his little legs watching me and waving his cane. That was different."

"I don't see why Monsieur Paul or I can't watch you?"

"I loved the *petit monsieur*. Didn't you love him, Maman?"

Maman ignored my question. I knew she would because this Mousis was listening. Couldn't he see that I liked *petit* Henri better than him?

"Monsieur Paul loves you like you were his own son." She looked up at fat old Mousis and smiled. He smiled back at her and patted her shoulder. She must have let him do it, put that awful thing into her last night. At that moment I hated both of them. Why couldn't he go away? But of course *he* wouldn't because *he* wanted to fuck her. My friends said he was doing that to her all the time. How I hated him, I really did.

"I don't want to play it anymore," I screamed and crashed down the lid. Then I slammed the door, kicked two tables over and ran out of the house shouting terrible curses. I had stored them all up for such an occasion.

I arrived back in Pierrefitte sometime in the morning. I had stayed the night on the Avenue Trudaine where the proprietor of the café opposite the Rollins school became my friend. There I drank all I wanted until I staggered in, and fell asleep on the marble floor in the goddamn entrance to the goddamn home I hated, on a marble floor I despised and which felt as cold as my feelings toward my new life here. Catherine scrubbed the floor but she couldn't remove my vomit. *Tant pis!* There's nothing that could be done about it. I never asked to come here, I figured it out that we could sneak out and go back to Montmartre.

But that Mousis tried. He certainly tried, I'll give him that.

When I reached fifteen, I heard them talking in the dining room. "Suzanne, I see no point in him continuing with his classes. We'll be driven mad and the boy appears to be getting worse." His voice was shaking. I suppose he was upset. "Look, I have some connections and I'll see to it that he gets work. I know of an opening as a shipping clerk in a factory which makes window shades which are painted later. He is young yet and perhaps a simple job will give him self-confidence."

Well I lasted at this position for a week. On the eighth day, I got fed up with it and never showed up. I became a delivery boy, and a grocer's helper in sequence. The positions lasted a short time. I couldn't stand the boring jobs and I arrived dead drunk at both of them. Then I lay about the house doing nothing while Maman continually shouted at me. I saw her tiptoe down to the cellar daily to count the bottles of wine I polished off. She didn't fool me.

This Paul obtained a position for me in a bank, The Crédit Foncier where I would spend my time copying and adding columns of figures. This work sounded less boring. "You can use your skill in mathematics, Maurice," he said smiling.

I nodded. But then he looked at me with serious eyes. "But you can't drink, and I can't emphasize this enough. You cannot come to the job drunk. They will not tolerate it. Do you understand?"

I shook my head. Of course he had to spoil it by saying that.

He insisted on taking me to his tailor, and I appeared for work in a stylishly cut jacket, high starched collar, vest and trousers and sported a new bowler. I looked quite handsome and Maman danced about me before the carriage took me into Paris. Monsieur Paul accompanied me to work that first morning and introduced me proudly as his son.

Frankly, I felt changed by the position. At the beginning, I stopped drinking altogether and strode about the boulevards in my new clothes. I felt that it was all part of a game. The young workers at the bank were older than I but were all quite friendly and invited me to bicycle races and boating parties; and I once went to a dance at the Moulin de la Galette. I put on quite an act as though I knew everything and knew little. I was Paul Mousis' son and that was enough. I drank a little later on, but one couldn't notice. I must say that my talent for calculating figures carried it all off. The work wasn't bad, better than being a shipping clerk.

What I liked most of all was not my job but my bowler. I loved it and watched it carefully, so carefully that sometimes I did nothing else. I tipped it to pretty ladies who reminded me of Maman. Mousis slipped me a wonderful allowance each week, and together with my large paycheck, I bought other hats, one a top hat which I wore to the nightclub Moulin Rouge with two banking companions to celebrate six months of working. I went there looking for the *petit monsieur*. We saw Cha-U-Kao the lesbian female clown and I caught a glimpse of Henri half drunk, his awful appearance shocking me, and next to him was his long nosed cousin, *le docteur,* always with him. Henri frightened me; he looked so ill and awfully pale. This wasn't the *petit monsieur* I remembered. What happened?

One evening, four of us went secretly to *La Sourire,* a café where lesbians gathered. The proprietress sat very regally behind her counter, and I was stunned when I spotted *petit* Henri again, this time drawing a pair of females kissing. I looked about at the lesbians, the *"little messieurs,"* the masculine females with their mannish jackets and stiff collars, short hair and cigars, while others looked more like women than the women. I was fascinated by the sight of so many females caressing. One female, half undressed was pulled away somewhere by her female partner who already had her hand halfway down her culotte. I was hypnotized by the scene. Poor *petit* Henri looked feverish and his body somehow was tensed up, but he looked at me and nodded. Did he really remember me? How I remembered him as very young and enthusiastic, the Henri of my childhood; the Henri who hopped about the piano waving his arms as he directed my struggles at the keyboard. Where was this Henri? While drawing a lesbian couple fondling, he muttered, "There is nothing as foolish as women making love to each other." But the lesbians accepted him and welcomed him into their circle. I heard stories that he once lived at *La Sourire* with the lesbians, but somehow I never believed it.

I was having a fantastic time but I knew that it would all end. It was much too perfect. Mousis's tailor whipped up more marvelous clothes for me and best of all, a half dozen bowlers which I took out every afternoon after work and touched and smoothed and counted with love. Not a dent, not a mark, not a blemish must ever touch them. They became a symbol for everything I ever wanted or ever would become. I cherished them with my life and I dreamed about them. And the dream finally shattered into a thousand pieces like one of Grand-mère's blue and white porcelain cups.

It rained that Monday morning. I came to work with a rain soaked umbrella which I placed in a stand. Then I carefully removed my bowler which was drenched by the shower, and placed it on a tall file cabinet to dry. From time to time I walked over to it, and felt the hat to see if it was dry. Then I sat adding up a column of figures. My goddamn supervisor, fat ass Paget, saw the bowler sitting atop the file, muttered something like, "What the devil is this doing here?" and threw it carelessly into a small wooden wardrobe where it fell on its side, the bastard!

I stared at the dust which covered the bowler. The closet was generally unused except by the cleaning woman who used it to store a pail, lye soap and a brush. The whole action was despicable. How could he do that to my beloved bowler? My cheek twitched and I felt like choking him. But I realized that my whole career hung on my controlling myself at this moment. I inspected the hat, my precious bowler and of course it was that butcher Paget's hand that dented it. Of course he didn't care what he did to it. He just didn't care. I shook with rage and felt a hatred I never felt before. In fact I was drowning in a pool of hatred. It was all because of that moron, Paget. I had marvelous fantasies of murdering him but I continued adding the column of figures. Mole face Paget sensed that something was wrong and began humming an obscene ditty. Did he think that singing would cover up his crime? Never! I made this bastard's collar grow tight as I sat staring at him hoping my look would destroy him. How I hated him. I hated the fact that he just didn't give a damn. A few more minutes passed. *Quel idiot*, now trying to be a good sort, turned and looked at me with a half apologetic smile wanting to make amends but I just sat and stared refusing to soften. When I looked at my poor bowler again, something exploded in my head. I just couldn't help it. I slowly put down my pen, got off my stool, went calmly over to my umbrella, then walked over to that son of a bitch, and crashed it down on his head! You should have seen that idiot's expression. He had it coming to him.

Of course I was promptly fired and I didn't care. The pleasure of the moment was worth it, and within the hour I went wild drinking in a nearby café, and returned to the bank, supposedly for my bowler, where I overthrew furniture and anything else within sight. All the months of restraint came to nothing. Then I went somewhere but I don't recall where or how I got there.

10

Suzanne
Nightmare

An unearthly calm prevailed in our home after Maurice lost his position, but it was a disturbing hiatus. Something was wrong. We all felt it like a gathering storm. Paul had already washed his hands of his stepson's future. So sickened by what had occurred at the Crédit Foncier Bank, he canceled all his business appointments for several days. I knew I had to save Maurice. It was a pressing foreboding feeling which tore at me. I began to sketch him as though my renderings of him would forestall the inevitable and a mounting panic invaded me. It was a feeling unknown and terrifying in its quality. And then an unfamiliar warmth pervaded, the kinship of protectiveness; it was a tender maternal bond cemented as though by magic, and it touched Maurice lightly and wrapped a tentacle about him. I must save him. He was mine and the feeling of closeness this time didn't evaporate after my drawing. My relationship with him changed. It would never be the same.

But Degas wanted nothing to interfere with my artistic progress. And when I visited him after Maurice's debacle, Degas was increasingly irritable.

"And what about your art? Is it to suffer with every whim of your son? *Dieu merci,* I've never had to deal with children. I don't even want to paint them. The thought of children about makes me positively ill. Oh, incidentally, Vollard wants another batch of engravings, and now that you're the famous, illustrious Valadon, you'll neglect me, like Cassatt."

"Oh, Monsieur, unlike Cassatt, whether you're a Dreyfusard or not holds no interest for me, and don't trouble yourself about Maumau. He'll be . . ."

"He'll be a constant disturbance to you. And now I've sad news to tell. Henri Lautrec has been sent to a *maison de santé,* the Château St. James, at Neuilly. But I understand he's producing a remarkable series of circus pictures solely from memory. So perhaps some good will come of it."

"*Maison de Santé* . . . an asylum, you mean."

"It's a rich man's term. How much can one drink? Bartholomé said they had to strap him down in order to take him."

"*Mon pauvre* Henri. I should have married him and it would never have happened."

"Your own son drinks. A marriage to him is absurd."

"Because he's a cripple? That would never have bothered me. I've told you that before."

"No. Because his problems run deeper than you could have solved. He's erratic, an extreme alcoholic, and has idiosyncrasies too numerous to mention, one of which is living in a brothel. But of course he's a genius who will die early as the others . . . one by one. And you, Maria, I just want you to continue painting . . . now don't give me your clever excuses."

He took a magnifying glass and scrutinized a painting. "You're improving, yes, you're developing a style, an amazing style . . . your paintings exude a peculiar sensuality, a sexual power, if I may be so bold to use these terms . . . most unusual for a woman. But then indeed you're a masculine painter, probably the most virile of the women artists I've seen in your use of line, color and subject matter. What d'you say, eh?"

"Am I to be flattered? Can one paint as a woman or a man? I don't believe that. I paint with the stubbornness I need for living, and I've found that all painters who love their art do the same."

"You can take it as such. What's wrong with being called virile? Virility is an admirable trait in art. Your paintings are realistic, your nudes unashamed and natural without the coyness I detest in women. This trait in you of always seeking the truth is a gift. You see life and have experienced it in its raw form without any sugar coating and you paint it this way."

"But my art has no gender."

"I don't agree."

He shrugged his shoulders as I gathered my things. "If your son disturbs you again, I'll give him a good flogging. I smiled and kissed him on the cheek. His reaction was one I didn't anticipate. He seemed startled for the moment, grimaced, stiffened, and seemed undecided as to what course to take. He fumbled with a paint brush. I left quickly, realizing that it was one of my few physical contacts with him.

The *gay nineties* ended. It vanished as the warmth of summer turned to the coolness of autumn, and time flowed relentlessly merging one season into the next. It was 1900. A century passed and in its wake Impressionism lay in a smoldering flame.

I was struck by the realization that I was thirty-five years of age. It wasn't possible. No, it wasn't possible. I felt like a girl of eighteen when I had Maumau. I looked in the glass at my reflection. I couldn't discern any aging. My skin was young, radiant, unlined and fresh, and my eyes lustrous, and figure, voluptuous. I was pleased. I would refuse to grow older. Age would cease to exist for me. *Voilà*, that was the answer. I would bury my head in the sand, then nothing would change. Nothing. The face in the reflection, the lush body and the luminous skin . . . the brightness of the eyes and the luster of the hair . . . the flash of even white teeth and the skin without a wrinkle, without a line and without a sag; and a perfect body of firm contours, always the same, always unblemished by time. I would *will* it. It couldn't be otherwise. Not to catch a young man's eye, not to invite an insinuating glance, not to titillate by a turn of the hips, a provocative walk, was unthinkable. Evoking desire in men was as natural to me as breathing. The absence of the physical charm destroyed by age, would be a kind of death.

And my life with Paul grew stagnant, another kind of death. It was under a warm summer rain that I climbed to the top of the Butte Montmartre, the same way I had done a hundred times as a child and sat on a stone bench which was placed there by some philanthropist; the rain stopped suddenly and there was a magnificent rainbow arching the watered grasses, blossoming chestnuts and poplars. The sight was breathtaking, and I sat and wondered that I still craved a deep love, a love which could obliterate everything else and blind my senses. How marvelous it must be to be really sure, without reservations, without doubts, like a fever sweeping through one's body. But, no matter, now my art is the balm for any misgivings. My drawings of the little animals who ran up the Butte Montmartre when I was a child, and the drawings I execute now of my son with firmness and surety, all fill me with an inexplicable joy.

Paul was in a somber mood as he sat on the satin coverlet of our bed in Pierrefitte; it was a rose satin trimmed with velvet bands. A *fleur-de-lis* in rose velvet embroidered the satin as the spread fell to the floor, its edges trimmed with tiny rosettes of pale blue velvet. On the windows of the enormous room were sapphire blue velvet swags draped in folds, each caught up at the ends by gleaming flowered rosettes of fine Limoges china. They fell over straight hanging rose satin, velvet banded draperies which puddled onto the blue and rose Aubusson carpet. In the center of the room hung a huge bizarre white and gilt chandelier, its arms encrusted with sculpted leaves on which cherubic cupids were perched, all endless ornamentation.

"I want you. And I'm entitled to have you," Paul said softly. "It's always Maurice and his damn drinking . . . let him be. Isn't it enough? Why do you sit so silently?" And slowly and softly he said, "I won't put up with this, Suzanne. You have to be my wife in every way."

I had a frightened feeling. I recalled Adèle's words, "You'll have to pay, Marie, for all that. You'll have to pay." I liked the life I led with Paul. I wanted to do nothing to jeopardize it, but the delicate balance I had to maintain between Paul and

Maurice's antics kept me on a perpetual emotional see saw. It was a juggling act in which I wanted to succeed and preserve the status quo. If I didn't feel passion for Paul any longer, if he left me cold, so what. I must fake it.

"You didn't answer, Suzanne."

I will submit to him, tonight . . . I must, I thought. I felt him caress my shoulders and then fondle my breasts. I felt nothing but feigned a response. I would have to learn this. I had to learn a new game as many other wives had done . . . the game of pretending pleasure. It certainly was a game the *prostituées* of the whore houses knew. It was repugnant to me . . . I, who always succumbed to the passion of the moment, had an instinctive abhorrence of anything contrived. What a bore.

"I love you but you already know that," he said low. His breathing came faster.

I became the actress and closed my eyes and parted my lips and moaned as he opened the laces on my bodice and put his hand under my skirts. I made it easier and stood and slipped out of my voluminous skirt and then out of my chemise until the mirrors about the room reflected my nakedness. Mirrored reflections from various angles showed that I was still firm, still beautiful and with the voluptuousness which had always characterized my figure.

"Suzanne, *ma petite* Suzanne, let me hold you and touch you."

I pulled away the coverlet and the satin sheets of the bed gleamed beneath. I looked away from his stomach which fell in layers as he sat on the bed naked. *Mon Dieu*, he stripped off his clothing so quickly, I could hardly keep from laughing. I whispered, "A minute, a minute *chéri* . . . get me a glass of wine, dearest, a glass of wine." Would that help me to warm up to him? Naked, he went to the cabinet for Bordeaux. His flesh quivered as he walked across the room. When did he get so flabby?

"Let's drink a toast to us, Paul," I said as a delaying tactic.

"Of course, *ma chérie*," he smiled. "*A votre santé.*"

I reconstructed Renoir, a young Renoir, and he came and rescued me from this graveyard of love. And then Miguel took me in his arms on the Butte Montmartre, passionate Miguel, and it was all working, the drink and the fantasies . . . and Henri . . .

how does one recreate passion? Ridiculous, I thought. Was all marriage like this? Why do I have to suffer his damn cock. I get no pleasure from it. It's death to spend one's lifetime without the excitement of a new love, the thrill of a new set of arms about you, and a young man's hardness taking you sometimes without mercy, sometimes tenderly. Why must I know every stale move he will make by heart until the final moment. *Mon Dieu*, I'd rather die! Even security is not enough to trade for this. I would sell my soul for one singing moment of passion.

"*Dieu merci*," I sighed deeply when it was over, the lovemaking a goddamn blur. I yawned into the pillow. His body next to me felt like warm pudding. He was suddenly quiet, fell asleep and snored loudly. Poor, poor Paul. He had gotten more than he bargained for. He certainly hadn't anticipated a drunken son, and he had been so patient with Maurice, I must give him something to please him . . . more of myself. What a bore.

Then I rose, took a hot bath and went over to my easel and mixed my paints. My art was what it was all for anyway.

Adèle with her customary intuitive sense paid me a visit not long afterward and questioned pointedly, "How is Paul?"

I replied softly, "You were right, Adèle."

"Oh, my God, please don't throw it all away. I know you. You're *fou!* Paul takes good care of you, your mother and son. Why in God's name can't you be happy? Look at me. *Mon Dieu*, look at me. I work like a dog at the Moulin Joyeaux and all I have is a restaurant and a pair of fat hips. Fake it with him if you have to, but keep him happy. If I had such a man as Paul I would make him feel that he spent the night with Venus herself. That's what women have always had to do for security since the world began. Give him plenty of fucking and he'll be happy forever."

"But I wont be happy."

"You're not supposed to be. You're too free thinking. We are only women."

"No, it's a new century and women are as important as men. I may be a woman but I want to do it all, Adèle. I won't be beaten. I want the world to know I've been here and made a mark through myself and my son. Is that wrong?"

"You have in Paul what most women would die for. He's given you everything. Get married if you have to. Why don't you?"

"Security isn't enough. I am *not* most women."

"What the devil do you want?"

"I want love."

"Love. *Merveilleuse!* How very noble. I've been deserted by twenty lovers who left for younger mistresses and who fleeced me of my money besides. We're not eighteen anymore, Marie. If you really believe that there is such a thing as love, you are *fou* and you will give up all this for nothing at all. I know you."

"I would give it all up for someone to love, *c'est ça.*"

"Then you're a fool. As long as we bear the children our lives will always have limitations . . ."

"Then we're no better than the whores."

"You would forget your lofty ideas soon enough if you had a big belly. You would be relieved then that Paul took care of you. These modern notions are only for rich women who can afford them. You can get yourself a lover and let Paul take care of you financially, and just be discreet. That's what the goddamn husbands do when they're bored. I have to leave now before I'm robbed blind at the Moulin Joyeux."

I reached out and touched her hand. "My dear, dear friend. I think when I'll take my last breath, you'll sit beside me and try to change me."

"You know I won't have to change you, you'll do it yourself."

Adèle slipped a mauve colored shawl over her shoulders and the long green moiré taffeta dress rustled as she walked.

She turned back for a moment, "Listen . . . in Germany, and I think America, the women wear a rubber pessary, a diaphragm which really does the trick . . . find out about it."

"And the man?"

"He needs nothing. Paul will never know the difference. You certainly don't want any more young ones . . . you just put it on before he bothers you. Oh, you'll have to be fitted by a doctor. There is a new science to examine women called *Gynécologie.* Find out about it."

" . . . you are right, we are born to suffer."

I watched my old friend walk down the path from the studio

with a familiar swaying of her hips and hail a coach.

"*Au revoir*, Marie," Adèle called waving a handkerchief and settled back in the plush seat; her face and body were becoming matronly. Her beauty that once Rodin extolled was convoluted somewhere between new mounds of flesh.

* * *

The new century drew on and with its dawn I saw an outrageous dancer, Isadora Duncan, perform a strange interpretive dance. But it was the Exposition Universelle which drew thousands of visitors to Paris.

I accompanied Degas to the Exhibition in the new Grand Palais, and when we left, "I'm amazed at how Gauguin was ignored," I said. "Did you see there was only one picture by Gauguin, and he rots in the tropics knowing this? And there were no paintings by Van Gogh or Lautrec. *Incroyable!*"

"The world is always behind. It'll catch up soon. That's the way it is. It's not ready yet, you'll see, my Maria, you'll see."

"I have little patience for stupidity. And not to represent Van Gogh or Gauguin at this exhibit is sheer stupidity. And how long will it take for the world to accept me? I belong to no movement. How long will it take? Will it happen in my lifetime?"

"One cannot tell but it will happen," Degas reassured. "Where is your courage, Maria?"

"I have it, I assure you."

He put an unaccustomed hand on my arm. "Have patience, my Maria; if you have enough talent the world will keep discovering it over and over again. Have patience . . . they'll listen to you because what you have to say is timeless."

I didn't answer but leaned back in the coach and I noticed how much older he had grown. "Mon *Dieu*, keep him alive," I murmured. My unaccustomed prayer surprised even me.

Spring rains showered down upon the Montmartre; it then dried up by the heat of early June, and Paris closed its shutters against the encroaching summer.

Letters from Degas were hand delivered to me by a servant and frankly I was relieved to escape the turmoil Maurice caused in the house at Pierrefitte.

March 9, 1900
Last night, my dear Maria, I had dinner at Bartholomé's home and we were saying that every year, on the same date, we receive a letter from Maria wishing us good things, except the pleasure of seeing her drawings and herself. Indeed are you still drawing, excellent artist that you are?
                                                                      Degas

June 25, 1900
My Illustrious Valadon,
Come to my rooms . . . I am doing over my whole arrangement of paintings. You can make me laugh, my little she-devil. I see few people . . . am virtually a hermit. I am suffering terribly with all sorts of ailments. Have some pity on me. You have become so elegant in Pierrefitte, that you don't want to know anyone from Montmartre.
                                                                      Degas

I took a coach to his new home on Rue Victor-Massé.

Degas began to live a hermit-like existence on the three floors of the old house. I couldn't see much difference in his arrangements. The entire top floor was crammed with his own and paintings he had purchased; they were stacked against the walls with no place to hang them. The floor below continued as his studio. There was an easel supporting his current work, a pastel of dancers at the barre. There was now a table replete with a collection of bottles of oil, paraffin, varnish and siccative, brushes and turpentine and all sorts of odd materials which could one day be used for props. His studio contained a bath tub, a cot, a chest of drawers with one drawer missing and a lectern. About the studio, I saw life size dancing girls of red wax, their tulle skirts coated with dust. Where had he found these figures? I smiled to myself. He could paint a girl in a tub without using a live model. I wasn't sure how I liked the idea.

One afternoon I came in on a shocked middle aged model who trembled as she gathered her clothes while wiping her eyes.

"I'm not using you anymore!" Degas said firmly.

"But you always said I was such a good model."

"Yes, but you are a Protestant and the Protestants and Jews are hand in glove in the Dreyfus affair."

"You miserable . . . miserable . . ." she began and left weeping. The incident and the empty spaces on his wall sickened me. There were blank areas where his old friend, Pissarro's paintings had once hung, and which were removed as a result of the Dreyfus affair. Monet's paintings also? Degas read my mind.

"I'm not interested in anything Pissarro has to paint."

"You can't hate Pissarro for being a Jew. I don't understand you. He's a fine artist and you've been friends with him such a long time. And Monet's paintings gone as well?"

"That damn Dreyfusard, Monet! Did you know he accompanied Zola to his libel trial? That's enough of the whole business, and I don't care to discuss it." I instinctively knew that I was treading on dangerous ground.

"They say you're an anti-Semite, Monsieur . . . the artists say it. And they say you cannot start your day without Zoë reading the hate against the Jews in the *Libre Parole*."

"Are you looking to fight with me, my Maria? I didn't write you to speak of Jews." He said this quietly but his face was flushed with anger.

"Alright, don't fret. You know I always speak my mind. You yourself have always wanted me to be truthful."

"I'll forgive you, Maria, because it's your nature. You've always been unafraid of saying what you feel."

"Well I have distressing news, Monsieur Degas. I fear that Henri is gravely ill. When he returned from the sanitarium, they said he became mentally unbalanced. When he moved out of his rue Tourlaque studio he left over seventy-five paintings he thought worthless and the landlord gave them to his cleaning woman who stuffed holes in her walls with the canvases and used the stretchers for kindling wood. I'm so sick about it . . . poor, poor Henri. I went to the little exhibition at his new studio on the rue Frochot and it was a terribly sad affair. Henri looked frightful . . . such an ashen face, and his beautiful eyes so heavily bagged, and he was tottering about on two canes trying to be the old Henri . . . my poor, poor Henri."

"Don't poor, poor Henri me. Damn fool! He's nothing but a damn fool who will die from it all. He was instructed never to touch a drop of liquor, but he'll never stop. He'll drink himself to death, *c'est ça!* A stupid ass, talented and brilliant who paints and whores in the brothel and has contracted syphilis as well, and now I hear he stayed with a pack of lesbians at *La Sourire*, another idiotic aberration. Damn fool. Must he live with those whores? Is he trying to prove that they're more grotesque than he is? All wasted talent." His hand was trembling with anger.

"Calm yourself, Monsieur. There's little you can do about it. Oh, I almost forgot, Émile Bernard said that Paul Gauguin rots in Tahiti with skin rashes and vomits blood every day . . . from the syphilis, no doubt."

Degas sighed deeply, "Another madman," he said low. "He will die early, like Lautrec, an abominable waste."

I began to leave and then turned back. "Oh, by the way, there's a new artist in Paris. I hear that he's only nineteen and from Barcelona. It seems he came in with some paintings for . . ."

"And who is this damn fool artist who deems himself so important that he's already presenting his works? Nobody. I could burst with anger at this nineteen year old swaggerer."

"I believe his name is Picasso, Pablo Picasso, an odd name."

"Picasso? Never heard of him and I hope he never bothers me. Spaniards have odd names," he mused.

"Yes, names like Utrillo," I said and left.

* * *

Maurice worsened. I felt a growing nightmare. I must get help. He threw more severe tantrums, drank more alcohol, ranging from red wine to cognac and then absinthe and back again. The gilt edged molding in the foyer had now turned green with the acid of his vomit. The stench about him was unbearable. At times he wouldn't drink at all, but mope, do nothing, or sit in a severe depression. Then the exigencies of the addiction would surge to the fore and he begged Maman for wine, or Paul, or myself.

I consulted Dr. Ettlinger who recommended various psychologists. They applied principles from this Dr. Freud who in 1900 had come out with *The Interpretation of Dreams*. Dr. Ettlinger called it an *Oedipal Complex*. And he claimed that some of Maurice's behavior stemmed from his attachment to me. It could become worse when he grew older. This Dr. Freud was *fou*, clear and simple. Perhaps it was something I had felt toward Puvis de Chavannes as a father, but then how could I have made love to him? Did it mean that Maurice was in love with me? What a terrible incestuous notion. It was a thought to dismiss from one's mind as quickly as possible as an unnatural abomination. Dr. Ettlinger was mistaken. Dr. Freud was misquoted.

One afternoon, I came in on Maman who kept rocking back and forth muttering incoherently and waving her arms. She pointed to her Maumau who was strangely flushed and seemed to be quite restrained, but to my horror sat with a butcher knife poised in his hand. Catherine was struggling with him. I screamed, "Maurice!" but he was oblivious to me. He watched us both from the corner of his eyes as he began cutting up furniture. All he said over and over again was, "I hate it! I hate it!" When he thrust the knife across the gold satin couch making a long slice into the shimmering covering, Maman began to scream and I watched him horrified. I bolted toward him and wrestled with him. He was too strong in his resistance. He cut the tassels off the arms, one by one. Maman began to wail, a low pathetic wail, as he started to saw off the legs of an ornate Louis XIII tapestry chair and its footstool, and changed his mind and carved a design into them. He looked up at us from time to time and laughed a wild laugh of lunacy. There was no point in trying to restrain him; instead I sent Catherine to summon César Gay.

César struggled with a wild Maurice who was dancing about, wielding a knife with a maniacal laugh and threatening to cut his Grand-mère if she didn't supply him with more wine. He grabbed Maurice by both arms and took the knife away. Maman stood by moaning. I called my neighbor, Dr. Ettlinger who pointed to the gold satin sofa already embroidered with a series of deep slashes and César Gay pushed Maurice down and held him. I watched in horror as Dr. Ettlinger administered a sedative with a hypodermic needle. The doctor reflected for a few moments on the marred sofa and then gravely looked up at me.

"Madame Mousis, you and I must talk, and when your husband returns, he must as well. I strongly advise that Maurice be committed to an asylum. There they will deal with his problem."

Flashes of Henri Lautrec whirled past me.

"No, no, no! I can't!" I screamed.

"But you must," the doctor insisted. "One of you might suffer bodily harm. It's for the good of your boy. They can help him in the asylum and stop his drinking. It's his drinking which makes him mad, nothing else."

"No! Certainly not! Never! My son will never go to an asylum like a lunatic."

"Yes, Madame, he must. It doesn't mean he's mad but that he is just an alcoholic. Just try it for a while . . . just a little while . . . you can always release him." His voice sounded soothing. A feeling of panic gripped me and my throat felt as though it closed.

I began to retch. It was an awful frustration, this futile fight against this incipient sickness which had invaded my son's soul. Even I, with all my bravado, could do nothing. I couldn't remember another instance when I was so completely helpless. Usually some inner courage came to the fore. Nothing seemed to work now. There must be an answer.

Slowly, reluctantly and subdued, I acquiesced. "What do I have to do, Monsieur? What do I have to do?"

"First, you will speak with your husband."

It was odd but I never thought of bringing Paul into the decision. It seemed as though he was never at all involved.

"Of course," I said. "I'll speak with him."

Dr. Ettlinger left when Maurice slept and then returned that evening and spoke with Paul. Maurice slept all of the following day with an additional sedative.

"I contacted Dr. Vallon at the Asylum of Sainte-Anne, and I have already sent a messenger, and have gotten an answer. You have just to sign some papers," he said and put the document in Paul's hands. "He'll be there for just a few months. His problem, I assure you, Monsieur Mousis, is not dementia but alcoholism, perhaps a maternal fixation. And there have been studies based on the new theories of Dr. Freud."

"Maternal fixation." I echoed, now more composed, "Rubbish."

"Perhaps, dear, he's right. Doctors know of these things," said Paul.

"Listen to your husband, Madame. Don't make light of it. You're entitled to your own thinking but allow the doctors to speak to his problem, and when he's released I would strongly suggest he be given something to do manually . . . manual therapy as it were . . . a good outlet. You agree, Madame?"

I nodded my head, assenting to the doctor's suggestions, not giving it too much thought.

"Well," and Dr. Ettlinger stroked his beard. "We'll have time for this *manual therapy* when the moment arrives."

At the age of eighteen, Maurice was committed to the Asylum of Sainte-Anne that day in 1901. He was put in the care of Dr. Vallon, a specialist in alcoholism.

After Maurice left, I returned to my studio in Montmartre and painted for several weeks with little interruption, either to eat or sleep. Then I returned to our sumptuous home in Pierrefitte and Paul . . . and a frightful emptiness.

Summer seared Paris in 1901, and the nightmare worsened. The heat assaulted with an oppressive smoldering cocoon of an orange sun which bathed the little twisted streets of Montmartre, and Paris shimmered and blistered in that blaze. The grounds about Sainte-Anne's Sanitarium where Maurice was committed, bleached out in the sun, and well kept lawns dried into tannish straw patches.

And all the while I felt that I had undergone some trauma, some awful disruption, and in my mind's eye, in my dreams and waking hours I felt the presence of my son in the asylum, screaming, sleeping, enduring the injections of white garbed attendants and doctors. And my mind conjured up the visions of the incubus with all sorts of terrible fantasies of what was taking place. There were dark circles under my eyes for lack of sleep, and I was distraught with worry. I imagined that the doctors would never release him . . . that I was duped . . . and I saw Maurice dying from loneliness and neglect.

It was a terrible aching new feeling for me, this giant spasm of guilt which overtook me; this desire for my son to be cured and released, and to be able to help him overcome the terror, the terrible terror which was destroying us all. And to add to my fears, while Maurice was at Sainte-Anne in late August, I received a note from Bartholomé dictated by Henri to his mother, the Comtesse Adèle, requesting that I see him one more time. I felt the urgency of the note. My poor, poor Henri.

* * *

Henri Lautrec was dying at Malromé, his mother's estate. Why was he leaving such a painful void in my life? He should not have mattered so much. I couldn't understand my own feelings. This emptiness was made even more acute by the dismal relationship I had with Paul, a kind of death. I leaned back in the cracked leather seats as the train pulled away from the station of Gare du Nord. It was an irony. Two men with the same alcoholism; my Maumau at Sainte-Anne and Henri on his death bed. There was the horror of Henri's fate awaiting Maurice.,

Bartholomé related to me that on July 15 when Maurice was confined, that Henri began to put his affairs in order, signing and gathering his canvases and leaving his beloved work in his studio. Henri de Toulouse-Lautrec, one year my senior, at the age of thirty-six, knew his life was ending. The fact that it was a terribly short life didn't seem to matter to him . . . the way he drank and his other excesses were bound to take their toll. We warned him, his friends warned him but he went on recklessly destroying himself. Somehow I always knew it would end this way, choking whatever life was left. And one night in that oppressive heat of August he collapsed with an attack of paralysis. And now he lay dying at his mother's home.

He is so young, I thought, as the motion of the train lulled me into a half sleep and I fell into a reverie. And I remembered those days when I climbed the stairs to his studio, when we made love on his mother's green plush divan. I looked out of the window at the passing countryside. I remembered how he had seen my drawings in disbelief, and he sent me to Degas, dear Degas. And I smiled thinking of the butterfly hat he had bought me at Madame Henriette's while the woman looked at us in astonishment, at such a mismatched pair. What a wonderful day! And how he had educated me, giving me the philosophers to read, and he was amazed and so proud of what I had written. I could have made him a good wife and been a marvelous hostess for him, and our friends would have been painters instead of bankers. And of course now I knew, I knew. *I love you, mon cher Henri*, and now it's too late.

It seemed as though an eternity had passed when the train finally stopped at Malromé, and a coach took me to the Château de Malromé. I was in the Girondé province near Bordeaux, a place of vineyards and hills that roamed far into the horizon. When I reached the Château, I caught my breath. Even as the mistress of the sumptuous house at Pierrefitte I was transfixed.

The Château was palatial in its approach, a turreted seventeenth-century mansion with its high wrought iron gates and garden walls protecting cultivated dahlias, geraniums and a profusion of other species all punctuating the rolling grounds with flurries of color. I could appreciate the flowers, some in full bloom, others already beyond their blossoming time. The Château's grounds were breathtaking with walks and ponds and flowers all rich in hue nodding in the gentle breezes of the lush landscape. At the side of the Château were the stables and mingling with it all were lily ponds chocked full of goldfish, glinting layer upon layer in the afternoon sun. I heard the crunch of the gravel as the coach made its way up the driveway to where Henri spent his early years, and somehow I couldn't connect this grandeur with the talented dwarf who had trudged up four floors to a studio blanketed with mounds of dust.

As I entered the Château, I saw Dr. Tapié de Céleyran, such a strange cousin, good naturedly always the butt of Henri's humor, his devoted, steady companion. Part of the Château was already electrified and he stood under a huge lamp as a servant handed him his gold headed cane. He tipped a tall silk hat acknowledging me, and without a word left the building. As I was led through the dim rooms I wondered that the remaining gas jets were sputtering and turned so low. Henri's room was the darkest of all, and Madame la Comtesse Adèle de Toulouse-Lautrec sat in a chair beside her son holding his hand. The Curé of Malromé had given him the last sacraments, bowed and left the room. In a dark corner of the room a nun was fingering her beads and praying. Beside her stood Bartholomé. When the Comtesse saw me, she turned and looked at me questioningly.

"I am Suzanne Valadon, his friend. Is he very bad, Madame la Comtesse?"

"Yes." The Comtesse had been visibly crying. "You can't stay long." She wiped her eyes and her cheeks were tear stained.

I greeted Bartholomé who had come on an earlier train.

"I'll ride back with you," he said. "There's a train leaving in two hours."

"My servants will prepare you some dinner before you leave," said the Comtesse.

Bartholomé took her hand. "What can I say except that your son has shown his genius to everyone. He's made a mark on the art world everywhere. You can be proud of him."

"My son will die and I'll die along with him. I've died hundreds of times with his afflictions. I died when I saw him grow up into a man who could never live a normal life." Her voice broke and she wept. "This will not be different. I'll die again."

Bartholomé waited for me outside the room. La Comtesse Adèle retreated into the shadows weeping. Such a handsome woman. It appeared amazing to me that this was his mother. I suddenly felt the anguish of having a deformed son and the pride of conceiving such a talent.

I approached the bed and spoke softly. He stirred.

"Henri," I touched his hand. It seared me. *'Mon cher* Henri." His face was ashen. I was shaken by his appearance, a face akin to a death mask but he opened his deep soulful eyes, his one good feature. I had never really noticed that his large nose was so bulbous, but it appeared purple now against the white sheet.

"Marie . . . it's you . . . you're still beautiful," he whispered hoarsely. He had forgotten that he changed my name.

I placed a finger to his lips. "Shhh . . . don't strain yourself, Henri."

" . . . you . . . paint?"

"Yes."

"Where is your . . . butterfly hat? Wear it, please wear it." He had lost track of time.

"Yes . . . my dearest Henri and I cherish your painting of me, and this." I fingered the locket he had given me.

"Good . . . good . . . want you to paint . . . " his voice trailed off and he closed his eyes.

"Oh, Henri, you should have married me . . . you wouldn't be so sick now. I could have taken care of you."

He beckoned to me to get closer to him. I leaned over.

"I . . . a cripple . . ."

"It didn't matter to me. I loved you but you wouldn't believe me. You changed everything for me, Henri."

"Your son used to . . . play . . . my piano."

He began to cough.

"Don't speak, Henri."

He closed his eyes and said "Marie . . . remember me."

"Remember you? Oh, Henri, I'll remember you always." I held his hand in mine and then for an instant put my cheek down on the sheet next to him. His pince-nez removed from his one good feature, revealed his luminous intelligent eyes now glassy and puffy with fever.

His hand waved weakly to his mother. He suddenly caught his breath and went into a spasm of coughing. Blood trickled from one side of his mouth. His face was a sickly greenish gray. His mother came from the shadows and bent over her son, wiping his lips with a lace edged handkerchief. I looked at her closely.

La Comtesse Adèle, a gracious lady with graying hair parted neatly, in a dark blue silk dress with buttons down the bodice, her nose, patrician in contrast with her son's bulbous one; and her skin delicate, in contrast to her son's heavy textured oily face. She looked as Henri had painted her in 1887 except an older version, much older, and there were deep shadows of grief and pain around her eyes.

"You must go," la Comtesse said. "You can see how bad he is."

"Good-bye, Henri," I called softly. "Good-by for now."

I doubted if he heard me at all.

I took my leave with Bartholomé, and gazed back in wonderment at the Château, this monument to a title, the Counts Toulouse, dating from Charlemagne's time. I marveled at Henri's eccentric father, Alphonse de Toulouse-Lautrec Monfa, a man who never believed in his son's talent, a scion of an old French family in contrast to his charming wife, his cousin, Adèle Tapié de Céleyran; this mismatched pair had an unbelievable dwarf for a son . . . and an artistic genius.

When Bartholomé and I returned to Montmartre, I spent some time with him in Degas' studio discussing poor Henri, and then went back to my studio at Rue Cortot instead of returning to Pierrefitte. And then something happened to me.

I was falling into little pieces. And to keep a firm grip on my sanity I began to turn out drawings faster than I had ever done them before. Clouded images of Maurice in the hospital and Henri dying at Malromé, a shell of what he once was, and my odd detachment from Paul Mousis came in like a tidal wave.

I sent a messenger back to Pierrefitte informing Paul that I would remain at my studio for several days, and then I worked myself into a frenzy of activity. After several days I returned to Pierrefitte. The huge house seemed strange, and unfriendly. Paul was concerned with some business project and I hardly saw him. Maman sat as a fixture in her rocker knitting a muffler for her Maumau and awaited his return while slurping her brandy. I found that I was unable to work and returned to the rue Cortot wading through my nightmare.

Montmartre revitalized me. In it I could fight the horror I felt at Maurice being in the institution, and the imminent death of a former lover and friend, Henri Lautrec. My world as I knew it was crumbling but I wasn't going to crumble with it. What was happening to me? I didn't understand it myself. All I knew was I was terribly frightened, a new emotion for me. Perhaps it was because Henri Lautrec was part of the world I once knew, one I really cared about, and he would soon be gone. Perhaps it was the realization that what I felt for Henri was really love. Degas had been right after all. But it was too late. I had to be strong and I inevitably turned to my drawing and painting as a source of strength. My art would enable me to transcend this horror, this incubus hovering over me. To draw and paint fast enough, to make all else cease to be; the art, a madness so that I no longer had any will; even my eyes and mind ceased to be and all was centered in my chalk or brush. I lost myself completely in my striving for self-expression and relentlessly and persistently turned out canvas after canvas in a paroxysm of activity.

I thought I heard Maurice scream out, but blocked it out. I took out another clean page, and returned to drawing. I banished all anxiety as I executed drawing after drawing. Lost in a blur of activity, I surpassed myself, and when I completed all the work at hand, I eliminated those I felt were poor and kept the rest. Then I began again and again, remaining now almost constantly at my studio, revisiting Pierrefitte at infrequent intervals. This continued all the months that Maurice was away.

And that September, I received the news from Bartholomé that Henri had died at Malromé. I paused for a few moments at my drawing and then resumed without tears.

I gathered up my drawings and paintings on the eve of Lautrec's death and brought them to Degas as when I first came to him, and he stood looking at them without comment. And then, "They're remarkable." And he managed to clear a space on his cluttered wall and put them up near those of Lautrec.

It was there I knew that the chapter of the little man with the stunted legs who had changed my life was closed forever.

Part Two
(1901-1917)

"She had amazing light eyes and hair parted down the middle and she seemed to dance rather than walk . . . like a fairy . . ."
André Utter, upon first seeing Suzanne

11

Henri

"Dying is so Damn Hard"

I died on September 9, 1901. I thought of Vincent Van Gogh before I died. We were both thirty-seven. At the time of my death a storm raged over Malromé and lightning streaked across the sky, and suddenly gunshots were heard. My papa, Count Alphonse was shooting owls from one of the chateau towers like a madman. Before my death he wanted to cut off my beard, an Arab custom. When he was stopped from doing so by Maman, he pulled the elastic from his boots and played some sort of insane game, taking aim at the flies about my bed. "You old fool." I said to him.

I suffered two attacks toward the end, the last one of delirium tremens and I was confined to a rest home in Neuilly. I recovered. I knew I was destroying myself and that the next crisis would be fatal. I wanted to see Paris once more before I died; and I felt death draw close like an icy wind coming from the distance.

When I reached Paris on April 15 and went to my new studio on the first floor of the Avenue Frochot, I thought of my first studio in rue Tourlaque and saw Marie-Clémentine walking up those steps as she had once done long ago. I was twenty-one then, young and full of exuberance. Now I was old and ill and my clothes hung loosely about my body. I was no longer the man she had known. No matter.

I barely struggled into the studio, and there was a wild disorder, and from it I extracted and stacked all my canvases, studies of women, portraits of friends, scenes in dance halls, posters, and all that I had accumulated and gathering dust in corners. There were a number of unfinished sketches which lay hidden for years, unfinished canvases were stacked high on shelves and flung carelessly across tables; dried jars of paint and stiffened brushes all had to be thrown out. I looked at the dust laden windows and remembered saying heatedly to Marie, "Degas has dust on his windows, every artist has dust on his windows." How long ago that was. It seemed so important then. It was in another time and another place.

Some of the work I examined seemed very good, and some poor. I sorted them into piles. I was extremely meticulous and worked without stopping against a dread event, my own death, and on July 15 I closed the door to the studio one last time, leaving everything in amazing order. It had the austere look of a museum.

Dr. Tapié de Céleyran, my inseparable cousin, who having taken his degree as a doctor of medicine now hinted that I had not long to live. The fool had the presumption of making such a diagnosis. I joked and reassured him, but I knew otherwise. The terrible finality of it all was drawing closer. One night in the heat of August, I collapsed with an attack of paralysis. My Maman took me back to the Château de Malromé on August 20th. I attempted to fight death but how much can one fight the inevitable? I climbed a ladder to paint but the brush kept falling from my hand. The paralysis was spreading over my body and now I could neither walk nor eat. I was too exhausted to be frightened. I began to hope that I wouldn't be alone at the end the way Vincent was, and that my friends would be at my bedside. Now I lay prostrate all the time, and the covers about me feel as heavy as lead and are crushing me.

Fevered dreams of the studio plagued me continually . . . of

Marie, of our lovemaking, all whispered their secrets . . . a worn green velvet divan . . . a woman's body yielding so completely, a face of beauty, sad yet defiant.

Would she come and where would Bartholomé find her? I still couldn't remember.

She came to my bedside, my petite Marie-Clémentine, and I wondered why she wasn't wearing the butterfly hat I bought her. She had wanted it so. Was that long ago? My memory fails me . . . I can't remember . . . once again, events rush into each other, and time, people and places become as one. I only remember her sweet body and her passion, her startling sapphire eyes, her sensual mouth, cognac colored sun-kissed hair, and full high bosom, and over and over again, our lovemaking in my old studio amidst the thick dust, amidst the wild disorder, amidst the easels, still wet with fresh paint. I remember that bliss that I never felt again. How I loved her then and that love faded leaving in its wake a delicious memory.

I was buried in the cemetery of Saint-André-du-Bois near Malromé. Of course my papa, the Count Alphonse, was eccentric to the end. At the funeral, instead of following in the procession, he took a seat on the box of the hearse, displaced the coachman by throwing him off and drove it himself to see that my body was conducted in a manner appropriate to a gentleman. He whipped the horse to increase his pace to such a degree that mourners who walked behind had to run through the muddy roads to keep up. Papa was a lunatic.

My critics blasted me after my death. "It is fortunate for humanity that there are few artists of his sort," wrote one. And another claimed, "His curious and immoral talent, that of a deformed man who saw ugliness in everything and exaggerated that ugliness." But what I saw in life was not ugliness but a passionate experience for all those who are willing to look at it with passion.

Yet after my death my paintings and posters soared in value. Most of my pictures, drawings and lithographs reverted to my parents. Maman was always supportive of my art while papa still waited for me to go hunting with him, and he waited until I grated out my last feverish gasp. I was a failure to him up to my end. Papa, not knowing what to do with the bulk of my art, and not understanding any of it, gave a portion of my work to my friends and ceded all the rights to publication to Maurice Joyant. Papa at least was honest at the end. He, who never approved of my work had no intention to benefit from it. "I failed to understand his paintings," he wrote to Joyant. "You believed in his work more than I did and your judgment was right." Papa finally did the right thing.

By dying, perhaps I did also. But I said to Maman at the end, "Dying's so damn hard!" It was the last thing I said to anyone.

12

Suzanne

Artiste-Mother

A dreadful fear of my son's drinking was heightened by Henri's death. Maurice left the Sanitarium of Sainte-Anne three months after he entered. He seemed strangely lethargic but he didn't drink. "You must have him do something with his hands, a kind of manual therapy as it were." Dr. Ettlinger's words came to me. "With his hands, with his hands, with his hands," I thought over and over again. What could he do? There was much he could do.

"Why can't you build furniture? I'll show you, and you love mathematics and can calculate the proportions, *n'est-ce pas?*"

He looked at me apathetically and was disinterested.

I explored other avenues. He rejected them.

"What can he do?" I asked Paul, but he had apparently washed his hands after Maurice botched his job with the Crédit Foncier.

Time was growing short. Maurice began to drink again. He drank in small quantities stealing wine from the well stocked cellar in the house, and panic mounted in the household. I was compelled to act.

"He must do something constructive with his hands that will also occupy his mind," repeated Dr. Ettlinger. "Otherwise, he'll lose himself once again. Perhaps he can do carpentry?"

"I already broached that to him. He's not interested."

What was the answer? Whatever the answer was, time was running out. It had to be done quickly else he would be back again in a sanitarium after making the household a living hell. He disappeared once and César Gay brought him back. He was becoming increasingly more difficult. A great panic gripped me.

And then it happened! It was under my own nose, on my own easel, part of my own palette It was so simple. The solution was so simple and I had never thought of it.

"Maumau, you're going to become an artist."

"What?"

"You're going to become an artist. I'll teach you all I know."

I refused to ask him his opinion as Dr. Ettlinger had suggested. Maurice hadn't agreed to any suggestions I made. I was tired of his negative responses. I simply informed him that this was to be his new vocation, and that's that. I didn't even know whether he had talent. Of course he did because he was my son.

Maurice just shook his head.

"Don't shake your head. I'll set up a palette of a few colors and you will learn, even as I did. You *will* do it yourself."

He stared at me apathetically.

"And if you don't do this and keep drinking, you'll get steadily worse and go back to the asylum and stay there forever!"

He looked frightened.

"Now I'm going to put a few colors on the palette for you . . . my own turkey red, two chrome yellows, a vermilion and a zinc white, and I'll teach you all that I know . . . how lucky you are."

He seemed in a trance and made no motion to cooperate.

"Well?"

He didn't answer. When I left, he sat for a moment and then took the paint tubes and flung them out the window one by one, and then returned to the divan. He reached up for a moment and pulled a small blanket over his face and fell asleep.

For the next few days he sat around apathetically, slowly inciting me into a deep rage. Then he began to read looking up at me from time to time. When his eyes met mine, his look was generally one of defiance, but I was determined. I found the pigments in the garden and threw them back at him.

"Have it your own way. Don't expect me to bail you out next time. I will, I swear it, leave you at Sainte-Anne's forever . . . to rot!" I shouted.

"Leave him alone," Maman Madeleine murmured. "He'll do it his own way."

"His own way? I know his own way. It's to be perpetually found by the police dead drunk and sopping with vomit."

"I'm not painting," said Maurice emphatically, suddenly finding his tongue.

"I better find you at that easel. I'm not going to wait much longer."

"I'm going to be a scientist, not an artist."

"I've decided you're going to be an artist!"

"Let him be. What's wrong with you? Can you force him to be an artist? Let him become what he wants to be," mumbled Maman. "My Maumau wants to be a scientist."

"You're Maumau is buying time. He wants to be nothing but a drunk. He gives excuses that I won't accept. He *will* become an artist. I *can* and *will* make him an artist. You'll see, I'll do it."

"You are *fou!*" shouted Maman. "Let him be."

"No, I've made up my mind."

Maurice looked at me with eyes that were deep immeasurable pools and then kept reading.

"Dr. Ettlinger said he must do something with his hands and he's my son and he must have some artistic talent. Who knows but he could be an artistic genius." Maurice glanced up again with a peculiar gleam in his eyes. "And if you throw the paints out the window again I'll have you committed," I said firmly.

Maurice kept reading for four days. When he didn't read he slept. *And if there are really miracles, the miracle happened.*

On the fifth day, with the daylight streaming through the window, and with the snow plaguing Paris and its environs that winter; with sheets of snow turning to ice so that the cold invaded every bone in the body; with the mercury plummeting and setting record breaking temperatures; with the countless scuttles of coal glowing in the iron stoves of the house, and the numerous fireplaces burning throughout Paris; and with the trees in the fields about the château looking all the world like white specters motioning to him while awaiting his verdict on his future, Maurice began to mix his paints . . . turkey red, chrome yellows and an abundance of zinc white the color of the snow clad trees. He put these on a palette and timidly applied them. It was so natural that he apply paint to the canvas. He refused to make any preliminary sketches.

But then the colors were too dark. He lightened them with the zinc white until all became very pale. He was hesitant and his first paintings were rows of dark red tiled roof houses and the beginning of his expressive leaden skies. I could hardly restrain myself, breathless at what I saw developing. The reds were still far too red and the yellows too yellow. He continued to use the white lavishly to tone down the vaguest of colors and he drew with a soft pencil and added a thick layer of color when the cardboard was half dry. Starting at the bottom he worked his way up . . . by instinct he became a landscape painter, a painter of houses and streets and of my beloved Montmartre.

And I watched from the corner of my eye and I bit my lip to restrain myself. Maurice looked up at me from time to time searching my face for approval, and I caught his gaze but showed nothing, my face a mask as I continued painting at my easel. But my heart pounded and my hand trembled in a kind of ecstatic excitement. I knew that this was a glorious moment which could be forever cherished . . . my son's first venture into painting . . . my Maurice's first labored strokes on the cardboard. And still I said nothing. I was afraid to speak . . . afraid to break that slender thread which connected my Maurice to his new discovery, his new found interest, perhaps to a revelation of talent. I would be silent. I would allow him to unlock for himself the joys of painting and then if he should come to me for instruction, only then would I intervene with the gentlest of suggestions . . . only then. But Maurice still worked in silence, alone.

He was still too timid to paint out of doors but later in the spring he would go into Montmartre and watch the artists painting *en plein-air,* watch how they mixed and applied their pigment. But basically he was unimpressed by the Impressionists and Post-Impressionists. He was drawn to something he had looked at every day of his life . . . the twisted streets of the Butte with the Sacré-Coeur still unfinished hovering in the distance. This is what intrigued him. And he struggled to express himself with thick layers of paint on canvas. His was a special art which was uniquely his own. And he became bolder by the summer and took his art to the streets and hills painting *en plein-air*, and he thickened the paint by mixing plaster or sand into the pigments. He pasted sticks and scraps of burlap onto the canvas, almost like a collage of a future decade, and he signed his painting, *Maurice Valadon*. He refused as yet to use the name, *Utrillo*.

And it all happened to him as in a dream.

And after a while he turned to me for help, and I gave him suggestions, many of which he wouldn't take. He seemed bent on his own course, a course which miraculously must always have been there. He enlarged his palette as the blues emerged. He couldn't seem to paint figures and his streets and scenes were empty of them. His painted figures appeared like little puppets with the full hips and large buttocks of my women. He supplemented Montmartre with scenes of Montmagny and Pierrefitte.

And with the seasons, Maurice painted. He forgot about the scientist he had dreamed of becoming, and he lived in a dreamlike state turning out canvas after canvas. He painted whatever his heart dictated, wherever his whims led him. In the course of a year he turned out one hundred and fifty canvases.

And through it all, I was nearby painting or watching, or suggesting, fearful that he would stop what he was doing by some curt remark or whim, or the demon which plagued his soul with drink. Was he a Pissarro or a . . . who was he? I couldn't place his style. But then, who was I? We both were unique.

And I wondered . . . I marveled that Paris didn't signal the event of his painting . . . the commencement of his work by a salvo from its now quiet canons, and even the "Bateau-Lavoir," a maze of rooms taken by the new artists such as Picasso, went its hectic way without noticing what had occurred. Why didn't Montmartre rejoice that in its midst, a thin twenty year old strapped an easel to his back and began to paint its streets like no one else had done, shyly at first, sometimes retreating back to the house at Pierrefitte, then venturing again into the hillside of Montmagny, the suburbs, and to painting in the Montmartre streets. It was an earth shattering event for me, why not for others? How was it possible that people in Paris didn't notice, couldn't share my joy that a mind had found itself; that a nervous energy wasted in tantrums and frustrations and buried behind the walls of an institution for the insane, now had a release through a simple thing like pigments and brushes and canvas. Why had not the world stopped? It had for me.

I knew my son was a genius. I could feel it and yet I accepted it easily, for Maurice was my child, and as I had always known, I, myself, was different, so too was my child.

I had become the all possessive *artiste-mother*, a new role. It was a role of quiet joy.

I often looked down at the canvas he was working on. I loved to see its progression from a void into the power of his marvelous streets some hung with surly skies. Yet I was careful in offering anything but encouragement. "I'm very proud of your paintings, Maumau. If you continue painting, perhaps by next year, I'll tell Paul to buy you a studio. Perhaps you can share mine on rue Cortot. It's certainly large enough. Would you like that?"

Maurice nodded his head. His eyes shone. He looked up and smiled. He had completed the *Butte Pinson at Montmagny*. The paint was thick on the walls of the little houses with their dark red slate roofs, and the picture was painted through a meshwork of nude twisted trees and empty branches, for autumn had descended upon the city. And he bent down and signed the painting *Maurice Valadon* in red paint.

I shrugged my shoulders and thought once again that the most important thing was his painting, not his name, for if anyone had resisted his craft, it was Maurice. That he was painting at all was a miracle. I spent whole days watching him paint and spent less time at Pierrefitte. With the passing season he shared my studio; and we would take our easels onto the Butte Montmartre, or he would explore the streets he had known as a child, always showing me the work in progress. And if I was not sure, I would ask Degas for his opinion.

In the spring of 1903, the warm rains and thaws ran in rivers over the cobbled streets of rue Cortot and drenched the fields of Montmagny. At Adèle's new restaurant, the *Moulin Joyeaux* I learned of Gauguin's death and for months to come I was haunted by his strong presence. I painted for a time, unconsciously using the broad flat colors of his canvases. I continued to outline my colors like a stained glass picture, very much like Gauguin whose luminous hues resembled cloisonné patterns.

The year 1903 passed swiftly into 1904 and merged with 1905 and the golden sunlight of a delightful Paris spring turned into a blazing inferno. In Montmartre, the aging baker Pinchot, still the roué, pulled his goods along to his establishment, squeezing the ample hips and buttocks of a young laundress as he passed. She screamed out as he laughed. Henri Lautrec's posters multiplied in the Moulin Rouge, and I hung his painting of me in the butterfly hat on a wall at Pierrefitte, this young girl painted twenty years ago. *Incroyable!*

The bitterness of the winter of 1906 saw the death of Cézanne. It was said that Cézanne died in a delirium denouncing all the dealers who didn't appreciate his paintings. With a springtime warmth, all Paris turned a tender viridian green. The walls of the Moulin Rouge now hung with Henri's posters of Yvette Guilbert; and the chestnut trees bloomed with an early promise.

And with the spring, Maurice finally accepted Miguel Utrillo as his father and signed his paintings Maurice Utrillo V, leaving a vestige of the name Valadon on subsequent paintings. "Miguel is an architect and that's why I can plan my buildings like an architect, Maman. I think he's really my papa."

He smiled and I forgave him everything all at once; and I drew him at his easel, my young man, to capture the saneness, the joy of this moment on canvas. He wore his bowler hat and long mustache and looking intently at the canvas, his eyes were intelligent and full of feeling. To draw or paint Maurice always gave me an incredible feeling of peace.

* * *

"Do you know something, *mon vieux*," I said, pushing a lock of curly black hair out of his eyes, "you're still a bit young but I really wish you would give some of your love to a good woman, perhaps a wife. I never hear you speak of *jeune filles*, and there are so many *midinettes*, for example, you could meet in Paris."

"A wife? *Sacrebleu!* I'm not going to add to my miseries by taking a wife! I'd rather go to a five franc whorehouse. I know I was not the Christmas present you expected, Maman. I've been difficult, but I'll try to make it up to you someday because I love you with all my soul and you are my goddess."

I felt a twinge of guilt for being placed so high in his estimation, just a passing twinge of guilt, and fear.

Undoubtedly, an abnormal attachment to me had never been resolved. Certainly the doctors who examined him saw his case as a classical unresolved Oedipal Complex as they now labeled it. But it all engendered an ambivalence for he both hated and revered me. My Maurice hated me? Look how he wrote a poem to me one afternoon, placing me on a pedestal as a goddess. My son hated me? He hated me? Never!

But the fact was, whatever the cause, he rarely spoke of women as paramours and seemed indifferent to the opposite sex. The only woman he responded to was myself. It was incomprehensible to me that I, his mother who had many lovers, who still found men enormously attractive, who still delighted in sexual pleasures, should have a son who would not do likewise with women. How could he be my son? And if his father were Miguel or Renoir or Puvis, they were all men of sensual bents; all men who had carnal desires. Maurice was in his mid twenties, and it was time for sexual experience. Suddenly, fear took hold and then a slow paralyzing panic began to grip me.

I might have a son who was a homosexual? Never, never never! A son who was that way? Impossible!

I found that I was experiencing an impasse in my painting

with canvases thrown about and never finished, and I found myself constantly uneasy about Maurice's alcoholism and fears about his virility. My friend Adèle dropped in one afternoon in rue Cortot and did little to mollify me.

"What's wrong with you? Have you stopped painting altogether?" A painting sat unfinished on the easel, its paint dry.

"It's everything, Adèle, and I'm sick to death of my life . . . and as you know, Maurice is still drinking. We never know when he might be brought in by the police. Paul has removed himself from the whole thing ever since Maurice moved to rue Cortot."

"I refuse to serve him more than two drinks at my place. By the way, he has beautiful men with him all the time, did you know that? He and this Modigliani came to my place."

"Oh, they're all artists.

"He's too familiar with them."

"I know what you're thinking, Adèle."

"If I were you I would take him to the nearest prostitute. Buy him some rubbers and then dump him there by all means."

"Let him find his own women."

"Well, it appears he's not finding any . . . only beautiful young men. You should see the face on that Modigliani . . ."

"My son is not *une tapette* . . . but I can see by your face . . ."

"Draw your own conclusions but do something, my God, do something, Marie. Don't leave it all to chance . . ."

"And do you think if he were . . . that way, I could change it?"

"Yes!"

"You're *fou*, Adèle . . . it's in the blood but the fact is that it's not in Maurice's blood."

"Blood? What do you think, that they're born that way? They learn it all from the deranged ones . . . they're taught, *c'est ça!*"

"I don't believe it and I don't want to think about it. My Maurice . . . never! You're completely wrong Adèle."

"Your Maurice is in love with Modi. Anyone can see that, anyone. You're burying your head in the sand, Marie . . . if he were my son, I'd take him as quickly as possible to the nearest whore and have him fuck her good and proper. That will cure him fast enough. Why do you stand there looking at me like that?"

"Because I don't believe it."

I stood still after she left with a familiar feeling of growing panic gnawing at my stomach.

Shortly after, a furious pounding on the heavy door of our studio reverberated through the corridors and brought me down the stairs. I swung the door open.

Only this Modigliani could look so tall and aristocratic even while holding up Maurice.

"Oh you're in luck, Madame," he said. "You're a beautiful mother or else I would have thrown you into the Seine."

I stared flabbergasted. "Of course, you're Modi. Come inside quickly. I remember you now. I saw you outside of Berthe Weill's studio. It's a shame that there was such a fuss made about your nudes that the police made her remove them from the window . . . a bunch of hypocrites these Parisians are. But Modi, do you have to make love to your models before you paint them? That's what I heard and looking at the faces, I believe it."

"When I paint a woman I possess her," Modi smiled and then began weaving and swaying and dancing through the rooms. He was as graceful as an inebriated satyr. He danced from one painting to another on the walls of the studio, touching the paint lightly with his fingers. "Quite good, little mother . . . quite good . . . and so is he." He motioned to Maurice, then staggered and fell into a chair.

Mon Dieu, Modi, let's sober you up with some café and I'll make it strong," I said.

"I'm not drunk."

"He's as high as a kite on drugs," Maurice mumbled.

"Then you'll sleep it off here . . . you can leave in the morning." I led him to a cot in my studio. I turned up the fluttering gas jets, flinging broken shadows around the room.

"My little mother . . . my dear little mother . . . how sweet you are." His handsome face smiled. He took my hand and kissed it. What I was unprepared for was his beauty. I was startled by it. His was an unearthly beauty, the chiseled face of the statue of a Greek god. Michelangelo would have used him for his David. He stood tall and poised, a dimple in his cheek as he smiled disarmingly. He wore a dark blue corduroy suit and an intense purple and yellow scarf and a wide brimmed hat of the Montmartrois before the turn of the century. He was in another time, another decade. It was an echo of Miguel.

"I'll call you my little mother. My own is in my *cara cara Italia*."

"You'll be my other son," I said and I reached up on my toes and brushed a curl off his forehead. He danced again about the studio, a lithe and languid extremely graceful figure, like a fawn, as though lost in a dream, moving to an inner music.

"I dance with joy. It's the hashish, little mother that speaks. Did you ever see Baron Pigeard's den in the Impasse de Delta? All the hashish in the world is there."

"He's a murderer!"

"Oh no. Not a murderer but a magician whose small house is fitted to recreate a Chinese opium den . . . just fifteen francs worth of hashish pellets lasts a lifetime, so he's a miracle worker . . . so dance with me and ease my burden, little mother."

"What burden?"

"The burden of my art . . . no one wants my art . . . come dance with me so I may forget my colossal failures, little mother," and he stretched out his arms to me.

"You're *fou*. Lie down on the cot and sleep."

I pulled him toward the cot and as soon as he touched it, he collapsed and his eyes closed and he was out. His Montmartrois hat had fallen on the floor and his corduroys were rumpled. His lips mumbled something and his cheek twitched as though he were dreaming a disturbed dream.

I took a blanket from an ancient armoire which stood on one wall in the studio and covered him. Modi's eyes closed in a skin of alabaster whiteness with thick dark hair curling about his temples. I found myself returning to that face, that amazing face.

I rearranged the blanket on Modi, kissed him lightly on the forehead, and turned off the gas jets in the studio.

"You'll be my other son," I affirmed softly.

Adèle was wrong. Modi undoubtedly loved women. And in time, he used my studio for his painting and whoring, and one of his prostitutes was named Claudette, who coincidentally once did some modeling for me.

But Adele's words about Maurice stayed with me. I had to do something. I had to try something. My very nature wouldn't let the matter rest. I couldn't wait for the inevitable, the dreaded moment when a terrible truth about Maurice would come crashing about my head. I began to think of Claudette.

I used Claudette's services earlier than anticipated. One afternoon I returned to find Claudette sprawled out on the sofa in my studio snoring. Modi lay in a heap on the floor in a miasma of cocaine and ether. I pulled the prostitute up by her arms. "Get up you drunken slut, get up." The girl snapped her eyes open and stared at me. "You drunken *putain*, get up. Put your clothes on your stinking body. My studio is for painting, not fucking."

The girl sat on a chair studded with nailheads and drew on a stocking as though she were in a trance. She was naked with full breasts and thighs and a baby face which was puffy with sleep, alcohol and drugs.

"I need money," she kept droning. "That beautiful one, that crazy Modi promised me twenty francs if I would pose for him."

"You're not worth more than two," I said. "You're nothing but a common street whore, so get out!"

"Have pity. You know I used to be in that five frank *maison close* in la rue Charlotte before it closed, and besides modeling, now I have to look for *michés* on the street . . . it's a hard life, easier to pose for artists. This crazy artist, Modi, promised me twenty francs for taking my clothes off . . . all the artists are *fou*."

"Well, what happened?"

"All he gave me was a good fucking."

I half smiled, "You'll get five francs and that's too much. The rest you drank in my liquor, now get out!"

The girl began to cry. "Do you know I'm only fifteen, Madame, and this one used me . . . he's crazy . . . he made me dance with him naked . . . oh he's a madman alright, from the drugs. I know a madman when I meet one, this crazy Italian, Modi."

I reflected. Something formed in my mind. Could she do the trick with Maurice? Would he like her? I watched her prepare to leave gathering together her flimsy outfit. Now fully awake, she brushed her badly dyed hair and dusted on some rice powder.

In a sleazy way, this slut was peculiarly attractive.

She was halfway out the door when I stopped her.

"Claudette, have you ever had the *visite* from the doctor when you were in the brothel?"

"Oh, I'm as healthy as a horse, and I have only been a lady of pleasure for six months . . . what have you in mind?"

"I want you to meet my son and make him happy that way. He needs a woman."

"A mother asks that?" She laughed. "Can't your son find his own woman?"

"He has a problem. You'll be good to him or you won't get a sou. First, Claudette, I want you to take a bath." I began to fill a round metal tub with hot water.

"I'm not going to bathe in that thing."

"You'll bathe in it and hold your tongue. And you'll be paid handsomely if you do your job. You'll get that twenty francs you want, but if he doesn't look happy when you're through with him, you'll get nothing and I'll personally see your pimp and tell him that you've been cheating and hiding money."

The girl's round blue eyes widened in terror. "Oh, Madame, I'll give him a night of great pleasure . . . only pay me my money."

"I doubt your talent. Now go bathe. My son is not steeping in another man's dirt." I handed her laundry soap.

"Madame have pity. That soap will tear my skin off."

"Scrub yourself with it."

The girl took the soap and stepped gingerly into the hot tub.

It took several hours for Modi to sleep off the orgy. The painting he had done of Claudette sat drying on the easel as he turned about winking at Maurice who arrived early in the evening, dragging his easel and paint box. Then he stared at Claudette attempting to bathe herself in the tub. "I must complement your mother on getting her into that thing. See now you can get the cleaner version of hell." he said winking at Maurice again.

"I don't want that tramp! If that's what my mother wants for me, she can go to hell. Don't think I don't see through her. If she thinks she can run my love life she's sadly mistaken."Maurice said, glancing at me with guilt.

Modi shook his head in disbelief at the profanity of his friend.

He turned to look at me apologetically and then patted Maurice on his shoulder. "I'm sorry to say I think she *can* run your life. *Sacrebleu*, Maumau...*foutre* any woman... it's time... what are you queer? I don't want a friend who can't fuck a woman."

"You're drunk, Modi!"

"Look who is calling me drunk. You're the greatest drunk who ever lived. I'm your friend and I tell the truth! Fuck some woman and give me a report. This is your assignment. That should be a good one." Modi began laughing uncontrollably, picked up his hat and easel, flashed me a marvelous smile, grabbed my hand and kissed it, whispering, "My little mother," and left.

Claudette got out of the tub dripping pools on the floor and I started screaming and ran for a towel to wipe up the mess. I was thoroughly disgusted. Was there really any hope for my son after all? What was he? God help what I am thinking. God help us all!

My poor Maurice. How your Maman has to arrange your life. My poor, dear artist son. But you always listen to me and love me because you know what I do is the right thing. Someday I'll find you a wife as well, someone who will care for you the way I do. *I, alone,* know what's best for you.

Oh dear God. Why can't you stay but a little boy and I a very young woman, modeling and drawing and standing by the fountains of the Place Pigalle. Don't you know that it's time which is our greatest enemy, only time, *mon cheri*. It's time which teaches us, shapes our destiny and then laughs at us in the end as it slowly shatters. Let's work quickly my precious one and leave something of ourselves behind. Call it our legacy.

Maurice

Maman, My Love

*To My Mother**

Suzanne Valadon, my mother is thus named,
She is a noble woman, as beautiful as she is good
In virtue, in beauty, In a word, a goddess of genius
In addition, endowed with His divine breath.

Then, He did not share the place among the false ones
In order that she could attain
Summits defying humans
Where are enthroned masters, alone the pure, a very few

With a firm and sure brush, defying matters,
She enchants, she animates the sky, flowers, stones.
Houses have a soul, their profound secrets
She embellishes in spite of what the Beaux-Arts decree.

*See Acknowledgments in Bibliography

*E*nchanting? Someone said she was enchanting. Of course, my mother enchants and I wrote about it in my poem. But sometimes I feel as though I hate her. The fact is that as much as I fight it, she has this power over me. I can't understand it. I paint the way she wants me to, and it's only to please her. When she doesn't approve of my work, I destroy it. But I still adore her. How I adore her. When I was a little boy I would beg for Maman's love, and when she wouldn't give it to me, I would cry in the quiet of my room. She is so beautiful who wouldn't love her?

I wrote this poem for her, my goddess, and she said nothing except that my poetry was atrocious, can you imagine, atrocious, and I would do better to stick to painting. Do you think I didn't know why she responded this way? The doctors told her that there's something abnormal about me . . . some kind of attachment I have to her. It wouldn't surprise me if she thought I was *pede*. I know that she'd like me to fuck some women, maybe whores. I can usually guess what Maman thinks. I hate her. I hate my goddamn saintly mother for trying to control my goddamn life. She's no goddess. She can go to hell!

And I don't care that I also love Modigliani. I love that Italian Jew with his handsome face and tubercular cough. He took me to the Bateau-Lavoir where I became friendly with Picasso and heard Apollinaire read poetry and discuss Cubism. And of course we would go to the Circus Medrano once a week and afterwards at the Lapin Agile where of course, I could get all the wine I wanted . . . and would you believe that some kind of political artist named André Gill blew his brains out in it after painting a *lapin*, a rabbit, over the door. I heard this Gill was *fou* anyway. By the time my mother's friend Adèle bought the place it became a cabaret and finally this wild character, Frédé Gerard, took it over and it still had the rabbit painted over the door and this crazy Frédé with his heavy red beard sits astride a barrel, strums a guitar, and sings or shouts, my God, the filthiest lyrics I ever heard. We all meet there and. I feel a part of them. Look on the walls, and you see my paintings and even those of that pompous ass, Picasso. I just drink the Corsican wine, join in the singing, and to tell the truth it makes me feel very important.

And it is here, at the Lapin Agile that I found my marvelous friend Modigliani, whom I call Modi. How I love him and he really understands me . . . he alone, and he listens to everything I say. He has sympathy for everyone . . . and he would give his last sou to a starving child. But *sacrebleu*, how mad he is for women. It makes me laugh. How can a man love women that much. He is always fucking them. He has one a day and he says he's going to get me one. You can have them. They're a big bother.

Modigliani was born in Leghorn a year younger than myself and the son of a Jewish banker, and poor fellow, he is full of tuberculosis. His damn friend Picasso made him come to Montmartre. Thank God for that but frankly, Paris is no place for a Jew to be since the Dreyfus case. To be truthful, I never thought much about Jews before meeting Modi, but now I see what he has to face. This anti-Semitism was always here in Paris even before Alfred Dreyfus was cleared. If you're not Jewish you don't really notice it. Now my friend Modi goes crazy with any reference to the Jews and he embarrasses the hell out of me. Take one evening at the Lapin Agile when a group of officers made anti-Semitic remarks. *Merde*, I knew I was in for it.

"Don't Modi," and I grabbed his arm trying to restrain him. "Don't get involved .My God, Modi, you don't meddle with officers, especially if you're a Jew," I whispered.

Mod's face flushed and his eyes narrowed. He frightened me. He strode to the officer's table and said, "I challenge you all!" His corduroy coat swung about his shoulders, a bottle of absinthe raised to crash down on a uniformed head. *"Je suis Juif, Je vous enmerde!"* he said loudly. "I am Jewish, I shit on you!"

"Don't, Modi," I whispered in his ear. I wanted to run out.

"Je suis juif," he repeated.

I ran over to the soldiers in a terrible panic and murmured apologetically, "My friend is a bit *fou* and doesn't know what he's saying, forgive him," and I pulled my friend away from their table.

"Sit down, Modi. Please, please . . . ," I pleaded shaking. Modigliani stood, his face twitching I pushed him down into the seat and his hands trembled as he opened a small case.

"What the devil is that, your dope?"

"It's hashish . . . they put it into pills." Modi popped one into his mouth. I was almost relieved . . . it would quiet him down.

I sipped some absinthe. "Why do the women love you so, Modi?" Good, let him talk about women.

"Women. They can't help it. They tear their clothes off and

pull me into their chemises."

"Christ. You're a lucky man, Modi."

"Don't envy me . . . I can't sell . . . you're the lucky one. You have a style, Maumau, you have a style. You love the streets of Paris and of Montmartre . . . you love the plaster walls, even those written on, peed on . . . you love all the dingy sordidness of miserable streets and buildings . . . you make ugly streets with ugly buildings beautiful. No one else could have done that . . . and as for me, I've failed and I'm sick to death of my carvings which I just threw into the Seine, and I'm going to die."

"I won't let you die, Modi. You're my friend and the greatest painter in the world." I downed another drink.

"No, You are the greatest painter in the world."

"I forbid you to contradict me. *You* are the greatest painter."

"I forbid you to forbid me and I'll kick you and . . ." He jumped up and hit me in the eye. The room whirled about.

"*Sacrebleu*, Modi, are you crazy? Never mind this shit. I'll really tell you something," I spilled out. "Do you know that it's true that I never had a woman . . . I never did. I never really did. What do you think? Is there something wrong with me? What am I? My mother thinks I'm a pervert." My eye swelled.

" You really never had a woman? So it's true? I thought you were joking. Are you really queer or something? Well don't put your hands on me. Let's pick up a *lorette* or go to a brothel. You'll fuck and I'll instruct. You don't know what you're missing, Maumau . . . we'll pick up a pretty pigeon." He slapped me on the back. "Just give it to her good and she'll love it. They're all alike when they're undressed, plump rosy animals. I'll teach you."

"You have no respect for women." I banged on the table and pulled off the cloth. The dishes went clattering on the floor.

Frédé motioned to two tall husky workers. The men picked me up by the arms while Modigliani sat and laughed hysterically, jumped up and danced madly about, his eyes wild, "Did you know, Frédé that my friend is a sodomite and I'm going to teach him how to fuck women. Why don't you watch? We're going to pick up a lorette and I'll give some lessons."

"Another dope addict," said Frédé. "Out you go, you *fou!*" Modigliani left the Lapin Agile walking with an unsteady dignity through the open door while I was tossed into the street.

Once outside I bent over the cobblestones and vomited. Modi turned in disgust and hailed a coach.

* * *

Of course Adèle convinced her that I was queer. Beside that, Maman was always after me to do something or other.

"Where were you? Where the devil were you? You're irresponsible as usual. Don't you remember you promised to sit for me? Now sit still while I sketch you. Sit down! You're not drunk, I hope. Frédé told me you were at the Lapin Agile the other night, with a handsome fellow, probably, Modi."

"I suppose he's handsome . . . what do I care."

"Of course you care. They're all beautiful, these men . . . "

"I told you, I don't care. I'm grown and you treat me . . . "

She suddenly seemed to crumple up. "You're *une tapette* aren't you, aren't you? It's always men. How can you do this to me, your Maman whom you put on a pedestal. How?"

I sat stunned. I never expected this from her.

"Tell me, dear Maumau, you're not *that*, tell me. Everyone knows it and even my friend, Adèle knows it."

"I don't know what the hell you're talking about!"

"Of course he's in love with you. Don't play games."

"Who?"

"Modi."

"That's ridiculous because you know he loves women."

"Oh I'm ridiculous, of course. Then what is he? Maman said sharply. "Is he a freak who makes love to women and men?"

"He's an Italian Jew."

"What else is his problem?"

"Dope. You know he takes dope!" I shouted. "He takes cocaine, hashish and ether all together. Didn't you see how doped up he was? What's wrong with you?"

"Never mind about that. My son is homosexual. You think I don't know what's going on?"

"You don't know what's going on if you think Modi is . . . or anyone else. My God, Modi can *foutre* one woman a day. Can't you see that? Go to hell!" I shouted. "Go to blazing hell!"

In fury, I kicked over two chairs and dashed out of the room.

Now I don't know how the devil Maman took it into her head for Claudette to fuck me. But of course Maman thinks I'm some kind of pervert. It's the fault of her friend again, who always refuses me her goddamn wine, who put it into Maman's head that I'm a homosexual, and this Claudette will set everything right. I decided that I was going to throw this slut out of the room if she took off one stitch of clothing. What right did Maman have to do this to me? I'm not a child. She can put twenty packages of rubbers on the bureau and I'll not use a damn one!

I set up my easel in my studio that evening, and looked for Modigliani, my Modi, but he was already staggering out.

"This Claudette is a good fuck," Modi whispered to me, his beautiful face glowing, "but don't give her more than two francs. *Bon* appétit."

He left his whore, Claudette, behind, goddamn her!

And I sat in my room and Maman turned the lights very low and she warned Claudette that only when her job was finished would she be allowed to come out. Maman handed her a packet of India-rubbers. "And if he doesn't use them, you'll get nothing," she said menacingly.

What did this *putain*, Claudette do? She pulled down her tawdry bodice, to show me her full cleavage. How awful the color of her hair was, a miserable dyed red, and it hung in fake ringlets about her head. What a vacant face she had with round light blue eyes like saucers, and she kept snapping them open and closed like a painted *poupée* in one of Maman's paintings. *Alors*, I started painting at my easel. She's Modi's whore not mine, I thought. Maybe she'll get the message and go.

Well this slut, Claudette, tried every trick she knew in her stinking trade to excite me, but I just sat like a stone in that chair with a paint brush in my hand. What a joke! As a last resort, she slipped out of her chemise, standing nude before me; and her hips swayed as she walked over to the bed. It all did nothing for me. She lay down on my bed and spread her legs apart pretending to moan. "Take off your clothes, *chouchou, vite, vite!* I can't stand it."

I began to howl like a dog scaring the hell out of her. Then I went to the door and tried to leave. It was locked from the other side. Go to hell, Maman!

"*Merde*," Claudette jumped up in terror. "You're *fou*, crazier than your friend. Your mother didn't tell me you were *fou*. What are you doing?"

She crept back on the bed and stared horrified, her eyes round as saucers.

I pulled the sheet off the bed from under her.

"What the devil are you doing? Stop! You're insane, worse than the worst *miché* who wants to beat me for only five francs. So that's why your mother asked me . . . you . . . you're *pede*."

I began to howl again.

"Let me out. I'm going back to my pimp." She quickly slipped into her chemise and what other rags she took off and smoothed her hair. How I hated Maman for this. The rubbers lay untouched atop the dresser. It will be a treat when Maman counts them.

This slut was determined to earn her money. She begged me to pretend that I made love to her and enjoyed it. "Pierre *le diable* has to pay off the inspectors at the *préfecture* . . . you know how it is . . . he'll beat me if I don't earn my quota. Please Monsieur, it's a small favor." She looked very frightened.

I felt a bit sorry for her and agreed, and Claudette knocked on the door to be let out.

"Well? How was it?" Maman asked.

"Oh, Madame, how he loved it. He said he never had such a good time in his life. We did it three times and he wanted a fourth; he's quite a lover, your son, even better than his friend. Now my money, please . . . all this lovemaking wears a girl out."

Maman glared at me. Of course, she always knew when I lied, so I said nothing but sat on a chair feeling miserable. Why was I so goddamn afraid of her?

"My money please," Claudette repeated.

Would you believe that the *Goddess* went into the bedroom and examined the box of India-Rubbers, all intact on the bureau? Then she slapped the girl soundly in the face which reddened

Claudette's cheek. and she threw five francs at her.

"You promised me twenty."

"You whore! You're lucky to get that much. You're a liar, in addition to everything else. You did nothing with him, you slut!"

"It's not my fault, Madame that your son is *fou*. He's *une tapette*, that's for sure. I don't *foutre* homosexuals."

Maman raised her hand again and Claudette ran to the door.

I watched that painted *poupée* run down the street and stumble once on the cobblestones. She turned around for a moment, dusted off that excuse for a dress she wore and screamed out at me, "You queer! Go fuck your boy friend Modi!"

Maman slammed the door shut.

* * *

Summer came on hot and steamy and days grew wonderfully long in which I could paint to my heart's content. And with the russets of fall, my still unfinished Sacré-Coeur, a mystical dome, stared at me from my canvas. I let it be and painted streets and buildings over and over again, always looking at Maman's eyes to see if she approved my art so that I could go on. Everything looked altered suddenly. How was it possible that I never noticed the marvelous texture, architecture and majesty of churches before this? My style was changing, developing under Maman's eyes but thank God she held back and left me alone, thank God. What a miracle it all was. I started the *Rue de la Jonquiere* and hesitated, but she read my mind. "It might be ugly when it's finished," I complained, waiting for her reaction.

"Make it ugly. It can't be ugly enough. I'm tired of those pretty, pretty scenes . . . as though these are the only ones that the academies will tolerate. Make it ugly but make it interesting. You have a talent for doing that. It will have a beauty all its own. Be honest in your painting and you'll truly be my son."

How I loved her for understanding. How I adored her.

When winter came, and our breaths made wispy lace patterns in the air, we trudged along in the snow with my paintings in hopes of selling them, and we found a former apothecary shop; in it was Sagot the Madman, a crazy baker turned art dealer. This lunatic Sagot merrily handed out drugs and medicines left on the shelves by the former owner in exchange for paintings. Would you believe that?

"Oh, such wonderful pills . . . for anything that ails you," and he winked as I entered the shop. Today I was alone, without Maman. There I saw Émile Bernard, once a painter, now the editor of *"L'Art Litteraire"* and a certain Louis Libaude, its art critic.

Sagot tried to push two vials of disgusting yellow liquid on me and grabbed at the work of art under my arm. Of course I wouldn't budge."

"Looks rather like you urinated in it, Sagot," said Libaude distastefully.

But then I sold a painting to this Bernard and I couldn't wait to tell Maman.

"You're Suzanne Valadon's son?" asked Émile Bernard on the way out.

"Yes."

"Utrillo? Miguel . . . of course . . . I knew your father. You certainly resemble him . . . and your mother, is she still beautiful?"

I grinned.

"He's Suzanne Valadon's son," he turned and said to Libaude.

"Who is she?"

"Oh, she was once a model, and she imagines herself a painter."

"Women," muttered Libaude. "Few women have any talent."

What an ass! But I couldn't wait to tell Maman.

A few days after, I painted the *Guingette at Montmagny* and Maman posted it in the window of a Monsieur Anzoli, a cobbler turned art dealer.

"My old friend," César Gay, the gendarme, embraced me as I pointed proudly to my painting in the window.

"See, I'm an artist," I felt very proud.

"Bien, then I shall buy the work of my old friend, and when I buy my bistro, you'll have the room above it. I'll always have it ready for you. You won't forget?"

I smiled and shook my head, "I won't forget."

"Remember what I said about your room. It will be your deluxe hotel," he laughed.

He paid twenty-five francs for the painting, tucked it under his arm and hurried away, my middle aged balding gendarme friend, his reddish hair thinning back from his temples, he, the father I never had, my dear, wonderful, wonderful friend.

That spring of 1908 painted Paris in a golden glow. We all attended the Theatres des Arts with Paul's banker friends to see the new play, *Candida* by George Bernard Shaw. My Goddess sat glowing in her box in an outrageous gown, a gleaming golden one-shoulder affair, and I was so proud of my beautiful mother. I couldn't take my eyes off her. I never felt so much love for Maman as I had at that moment. I just wanted to embrace her and hold her safely in my arms, away from Paul.

I know she felt that her life with Paul was stagnant and empty, but the deal had been made, *voilà*. Who told her to do what she did? What a pity my beautiful Maman had sold herself in this way. What a pity she had to make love to *that*. How I hated him and everything he was doing to her. How I hated him. When I thought of every time he touched her, or embraced her, my beautiful Maman, my eternal Goddess, I became sick. If I thought of it enough, I would retch. No one should touch my beautiful Goddess, certainly not the honorable Paul Mousis.

Why do I feel so differently about Maman from day to day? Of course my Goddess thinks I'm some kind of *intermediate sex* which some doctor wrote about not too long ago, and mouths something whenever I mention a friend. It's insane. Damn her, damn her, damn her! The fact is that I'm not drawn to women except Maman. *Tant pis!* As a matter of fact, I find myself hurling insults at women in the street, and the pregnant ones make me furious. Perhaps it reminds me of what this Mousis could do to her. And as far as women are concerned, it's none of Maman's goddamn business whom I fuck. If I had half a backbone I would have stood up to her. I don't know what the hell is wrong with me. All I know is I love Maman, I truly love her. No one is like her, not one. Modi says I'm abnormal the way I carry on about her. I don't care. She's a veritable Goddess.

But after my fiasco with Claudette I knew I was in for it. Maman would try again, and if I were man enough I would tell her to go to hell to her face. She's up to something and for once I'll fight her. I'm ready for her little scheme. Damn her!

Maman spoke of Lautrec's paintings in the brothel. Now I can see what's coming. Henri had lived at the most luxurious, most extravagant of Parisian brothels, sleeping with each girl while doing his drawings. She mentioned the large painting he had done in 1894 of the classy Salon in the *Rue des Moulins*, of the whores waiting for their customers. If she thinks I'll go there, she has another thing coming. Of course, I knew that Maman would never take me to a sleazy five franc whorehouse.

She stood before me in her mauve silk walking suit, with its draped skirt and she wore a hat made from the same silk with feathers gracing the crown. When she said, "Cheri, we're going to the rue des Moulins," and tapped the floor impatiently with her flowered parasol, I exploded and couldn't believe it. My own dear mother was doing this? Of course, I expected it from her. *She* could do anything. I put on quite a show of anger. I'm good at that. Perhaps I'll smash something.

"You'll go if I have to drag you," she said quietly. Her calm tone made me more afraid.

"I won't make love to a prostitute!"

"You won't make love to anybody . . . that's the problem."

"I'll get the clap."

"You'll take along those India- rubbers."

I shrugged my shoulders. What was the use? "Have it your own way. But first, I want a bottle of wine."

She unlocked the door to a small cabinet and took out a bottle of Beaujolais. I drank it slowly, savoring every drop. Halfway down the bottle, she pulled it away. "Enough. You can't perform when you're drunk." I reached for the bottle and she slapped my wrist. "Now get dressed. Put on your new hat, Maurice, and carry your new cane."

"I have to dress for a goddamn whore?"

"No, but when we enter, it helps to look distinguished. You'll get a better girl."

Why couldn't I fight her? How I hated her at that moment.

But I looked quite good in my new dark blue suit, a stiff white collar, cravat and new derby. Maman bought me a hand carved cane and white leather gloves. My derby made it all bearable.

She looked approvingly. *"Bien*, now you're a man about town. Let's go."

A sudden disturbing thought went flying through my brain. "Maman, please don't tell Modi if he comes here . . . he'll tell the whole Bateau-Lavoir gang and I'll be laughed at."

"I won't *mon cher* Maumau."

I could run out on her even now . . . the goddamn Goddess. I could go to a café and drink up a storm. But I don't dare.

I dutifully followed her as she hailed a *fiacre*.

We reached 24 Rue des Moulins and stepped down from the coach. I felt anxious as I looked at the façade of the brothel.

"I'll make the arrangements. You don't have to say anything."

"Go right ahead, but I'm sleeping with none of them."

"You'll do as I say."

I shook my head, muttering. Of course I would comply. Oh, how I hated her! How was it possible that one could hate and love a Goddess at the same time? Was that possible?

The salon in the brothel had changed little from Henri Lautrec's painting years before. The original palette was there and it was as though time stood still. My eyes wandered about the room drinking in the marvelous tones of color Lautrec had lived with. I thought of the words, tonal symphony, I had heard somewhere. Of course, Maman had said it. I looked about at the mauves and lavenders for the walls, and the striking greens and whites of the archways and columns. All kinds of women were resting against plush vermilion cushions . . . some exposed their intimate parts . . . most did not. One whore had a red bow pasted to her cunt. I nearly died keeping in my laughter. The whores tried to appear very classy but they were whores anyway, and they performed any *spécialité* you wanted for a sum. A whore is a whore in my book.

Marie-Victoire Denis, the mistress of the establishment, sat elegantly in rose satin with some cheap beads glittering at her neck and running down the front of her dress, or whatever she was wearing. Something shone at one shoulder and a Bakst gold turban circled her head, anchored with a phony ruby pin. Her face fascinated me with her heavy powder crinkling into a mass of tiny wrinkles when she smiled. I wished I could paint her.

Maman waved me to the side. I leaned against one lavender hanging nearby, close enough to hear both of them. Truthfully, I was more curious than frightened.

"I have a special purpose for coming, Madame. I'll come to the point."

"I'm Madame Denis. Your name?"

"Pinchot, yes . . . Madame Pinchot. I want a young beautiful woman for my son."

The woman looked surprised. "Your son? Where is your son?"

"He's over there against the tapestry. He is only . . . twenty-one and still innocent."

I felt my face grow hot. Perhaps I'll run out. It's not too late.

"Madame Pinchot, I assure you it doesn't matter to me . . . I have all kinds and men who want all sorts of *spécialités* . . . I'll give you Odette who knows all the tricks of the trade. See, she sits there, the one in the mauve kimono. She's . . . quite young."

Young? The whore, even in the soft lighting of the room seemed well past forty.

"I save Odette for my most important customers. But," and she leaned over, "you can confide in me . . . he's not that way, you know . . . effeminate?" Her voice was hushed and intimate.

"Of course not!" Maman snapped back. "And what about your girls . . . are they clean?"

"You insult me. All over Paris we're known as the cleanest, best known house in France. Every Monday morning we have a *visite* by a fine doctor, and if the girls are infected, out they go. A man has no fears when he comes here. And my Odette is a genius. There are geniuses in all walks of life, Madame, but in this business which, is a difficult one, a genius. In her cradle she vamped the doctor, I've heard, and she was only two weeks old. She's already a legend in her own time."

I cleared my throat, stifled a laugh and cleared my throat again.

The whole situation was *fou*. Even Maman kept from laughing.

"You'll have to pay in advance, Madame. Of course our girls don't come cheap. This is the price," and she scribbled a number on a piece of paper, "and any *spécialité* is additional, of course. And if he spends the night with her of course you'll add a sum."

"Just let it be successful and you'll get more than your due," Maman said as she opened her purse and winked at me.

The room I entered looked like an Arabian tent covered with awful red paisley and gold hangings. Ornate gilt edged mirrors hung on a red brocaded wall covering. Gold tassels hung from plump cushions everywhere and the folds of red paisley came to a center over the bed forming a canopy held by a huge shining round gold crown at the ceiling. Wherever I looked there were statuettes and carved candlesticks. Tapestries of nude lovers fucking each other were all over the place, each group in a different position, and a thick bright red Persian carpet blanketed the hardwood floor. *Sacrebleu!* What a whorehouse!

I sat stiffly at the edge of the bed while Odette stepped out of her chemise. I watched her and felt like screaming. I could still get out. Why the hell should I be in this place, why? In my mind I escaped down the red carpeted plush steps of the winding carved staircase. But I didn't want to see my mother's face as she waited outside, I just couldn't face her. The brothel was the lesser of the two evils.

The whore at close range was older than I imagined. I wondered why my mother agreed to her, but the fact that she was older calmed me. I was struck by her long red hair . . . and her breasts had begun to sag. Something had stretched her belly so that it was a small mound of jelly, like a soft sponge crossed with bluish marks. Had she given birth? Did Maman look like this?

I lay still, feeling nothing as she fondled me and slowly removed my clothing. I dared not breathe. I could still run out, this time naked. Why shouldn't I, and it would punish everyone. My mouth ran dry. Her hands and mouth were all over me, kissing my belly, my chest and my genitals, mouthing, stroking, sucking, slowly, gently, enveloping me with a kind of symphony of incredible sensations. She narrowed her eyes with understanding when she felt me tense up.

Suddenly she drew away. "There's no hurry, *chéri*, no hurry."

I looked at her as she sat quietly doing nothing more, and a strange calm spread over me. There was no urgency. She seemed to have much time at her disposal. My mother must have paid much for this time. Slowly, I relaxed.

She seemed so maternal, like my own mother and she cradled me and held me to her breasts singing me a lullaby that mothers sing to their babies, a lullaby my Grand-mère once sang to me.

"You smile, *mon petit*. Why do you smile?"

"My Grand-mère sang that to me."

"Then she came from Limoges as well, *mon petit*. Well then I will be everyone rolled into one . . . your Maman, your Grand-mère, and of course your mistress. Oh how I shall be your mistress if you'll let me."

Her hand caressed my body, so slowly, so unhurriedly that I felt myself being lulled into a dream by her touch. The foreplay was not so bad after all. If it didn't excite me, it relaxed me. "Now, don't go to sleep on me *mon petit*." Her voice was low and soothing. Then, slowly, a wall melted and I felt a rush of desire.

I felt myself breathe faster, holding her body to mine and took a woman hesitantly, fearfully, for the first time. It was over quickly. I fell back exhausted and ashamed and covered myself.

"*Alors*, my young one, my innocent one. You see, it's not so bad, *hein*? I won't beat you and I won't force you. You're so beautiful. Don't cover your body. You're like a son to me, but we can make love anyway. You'll become experienced, a man of the world. All the *midinettes* and *jeune filles* will be after you. They'll see the experience in your eyes. Now if you want, you can nap."

I smiled and lay with my head on her breast cradled as though I were a child. A warm odor emanated from her body and it soothed me. She sung me the lullaby my Grand-mère had sung. And I fell asleep.

"Sleep, *mon petit*, sleep my little one." Odette kissed me on my brow, just like Maman.

I went back to Odette from time to time, gathering more courage each time I went and we always played the same game . . .

she was the protector, the mother, the older aunt, the grandmother who sang me lullabies . . . and I learned to be her lover. Odette was a good listener and sympathetic, and when I threw my first tantrum, fell into my first drunken stupor, she held my hands as Maman did and listened patiently to my ranting.

When I was sober I said, "I wish I could paint you, Odette but I can't. I can't do women, only buildings and streets."

"Oh I was painted, *mon petit* . . . *alors,* I remember it because it was the turn of the century. I was painted by a funny little cripple with a pince-nez . . ."

"Lautrec! Lautrec painted you? He was a Count, you know."

"Lautrec? We called him *petit* Henri. He was a Count? Why I thought he watched every sou. Poor cripple. We loved to hear his little cane tapping on the staircase, and every time he came he brought us an armful of cut flowers. He would sleep with a different girl each night and then paint her in the morning. Do you know what he called his painting of me? *Madame Poupoule. At Her Toilette.* That's my name, Odette Poupoule. He painted me combing my hair. He said that the painting will hang in a museum one day. *Dieu,* it might be hanging in one even now. He loved my red hair," she smiled. "Do you know that he gave me money once to take care of my little daughter? *Mon Dieu,* and I thought he was a starving artist. How sad and how swiftly time passes. You know, I was once going to own a millinery shop and instead I deal in men's pleasures. This is an art, as well."

"Do you ever see the child's father?" I asked.

"Oh no, he's a bad one, a rotten pimp! I escaped from him. He threatened to kill me if he found me."

I lay back with my eyes closed thinking of how I played on Henri's piano in rue Tourlaque; how I climbed the three flights to play that afternoon and saw my mother naked kissing the *petit monsieur.* How horrified I was to see the midget's legs yet at the same time I loved him.

I stared at the ceiling feeling choked with a nameless sadness. My cheeks seemed to burn with my tears.

"Don't cry, *mon petit* don't cry. It will all be alright, you'll see. Just paint. She's a very clever woman, your Maman, to make you paint, a very clever woman."

Odette cradled me in her arms like a baby. I felt safe but wondered when I would return.

I hadn't visited Odette for about two months. Then one afternoon I had a sudden wish to see her, more to talk to than to satisfy any sexual desire.
Madame Denis sat at her post, looking sadly at me.
"I have dreadful news for you. Such a pity. She's gone."
"Where did she go to, Madame?"
"Didn't you read about it . . . all over the newspapers, it was. It was horrible!"
"What!"
"She was murdered by that mad pimp . . . by the father of her child." She motioned with her eyes to the room above . . . the red paisley room with its tented ceiling where I had been cradled in her arms.
"He made his way upstairs as though he were a customer . . . with a concealed knife. If I had only known that he was looking for her. Such a mess it was to clean up. She was carried to a hospital she was, but she died anyway . . . at least the murderer was caught and the guillotine does its job well. I know it's a cruel blow to you, Monsieur, a cruel blow . . . she was so good for you. I have here a note for you. She became afraid toward the end . . . women know such things."
I held the torn slip of paper with shaking hands.

Mon pauvre . . .
I want you to listen to your Maman, always, and do your painting. I love you as though you are my son . . . think of me a little, just a little.
Odette

I sat down on one of the divans in the huge salon and I began to sob like a baby. The prostitutes milled about, and some stared at me with curiosity.

* * *

And several months later our lives changed forever . . .

Our lives changed with the first words he uttered; he, a good looking young man; *he*, probably my age of 25 who stood behind me in the street smoking a pipe; *he*, whose beard was light and who tossed back a lock of his sun streaked hair from his brow. *He!* And I liked his manner and his perfect teeth and I liked that he was pleasant and easy going and he really was interested in what I was painting.

"Well . . . that's amazing. How do you do that?"

He watched me mix plaster with my zinc white and apply the mixture in thick layers onto a cardboard. I had taken to using cardboard in these early paintings.

"Oh, my name is André Utter, and yours?"

"Maurice . . . Maurice Utrillo."

"Have you had training?" he questioned.

"No, but I'm applying to the Beaux Arts."

"I really hope you make it. You're quite good. Just call me Dédé, everyone does. By the way, did you ever see Cézanne's Memorial Exhibition at Bernheim Jeune?"

I didn't answer.

"Sorry you missed a fantastic group of paintings, over forty-eight of them."

"How did they get them?" I questioned.

"From his sons, and from Maurice Gangnat, you know the man who collects Renoirs, and from Émile Bernard who worshipped him. Did you hear what Cézanne wrote? It's mathematical or something like that and it's influencing all the cubists."

"He wrote that everything in nature is modeled on the sphere, the cone and the cylinder," I said with authority.

"Well, you're a bright one. You know it started a whole group of cubists, Picasso, Derain and Braque. Have you ever seen anything of Picasso?"

"Yes, but it wasn't cubist," I said." It was a blue painting."

"Forget that," André laughed. "That's old hat. What I like the best is Picasso's *Woman With Pears* . . . Now there's a piece of art that tells something. It's fantastic."

"What does it tell . . . nothing. All I see is nothing. Where is the woman and where are the pears? Her face looks like it was in an accident. I don't know what the devil he's trying to do. It's not a piece of art. It's a piece of shit."

"A piece of shit?" André laughed. "Well . . . you just don't understand that it's all new and exciting . . . new art is always exciting. Perhaps I should become a collector? I'll wager these works will be worth something some day. Anyway, I enjoy talking to you. Visit the Circus Medrano some evening with me . . . the whole Bateau-Lavoir crowd comes."

"I've been there with my friend, Modi. You should meet him."

"Modi? Oh, you mean Modigliani. He's the handsome Italian painter . . . a Jew, I heard. I met him with his friend, Picasso. Well, you can join us if you like and bring this Modi with you. How about some wine to seal our friendship?"

"Wine? That's a great idea. Wine. I'd like the drink now, right now, and you can call me Maumau, everyone does."

"Does having a drink excite you that much? Where do you want to go?"

"My mother's friend, Adèle, owns the Moulin Joyeux." I closed my paint box, collapsed the legs, picked up my easel and took Dédé with me to rue Cortot to drop it off.

Then, an amazing thing happened. Several moments later, Maman passed by quickly. She carried a huge parcel of paintings and André stared at her mesmerized. She stood in the sunlight waiting for a coach, her reddish brown hair twisted back into a chignon under a blue feathered bonnet. André ogled her rounded figure. Oh, I saw how he looked at her, my Maman.

"Is this nymph your sister, Maurice? She's certainly not mortal. She has the most amazing skin and fringed eyes the color of sapphires. My God, she's beautiful. I saw her hailing a carriage and then heard her giving directions to the *cocher*. Did she say, 'Degas . . . Rue Victor Massé'. You can't tell me she is visiting Degas. Did you see her? Why didn't you tell me about her?"

I didn't answer. I somehow enjoyed my little game.

And as for Maman, she must have caught but a brief glimpse of this André, as she stood waiting for the coach. And I noticed a peculiar, warm sweet ripple of a flush sweep over her face. The look lasted for an instant and then it was gone. How could André have affected her in this manner? Maman was mine alone.

André Utter was three years my junior but he looked older. He was quite a student and he first disappointed his mother by wanting to be an artist. She wanted him to enter one of the professions and his father owned a plumber's shop and wanted André to work in it, but André a plumber? Ridiculous. His friend, Max Jacob introduced him to the artists at the Bateau- Lavoir, and he joined them and whored with them . . . and sipped absinthe and learned to take ether and hashish. Garbage. Give me a good glass of wine anytime. An Aunt Louise, a spinster who came to the Sacré Coeur for mass on Fridays decided to make him an artist. She dragged him to the Louvre and made him study painters like Raphael, Rembrandt and Da Vinci. Well, he convinced his mother that he was indeed an artist, and she helped him move to No.6 rue Cortot, near our studio.

I loved hearing André speak and hung on every word, and we became inseparable. He was a real friend like Modi, and it was a marvelous feeling to be able to have someone else to confide in and to share your views for a change. We ate together and caroused together, and when Dédé saw that I had gone beyond the drinking, he cut short the order for wine. It frightened him to watch me being possessed by the demon, as he called it.

And then one afternoon André caught another glimpse of Maman entering our studio holding a painting.. "My God, who was that lovely creature I saw entering your studio yesterday afternoon? Do you have a sister who paints? Who is that woman?"

"What?"

"I've seen her before. Who is she? I must find out."

I smiled. I'll tell him and be done with it.

"She's my mother."

"Your mother? What! Your mother?" he repeated. "She's beautiful and so young. I don't believe you. She's an artist? Truly amazing."

I stood grinning, ear to ear. The little deception was over.

It was autumn of 1909. Maman and I sat before our easels on the lush grounds of Pierrefitte before the Chateau of the Four Winds. A hillside grove of young poplar trees flowed down to the valley, trees that caught the dazzling light from a huge crimson sun across their bark. A rosy glow tinted the zinc whiteness of my painting. I shielded my eyes against the sun's glare with one hand and stared at her.

"What are you thinking, *mon vieux?*"

"I forgot to tell you, my friend's name is André . . . André Utter. Call him Dédé."

"I'll call him André," Maman said. "But why can't you ever meet a woman? You speak of him as though he's a woman."

"Leave me alone. You did enough."

"You're already twenty-six . . . it's unnatural."

"I have you."

"That's not what I meant. I'm your mother."

"I love Dédé . . . is there anything wrong with that?"

She ignored me and then said grimly, changing the subject. "I know you'll be admitted into the Beaux Arts."

"And what if I'm not?"

"Then you'll go on painting. Let them all be damned."

We painted in silence.

"I told Dédé what a good artist you are"

"I'm more than a good artist, Maurice."

"You are immodest, Maman."

She smiled. My answer was part of a game we played.

There was a silence.

"Where were you last night?"

"To the Bateau-Lavoir with Dédé. You wouldn't believe it. I saw Picasso, Max Jacob and a Dutchman, Van Dongen . . . then a critic, Coquiot came in and a peculiar looking American, Gertrude something, who was sitting for Picasso . . . people come and go in the most awful dark rooms. It's unbelievable."

I found myself spilling out my words and trying to see Maman the way Dédé saw her.

"Why do you stare at me like that?"

"Dédé saw you going into the studio . . . and it's funny the way he speaks of you."

She put down her colored chalk. "What do you mean?"

"It's as though . . . he . . . he's in love with you or he thinks so . . . I don't know . . . it's so peculiar . . . it's ridiculous."

"I thought he was in love with *you*, Maurice."

Her words cut through me like a sword. Why was she so cruel?
"I never said that."
"Oh, I'm sorry, I confused it. You're in love with *him*."
"I love him as a friend. There's a difference. Why are you torturing me?"

There was a pause. I shrugged my shoulders and waited for her to react. She smiled, raised her brow and continued working. "So your friend is interested in me? Your Maman is not so old, *mon pauvre*. But he's a little young for me, *n'est-ce pas?*"

"He's twenty-three but everyone thinks he's older."
"That makes it alright, then?"
I laughed uneasily and felt myself flush.
"Invite André to Pierrefitte for dinner some time. It will be interesting to meet him."

I said nothing but nodded. For some reason I hesitated.
"Invite him, Maurice," she repeated.
I nodded and felt a ripple of fear pass through my body. "Ill invite him . . . sometime this winter."

Maman only smiled but I remembered her odd look when she first caught a glimpse of André. The memory unnerved me.

14

Suzanne

Of Love and Art

One hand was placed in a protective manner on Maurice's shoulder as André stood gazing intently at me. He had an open friendly handsome face, crowned with sun streaked hair. His manner was buoyant and his eyes glistened as they caught mine. I felt uneasy.

If I felt undressed beneath his steady gaze, I was far from it. I greeted André in a rose silk Doucet afternoon dress whose lining of matching silk taffeta rustled beneath. The outfit had a filmy appearance with its striking bodice of lace inserts. My hair was swept up in curls and reflected gold and russet lights in the ornate mirror as I passed. It was an elegant and expensive costume, but in my mind's eye I was Marie-Clémentine, with hair simply brushed back, wearing a dark gray muslin skirt under a black weskit covered by a painter's smock.

"How do you do, Madame. I . . . I believe I've seen you before."

"I certainly would have recalled you if we had met." I smiled. Of course we had met. Why was I playing such games at my age?

"Oh, I could never forget you, Madame Mousis," he said fervently. I was surprised at his candor coupled with an uncomfortable ardor.

"You don't think me ordinary?" How absurd this talk was.
"You, never."

Maurice watched but didn't smile. André said nothing after that. The tension was mercifully relieved by Catherine who supervised the meal, running to and from the kitchen.

Paul arrived late to the proceedings, pecked me perfunctorily on the cheek, looked tired and somewhat irritable, and expressed repeated sentiments that he had a difficult day.

I introduced André to Paul. Paul hardly acknowledged him and took a seat at the head of the table next to me under a huge crystal chandelier; it hung from a ceiling bordered by a frieze of diaphanous shapes. I was always fascinated by the jagged patterns of light which were thrown onto the Battenberg lace tablecloth. Gold moiré hung at the windows, tied back with floral tapestry bows. The Louis XIV chairs were antiques, white and gold with rose damask seats. A huge tapestry covered part of a wall gleaming with gold flocked paper broken up by square ornate moldings.

André Utter sat seemingly unimpressed by this dining splendor, his eyes always on me, drinking me in as though he couldn't have enough of me, and he made me uncomfortable. Something was happening to me. What was it?

Maurice became visibly more nervous and fidgeted in his chair.

And then I felt myself grow warm, my body coming alive with something that had long been dormant. *Merde*, I thought, this boy could be my son. Careful, careful . . . don't be foolish, but then what is age . . . a state of the mind and body, and I feel like twenty not a day older . . . only Paul makes me feel like an old woman with the fires of passion gone out. The *orgasme*, that marvelous explosion of feeling, that wonderful wild unbelievable burst of fire . . . *Mon Dieu*, how long has it been . . . how long since I have felt such a feeling? I can't even remember. What a mischievous imp this Utter is. Perhaps I can use him as Adam in one of my paintings. And I could be his Eve. What a marvelous looking man. A wonderful Adam with his light hair and beautiful teeth and hard muscles . . . what was it? I felt as though I were on fire.

"And my mother wanted me to go into the priesthood . . . me, a priest, can you imagine?" André was saying. "It's all because I did so well in school; and my father wanted me to become a plumber."

"Plumber? And are you?" Paul suddenly asked, smiling.

"Dédé is an artist," said Maurice proudly.

"Who has to support himself by doing electrical work and odd jobs. Certainly my painting doesn't support me."

"Well, the plumbing business would probably pay you more money in the long run than art." A bored Paul examined the chandelier.

I noticed that beside André, Paul looked old and stodgy.

"Probably," André said with a flourish. A smile lit his handsome face and he looked intensely at me. I felt an odd quiver in my cheek and I looked down at my soup.

"Is everything alright, Madame," Catherine asked sensing something in the air. She grew apologetic about the vichyssoise. "I caught the girls in the kitchen napping and gave them a tongue lashing."

"Everything is fine, Catherine. It couldn't taste better. This vichyssoise is delicious, isn't it Paul?"

"It couldn't be better, Catherine," he echoed.

"I understand Madame Mousis, that you knew Lautrec," André said breaking an awkward pause.

"Yes."

"He had quite an infirmity . . . I mean . . ."

"I know what you mean. He was a giant . . . I never paid much attention to what he looked like."

"You were fond of him then?" He glanced at Paul who was slurping his soup. "I understand he was difficult to deal with."

"I was the difficult one. Posing for him was always a pleasure. And Henri had a genius for friendship. He changed my life."

"André's studio is near me so we can paint together," Maurice stumbled, changing the subject.

André looked up at me again and his eyes met mine, and I felt their fire. A torrent of warmth poured through me as though his body reached out to touch and hold me. How ridiculous this all was . . . my son's friend . . . and yet I was being sucked into a maelstrom of sleeping desires submerged under this cloak of bourgeois respectability. Something fearful was being unleashed inside of me, unfettered, awakening, familiar with a poignant longing . . . it was sweet, unutterably sweet.

"Madame, your art is beautiful like you," he said in a low voice.

There was sincere adulation in his tone. But he was again too familiar. Paul seemed mildly amused, but Maurice became visibly annoyed again.

I said nothing but my eyes returned to his involuntarily by some magnetic pull, and then, "Would you like to pose for me sometime, André?" I hoped none of them would detect the emotions I felt. Could they detect desire? "Maumau, what do you think? Wouldn't he make an excellent Adam?" I deliberately drew my son into the discussion as though his approval would sanctify my intentions.

Maurice was agreeable. "Excellent idea, Maman. I think you would be a wonderful Adam, Dédé. I would love to see the painting when it's finished. Maman does marvelous figures. I paint empty streets. We are so different."

"I would be happy to pose for you, Madame."

"I share my studio with Maumau and I'll be there next Monday morning."

He nodded. He needed little coaxing.

I leaned out of the window of my studio and called, "André come up." He looked upward and smiled. I ran down a flight, opened the huge door, and then we ascended the wooden staircase passing a pile of coal on the landing to my quarters. I put a small scuttle of coal into the huge stove in the large studio room.

"Let me get you some café au lait. You look frozen."

It was a cold day in February when André sat in a huge chair on a worn Persian carpet which lay on the floor. Beside the old stove in one corner of the room was Maurice's easel with a painting of the *Rue Ravignan* unfinished, the paint still wet. Assorted paintings by myself and Maurice were on the walls. Several easels of different sizes were in the room. A tall chair decorated with brass nailheads sat next to a buffet, its top laden with statues of various sizes and a bowl of dried flowers used as a prop. Several Louis XIV chairs with velvet seats were lined up at one side of the room as though to witness a performance of a play. A group of draperies used as backdrops in various colors and patterns were draped over an easel. But where I painted, a canvas at least five feet high and four feet wide was being prepared for paint and this was to be the *Adam and Eve*. My Adam was now sitting in a chair calmly finishing his café.

André's gaze took in the room. "This studio suits you more than sumptuous Montmagny with its thick Aubusson carpets. I'm quite at home here."

"Not in that palace of bourgeois decadence?" I smiled.

"You belong here, where your art is about you . . . I want to learn about you here."

I shivered, an expectant, delightful tremor.

He disrobed while I began to set up my paints. I sketched him, and in the light of that cold March morning, his fairness shone with a luminescence I tried to capture. I outlined his figure on the canvas and my strokes were incisive, the strong dark lines of his body executed swiftly and with boldness.

Utter was a good subject. He posed patiently, engaging in endless conversations. I remembered that Maumau had said that he loved to expound his ideas. I also got a description of every facet of the happenings in the Bateau-Lavoir, all of which fascinated me. And he told me of his dreams and theories of art and his relationship and impressions of Maurice. He questioned me about the influence that Lautrec and Degas had on my art, and he sensed that my involvement with Henri went deeper than expressed, but he drew the curtain there. I spoke of my modeling days and the wonders of the fountain in the Place Pigalle where the models stood waiting to be selected.

As I drew the planes of his face, I felt the full impact of his beauty. The feeling of warmth which coursed through my body days before was becoming familiar and welcome. It was so long, so long since I felt anything like this. There was no question that there was a tremendous physical current passing between us, a peculiar energy which seemed to generate from him . . . his touch on my arm, his step, his holding of a pose, his very movement unleashed a boundless sexual response simmering in my body waiting for release. He was young and buoyant and welcome to any new experience with a zest and passion for life, but his sensitivity to another's needs made him seem far older than my son, far more mature. And it was mad. Any thought that he could become my lover was *fou* . . . and marvelous.

And each day André seemed changed to me. Or was it all an illusion? What was happening? Today he had become Renoir, my once carefree, handsome, spirited, good natured Renoir, and yesterday I had felt a passionate, sensitive, tortured Henri Lautrec offering suggestions, making witty comments; poor Henri now gone, only to be resurrected through his paintings plastered in the Moulin Rouge, and through delicious, nostalgic images of rue Tourlaque and the insane upheaval of his studio. And sometimes a lusty Miguel Utrillo peppered my meetings with André in his zest for life . . . these intruders changing André's image in so brazen and clandestine a fashion . . . almost rendering André a figment of my imagination. It was a fever from which I would recover tomorrow, and tomorrow came and nothing changed.

But my desire swelled and obliterated all resistance to his taking me and using me and making me a part of that firm, sinewy body, that youth I once had. I bit my lips and continued painting, the brush caressing the flesh of my Adam on the canvas with long loving strokes. I was indeed *fou,* a forty-three year old woman desiring the body of a twenty-two year old youth. If I were mad, then *Mon Dieu,* make me a slave to that madness, his slave, so that my mouth might caress his body from the light curled hairs on his chest, my tongue finding the cleft of his naval and will follow the trail of hair to his lovely cock so that I might devour it slowly, bit by bit. He must feel what I feel now, he must feel it.

"I think we're finished for the day, André; then tomorrow we can begin again," I said aloud, quite primly. And I was discreet, and still remained the older woman, the mother of Maurice.

And when he returned the next day, I asked him in a cool

impersonal voice as I mixed my paints and he disrobed, "Maurice, where is he? I haven't seen him for several hours."

"Madame, I saw him on the Rue Norvins."

"Don't you think it's time you called me Suzanne?"

"Suzanne," he said softy, nothing more.

I looked up at him again with the painter's objective eye. But his face was flushed and he appeared very perturbed.

I looked away, but a delicious current swept through me and seared my very being.

I remembered my conversation with Adèle.

"Be careful, Marie, he's your son's friend. I said you should take a lover but I never mentioned one of twenty-two years of age," she laughed. "What is wrong with you? Your brains are still between your legs."

"It's madness, I know. I can't help what I feel, and he feels it as well."

"He's a baby, like your son."

"No, he seems much older than Maurice. He's a man."

"If you have to have someone, for God's sake there's plenty in Paris who would wait in line for you. Did you hear me, Marie? Don't fuck your son's friend, it's a sacrilege. What would Maurice think? You would be ashamed to face your own son. Perhaps you should send your Adam home."

"No!"

"Why? Can't you complete the painting without him?"

"I want him, Adèle, I want him so. Is that madness?"

"Yes, it's a sickness. Go away on a vacation with Paul, or by yourself. Run Marie, run before this disaster overtakes you. This time, you will definitely affect your son."

"I can't help myself."

"*Merde*," Adèle said, shaking her head.

I came to the studio from Pierrefitte that afternoon; it took me forty minutes driving in my mule drawn tilbury. Along the way I vowed to myself that I would keep my relationship with him restrained and discreet. When I arrived, I impatiently threw off my silk taffeta and slipped into a long smock covering a simple cotton bodice and skirt.

He entered the studio scarcely looking at me and stripped off his clothing. He stood nude, the fine texture of his skin, and his lean muscular body reflecting the morning light. I set up my paints. When I glanced up, my eyes met his and I looked away at the painting. It was an idealized version of the garden of Eden. I was Eve, to André's Adam. The painting combined the realism of my craft and the allegorical. The paintings of Puvis de Chavannes somehow shadowed this work as though a voice from my past seeped through.

"Don't stare at me, André. You're spoiling your pose."

"I can't help it."

"Stop it. Do you want me to finish this work?"

His body suddenly relaxed as though he had stopped fighting something and he approached me, his nude flanks firm and muscular.

"What's wrong, André?"

"You."

"Please continue posing, André. You must continue . . . don't you see, you must continue." I visibly trembled.

And my thoughts were fevered. It was no use, I couldn't fight it. I would burn in this fire and my body would perish in the flames. I throbbed now with unbelievable anticipation . . . what undeniable exquisite pleasure there must be from the firm thrusts of his marvelous cock; and I grew wet with longing . . . my own deliciously young André, my beautiful André.

I dropped my brush. As I began to pick it up I felt his mouth and tongue on a little place behind my ear, and a surge of wanting shot through me and he faced me, drawing me to him, half lifting me, and holding my body tightly against his. I no longer had a will or resistance and the fight went out of me as I closed my eyes and was immobilized by something delicious and wild and intense; something I had half forgotten charged through me.

"Please . . . please . . ." he begged . . . but didn't he see there was no need to beg? "Do you know I've not been able to sleep, nor to work, nor even to breathe . . . you're always with me, have been from the first moment I saw you standing in the rue Cortot with your parted hair and startling light eyes . . . no, don't draw back, just hold me," he murmured as he held me fast with his youth, his promise of what delights were yet to come. "My sweet, sweet darling Suzanne . . . my adorable *chérie* . . . my wonder of wonders . . . your body, your voice, your talent, your beauty. Oh I so long to possess it all . . . don't draw away, my God, why do you draw away . . . please don't draw away or I'll die, as there's a sun in the heavens, I'll die from longing."

I was breathless. "You're my son's friend."

"No, I want to be your lover."

"I'm older . . . "

"Don't speak . . . it doesn't matter," and he put his hand on my lips. "You'll always be young . . . age plays no part in love for me, my beautiful one, my precious petite Suzanne, you'll always be mine forever . . . can't you see that? God meant it this way. I have a thirst I could never quench . . . I'll go mad in wanting."

"There's no need to go mad, no need," I whispered. I knew that I would surrender; I had known it from the first moment, and how I had longed for this. I opened my smock and several of the laces of my tucked bodice, and held him against my partly exposed breast. "My wonderful André . . . *mon cher* André, my sweet André," and I felt his mouth on mine and drew in the moistness of his tongue as it probed mine, exploring deeply, relentlessly. His kisses were on my throat, and he tore open the remainder of the laces of my bodice as he sank to his knees before me, and his mouth ran over my breasts, kissing each nipple in turn until they both stood erect. His hands ran over my body as he picked up my skirt. *"Chéri, chéri,"* I whispered over and over again, and I flung the smock over the easel and slipped out of my skirt and chemise and stood nude before him. I stood as I did in the painting. I was now his Eve.

And I guided him to a Récamier divan where he held me to him caressing my flesh. *"Ma petite,* how I will devour you until there is nothing left but a little voice." He kissed my body, my full lush breasts, my rounded belly and explored each shadow, each fold, the dark moist triangle, probing with his lips and tongue . . . with both lust and tenderness . . . when I parted my thighs and arched my body to meet his, he took me gently and then fiercely, and it was as though I had never been made love to before... not like this... not like the youth rejuvenating me as though I drew my strength from his virility and young ardor. It had never really been like this, for all the men I had loved were either my contemporaries or like Puvis and Renoir, much older and flaccid, so as with Paul, I looked away from their flesh. But André was young, the youth of my youth which had fled, and he restored a time which had gone.

Was it indeed insane to make love to a man younger than my son, twenty-one years younger than I? If so, I was indeed insane. But if my lovers, Puvis and Renoir had been so much older than I, why couldn't the same rule apply to a woman? I was certainly at the full expression of my sexual powers and I couldn't express them with Paul. For the first time in years I felt truly alive. And I marveled at the young hardness of him as he quickened his thrusts and I felt myself soaring and finally bursting into that glorious climax of feeling... that wild *orgasme*... I cried out and stiffened in ecstasy and lay with my legs wrapped about him, his semen running down my thighs. Locked in one another's arms, we savored the aftermath.

"I could still become pregnant," I murmured.

"It doesn't matter... I would marry you."

I lay still for an eternity, my body entwined in his and then said gently, "I have Paul, André."

"No, I haven't forgotten and you'll leave him."

"What!"

"You'll leave him and we'll stay in Montmartre together."

"I have to think about it. What will we live on? And he's been so good to me and to Maurice... I don't want to hurt him."

"It will be easy for you because you don't love him. There's nothing between you but money."

"Money counts for something. It puts a roof over Maumau and my mother."

"And you?"

"I can take care of myself."

"Maurice is a man," André said. "He should stand on..."

"Maurice is a baby, a difficult, erratic talented baby, but one who has to be watched, cared for and nursed through his alcoholic binges. You may laugh but he'll become a difficult son for you to deal with."

"It's you I want, Suzanne. Nothing else matters."

"My sweet André," and I ran my hand through his tousled hair and kissed the curled ringlets on his chest now damp with sweat, and held him close to me. I knew at that moment that I would leave Paul.

And then one afternoon on a warm spring day, the late sunlight bathed the studio, and a ray of light threw oblique shadows across the room. André had just completed posing for the Adam and Eve.

"The painting is finished, *voilà*, my Adam," I laughed and signed my name in the lower left hand corner. Then we opened a bottle of champagne and toasted one another.

"*Salut, ma petite chérie*," André said and I perched myself on his lap. I lay content against him and traced his features lightly with my hand, and ran my hand down the long slim flanks. How I loved touching him. It was a wonderful fever that raged through me that I succumbed to so easily. The battle was over before it began. Oh how I loved the feel of his hand on my body as he undid the tiny pearl buttons on my bodice and bent and kissed my breasts which fell exposed from my chemise. How I welcomed that treasured rush of desire that was dormant so long. We went again to the old velour Madame Récamier divan, its contours enlivened with gold nailheads. He kissed me deeply and he made love to me again and then again, and we lay locked in each other's arms.

When Maurice came in unexpectedly, he surveyed the scene, our nude bodies intertwined . . . Adam lying between his mother's legs and his mouth formed some words and his eyes opened wide. Then he stormed out.

For two days Maurice went on a drunken binge; he found his way to the high walled cemetery across from Lapin Agile where he polished off countless bottles of wine. César Gay, still in his uniform finally found Maurice and dragged him to my studio. From there, I removed him to the house at Pierrefitte where Dr. Ettlinger gave him an injection to calm him. It took several weeks of Maman's care, a series of injections of some sedative by the doctor, and explanations by me as to the state of my liaison with André to return him to a painter's life and some normalcy.

André attempted to explain himself but Maurice wouldn't listen. He just stared at him as though in a trance.

"Goddamn the two of you! I hope you both burn in hell," he said scarcely looking at us.

Finally, he went over to his easel as though nothing had happened and completed the *Rue Ravignan*. He never spoke of the incident again. It was as though it had been entirely blocked from his mind.

My painting, *Adam and Eve* was to hang in the Salon d'Automne which was in the basement of the Petit Palais on the Champs Élysées. Before doing so, however, I was told to cover my Adam's "all too prominent genitals" with grape leaves. I fought bitterly against altering my painting but I battered against a stone wall, and finally relented. Hanging beside my painting was the *Rue Ravignan* by Maurice, and he was elated. It was his first exhibition and I didn't know whether I felt prouder of my Maumau's painting or my own. Maurice strutted through the Petit Palais as a boastful child and commented now with an assumed authority as to the relative merits of each work, sporting a cane with which he pointed to each in turn. I stifled a laugh.

And it was here, while looking at my painting and that of Maurice . . . it was here that I decided to inform Paul Mousis that I was leaving him. The estrangement was there. The shock would certainly not be too great. I was wrong.

* * *

Paul sat at the edge of our bed, his nerves completely frayed. "I won't put up with Maurice destroying us . . . my God, he's drunk again in spite of the exhibit. Doesn't he have a studio to go to? He's even provided with an allowance. Perhaps he shouldn't share the studio with you. I'll get him one of his own. He's almost twenty-six and he's a man. I had a responsible position at twenty-six and was making lots of money. Why aren't I an example for him? What more can I do? Tell me."

"I know you've done all you can, Paul and I'm grateful to you."

"He shouldn't have to be taken care of, damn him!" he shouted. "You accept his drinking as nothing. You make less of a fuss when he comes home drunk than when he distorts a perspective in his painting. I don't understand, Suzanne. Someday you'll have to choose between Maurice and me. Let him be."

"He's my son and a great painter. I must tend to him."

"And what about your duties? What kind of life is this?"

A voice from Adèle whispered in my ear. "He'll expect things from you, Marie."

"You haven't entertained in months. All you do is paint. Of course I'm proud of your painting but you stay for weeks at a time at your studio and neglect your duties here. Some of the wives of my business acquaintances think you're mortally ill and they don't believe me."

"Damn them! I'll entertain when I choose . . . those empty headed imbeciles."

"They are important clients' wives . . . how can you talk that way?"

He held his head in his hands. I felt suddenly very sorry for him. Leaving him would be merciful. Poor, poor, kind Paul who wanted a gracious life in Pierrefitte, and an elegant hostess dedicated to being the mistress of the Chateau of the Four Winds, and he got *me*, erratic, willful, absorbed in my art, deserting his bed, unfaithful, and presenting him with an alcoholic nightmare for a son as a dowry. Poor, poor Paul.

I would take him out of his misery. "Paul," I said aloud.

"Yes?" He looked up, his eyes bloodshot, a desperate man.

"Paul, I've come to a decision. I've decided to leave."

"Good lord, you're not serious."

"It'll be a favor to you. You won't have to contend with Maurice; and in all fairness I really haven't been much of a partner to you. I've really gotten more from this arrangement than you have. We were never married so you owe me nothing."

Paul turned white and his cheeks sagged. He suddenly looked very haggard. "You're all I want, Suzanne. We'll work it through.

We'll marry and everything will change. I lost my head."

"When was the last time I slept with you, Paul?"

He sat, his mouth open, his face full with the weight of the encroaching years. I couldn't believe that I had ever made passionate love to him . . . when . . . how? I tried to recollect how he had once been but all I felt and saw was André.

Then suddenly, he began to cry like a child.

"Oh, please don't sob, Paul. You've been such a wonderful father to Maurice and so good to me . . . you have nothing to reproach yourself for. It's all my fault. You need a woman to appreciate you, who will entertain and perhaps even have children for you, not a woman such as I who . . . *who has been with André* . . ." I caught myself but the words were out. I held my mouth and waited for the impact.

He stared at me and his cheek suddenly twitched and a look of disbelief came over his face. "André?" he said quietly. "André!" he shouted, his eyes turning glassy with emotion. "You made love to André! So that's it! That's what Maurice was babbling about when he was drunk. You made love to André! Yes, that's it. Be damned! Be damned in hell! Where does it go on, in your studio? You fuck him in your studio? That's why you don't bother to come home? Tell me, is he good . . . is he better than I am? So you don't deny it. He's certainly much younger. So you need a young cock now? I'm too old for you? Damn you!"

I sat, my eyes searching his out, but Paul's face became a mask.

"It hurts, Suzanne. Don't think it doesn't hurt. I thought we'd have a life together. I gave you anything you wanted but it wasn't enough. I would give you anything now, anything because I love you. I don't mind losing you to your art but not to a boy young enough to be your son . . . you know you have lost your mind, that it's totally insane. You won't get another sou from me. You can be sure of that. Infidelity is not my cup of tea." He was whispering now, a terrible whisper flooded with hurt and rage all at once.

He left and slammed the door to the bedroom.

I sat quietly with a peculiar feeling of emptiness when he was gone. I looked at the lavishness of the room about me, at the life I was leaving. I thought of Adèle's plea, "Don't throw it all away.

Take a lover, Marie, take a lover if you're bored." Well, I had, and now I wanted more than the life Paul offered me.

For if I could not live with André openly, could not hold him each night, feel his lips pressed against my bosom when I cradled him in my arms murmuring to him, could not touch his glowing skin and feel his young taut body, and hear his soft melodic voice criticizing my work, offering me suggestions, and then relishing his opinions . . . if I could not have him totally without reservation, I could not go on. The thought of him made me grow warm with desire and my body began to ache for him. I leaned back and smiled and the luxury of the house and all it represented, dissipated into nothingness.

A disgruntled Maman shook a bony finger and took a swig of brandy, and the doom she predicted had arrived; judgment day was at hand.

"You're *fou!* You're *fou* and I always knew it. Where will we go? He'll throw us out on the street, that's what Paul will do, throw us out on the street . . . for shame . . . carrying on with a boy young enough to be your son. What have you got between your legs, Marie, a fire? We live in a palace but it's not good enough for you. What you really want is to throw your mother on the street with paupers. Mary, mother of God, Who will take care of us? Who? Not André, and certainly not Paul."

She began to drone and rock back and forth, the bottle of brandy missing her mouth and the liquor running in dark amber rivulets onto her chin and body.

"You don't understand how I feel."

"How you feel? And what about Maumau? Paul has been so good to him."

"Your Maumau doesn't like Paul so rest easy. And Paul is fed up with Maumau's drinking, and anyway, we don't even sleep together anymore."

"Madame Pinchot didn't sleep with the baker since the last child was born. What makes this so different? Women all over Paris don't sleep with their husbands."

"Oh listen to this wise woman. That's why men take mistresses and Pinchot goes to prostitutes. I don't want to live like that . . .

like these other women."

"If he gives you money, you should kiss his feet."

"No, it's not enough."

"You live like a man lives, not like the mistress of a mansion."

"I live to please myself. I'm not one of your empty headed wives from Montmagny. I won't be caught in a trap set for women."

"A trap was set for women long before you were born. Take care, Marie, take care or you'll soon walk with a big belly, even at your age, and André has nothing. The devil has made you scribble, *c'est ça!*"

"What in the world has my drawing got to do with it?"

"It's shameful to have André pose naked for your painting. It's shameful a woman painting a naked man."

"I can't explain . . . you wouldn't understand. We're leaving here. I told Paul."

"And where will we all live?" Maman moaned.

"We're going back to Paris, to the Montmartre where I belong. We'll manage to survive."

Maman began to plead, "Please, Marie, ask Paul for money, perhaps he'll be generous. Perhaps he'll forgive you."

"I'll ask him for nothing. We'll live on our paintings."

"Will the saints preserve us . . . Marie, please make up with Mousis, Marie, Marie . . . please or we will all starve . . . you are *fou* . . . running away with a penniless boy . . . God help us all." My mother moaned and wearily fumbled in her huge canvas bag for a flask.

"I have everything I want. I have André and I have my son."

I wrenched the flask from her hands and hurled it across the room. A shower of brandy splattered the wall but the flask remained remarkably intact.

Maman muttered, crossed herself and wearily picked up the flask.

For a moment, something about her touched me. "Now pack your things, Maman . . . we're leaving in a few days."

"All this beautiful furniture," she moaned.

"Fuck the furniture! I'll leave as I came . . . with nothing but my easel and paints and my son, Maurice. But I'll take my lover,

André with me."

Maman finished the few drops remaining in the flask, a look of horror never going out of her eyes.

June had begun when I packed some of my collection of china pieces, my gowns and my easel and paintings. For some reason, leaving Paul in the large lavish home seemed simple. Perhaps it was my own nature which made it simple or my desire to live with André, but in my forties, I had a sudden rush to live and love and experience passion before it was too late.

I left Pierrefitte with a German sheep dog, two cats and a goat. For a moment, just a brief moment, I paused on the way out to run back and take a painting from the wall, Henri's painting of a very young Suzanne Valadon in the butterfly hat. It was a tribute to that glorious day so long ago. I tucked the canvas possessively under my arm.

When I walked out of the marble entrance at Pierrefitte, it all seemed part of the past, of something I was done and finished with; my paintings would always be reminders of the unbelievable life I had once lived.

On the way to our new apartment, a cleaning woman questioned me on keeping a goat.

"Oh," I replied, "it's to eat up my bad drawings." André and Maurice laughed, Maman shook her head mournfully, and the charwoman threw up her hands in affirmation of the insanities of artists

We moved into 5 Impasse de Guelma which resembled the Bateau-Lavoir. It was chock full of artists . . . Raoul Dufy, George Braque, and Gino Severini who was noted for wearing sandals and outrageous socks. Empty wine bottles dotted the landings, wild parties punctuated the nights, and no one locked any doors for keys didn't exist. It was *la vie de bohème* in full flower, a renewed delight for me, certainly a far cry from the lavish frieze decorated ceilings of the château at Pierrefitte hanging with glittering chandeliers. I had left the servant, Catherine, and all the staff with Paul; and Maman was again to do the work of a cleaning woman in the studio. And Maman Madeleine watched it all with jaundiced eyes. She had little faith in it, but she was pleased with André's influence on Maumau. He was painting and his drinking had abated.

The new year of 1910 dawned with a chilled uneasiness which pervaded when the ballet *Schéhérazade*, was introduced to Paris by Rimsky-Korsakov and was attended by André and myself. I sold one of my canvases to pay for the admission. Another canvas paid the groceries. The artist, Bakst, set Paris on its ear. Bakst, although a Jew, was already noted as an artist in St. Petersburg. The semi-oriental fantasies he provided in *Schéhérazade* influenced Paris for years to come.

We saw Nijinsky dance the *Specter of the Rose*, with borrowed funds that year. We had come repeatedly to Dufy, who now had steady employment designing fabrics for Paul Poiret, a name in *haute couture*. Dufy was often our mainstay keeping us fed for days. And we visited the Bateau-Lavoir where we became friendlier with Picasso and heard Apollinaire read poetry and discuss Cubism. At the Circus Medrano the group sketched the clowns and acrobats. Afterwards we went to the Lapin Agile and madness, wine and absinthe flowed like a river.

And I floated on my dream. For both André and my son were with me and André seemed incredibly versed in all matters and never ceased to dazzle me with his lively wit. I had an increasing reliance on his opinions. When his easel was near me and I smelled his pipe, I found myself glow. We walked through the Louvre to see old masters, a new experience for me.

We believed we were the world's first lovers.

* * *

Our life with Paul at Pierrefitte was a placid dream which was rarely mentioned. The dream faded slowly replaced by a new cast of characters and some old ones drawn from the past. Modigliani became my son again and he joined us often at dinner.

"Picasso made me come to Paris, that confounded egotist,"

he said one evening at the Lapin Agile. How his vehemence altered his beautiful face. I marveled at the perfection of his features. I must paint that face before he disappears into the atmosphere like a puff of smoke. As though to confirm my thoughts he fell into a spasm of coughing.

"Nothing bothers Pablo, but things bother me," he continued, wiping his lips. "Why is it that Picasso sells, but I can't, André? I wish I had your self-confidence, Madame Utter. So I trade my pictures for a few croissants. You know the saying in Paris, 'Tell me where you eat and I'll tell you how you paint.' Just look at the walls and you see how many times I've eaten; I'm here and I'm a colossal failure. You know poverty when you have to paint on both sides of the canvas." Modi grew increasingly restless as he spoke.

"What's wrong, Modi?" asked André.

He ignored the question.

The *garçon* arrived at the table with a tray of drinks. "Let's make a toast to our friendship again . . . to my family, my beautiful family of artists," said Modi.

"*Salut!*" André and I toasted. Maurice murmured in assent as he feverishly downed his drink.

"How did you learn to drink like that, Maumau?" asked Modi.

Maurice looked up at me and said nothing.

But Modi was in another world. He began to draw again becoming more agitated, riveted to the seat as his charcoal sketched the woman from the next table. He was about to crumple it up again. He pounded his fist in exasperation on the table.

"Calm down, Modi," gestured André with his hand.

"It's something I can't explain. I felt in the last drawing . . . like . . . like . . . remember I spoke of style? I have to evolve a style." He sipped the drink.

"I don't understand. Just draw what you see, *voilà*," I said.

But Modi blocked us out as he drew faster, his charcoal redrawing the eyes, reshaping them and then the neck, sketching, altering, realtering . . . proportioning, reproportioning, the charcoal constantly moving . . . and then the eyes became almond shaped and the proportions of the body altered as the neck was elongated and the head, egg shaped.

"I don't think you realize what I did, my friends." He spoke low, his voice charged with emotion. And then with one burst of excitement, "Do you see what I did?"

Several tables of artists turned around.

"Is he trying that out on you now?" shouted someone from a nearby table. "He tried that out on us last week."

"He wants to get your reaction," shouted another. "Don't believe him. His long faces with the almond eyes are a sure sign of lunacy. Even Rosalie wont accept them in exchange for anything. He'll surely starve to death."

"Don't listen to those two, they're jealous of my talent." Modi turned and shouted, "Why don't the two of you shut up and go home and learn to paint!"

Maurice looked at him, a smile spreading over his face. "You're *fou*, Modi and it's the absinthe . . . why did you stretch out her neck? No one paints a neck like that. Maman, look at that neck."

I leaned over, "Perhaps this is to be your style, Modi."

"It's a glorious night and I owe it all to you. Aren't you impressed?"

"I think personally it's a pile of shit, Modi . . . a long neck and two beady eyes," laughed Maurice.

"If you don't recognize genius what can I do? You're my friend, so I'll forgive you."

And back at the studio, Modi said, "Well then, little mother, please just let me sit at your feet and watch you paint. See, I have a book with me. I'll read Dante to you and translate it into French, and I'll sing you an Italian song. Just let me sit at your feet."

I reached over and kissed him on the cheek.

"Now just be quiet," I said as a mother would to a child. Certainly this artist lying still on the divan with a face of ethereal beauty, was completely mad. Suddenly he coughed, the tubercular dreadful, feverish cough of the consumptive, and the sound pierced the air with an awful portent. My poor dear Modi, my beautiful one. His was a face bestowed by the Gods.

Modigliani's excesses became worse. His breath stank of absinthe and ether. It was generally deemed that intoxication and drugs was the food of genius. Ether was very available in the pharmacies of Paris, tasting hot and sweet. It was highly explosive and when one of the art students forgot her bottle by a stove, the wall of her studio blew out. At a New Year's party at the home of an artist, wine and hashish were discussed as a means toward the multiplication of creative capacity; at the door, Modi offered each guest a green bullet of hashish, the new concoction by Baron Pigeard. A kind of madness took over. There was a huge vat of punch under the Christmas decorations, and when Modi was at fever pitch, he poured kerosene on it and set it afire to have a great punch flambé. Then the decorations caught fire. Everyone panicked, screamed and cavorted around crazy, whipped into a frenzy by Modi's pills. But Modi just danced before the fiery vat and shouted lines from Nietzsche as though he were weaving incantations; then he grabbed a woman he had been sleeping with, stripped off her clothes, slung her over one shoulder, and disappeared into a nearby shed. My poor Maurice drank one bottle after another and then darted out in a drunken stupor, fear lending wings to his flight back.

Modi became even more erratic, more disruptive and sadistic, even when not under drugs. Finally Frédé, the gentle proprietor of the Lapin Agile wouldn't admit him. And then, my poor, poor Maumau's only friend, Modi, moved, following Picasso over to the rue Montparnasse where he joined a group of Jewish friends . . . Quisling, Soutine, and Max Jacob. He finally got a cell-like room on the ground floor of a collection of rooms called *La Ruche,* which proved an inferno in the summer and freezing in the winter. How my poor son suffered from the loss of his friend. How he suffered. I persuaded Modi to come over from Montparnasse from time to time bringing canvases. But Maurice rarely returned with him. But it was at those times when Modi came back to show what he had done, that he sat at my feet and watched me as I painted, and he sang his Italian songs. He would tell about his new friends, much to Maurice's sadness, and complain about *La Ruche* where Chagall, the new Russian painter, worked at night stark naked. To hold onto his friend, Modi asked Maurice to join him in his small studio. It was a last desperate ploy. I wisely put a prompt end to it. "You will live like Van Gogh lived with Gauguin, and in the end, you will be at each other's throats!" I shouted.

Maurice sat still and listened, and smiled miserably to himself, flattered at his friend's invitation. He would never leave Montmartre or me. Certainly he would never leave me.

Then Modi began to come less often. I had expected that this would happen. Maurice became desperate and once went over to Montparnasse; and finally it all stopped, but the memory of their former friendship remained like a low flame, smoldering, awaiting rekindling. How I missed that talented being so full of life and passion, dousing his brain with drugs. Amedeo Modigliani, my other son.

* * *

There was unrest in Paris and the news from London of the First Post-Impressionistic exhibition didn't help. But I'm glad I came away with him and left all that boredom behind. Everything now was so new and exciting. When in 1911, there was a startling bit of news in the art circles that the Mona Lisa disappeared from the Louvre, frame and all, it added to that excitement.

And amidst this turmoil, my André and I continued a protracted honeymoon, and went to the Theatre des Arts and saw Dostoyevski's *Brothers Karamazov*. And the following week saw Nijinsky make a soaring exit through the window in Petroushka. I often wondered if André felt the thrill and longing to create which I felt. I knew he was thrilled at what we had done to be together. It hadn't been easy to substitute one life for another but it was all so glorious.

Our life and love gave wings to my art. I will paint now . . . how I will paint. AndI began painting huge canvases. *The Joy of Living,* showed some influence of Chavannes and was exhibited at the Salon d'Automne, and my beloved portrait *Grandmother and Grandson* was exhibited at the Salon des Indépendants. How I loved this last painting, my Maurice with a far away look in his eyes and Maman's so quiet expression succumbing to her lot and the dog sitting in passive wonder of it all.

Amidst all this turmoil Clovis Sagot, the madman baker turned art dealer, was persuaded to have "A Valadon-Utrillo" exhibit. "By God, it has a ring to it!" said André excitedly.

It proved a disaster. No one came. Maurice stormed out extremely agitated and was restrained by André. The exhibit closed drearily.

How could I pacify him? "We'll go to the Gallery Druet, Maumau, and take your paintings with us."

But at the gallery, Druet looked down his pince-nez at his work and made a terrible face.

"Don't you see the talent, the promise in my son's art? He has painted a masterpiece in this one." I held out the *Street at Montmartre,* an oil on cardboard as my mouth quivered with anger.

"Surely you are joking? You call this a masterpiece, *this*? He's your son but I must say it. It's amateurish and that's being generous. The walls . . . empty . . . streets so dismal. This one, for example . . . to paint such an ugly desolate street is a breech of esthetic judgment." He pointed to another painting. "Why there's not even a figure on the streets . . . so bleak, so colorless . . . "

"Enough, you stupid boor!"

"You call me a boor? Your son would do better to study another trade, perhaps electrical work since he seems to be able to use his hands, or baking. He could be an excellent baker, if he would mix his dough like that hodgepodge of plaster. Yes, a baker would be a suitable trade."

"A baker? Save your bleeding heart, Druet. Someday, I assure you, you'll beg for my son's work . . . and I want to be there to see you do it. These paintings are the work of a genius."

"A genius, your son, a genius? I'm so sorry for you."

"You uncouth pig! You're sorry for me? You'll be the sorry one," and my voice grew hoarse with rage.

"I'm busy and you've taken up a good deal of my time."

"Don't put on any airs with me, Druet. I remember you when you worked in a café and dealt with drunken patrons."

"And that's precisely why I can't tolerate your son."

A gentleman stood by, impeccably dressed in a tall silk hat.

"Can I see that one, Madame?" He pointed to a painting I held.

I recognized him as Monsieur Jourdain, the art critic.

"Oh, Mademoiselle Valadon, we meet again. Whose work is this?"

"My son's," I boasted looking significantly at Druet.

"He's quite amazing."

Druet's eyes clouded over. "Ah! Monsieur Jourdain, welcome. We certainly have other work. There is much I can show you."

"I'm interested in this painting . . . it's . . . different. Don't you see . . . its very starkness . . . its simplicity has in itself a beauty and the heaviness of the paint . . . he applies it like plaster itself. It's as though he constructs his buildings."

"I don't know what to say except the artist painted a dreary street," said Druet.

"That's just it . . . it *is* dreary and somber and lonely. I like it. Have you others? I should like to see more, Monsieur . . . Madame?"

"You'll come to our studio . . . 12 rue Cortot and we'll show you others," I said smiling vengefully at Druet.

Jourdain visited our studio several days later accompanied by three friends, Paul Gallimand, a publisher, Octave Mirbeau, a novelist, and Elie Faure, a critic. I brought out the thirty-six paintings which had been at Sagot's Gallery plus others with the paint not yet dried. I felt my heart pound. Maurice sat by in a trance without speaking.

"They have a haunting loneliness about them," said Gallimand.

"I think them superb," said Jourdain. "Superb. Look at the slathering of paint, like the façade of a building," he said as I trembled with expectation.

"How does your son do it . . . make the paint so thick?" asked Faure.

"He mixes plaster in with his paints, or sand, and applies it with a palette knife. Have you ever seen anything like this . . . oh I warrant that once the others get the hang of it there will be many copies," I said.

They all bought paintings at fifty francs apiece and afterward wrote about his art in their publications. What joy I felt . . . what great joy. I would have liked to stuff every frank I received down Druet's throat. No matter, my marvelous Maurice was getting noticed. I repeat, what can measure a mother's pride in her child, her accomplishment? And when your child is a failure, nothing else matters.

Clovis Sagot, the madman, died. And Louis Libaude came into our lives. He was a bastard, a scheming, sniveling bastard. He was the art critic from *L'Art Littéraire*, former horse auctioneer and fanatic collector whose flat at No. 6 rue Boudin was chock full of paintings, antiques and fine porcelain. *Dieu*, everything including his bed had a price tag on it. And his motives were devious. He had earned the name, "Wily Libaude," by hatching suspicious schemes, known only to himself. I repeat, he was a bastard. At the very least, he was a fawning, unctuous man of fragile health, and he made my flesh creep. I would like to stamp him out as one does a bug, a son of a bitch. But he had a superlative eye for talent that one, and this made him a small fortune.

He wanted the entire production of Maurice's paintings in exchange for a modest monthly retainer to be given entirely to me. As an enticement, he promised me a subsequent Utrillo one-man show.

A short while after, a contract was signed with my son and it was a terrible mistake. Libaude proved the most tyrannical of dealers. He began to dictate even the signature on Maurice's paintings, insisting that it be executed in a neat, precise hand. I found myself threatening to wrap my fingers around his scrawny grimy throat.

But in the end I was defeated. Somehow I knew I would be. Maurice was drinking and was in need of medical care and we needed the money. There were increasing disturbances and frequent calls from the police station. This time there was no César Gay, who had always been there to take an interest in him to carry him home. My poor Maurice was becoming sicker. I felt the storm coming on once again.

The pace quickened.
Maurice was at the peak of his *manière blanche*, his white pe-

riod, and he revised his palette, continued to apply his paint with a knife and mixed his plaster with his zinc white to make his walls more authentic. He was producing a painting daily. It floored me. One day he painted several views of the *Rue Norvins*, another the *Factory at Saint Denis* with its stark loneliness. I realized one day that Maurice and my paintings at this time had the same organization, the same materials, the same method, the same harmonies and that only the subjects and the motives differed. Of course it was so because it was the Valadon palette.

Most of his paintings now sold from one hundred to two hundred francs. Aside from this, he was a lost soul when he was committed again to the Sanitarium for the Insane at Villejuif; but this time not as an alcoholic but as a lunatic.

A lunatic? Yes, would you believe it, my son was now considered a lunatic for peeing on a statue. How we all have moved up in this world. Frankly I'm tired of fighting the authorities and poor Maumau's long pattern of alcoholism has left its mark on me. I longed to paint without the persistent distraction of a drunken son as much as I wanted to protect him. Somehow I felt that I would always be tortured in this manner.

I had heard disturbing rumors about his treatment. Alarmed, I went to Villejuif Sanitarium that afternoon. I alighted from a carriage and walked briskly onto the carefully cultivated grounds. Here, they made no allowances for artists; nobody, but nobody would be cruel to my Maurice, my genius, no one. I was the lioness fighting for all the protective mothers of the world, fighting for the well being of my cub. But what I saw and heard unraveled me for days after.

I passed weeping willow trees which stood in the midst of ovals of earth and grass with benches scattered randomly about; and I looked for my Maurice but he wasn't out of doors. There was a calm here, but as I walked and entered the cold gray stone building with the brooding façade, the serenity shattered, and the stillness was rent with the terrible screeching of a woman. The blood curdling screams tore through me chilling my very being, and as I passed a barred room, the most awful wails of terror were taken up by the woman's cellmates and inmates nearby. *Merde*, I must get him out of here. I covered my ears to shut out the din of wild haired creatures tearing at filthy clothing and clutching at the bars of their prisons. I couldn't bear it. Where was my son? What had I done to him? A sudden calm and serenity startled me by its very stillness; a quiet atmosphere suddenly prevailed where attendants dressed in white shirts and green trousers walked about with huge bunches of keys jangling from thick belts. What would they do to my son if he disobeyed . . . beat him? I dared not think.

"Are you looking for someone, Madame?" an attendant asked putting aside my thoughts.

"Oh yes, for Section C . . . Maurice Utrillo, the artist."

"Oh, of course." He took me down another long corridor where newly installed electric lights threw elongated shadows on the wall.

He unlocked a door with a key taken from the assortment he had hanging from his belt. The keeper grinned and waited outside. I entered a cell like room and in a corner sat a pitiful dwarf like creature huddled in a fetal position with paint smudged around his mouth. And at his easel, Maurice sat before the window with a vacant expression. He barely acknowledged me and appeared to be under some sedative. What had I done to him? "What have I done to you *mon pauvre?*" I murmured. I embraced my poor Maurice and held him to my breast like a baby. And then I noticed something else, and swiftly I pulled a tube of zinc white from the gnome's hands. "What are you doing, you idiot?"

"He eats the paints, Maman. And they feed them to him. Look at his mouth."

The creature looked up at me, a huge white smear encircling his mouth, stuck out a frosty tongue, and began to dance around me while Maurice sat and put his head in his hands, so sad, so totally dejected.

I pushed the creature away. "I want this . . . this thing out of here!" I shouted. "I want him out of this room . . . guard? Where is there a guard?"

Maurice shook his head and then looked frightened as he pointed to his easel.

"I see nothing on it. How much painting have you done? Why

is your canvas all smudged this way?"

I turned to the little mad figure who was hopping up and down in a corner.

"No, not him," Maurice said and began to cry.

"Who then? Who smudged your canvas . . . I'll kill him!"

"Maman, Maman . . . please don't say anything. They'll beat me."

"Who did this?" I repeated. "Who did this terrible thing?" I went over to Maurice and shook him. "Who ruined your painting? Tell me."

"No," he said in a meek tone.

I slapped his face. Then I held him to me again as he cried like a baby in my arms. "It was the guard, Maman . . . the one who was here," he whispered. "Don't say anything to him . . . he's a mean one."

"What?"

He motioned with his eyes toward the door. I released Maurice and stepped out into the corridor. I took the guard quietly by the arm and took him into the room. "Are you the keeper for my son?"

"*Oui*, Madame."

I looked at my son and he nodded significantly.

"And you've watched over him while he painted?" I said quietly restraining myself.

"Sometimes, Madame." The guard grinned and slumped somewhat.

"Then why do you let this creature eat his paints?" I said.

"Why that little animal is *fou*, Madame . . . that's why he's here."

"And you . . . why did you smear my son's painting?"

"What? I . . . I smeared your son's painting?"

"You heard what I said. Why did *you* smear it?"

The insistence in my tone unnerved the guard for several moments and his mouth hung open. When he regained his composure, "It . . . it's part of the treatment. He must be taught a lesson."

"You're a liar and a sadist," I said slowly. "And I'm going to have you fired." I lunged at him. "You deface my son's art? Damn you!"

I picked up a tray on which there was still some food and threw a bowl of tepid soup in his face and smashed the tray down on his head!

The little elf cackled hideously, dancing about in the dim light of the cell.

The guard wiped his face. "You're *fou* like your son."

He ducked as I threw a wormy apple at him.

"So I'm *fou!*" I screamed. "You ruin my son's art you sadistic butcher! You savage beast! You . . . you . . ." I hit him with my umbrella, making a gash near his eye. He darted out of the room and down the corridor. Several moments later a chief official of the hospital, a Dr. Moreau ran into the room. He bowed.

"You don't have to bow to me, Doctor Moreau . . . that monster ruined my son's painting. He was taken here as one of France's greatest painters, and a painting of his is worth five thousand francs. I want him out of here by tonight."

"He's not ready yet."

"He'll never be ready here. I'll pay for the rest of the month and I want him out."

"Have it your own way," he said stroking his beard. "But you'll have trouble, I promise you. He has a terrible alcoholism."

"I want him out!"

"*D'Accord!* I won't stop you."

"And Doctor Moreau, put that poor creature in with a banker. Perhaps he'll eat francs instead of paint. It's far better for the digestion."

Dr. Moreau smiled an uncomfortable smile.

That evening Maurice dragged his easel and his folded paint box behind him back to Montmartre. André stood before the studio, smiled weakly and then sighed, "Your *Place du Tertre* sold for four hundred francs."

Maurice shrugged his shoulders completely oblivious to it all.

* * *

Paris tossed with rumors of war. I felt the stinging winds of change approaching that year of 1914, and I shivered in that bitter winter.

By springtime, scandal broke. Madame Caillaux, the wife of the ex-premier of France went to her hairdresser and had a new coiffure and nails done, after which she purchased a gun and proceeded to shoot and kill Gaston Calmette, the editor of Figaro, who had charged her husband with corruption while in office. Sympathy for her reigned, for even her husband's first wife gave her moral support in court. She was acquitted and the bohemians of rue Cortot went wild, but other matters came to the fore.

Paris was seething in political turmoil. On August 4 the Germans invaded Belgium and France and terrorized and massacred the peasants. War was everywhere and now patriotism came to the fore in full force. Everyone talked about enlisting. I held my breath that it didn't touch us. But the prospect of putting on the blue uniform of the Republic was fraught with a romantic fervor. The youth of France rushed enthusiastically to the recruitment headquarters in each town.

And before I could digest what had happened, my André joined a group of rue Cortot artists and writers. After remaining in temporary shelters they were to be sent to the 158th Infantry regiment at Fontainebleau.

I was stunned at André's enlistment.

"You never told me," I cried. "How could you leave me this way?"

"I would have been called anyway."

"You don't love me, André. I thought you did."

He embraced me. "Of course I love you, but it's something I must do. I knew it would upset you if I mentioned it."

"It's cruel, all the same and . . ."

"It's not cruel, Maman. I might go also," interrupted Maurice.

"You'll both leave me all alone? You will not enlist, Maumau.

I want you to be safe. Never. I don't believe in this killing. I just can't believe you would do such a thing. I have a drunken senile old woman of eighty-four who never speaks, for a mother . . . that's what I'll have left." Maman sat staring in a semi-catatonic stupor. Maurice kissed her on the cheek and her eyes flickered with a soft light.

"But I'll make you happy, Suzanne. We'll marry quickly with only Maurice and Maman Madeleine present," he said. "There, after all these years, I'm asking you to marry me, Suzanne, and you say nothing."

"I don't care a damn about the marriage. I don't care a damn. We've been together for so long and it's all the same to me . . . I want you home."

"I can't stay."

"You did this to me, you, my dearest friend and lover. You did this," and I turned away.

We were married at the *mairie* that August on a hot summer day. André gave his age as twenty-eight. I was forty-nine. Somehow, I took small joy in the marriage. But he held me with a terrible possessiveness that last night before he left for the front.

"When you come back, *chéri*, I'll be an old woman to you," I said.

"You'll always be young to me, and I'll love you always."

"It's all words, André, all words. You're young and I'm old. Sometimes, you look so young, André, it frightens me."

"Nonsense." And he held his hand over my mouth. "You're always worried about age differences and I never give it a second thought. I don't want to hear it."

"My own dearest, dearest André," I said looking up at him and nestling my face in the light curly hair of his chest. "You know I'll love you forever. Why wasn't I twenty when we met?"

"*Sacrebleu!* When you were twenty I was a thought in my papa's head."

I began to laugh as he joined in. But it was bitter laughter and I fell asleep with an empty feeling. Somehow, our idyllic relationship, our closeness, our being an integral part of one another's art . . . all this was ending and I, who always wanted to be in control of every situation had to wait . . . to wait.

"I'll write to you, Suzanne . . . " he shouted as the train pulled away from the station at Gare Montparnasse, his voice lost in a deafening roar.

And when André's train was gone, I felt a part of me die.

15

Maurice
Alcoholic Aberrations

Oh dear friend, César, what would I do without you? Well, this police sergeant finally retired and purchased his small bistro, the Casse-Croûte in the rue Paul-Féval. And he kept his promise. In the early part of the year he reserved a room for me above the bar where Maman sent me to recover. I began to think of it as my home.

"It's my hôtel deluxe," I laughed.

"I waited for this day, my dear artist friend," he smiled. "Now your work will fill my walls. I'm the friend of a genius. It's an honor bestowed on me."

But it took a short time for me to beg for a drink and César to refuse. I picked up a cup and smashed it against a wall but he was ready.

"You don't frighten me, Maurice, the *artiste-peintre*. I'll strike a bargain with you. You want to paint, *hein*? And I for one, enjoy sitting and watching you paint. We'll make an agreement. When you finish a painting, you'll call down to me and I'll come up and give you a liter of wine, not before."

"That's too much. It's too long to wait."

"That's to be our agreement, no more, no less."

I pouted. Perhaps he would change his mind?

"*D'Accord!* Then sign this."

César took out a sheet of paper on which had been written, "I, Maurice Utrillo V agree to complete a painting before obtaining wine from César Gay, proprietor of the Casse-Croûte Bistro."

I laughed and affixed my signature to the document. What a character he was.

"Now it's official. You look happy now but you're caught like a fish on a hook."

I sighed deeply and went to my easel. This good man was relentless.

"Oh, your mother has sent these pigments for you." He handed me a parcel. In the bag was a huge tube of zinc white among other colors.

"*Bien*, she didn't forget," I said.

"You have an exceptional mother . . . so concerned with your art. And *artiste-peintre*, if you would be ever so kind, please take a few minutes of your time, someday, and teach me."

"Teach you? What can I teach you?"

"Why to paint, *artiste* Maurice, to paint, of course. Don't laugh . . . I would like to paint like you . . . just like you. I'm not joking."

I was surprised and then pleased. "My dearest friend . . . it's little compensation for the goodness you have shown me all these years. I'll certainly teach you how to paint."

In a few days, I reneged on my written agreement. I demanded the wine with a canvas half finished. I stamped on the floor to get César's attention. He ran up from the bar but when he examined the canvas, he shook his head and locked the door.

I pounded on the door and began to yell hoarsely. César opened it and shut it again with hardly a ripple of agitation on his face. In an hour he sent a serving girl with a tray of food to my room. I chased her down the stairs and made her scream. With a signal César had his employee, Victor, force me back to my room.

"He smells so sweet," said Victor. "It doesn't smell like alcohol, what is it?"

I had my little secret hidden under my mattress. Let them all be damned. I grinned, danced crazily and laughed loudly. What fun. What delicious fun.

That old hag came running up the stairs. Ugh! That shrew.

"*Ma fois!* What do I smell on his breath? It's so . . . so familiar."

Suddenly, she shrieked, ran into her bedroom and returned breathlessly.

"What's wrong with you, Marthe?"

"What's wrong? What's wrong? *Incroyable!* You take him in, César, from the goodness of your foolish heart and he, he . . ." she looked on the floor of the room and found it. I tried to kick the evidence away and she screamed again. "Look what he's done. Look what he's done." I laughed madly. "You stupid fool!" she screamed.

I laughed louder. This woman with her wild beady eyes and stringy hair was a sorry sight.

"Marthe, have you lost your senses?" He scowled at his wife.

"It's my cologne. He drank my best cologne, and I used it only once. I've been saving it for the theatre. He drank up my cologne. I don't want him here. I want him out at once. I'm sending him back to his mother. He's an animal . . . an animal!"

A witch, that's what she is, a witch, I thought, laughing at her.

"You must be patient. He's a great artist," César protested.

"I don't care if he's the greatest artist in France. I'm throwing him out. His mother will buy me a new bottle of cologne."

"In hell," I muttered and then the room whirled around and I flopped to the floor in a semi-stupor. With the assistance of Victor, I managed to get to my cot.

César shrugged his shoulders, "I'll have to send for his mother again. When he recovers, Victor, we'll give him a bowl of bouillabaisse which my wife makes like an angel." He put two fingers to his lips and made a smacking noise as a kiss. "And then I know he'll begin to paint again. This time he'll teach me."

"Oh, no I won't. I won't touch a pot my dear husband. When he wakes up," the witch shrieked, suddenly returning, "I'll give him nothing! I don't care if he starves!"

"Go down to the kitchen, Marthe, and make him some soup."

"Never. I'll see him in hell first!"

"Be damned in hell!" I yelled out hoarsely, "Be damned you old witch!" The outburst sapped my energy and I drifted off.

But when I woke up, I saw that Maman had been called and was having the confounded bouillabaisse.

I looked at Maman and she appeared as a fairy princess shining in the light.

Well, the old hag finally had her way and sent me home. Poor, poor César lost his battle.

When I finally came home, Maman seemed desperate, grasping at straws. She got something in her head that what I needed was a wife to take care of me and all my problems would be solved, and would you believe that she picked Paulette?

My God, Paulette? How could Maman ever have thought she could give grace and breeding to a pig? What was Paulette, really? She was a large, overweight girl from Brittany, with a big bosom, large buttocks and fleshy thighs who was told how to keep house by our English maid, Lily Walton. Maman decided to use her as a cook, cleaning woman and nursemaid, an all around *bonne* who came with good references and was quick to learn. Pierre, my bodyguard and nurse had left, and Paulette now took on some of his duties. Occasionally, Maman used her as a model. The girl was pleasant, really not bad looking and I figured out that perhaps she wasn't all that stupid. But she'll be Maman's daughter-in-law who would give her grandchildren? Over my dead body.

I imagined what must have taken place between Maman and Paulette. Maman must have come into the room where Paulette was cleaning and Maman seized her golden opportunity.

"Do you like my genius son, Maurice?" she asked.

"Oh yes, Madame. He's quite good looking you know."

"Paulette dear, how would you like to marry him? We're not such poor people you know, and we would make life comfortable for you. But you must take care of him. It's not often that a servant has this opportunity to move up in society. You'll be a lady, a real lady with a maid of your own." Of course Maman would have tried to bribe her with this great offer.

Paulette must have been amazed. "I . . . don't know. I have to speak with my mother . . . he's so very handsome, so handsome. But he drinks so . . . how wonderful to have a maid of my own. Maman would be happy."

"Your mother could brag about it," Maman surely said.

"But there is one thing, Madame. It's very important. I would love to wear a cerise colored satin for a wedding dress. I couldn't marry without it." What an idiot she was.

And Maman went along with it. "Of course Paulette. Why, we'll look through all of Paris for a cerise colored satin. You'll be a daughter to me."

This girl was really stupid. And would you believe that she wanted a wedding gift and a kiss from me to seal the engagement? Wild horses couldn't make me kiss her. Frankly I would rather kiss a hippopotamus."

I had returned to Cesar Gay's bistro closing my eyes and ears to that old witch, Madame Gay. One evening, Maman came there to my room and sat down in an old rocker in the corner. I was painting from a postcard at an easel by the window and I knew what was coming . . . my marriage to a hippopotamus.

"I want to speak with you. I found someone, a gem for you, Paulette . . ."

"*Sacrebleu!* A gem? She's a gem? She is a clod . . . the *bonne* who cleans my room . . . are you mad, Maman? I could split my sides laughing. I don't want to hear about her or her damn wedding dress."

"What's wrong with her? She's strong, not bad looking, a little plump but you like them that way and I think she's a virgin . . . she knows little of men. She'll bear you many children, all little artists, and she adores you, Maumau, she adores you."

I threw down my brush. "Damn! Let me be, Maman."

"There's nothing wrong with her."

"Well, she's certainly not like you, Maman . . . not my idea of a wife."

"Of course she's not like me. You're not marrying your mother, Maumau."

"She's not beautiful like you."

"She has her own . . . eh . . . buxom charm."

"I won't sleep with a pig."

"You don't sleep with anyone, that's the trouble."

"That's my affair, not yours."

"You have a tongue now, have you? Well she's better than an asylum and will bear you children. She'll take care of you and I'll manage the whole thing."

I should fuck her? I thought. I began laughing hysterically.

"Marry her . . . she'll be good for you and . . . be good to your mother, Maumau. Show me how much you love me."

"All right. All right. Just don't bother me."

"That's a good Maumau . . . oh . . . she wants a cerise satin wedding gown, a small gift and she wants you to kiss her."

"You kiss her, and I wont marry anyone in that dress."

"How will you have children with her if you won't kiss her?"

"I'll have to engineer it" The thought amused me and I rolled about waving my arms and purposely laughed a wild, hysterical laugh.

"You sound like an idiot, Maumau."

"If I married her I'd be an idiot."

César Gay heard me from the bar.

"Oh, my dearest friend," Maman said when he entered the room, "I want to announce the engagement of my son to my . . . model, Paulette."

César Gay was startled. "Is it possible? When? How? *Incroyable!* Oh, my beloved Maurice who has been like a son to me. How happy I am for you, how very happy. *Mes complements.* I am so happy for you."

Don't be so happy for me, César, you poor old fool, I thought. But I played along with the game.

Would you believe it that Paulette and Maman finally found a cerise gown at a dismal shoppe, a mass of glitter, ribbons and cheap lace. This dress amazed me; it was the dress of a whore at the brothel I went to. But even whores dressed in better taste. The proprietress, Nina, advised against it, but Paulette was stubborn as a mule. She got Maman to finally buy it.

The very next day, Maman dragged me along with Paulette to the *mairie* to announce the wedding.

Afterward Paulette looked at me and sulked. Maman asked her impatiently, "Don't you like your dress?"

"I was thinking, Madame, why are you all so good to me?" The cow was growing suspicious. "I'm really a nobody. Do you know that they really put my mother away? She became *fou* and she's in an asylum. She imagined people were chasing her, and she drank too much. I lied to you. After all, I'm only a servant. I have no dowry and you're a fine family of artists, you and Monsieur Utter and Monsieur Maurice." So she wasn't as stupid as everyone thought.

"Well if your mother drank then you should understand him," Maman said motioning to me.

I secretly wished that Maman would shut up.

"Oh I do, I do. That's why he doesn't frighten me." But it wasn't true. She looked at me, scared out of her wits.

"Then what's wrong?"

"I don't know. It's all so fast. I didn't count on getting married yet, and he should still give me a small token, perhaps a ring."

"He's done a painting for you as a gift."

"I saw it and it's not the same as a ring," she whined. "I don't want anything but a ring. A painting is the wrong gift for a bride." She looked at me angrily.

Maman was furious at her colossal nerve. Let's face it, what did Paulette know about painting? Maman made a big mistake. She was glaring at Paulette. Then she stopped herself. "I told you that you'll be the daughter I never had," she said sweetly trying to amend what couldn't be fixed. It was too late.

The remark didn't make a dent in Paulette. She gave me this awful look and turned her back on me. Couldn't Maman see that this future bride was a monster? No way would I ever sleep with her.

The next morning she was gone, thank God. She fled in the middle of the night and left my painting on the bed but the cerise satin gown was nowhere to be found.

When I heard that she took off, I felt that a load was taken off my back and I promptly forgot about her the next day.

The painting she left behind was later sold for over one hundred thousand franks.

Several weeks after this fiasco with Paulette, I got word that my application for study at the École des Beaux Arts was rejected and I don't remember how it happened but somehow I found myself in Villejuif again. I remember drinking up a storm and then scaring off a nun coming from church and shouting obscenities at a pregnant woman. But let's face it. How many drunken binges can one have? I was sent from Villejuif to Picpus Asylum for the Insane for peeing on a sacred statue.

16

Suzanne
A Rage against Time

*T*ime, that relentless dimension was my nemesis. At fifty-two I desperately fought it, laughed at it, behaved at moments like a foolish ingenue among my friends, always attempting to prove my youth, always mocking the elements, the forces that would not be mocked, and in the end I knew I would be shattered. Time, that relentless dimension would destroy what beauty I had. It was inevitable. Why was it that in my early years, Time seemed to stand still; it moved but a fraction in one's perception. Every moment was trivial, glossed over when the world was young. There were so many other moments yet to come. And I in my youth laughed always at age; looked with contempt on the shriveled body, the shrinking bones and the prospect of growing older didn't exist, was completely out of reach. One didn't contemplate it when one was young. Why didn't I know then that I would grow old? Why didn't someone tell me to savor the moments, to treasure my youth, a youth never to return? Was youth such a trivial thing that no one deemed to mention that it would soon flee and something else would take its place; something fraught with lassitude, illness and the loss of beauty and vitality. The withered old woman, bent and struggling would die and I would take her place, withered, bent and struggling. Why didn't someone warn me?

But in my mind, I didn't change. I still sat with Adèle in Place Pigalle, basking in the delicious shimmering light of the waters of the cascading fountain waiting for new modeling chores. And we giggled about lovers and artists and nothing at all. And if my mirror belied me, reflecting someone younger than my actual years, it was only in my paintings that I portrayed the harsh reality of what I was. But I wouldn't permit Time to pass at a furious, dizzying pace, but would hold it back and savor every moment as before; enter every experience with zest. I found myself resisting a force which dragged me downward in a persistent undertow, and swept me helplessly along so that my skin began to line and body sag, and a fine network of wrinkles appeared about my eyes, waiting, waiting for the signal to spread over my cheeks, the luminous glowing cheeks of my youth. The demolishing Time, fading and destroying youthful impulses and blooming beauty in its ensuing path; ever quietly creating a wasteland in its wake.

"For a woman, age is deadly," I often told Adèle.

"What can we do?" Adèle had answered. "Can we hold onto our youth? A man can grow old . . . never a woman, *c'est ça*. It's a bitter truth."

I thought of André and grew afraid. Something stayed me. I was more reflective. Some of the old fight was gone.

And in my fight against the ravages of time, I thought about Renoir. Why should I have cared that I was older except for the fact that as a young model, a bright, fresh Marie-Clémentine who posed for his *Dance at Bougival*, I had once loved him. It was so long ago. Would he see me now so changed?

I had heard that Renoir was free of financial worries in his sixties, but the horror of his rheumatoid arthritis became steadily worse each year. He was still able to walk by the use of crutches. However, he was a financial success and his paintings sold for huge sums. A gentle old man, he was venerated by the young artists who came to Cagnes to pay him homage. Occasionally, he came into Paris and stayed in the home of his friend, the collector of his works, Maurice Gangnat. I took several of my own and my son's paintings to Gangnat. I had heard that Renoir was a house guest but what I saw stunned me.

I remembered a happier, dapper, dashing, impeccably clad young man over whom the *midinettes* fussed and with whom they flirted outrageously. That Renoir was gone. The recollections of walks on the Boulevards and lovemaking in the garden of his studio, and the Renoir who evoked a whole panoply of breathless, youthful romantic images for me disappeared somewhere, submerged, changed. Was this possible?

Those limp arms and the gnarled hands slowly being made useless by this crippling disease; the deeply furrowed face with its sunken cheeks, and the nose which seemed to have grown much longer; lips changed with the set of new teeth; that snow white beard, and heavily bagged eyes flooded with pain. Was that the Renoir I once knew? At seventy-four, he looked a haggard ninety. A network of wrinkles moved from his brow, down his cheeks and meshed with his beard, and it appeared to me that he grew thinner as he spoke. But behind the rheumy eyes, there was still flashes of his zest for life. Something of my former lover came through. It was the spirit that shone.

And for some reason I hadn't expected to see Aline. It was unreasonable for me to have ignored the fact that he had a wife who had borne him three sons, yet when I saw her, it seemed a cold hand from the past touched my shoulder. I looked at her and remembered the time when Aline's arrival forced me to leave Renoir's home. How I had hated her then. I had shrugged it all off, had put my memories of our lovemaking out of my mind repeatedly, but Aline's presence now started it up, tearing open an old wound. Aline was my age, yet she looked dowdy and rather like a woman of seventy. Where was the bright haired, fresh cheeked young model who had defied me once for her place by his side? She had grown fat and shapeless with the years and her dress hung loosely about the low slung sagging breasts. And I had heard rumors that she was diabetic and had a short time to live. Was that really true? Aline, about twenty-one years younger than Renoir could precede him in death?

Then I looked back at Renoir. Had we really once been lovers? He looked at me now as though he remembered.

"My beautiful one," he smiled and turned to Gangnat. "I

painted her in my *Dance at Bougival*, and in *The Bathers*, and ..."

"I thought I posed for *Dance at Bougival*, Pierre," said Aline. "Didn't I pose for that one, *chéri?*"

She threw a blanket over his legs and kissed his forehead.

"No, my dear Aline, you just erased the face ... don't you remember?" I said sweetly. Renoir muttered something and let the subject rest. Aline put her hand in his and looked straight into my face with a glance that told all. This was her husband, all hers, this dear man, this great painter. He had been hers, as ill as he was, all through the years, and the look directed at me, cool, detached and confident of her position as his wife, was the same look she defied me with years before.

"Would you believe," Aline said, "that Pierre apologized to Monet for accepting the Legion of Honor, silly man," and she held his hand continually.

I sensed the closeness of the couple, and it made me long for André to return. All my sharp innuendoes had fallen harmlessly by the wayside. Theirs was a marriage of solidity graced with three high spirited sons, Jean, Claude, and Pierre. And Aline catered to her husband's every whim and nursed him like a child.

But my visit to Renoir left me with an emptiness, a loss of something past, and I felt a pang of longing suddenly for the bohemian life I once lived. Renoir was a magic symbol of my youth which had vanished.

Six months later I heard that Aline had died.

Several months after I returned from my visit with Renoir beloved Grand-mère, my brandy sodden mother, an eternally despairing, wizened figure in my paintings, helping, dressing, and consoling her Maumau ... joined Aline in death. She, who dried his childish tears and sang him Limousin lullabies, was gone. She sat in her rocker mending his socks, and her head fell back and she snored gently at first. When I returned to the room, my mother was quite still; the look on her face was tranquil and I knew. I didn't have to be told.

Maman understood about her Maumau, her darling grandson whom she had nurtured from birth; the Grand-mère who slept with him when he was young; a child sitting on her lap listening to her speak and ever fascinated by her droning voice. "Just speak, Grand-mère, just speak . . . I like to hear you speak." I can hear him now. Poor Maman . . . the only gift I could give her was not my art which my mother never understood, but my son, her Maumau, who was always perfect in Maman's eyes.

Maman was a veritable hag, gnarled, shriveled and lined, completely oblivious to her rotting teeth, her untidy hair and finally to time itself. I always remembered Maman as a plain looking woman, even in my youngest years, forever awaiting the fulfillment of a scenario where we would all be put out on the street disgraced and rejected.

This mother was indeed a drunk whom I frequently detested but always expected to be there in the shadows, just a fixture quarreling with me. Yet for all the years of her life, she lived only with me, as though she existed just to defend her Maumau against my quixotic nature. No matter what his drunken orgies were, no matter what his tirades became, she was always there, always shaking her head in disapproval of the general bohemian life of the artists in which she found herself; and through it all, she sipped her inevitable bottle of brandy while cursing her one time lover. This father whom I could only imagine, always lurked somewhere in Maman's mind, in her oaths, always killed by some horrible means.

I buried her in Saint-Ouen Cemetery in a new family plot and resolved I would not tell Maurice until he was released from Villejuif.

After my mother's burial, I sat still and then walked over to Maman's perennial rocker and sat in it trying to imagine what my mother had felt. I sat in it very still, for the rooms were deadly quiet; the clock chimed low. The stillness was deafening. Never had I felt so alone.

Somehow I resented my mother's death.

A mother just didn't die. No matter what you felt toward her she was solid and immortal, not an ephemeral being like all the rest. She was there to serve, to reprimand, to protect, not to die. A mother didn't die, particularly when she had a daughter, for although my relationship with my mother was strained, I was still a daughter, and that mysterious bond which connects mothers and daughters could never be broken. For the daughter was always an inch away in distance from the mother, and as time progressed and the daughter aged, she inevitably, as much as she might fight it . . . she inevitably became the mother even against her will, and the sins were perpetuated all over again. A tear splashed down my cheek, and then another. It was the first of tears shed. I had not cried at the burial, for the burial seemed too urgent a chore to me. After the next tear came, there were no others; it was the last of them and now what was left was only an emptiness.

With André away, and Maurice again at Villejuif, and now Maman dead, I felt an unbearable loneliness. I would have welcomed my mother's gloomy predictions. How I would have welcomed her voice, but there was the cursed deadly silence which answered me. And with the loss of Maman, the acute loss of my friends from the past hovered over me.

I was very much alone and in my desperation I remembered and reached out for one other I could turn to . . . César Gay. He would rescue my Maumau.

My Maumau? I found I used Maman's pet name for him more frequently since her death. Was I becoming Maman Madeleine?

And when Maurice was released, César Gay went to Villejuif and took him to the small room above his bistro, and there we told my poor Maumau about his grandmother's death. He sat in a trance for a moment, gave a little sob and then I took him home to his painting.

But when he slept, I covered him with my mother's hand sewn quilt, made for her Maumau with the muslin squares saved from countless sheaths of fabric she had stored from the time she was at Bessines. It held new meaning for me with her death. It seemed to me that this patchwork quilt was part of the fabric of our lives, with its silky bright thread; its patterns repeating randomly, desultory, one bright flowered motif here and then another there, dark and inky, and then the first reappearing later with a kind of shining unalterable resilience. It was our art, my son's and mine, which always reappeared unscathed; our art which coursed through the frightful phantasm of Maumau's commitments, ultimately standing up against the deep shadows of his illness, unblemished by the winds of change. While he slept, I smoothed the quilt's faded patches, all flowered with sad bits of my mother's dreams and pushed a lock of hair out of his eyes, kissed his brow, and forgave him. He murmured, "Grand-mère," in his sleep.

As the war dragged on, I painted without stopping and my style developed, and as always, my art was brutally truthful. In my paintings of women, I didn't coat, didn't soften, and my portraits, even of myself were usually unflattering ones. My portrait of Mauricia Coquiot, the wife of the art critic, was no exception. It commanded attention with an honest vigor. I never lessened her ample bosom, never slimmed her with deceptive shadows. The painting of *Madame Coquiot* went into Berthe Weill's first one woman show of my paintings. It was acclaimed by the critics, including Gustave Coquiot, the husband, who examined the expansive portrait of his wife with a jaundiced eye.

There were echoes of Gauguin in my paintings . . . his rich flat color surfaces clearly separated by black lines in the manner of stained glass. I felt Gauguin was a pioneer who freed line and color for me and others. His semi-oriental rhythms were reflected in my work. Both in his nature and art, he was my idol. He was a genius, and if I emulated his paintings, it was an unconscious act, for it was colored with my own striving for truth, my own *joie de vivre*.

I painted the *Sacré-Coeur* seen from the *Gardens of the rue Cortot* from my window. It had been a scene which I painted countless time and would paint time and time again; the colors were bright and clear and the opaque whiteness of the basilica stood clearly visible above the old rust tiled roofs and the lustrous greens of my leaves. The clarity of the azure sky offset with a fluff of white clouds, contrasted with my son's leaden gray blue skies and pale colors of his white period.

And with the exhibition of my painting, I received acclamation from various critics. I experienced a certain satisfaction in my work stemming from the fulfillment of recognition.

It was of course, a grande culmination of the years of struggle to achieve artistic expression, and the glorious fulfillment of recognition.

* * *

It was to Degas, still my mentor, that I brought my work once again, awaited his suggestions, listened to his complaints, related the gossip of artists which lessened his loneliness and still savored his friendship; a friendship now tinged with the sweet nostalgic echoes of a past shared. He helped me broaden my palette and crimson lake and ultramarine were lavishly used, as well as my turkey red, cobalt blue and several greens.

One morning I received an urgent note from Degas. His house at 37 rue Victor Massé was to be torn down and he was lost. He went looking for an old-fashioned home which was like the one he had lived in for twenty-five years. Zoë, his housekeeper was now old and ill and he released her. Everything had to be torn apart and removed including his enormous collection of paintings, yet he had not found a new place. I took charge of the proceedings and the search for another studio; it was no easy task. Degas refused to leave the Ninth Arrondissement. I kept at him and he finally relented and I found him a home at 6 Boulevard de Clichy, across the street from the Cirque Medrano. Durand-Ruel sent movers to transport his furniture and paintings. What a monumental job. I prayed that Degas would never move again.

But after he moved it seemed that Degas was always there, always in the background still orchestrating my art and if I sometimes forgot him, I would receive notes to remind me.

Tuesday

My she-devil, Maria
I stay in bed more than I get up. I am declining, my wicked Maria. I am declining and old . . . yet you don't care enough to visit me. Come next week and bring some of your wicked drawings so that I may put them up on my wall. I hope your son is well.
Degas

Friday

My Wild Maria
They tell me I am still delicate and must beware of cold on my left side. You must, in spite of the illness of your son, bring me some of your supple drawings.

Degas

By 1917, Degas visited me quite infrequently. He bemoaned the years I had been at Pierrefitte "with that rich clod" as he once called Paul, and considered that I certainly abandoned him with my new marriage to that "boy" André.

When I visited him now at 83, I found him almost blind and somewhat deaf. Of course he felt I never took his illnesses seriously, thinking him a hypochondriac. He hadn't changed much with the years. Even now, he was the same carping, acid tongued neurasthenic Degas, but the symptoms had become more extreme, more debilitating. The aging process had seized Degas in its wake. He had stopped cutting his hair and beard and had trouble with his bladder, having to urinate more frequently, several times during the night and sometimes this elegant artist whom I remember as being so dignified, left his fly open. He would surprise me with questions like, "How many times a night do you have to get up and piss?"

He still reviled the Jews and never forgave the government for exonerating and reinstating Dreyfus in 1906. He felt that it was all part of a Jewish twentieth century conspiracy, a sentiment, no doubt shared by the anti-Semitic *La Libre Parole*. Aside from this, he deeply resented the fact that he had to abandon drawing and painting and suddenly admitted that as a young man he had a dose of the clap. This revelation shocked me. His clothing was sloppy and *Mon Dieu*, how cheap with money he became. Yet one of his works commanded one of the highest sums paid to an artist in his lifetime and others sold to galleries and collectors for huge sums. Yet, he ignored it all and doled out only five francs a day for food for himself and a peasant girl who did the housework. He became restless and wandered the streets aimlessly for hours, or sat on omnibuses riding from one part of Paris to another. I had heard all sorts of tales of his wanderings. But I saw him sitting alone in his fifth floor studio with long white hair and white whiskers, reminiscing. I found my beloved mentor muttering incoherently to himself.

He was indeed an old man, unkempt with a snow white beard and hair, but with the same bitter ingredients that were familiar to me. And sometimes he made the trip to my studio.

I heard him shuffling up the narrow staircase one afternoon.

"Monsieur Degas, let me take your cane. How good to see you." In my mirror, a paint smudge shadowed my cheek and my smock was smeared with the greens of my palette.

"Don't give me that insincere greeting. I know you far too long, my deviltress, Maria. Where the devil have you been?" He gave it to me good and proper. He had stored it all up. "When did you last come to see me my terrible one? Let me see you worm out of that one with your clever tongue. When have you last brought me your paintings ... although God knows I hardly see anything with these eyes. I am so alone, Maria. I just sit alone in my rooms and think endlessly about the past and come to no conclusion. Do you care? No, you don't. I can answer for you." He was suddenly out of breath and paused, falling into one of the old wooden chairs with such force I became alarmed it might break. "And why the devil can't you buy a comfortable chair? My back is aching so. No one, not even you cares about me ... would you believe it, would you believe it if I said my friend, Pissarro came to see me?"

"Pissarro?"

"Yes, Pissarro. He must have had a change of heart. He heard I was sickly. I might forgive him for being what he is."

"And what is he?"

"Jewish. He's one of those."

"You haven't changed, always the same, Monsieur Degas.

"I do and say as I please. I have little in my life to look forward to but death."

"As long as I know you ... always whining and complaining, yet you look well."

"I have much to complain about. I grow more feeble and I cannot see or hear."

"You hear me now ... I can't believe you. And you see me

now. And you always look the same, no older."

Well?"

"Well, what?" I asked.

"News. What do you think I came for? News, what d'you say, eh? News feeds my poor soul which craves for some marvelous gossip from you. I didn't struggle here to just see your paintings, although you know, Maria, that you're the only woman I can tolerate now."

"Why didn't you come to see my group show with André and Maurice at the Bernheim-Jeune Gallery, or at Berthe Weill's last March? You certainly deserted me."

"I lay in bed with intestinal virus, but would you know? Of course not. You care for nobody but yourself and your precious Maumau, or whatever his name is, and that boy, André, you're living with."

"That boy André, just got wounded for his country."

"A fool. He had no business getting wounded."

I laughed. "You're a prize. What about Mary Cassatt? Doesn't she visit you?"

"An old woman . . . I hardly see her. She's virtually shut herself up in her damn château which is really a fortress and never visits anyone. Such a pity and such a talent. She holds the whole Dreyfus case against me . . . a Dreyfusard, clear and simple. Those damn Jews! I'll tell you that I won't walk into a Jewish owned shop or buy from Jews, and I just saved Vollard, from being fleeced by one."

"It's not because of the Jews that you don't see Cassatt. What have Jews got to do with it? A spinster is a spinster, *voilà*, and that's how it all ends for them, alone."

"For once, you might be right. It's all very depressing, Maria. Show me a painting . . . near the light." He walked to the window. He held up my painting of *Sacré-Coeur.*

"I don't care if you like it or not," I said observing his frown.

"It's good, it's good, my Maria, but you're painting landscapes now . . . why?"

"The next one will be a figure, are you happy now? Now I'll tell you a bit of gossip . . . now do you know that Maurice, André and I are called the unholy trinity? André is gone to the army and still their tongues wag."

"Don't tell me about your odd household, my Maria . . . a woman who lives with a husband over twenty years younger, and with a drunken son the age of her husband, certainly deserves to be talked about, what d'you say, eh?"

"Let them talk, the fools. How is Renoir doing?"

"It makes me ill. The way those young upstarts who call themselves artists, fawn over him in Cagnes, makes me ill."

"Oh don't be such an old grouch. He's sicker than you. He paints with a brush strapped to his hands. And the young artists would visit *you* in droves if you let them just to learn . . ."

"Who wants them poking their noses into my collection?"

"Oh, you would love it . . . the adulation. And what do you think of the new art?" I asked, changing the subject.

Degas growled. "*Sacrebleu!* There was a time that art was recognizable. That's not true anymore. All sorts of aberrations float about canvases in the name of art. This abomination, Rousseau, who passes for an artist is being exhibited illustrating the most infantile of delusions on a canvas . . . it makes me ill to speak of him . . . the ravings of an inmate of an asylum. And the art of today, this Cubism, Surrealism and any other derangement of the mind, is an insult to all we have attempted to do in art. I'll take one drawing by you, my illustrious Valadon to one hundred Cubist gyrations. At least you have something to say. It is a desecration of centuries of art . . . a scourge."

"Isn't this what they once said about Impressionism? I heard these words from Cormon, himself," I smiled.

"Impressionism? Don't mention Impressionism in the same breath as these wholesale distortions on canvas. Impressionism was a thing of beauty. And it's too bad that damn Renoir had to pretty up those damn women. I'll never forgive him for it but his pretty faces will be forgotten anyway with time. How long can the world digest them? Can't he make a woman plain if she is plain? Most of Paris is filled with plain women. And this Picasso fellow is a bona fide lunatic together with his colleague, Braque. Why must art be reduced to these terms? It's trick art, this cubism, trick art . . . a ruse of gigantic proportions."

"I think this cubism is very significant, and I think it will influence all movements to come. You can't ignore it."

"I can ignore it, I assure you, but of course you always say what you think," he said resignedly.

"By the way, did you see Monet's work at the last Durand-Ruel exhibit?"

"Do you know what I said to him? 'Let me get out of here! These reflections in the water hurt my eyes.' His pictures always were too draughty for me. Any worse and I would have come down with a terrible grippe."

"So you have made up with him?"

"I only did it for convenience. He's still a Dreyfusard. Let's speak of other matters before I become ill . . . about your son, of course he's driving you mad as usual so you can't paint? He needs a good flogging. If he were my son, he'd certainly get a sound flogging with my cane. He'd be cured immediately. There's no discipline in these times, no discipline . . . that's the trouble."

"Your theories of bringing up children are superb. I'm sure if you had one of your own, you would have pampered him terribly."

"Never!"

"Well, my Maurice has still turned out hundreds of canvases. He's a great painter."

"He's not as great as his mother . . . paints, I hear from postcards . . . why don't you stop him?"

"It doesn't matter. He'll surpass me anyway, and I don't care."

His voice softened. "My Maria, I've never thanked you for getting my house on the Boulevard de Clichy, but I've never been the same since they tore down my building in rue Victor Massé. To change the subject, let me tell you how terrible it is to be old. Oh, you'll get there one of these days, so don't be so smug about it. I'm going to die soon, a horrible thing to contemplate. I have so many drawings, pastels and paintings unfinished. Ach! My aches and pains run their little knives through my body".

"You'll live another twenty years. Only those who don't complain die young."

"Your philosophy is indeed unique, Maria and a bit comforting. Give me a painting before I leave and I will study it on my wall . . . and I'll send you what I think it's worth. But don't expect too much. It's sad, my Maria that everyone I once knew is gone and only the new upstarts are here. Only Renoir is left, and in what shape is he? What happened to the Impressionist movement? It disappeared down the toilet. Bah! It's all the damn critics' fault, anyway." He rose to leave. I walked with him to the door. "No, don't come with me, my little Maria. I will struggle downstairs alone. Life, anyway, is a dismal struggle and I'm used to it. *Au revoir,* my deviltress." I ran to my easel, and placed a painting into a giant portfolio which he put under his arm.

"And don't forget your cane, Monsieur," and I held up a gift from Gauguin, a carved cane from Tahiti. I kissed him on the cheek. "Good-by and God take care of you, as you have watched over me. *Au revoir,* and I love you in spite of your evil tongue. I'll come visit you soon," I said softly and felt a sudden sinking feeling as he shook his head.

"You'll never visit me as you promise and you'll never answer my letters; not for almost thirty years have you answered my letters, not one. I know you, Maria, I know you ... but, what can one do? You're a she-devil who was never tamed." He shrugged his shoulders and hobbled down the narrow, winding stairs, stopping at each step poking with his cane, muttering constantly. He was a crusty old man, a complaining, moody, despondent, bigoted, old man with a sharp biting tongue, but I loved him, how I loved him. With all his complaining, hypochondria, sulking, and suspicion of anything smacking of a modern movement, a paradox to his own art which had been ahead of its time; for all this, he was the father I never had.

"I'll visit soon, Monsieur Degas," I called out the window.

He paused for a moment, waved me off with his cane and boarded an omnibus.

I suddenly experienced an awful premonition followed by a feeling of intense loss.

* * *

Most of the Cubists were in the army by 1917. Braque was wounded and released as an invalid; but in the spring Picasso went to Italy and then Spain. There, he presented a work to the

Barcelona Museum. He escaped the war. And on May 1, my André was wounded in the shoulder.

I left for Belleville sur Saône near Lyons, and our reunion was idyllic for we were carefree and alone. It was as though we had begun our relationship anew, this time free from the horrors of Maurice's alcoholism and the hectic life of the Butte. I wore a naive rose and white striped cotton day dress with a piping of plain gingham, and pearl buttons running down the front. My low chignon peeked from behind a flat brimmed hat trimmed with bright feathers. I felt young, as youthful as a girl of eighteen; and the Lyonnais pastoral setting became a part of our joy in one another. We painted together and walked together, and in the evening we made love in a small room in a country inn. It was a reunion filled with magic.

"My beautiful, beautiful André," I whispered repeatedly to my thirty-one year old husband, and the night was filled with his nearness and the rapture of his body as though this was the first time we made love.

"Suzanne . . . my beautiful little gamine . . . I told you I will love you forever," he whispered over and over again as we clung to one another, and the years melted into the eternity of time, and then it ended abruptly, too quickly . . . it seemed but a moment . . . and he was gone.

And when he left I noticed the shadows of age in my glass, the hallmarks of time.

Part Three
(1917-1938)

"... everything under her brush comes to life, breathing and pulsing; this extraordinary woman is passion herself and one seeks in vain for someone to compare her with..."
André Tabarant, art critic - L'Oeuvre

17

Degas

Bitter Exit

*E*nding it all, I died . . . my thinking of that ungrateful little one, Maria, my wild Maria who never visits me; and that irritating pro-Dreyfusard, Cassatt, my disciple, who appears to have vanished; amidst my sorting out a whole series of my wax and clay figures; amidst some unfinished pastels and drawings and several paintings once begun but still stacked with their paint dried; amidst it all . . . I died.

It was a shock to everyone . . . everyone except myself. With all my ills, I was frankly tired.

I died on September 26, 1917 of what the damn doctors who never believed me, called cerebral congestion, whatever that is. I died in an austere bed in an austere room whose only adornment was part of my collection of art on the walls. Above my bed were drawings by Ingres, two small Corots of Italian scenes, a sketch by my Maria, and two masterpieces by Manet.

At my death my art collection was recorded, and it was larger than anything I had ever conceived of. In fact, I venture to say it boggled the mind. There were Daumier prints, eighteen hundred lithographs, etchings by Manet and Millet, woodcuts by Gauguin, drypoints by Morisot, works by Pissarro and Whistler, eight Gauguin paintings and others by Van Gogh, Cézanne,

Bartholomé, Lautrec, Cassatt, Daumier, Morisot, Puvis de Chavannes, Renoir, Rousseau, Sisley and of course, Valadon. I had thought of a donation to the Louvre, or of creating a museum of my own but I couldn't do it. The thought of anyone touching my precious work with gauche fingers, exposing the art to faulty temperatures, filled me with terrible anxiety. I knew what untalented oafs abounded in the art world, particularly the self-styled art critics. So I safely kept my art work, but at the end my painting suffered as the darkness of blindness closed in about me. I turned to sculpture as an outlet.

My wild Maria was my last disciple. It was the end of an association with her which had begun in 1887 when she stood before me and watched me take each drawing from her portfolio, and I remember saying, "Yes, you are indeed one of us." I felt it was quite a significant thing to say and I watched her face glow as I said it. She was a talent, my Maria, a talent to be sure. But she was an ungrateful one and for that I visited her little.

I was buried in the brilliant sunshine, in the midst of a war which concerned me little, in the Degas family vault in the Montmartre Cemetery.

Several weeks later Rodin died, a fitting postscript to my passing, and my world being destroyed by aberrations the artists sickly called new movements. What artistic chaos. There is some consolation in not being around to witness this terrible upheaval. Mercifully I won't have to deal with it. Everything has gone, everything. They call themselves artists, but I have serious doubts that the whole lot of them can paint.

The terrible thing that I have dreaded all my life is about to happen. The auctioneers will undoubtedly get their filthy hands on my work. Every dilettante who ever bought anything will profit. Every piece of art will be destroyed. My pastels will be ruined and my paintings exposed to the most extremes of temperatures and the canvases will curl and crack in protest. Because I have no heirs to salvage what I have done, and even Zoë is dead, it won't take long . . . it won't take long.

And after the last of my precious work disintegrates, the world will never hear of me again.

18

Maurice

Finding Poor Modi

On Christmas Day I escaped from goddamn Picpus before all my paintings were robbed. I was committed here because the psychiatrists claimed I was in a depressive state. I was drunk, that's all. Couldn't they tell when a man was drunk? It was the drunken binge that made me hurl insults at the pregnant women, so what. What an imbecile that doctor was and I can tell you that I had to get out of this place.

Why shouldn't I have celebrated my birthday in freedom, and so I escaped and headed for Montparnasse. On Christmas Day I found Modigliani at Rosalie's, and we resumed our friendship immediately. It certainly was marvelous to see him again.

Of course Modi had left the Butte for Montparnasse with that arrogant bastard Picasso leading the way. He was happy there because he found a group of Jewish painters like himself. The anti-Semitism following the Dreyfus case was pretty terrible but Modi found a haven there in Pascin, Kisling, and Chaim Soutine, all immigrant artists living in La Ruche. The Polish poet, Leopold Zborowski became his friend, even went into debt to buy him paints, and handled his paintings as an art dealer. I was very happy for Modi, but I missed him in Montmartre.

Rosalie's restaurant in the Rue Compagne-Premier was known

for her generous feeding of starving artists. Modi and I embraced one another warmly and we talked excitedly. He babbled endlessly about his life and friends, never stopping. I listened the way I always had as Modi still spoke of *"Cara cara Italia."* And he spoke of returning to Montmartre with me to see Maman, his "little mother," and laugh as though the years never passed.

"But first we will drink and drink and drink," laughed Modi, but I felt it was a forced laughter of long suffering and defeat. He described Jeanne Hébuterne, an art student who gave him a daughter, and I told him of my sale of a painting for 1580 francs.

"But how can I be rich like you, tell me. Would it help to die first, and then be famous like Cézanne and Van Gogh? Would you really care, Maumau, if I died? You see everyone sitting there? They wouldn't give a shit! I'd be one less artist."

"My dear, dear friend," I cried. "I care . . . and each time you cough, I hurt inside. You'll do pictures and I'll sign my name, and you'll make money. I fixed up some of Caesar Gay's pictures and he's making money. I'll paint Modigliani's . . . the long necks and almond eyes and egg shaped heads . . . I will by God, I will, and sign my name and they'll all sell, *voilà.*"

"And the forgeries will take over like cockroaches and the damn critics will choke on their damn ignorance as they praise the fakes and condemn the originals . . . they can't tell the difference between a Utrillo and a *pissoir.*" Modi banged on the table.

"By God, that's a great one! A Utrillo and a *pissoir.* You're a genius, Modi," I laughed slapping my friend on the back.

Rosalie Tobia, a short, plump, dark haired full bosomed Italian with a prominent nose, came to the table and threw up her hands. "Still a handsome devil but you have no money, Modi. You stink from absinthe and have probably fucked every woman in Montparnasse. But I'll be kind to you because it's Christmas."

"Christmas? What do I care, I'm a Jew, remember? But anyway you owe us a Christmas dinner."

"I owe *you!*" *she* screamed. "I owe you nothing. You're nothing but a bum . . . and I know this bum, too. He's Litrillo."

"Utrillo and he's a great artist. Rosalie . . . you with the sweetest cunt in . . ."

"Shut your foul mouth," she cut in.

"You don't realize that you have the great talents of two great artists to paint a mural on your ugly bare wall . . . but first, that dinner, but I heard that the rats ate half your cheese."

Modi squeezed her buttocks and thighs and searched into her bloomers.

"Get your filthy hands off me and your fingers out of my privates, you devil . . . can't you get enough women to satisfy you? Do you know I'm over sixty? Ach! To think that I used to be a model and that Bougereau, there was a painter and he did beautiful paintings of me. Look what I have now . . . a hole in the wall with 4 tables, 24 chairs and big spoons for your soup. Alright, go ahead and scribble first, but you're not going to worm out of this one . . . and if I don't like the painting I'll throw you both out and you'll get nothing to put into those empty stomachs. And I don't like your friend Litrillo. He looks like a thief to me."

"It's his birthday and you're so cruel," Modi said nodding in my direction.

"You're friend is a lunatic and a drunk and he's still got his prison clothes on . . . you can't fool me. But I can tell you I only serve people I like and I don't like this Litrillo. That's too bad for him. When I decide to like him I'll give him a big bowl of soup. Everyone loves my soup. Get on with your smearing."

Modi descended unsteadily to the basement and carried up his paintboxes, a packet of brushes and several tubes of pigment.

"You paint the buildings of Montmartre, Maumau, and I'll paint the figures. It'll be a phenomenal mural." We began and we fought over the mural like children until Rosalie threw up her hands.

"Who cares? You both give me *agita!* You can't even get together on it. I've had enough of you. It's a miserable mural and I'm throwing you both out. But first, take this rag and erase my wall."

"We both refuse to deface such greatness don't we Maumau?" Modi pulled me out of the restaurant, into the bitter cold and into his room, smeared with paint and discarded canvases; he became high on cocaine and I, in my drunken stupor vomited on a pile of rotting bedclothes. I finally returned home bareheaded without my coat, wearing only my shirt and hospital trousers. Maman saw me, a bedraggled figure at the door dragging my easel, shivering with cold, and said nothing, her lips firm and face grim. She got me undressed and into bed, wrapped me in blankets and poured hot drinks down my throat.

"What are you doing to yourself?" she asked wearily as I opened my eyes that day after Christmas. "More to the point, do you know what you're doing to me? When Picpus notified me, I ran through every street looking for you. Where were you . . . certainly not in Montmartre."

"I was with Modi."

"Modi, you found Modi? Of course, in Montparnasse. I should have known. Did he at least take you to some women? Is he whoring around as usual? What did you think you were doing, running out of Picpus? How long before they find you . . . how long?"

She sat at the edge of my bed, and her appearance shocked me. I saw my beautiful Maman bedraggled, her hair wild and heavy shadows under her eyes. Even her clothes looked like they had been slept in. Where was my beautiful Maman? Was I responsible?"

"What happened?" she asked shaking me.

I became afraid to answer.

"Answer me, dammit!"

"I—I—they stole my . . . I was celebrating . . ."

"What the devil were you celebrating?"

"My . . . my . . . birthday and . . ." My God, I don't have to apologize to her, I cursed inwardly.

"So you escaped . . . with your easel . . . and I have to suffer for your birthday? Well lie down and sleep. Nothing can be done now."

"Yes," I said low and closed my eyes and grew very weary. And suddenly I felt the touch of her lips on my brow and I felt safe.

19

Suzanne

The Winds Of Change

Degas rarely left my thoughts and it was a turning point as though a part of me had died. At his funeral, among others, were Bartholomé, Cassatt, Vollard, and Daniel and Louise Halévy, both Jewish, who had overlooked Degas' antisemitism after the Dreyfus affair. Bartholomé was deeply affected. Renoir was too ill to attend; he remained at home in Cagnes strapped to his wheelchair, painting his goddamn pretty women, no doubt.

When the funeral was over, I glanced at Mary Cassatt for a moment, and our eyes met significantly and I was startled by Cassatt's changed appearance. Before me was a somewhat blinded, stooped, seventy-three year old woman with an air of reclusiveness about her. She smiled briefly at me and took my hand. I embraced the bent artist who seemed to shrivel before my very eyes.

"You must visit me at rue Cortot," I said. "I should like to show you my own and my son's work."

Cassatt didn't answer.

When the Armistice was signed, André returned and I attempted to intensify the flame which burned so fiercely during our sojourn in Belleville. But rue Cortot was not a pastoral idyll.

A group of writers lived on the ground floor, and neighbors such as Braque, Derain, and Nora Kars, now my close friend, would drop in unannounced. Our studio became the focal point for bohemian life in Montmartre. It was always open house at the studio, hectic with laughing and drinking, and often I would spread a cloth on the floor of the studio and my many visitors would have a picnic. I could paint with a whole host of guests passing through. Entertaining was as natural to me as breathing. I made informality a creed and everyone felt free to come and go at all hours of the day or night. I suspected that I had become a legend in Montmartre.

At 54, I held on fast to my waning beauty and my full voluptuous figure, and tried to project being younger than my actual years. I tried every extreme measure when I sensed that my relationship with André had soured but I couldn't hold back the storm. He spent wildly and so I held the purse strings, doling out money to him from a tiny bag sewn into my skirt. I went on tirades, my success only giving fuel to the discrepancies in our relationship. I carped at him and regretted it, criticized his pipe smoking and regretted it, drowned him out in any conversation with friends and regretted it. And I had a terror of losing him, for André, now thirty-three was in his prime. He appealed to women with his good looks and outgoing manner, and I was aging. Age was all consuming. It affected not only the body but the mind. Perceptions and attitudes toward life were altered insidiously and one was not really aware for it occurred so gradually, like a light breeze whispering its message softly and obliging the body to obey . . . gently . . . gently.

In December of 1919, Renoir died in Cagnes. I had terribly mixed feelings. Had we really strolled between the chestnut trees which lined the Boulevards in the spring? Had I modeled for him and made love to him in a garden behind the rue Cortot? Dear, dashing, handsome Renoir. How gnarled those delicate hands were when I saw him last. How crippled the arthritis made him, and how he had changed. I thought of Aline and her devotion, sitting with her hand in his, this once fresh faced model who had usurped my place and died unexpectedly before he did. What did it really matter? Renoir was the last of those I sat with at la Nouvelle-Athènes; Cézanne, Van Gogh, Lautrec, Degas, Gauguin and now Renoir, all gone, fading into a mist.

And that afternoon, almost as a solace for an era now gone I turned to Maurice. I caught that evanescent moment when he seemed at peace with himself, a time so fleeting, so difficult to capture and I posed him at his easel and called the work, *Maurice Utrillo Painting*. I painted him with his crushed brown felt hat, a thirty-five year old Maumau intent on what he was painting. My affection for him mixed with my pigments for this was my real son, the calm one, the one I should have had, the one he really was beneath the dreadful alcoholic miasma which cloaked him. He painted with an intense, passionate, familiar look, with the deep furrow between his brows. "Miguel," I whispered. It was Miguel of years before come to life.

And December passed and the new year rolled into Paris that 1920 with a terrible blizzard and Modi, dear, dear Modi returned. *Mon Dieu*, was it for the last time? The snow piled up in drifts, and mounds lined the boulevards glinting with a bright cold sun and streaked gray with urban soot; the wheels of the automobiles crunched trails in the snow bravely announcing their presence.

He returned and I heard his awful consumptive cough break through the icy stillness as Modi burst into the studio dragging huge oils under his arms. "So unexpected, Modi. *Comment ça va?*" He shook the snow from his coat. "*Mon pauvre Modi*, why are you out on a day like this? Look at you. Good God, look at you." His haggard fatigued appearance, his green skin, the dark shadows under his eyes and loss of weight stunned me. Of course his years of drink, whoring, dissipation and drugs would have taken their toll. What did I expect? I was heartbroken. At 35, he looked almost 50.

He put his paintings down and I could see that they were all very mannered with the almond eyes and elongated necks, but I could also discern that his work had matured in recent years. "These *are* your best works, Modi. Who is this?" I looked at a painting of a young woman who had an innocence and helplessness about her. She seemed almost not of this world.

"It's Jeanne Hébuterne. I have a little one with her and she's having another." Jeanne was painted in shades of browns and blues with distant brilliant blue almond eyes and red-brown hair. Her thick yellow sweater clothed a graceful slim body. Her elongated figure with its characteristic attenuated neck couldn't hide some personal beauty.

"You did the painting of her with affection. You love her."

"At times. I've done many paintings of her."

"Oh, you wicked one, how did you meet her?"

"She was a student at the Colarisse Art Academy, but she clings to me. If I die, she'll be nothing . . . there's a weakness."

"Modi, you've been talking about dying for years."

"Look what's happening to me, little mother," and he suffered another spasm of coughing which slowly reddened a handkerchief held to his lips. *Dieu*, I was afraid to look. There was a crust of fluid at the corner of his mouth and his frayed collar with old stains of dried blood turned my stomach.

"Oh my poor Modi . . . you need a doctor."

"Don't trouble yourself, little mother . . . only my tuberculosis . . . only that," and he sank into a divan and placed the paintings at his side, with a face ashen and shaking. "I'm in trouble."

"Of course. You're killing yourself with cocaine and ether."

"I keep myself going that way."

"Come, *mon vieux*, I'll make you some *café au lait*." Modi dragged himself into the large kitchen with its blue and white checkered table cloth, and white pine open shelves. Long shutters of white pine at the windows opened to a view of the gardens cloaked with a mantle of snow blowing about in bitter gusts. I heated the water atop an ancient coal stove. "These are Adèle's croissants, the best of course in Paris."

He sipped slowly, munched on the pastry and then pushed it all away. "I can't sell! Perhaps I'm a fraud . . . tell me that I'll sell, tell me little mother, tell me."

"You'll sell and I'm sending you to a doctor friend; you need medicine, and don't worry, I'll pay for it.

"You can't save me, little mother, it's too late."

"Modi! Don't!"

"Because I know. I know it's about to happen . . . it's too late." He coughed again. A peculiar rosy glow spread over his skin.

I bent over him and put a hand on his brow. "You're feverish, *cher* Modi. I'm going to put you to bed. Stay here for a few days. Maumau would love it."

"Why am I so frightened, little mother . . . you're always so good for me, tell me . . . I know it's death. I feel death coming."

"Ridiculous, you're only thirty-five. You're not going to die."

"I am, little mother, I am."

"And I won't let you." I embraced him. "Come, you can watch me paint, like in the old days," and Modi sat at my feet again as before, an older Modi, eaten up with drugs and alcohol, still carousing and dying of consumption, still wearing his rumpled corduroys and battered hat . . . my poor Modi, still fighting the battle of the individualist, and still losing the battle.

I looked down from my easel. "My dear, dear Modi," I whispered, and when André and Maurice entered late that afternoon, Modi was still sitting at my feet. Maurice greeted his friend and never left his side.

And then slowly and barely audible and gradually rising in volume, with a tremulous melodious voice, Modi sang, but instead of a song from Italy, an odd song, rather a wail emanated from his throat and filled the quiet room.

"What is that?" I asked.

"It's the *Kaddish*, a Jewish lamentation for the dead, because there's only one tragedy in my life," he said, "and it's not that I'm dying . . . but that I haven't been recognized for what I am, a good painter . . . it's not fair." He turned to me and put his head on my shoulder.

His words came back to haunt me repeatedly, as did his still handsome figure and beautiful face which melted into the twilight that afternoon as he left.

About ten days later, Modi had terrible kidney pains and went to bed. Leopold Zborowski paid a visit and told me that Jeanne Hébuterne sat watching Modi in an ice cold studio on a bitter day that January, her belly huge in the ninth month of her pregnancy. Jeanne kissed Modi's face and closed eyes over and over again and then sat helpless and did nothing, nothing. Finally, a physician came and examined him. "He has tubercular meningitis," he said to Zborowski who carried him downstairs and to the pauper's Hospital of Charity where he died on Saturday evening, January 24th.

"He died with the words, *Cara, cara Italia,* on his lips," Zborowski said wiping his eyes. "He died from tuberculosis, carousing in the cold and rain and those damn drugs."

"He died from heartbreak," I said. "That was the real cause."

"And then . . ." said Zborowski, wiping his eyes again, "Jeanne Hébuterne was acting so peculiarly . . . so strangely that her parents took her home and sent her brother to sit up with her. My God, he fell asleep and she tiptoed out of the room and threw herself out of a fifth story window. Who could have stopped her? She was only twenty-one, that one . . . the baby died with her, and some say it was a pact."

All I thought of was the painting Modi had done of her with such love.

From Rome, his brother Emanuel telegraphed, "Give him the funeral of a prince."

And that it was . . . the funeral of a prince.

What recognition Modigliani had not received in life, he got in death. The procession passed slowly through the streets of Montmartre to which he first came in 1906, out toward the Père Lachaise Cemetery. Policemen who had arrested him for disorderly conduct tipped their hats to his coffin. Carriages filled with flowers lined the streets. Artists came out from the studios of Montmartre and Montparnasse, from all the little bistros where they traded their paintings for food; from all the little rooms where they lived and died.

A rabbi said prayers at his grave.

Only one very good friend was missing from the services, Maumau. He had become too drunk to attend. He sat in his studio in rue Cortot muttering to himself and staring out of the window in remembrance of something lost, his dearest friend. He had the same expression on his face as when told that his Grand-mère had died.

But what happened afterwards was a phenomenon. Every artist in Montmartre was flabbergasted. And for Modi, who could never sell his work, it was a bitter victory in death. Almost immediately, the price of his paintings soared. When the rumor spread of his death, wily Libaude dashed about Paris buying up all the Modiglianis he could lay his slimy hands on, and the news was that he celebrated the death of Modi with the finest of wines. He made a huge profit. The dealers and the tourists who collected art couldn't buy enough of him. Modigliani became a legend. The dealers began to forge his signature on paintings he had left unsigned. Rosalie screamed and ranted because of the work destroyed by rats in her basement. There was comment that the prices of his work would reach fifty thousand francs in ten years, an increase unparalleled in the history of painting.

"Poor Modi," I said over and over again. "Poor Modi. He had never lived to see this success." It became a constant refrain.

Modi was indeed buried like a prince in the Père Lachaise cemetery, but Jeanne Hébuterne was buried a suicide, without a priest by a stern father in the dismal burial ground at Bagneux in the suburbs, *voilà*. A while later Modigliani's grave was reopened and Jeanne Hébuterne was put to rest beside him.

After the death of his friend, Maurice went on a rampage, and by July he was confined by the courts to Picpus once again where he remained through the summer.

* * *

After the Armistice, Paris was deluged with all sorts of collectors deeming themselves experts. The layman threw around terms like Impressionist and Cubist without the slightest notion of the movements. They converged on Paris in droves. It was now chic to collect art and the collectors heard of the rue Lafitte which was the street for great bargains. Prices soared. Utrillos that had sold for one hundred francs before the war, now sold for one thousand. And bogus artists flourished. Hundreds of cubist paintings were passed off as Picasso's, and large sums were extracted from gullible tourists who would never pass that way again. Hundreds of painters signed Utrillo's name to the most primitive paintings of streets; and works of Cézanne, Van Gogh and Modigliani, were copied eagerly and passed off as authentic to the tourists; they commanded higher sums than the original artists had ever seen in a whole lifetime.

And in the endless hunt for bargains, two such bargain hunters knocked at our studio door one afternoon. It was a Belgian banker, a Monsieur Pauwels, and his wife *Lucie*.

Their casual visit was to change all our lives forever.

Lucie Pauwels sailed into our studio wafting an expensive cologne into every room. Maurice must have smelled it for he shyly entered the huge studio and sat down on a wooden chair in a characteristic pose, his head in his hand. Lucie wore a hat with tall ostrich plumes. She wore it with magnificent panache, and she shook it vehemently to emphasize her words.

"Oh, my dear Madame Utter," said the woman, "I want you to meet my husband, Monsieur Pauwels, the Belgian banker. Surely, you must have heard of him . . . he's so well known."

"Of course I would have heard of him . . . " I said with tongue in cheek. "He is well known in every studio in Montmartre."

"Oh, my dear . . . I knew you had heard of him. But I must stop for a moment." The woman was breathing heavily with a bosom adorned with the most expansive assortment of crystal beads I had ever seen.

"Do sit down, Madame Pauwels."

"Call me Lucie, my dear. As I was saying, *mon cher mari* and I have been running up and down Montmartre to find you. My husband is a great collector, but then you know that."

"Of course," I smiled fascinated by her brashness.

"But wait, I'll give you my coat." She removed a fox lined coat of turquoise blue and draped it over the arm of our new servant, Lily Walton, whose eyes disapproved. Lucie exposed a very stylish silk taffeta with a voluminous skirt; her fragrance a mixture of violets and jasmine unleashed itself again on the studio. Maurice seemed hypnotized by the rustle of her dress as she moved about, swaying from side to side. She rapidly examined one painting after another. Then she opened her purse with fingers covered with huge rings of every size and shape, and a massive cocktail ring of diamonds and rubies flashed on her little finger. A host of diamond studded bangles adorned her wrists with circles of glitter. She carefully spread a lace edged handkerchief saturated with the jasmine scent, before sitting.

I was mesmerized.

"To come to the point, my dear husband and I want to purchase some of your paintings and of course those of your dear son. We are both marvelous collectors." She fanned herself.

Her husband said nothing but sat listening to his wife.

"Are you really a collector, Monsieur Pauwels?" I asked.

He nodded and seemed to fall asleep.

"My dear, don't even ask him . . . he is so modest. He collects fine horses, flowers, birds and we have quite a few Utrillos. And to think that you are an artist as well. It's too much to ask for . . . well, you're so fortunate to have such a handsome son," she tittered as Maurice glowed. "We have no children, but as is commonly known, I'm a woman of the theatre."

"Well, I could see that you must be talented." I stifled a desire to laugh.

"Oh, yes, a woman of the theatre whom my dearest one rescued, *mon mari*." She smiled at him but he barely saw her through half closed lids. "I deserted the stage for a marriage of real distinction. It's an honor to be married to a famous man like my love. I could not do otherwise my dear," and she moved closer to me. She put one arm around my shoulder. "We must become the closest friends and I want to be a real part of your life. You must call on me if ever there is something you need."

"But you scarcely know me," I said.

"I have infallible judgment about people. Well, I already see three paintings I would like to own. You'll find me very observant and quick to make decisions, and my taste is very cultivated. Monsieur Pauwels will discuss the financial end."

She rose, a woman of about fifty, buxom, with a dramatic flair. Eternally on stage, she was ever preening, her voice ever rising and falling. She glided with a flourish and kissed Maurice on the cheek as he sat watching her enraptured. "And you're the great Maurice Utrillo all Paris is talking about."

"Am I?" He seemed in a trance.

She bent over her husband who was still sleeping and handed him his gold tipped cane. "Dear heart, you must open your eyes now. It's time to go."

He snapped his eyes open as if on command. Amazing!

"And dearest one, do make the proper arrangements for these paintings." He obeyed her instruction.

Lucie Pauwels chose two of my florals and *Le Lapin Agile* by Maurice in an easy sale. "By all means, come again," I said.

"Well . . . it's time to go, dear heart," she turned to her husband, "and let these marvelous artists work. I will definitely call on you again. Call me Lucie and I shall call you, Suzanne. And someday, I shall paint and be one of your precious artists."

"That would be marvelous," I said anxious for her to leave.

"*Au revoir*, dear artists, my new found friends," Lucie bubbled and left a trail of jasmine scent behind her.

"*Merde*, she postures like a peacock."

"I liked her," said Maurice.

"Well, you certainly have a great deal to learn about women."

"I really liked her, Maman."

His expression completely baffled and distressed me.

As the months passed, André couldn't seem to reestablish himself as an artist. His years in the army had taken their toll and he began to drink and shouted loudly denouncing all his enemies. But how could I blame him? To create and not be recognized was a terrible frustration; this agony of Van Gogh and poor Modi and how many others?

"I can't stand my life anymore, Suzanne, and don't you realize how much you've changed toward me? You and Maurice are the ones who are important and I am nothing, nothing . . . I can't sell and you know it."

"George Coquiot wrote that you reminded him of Van Gogh."

"Small consolation. I'll be like poor Vincent and never sell a painting in my lifetime. Damn! I'll paint what I want."

"It'll come to you like it came to the others . . . Lautrec and Renoir and Degas."

"Or perhaps when I'm dead like poor Modi and Vincent. Those

pigs only buy you when you're dead, like vultures over a corpse. I want success now, damn them! I want success."

I embraced him. "I love you André . . . and your success doesn't matter to me. I know I'm difficult sometimes, but you know I'll always love you." I perched myself on his lap and leaned against his cheek. "Let's go away again, André. Let's go away. You'll see . . . everything will be fine again between us . . . we'll paint together and it'll be as it once was, you'll see."

"You think so? My dearest Suzanne . . . my petite lovely elf."

He held me to him and then began unbuttoning the bodice of my blouse. I noticed as I looked down that when he bent and lifted and kissed each breast in turn, they no longer stood outright but had begun to sag. I pulled away and leaned against him, taking his hands in mine.

Although André's paintings still didn't sell, he wasn't crushed for long. He never thought highly of Maurice's artistic talent, but he knew that Maurice's paintings sold. Something formed in his mind and he began to veer toward the business concerns of the family. He painted less, and he said to Francis Carco, "Maurice Utrillo is the prettiest piece of business to appear in half a century," and he proceeded to collect *Utrillos*. He roamed all over Paris, to the little bistros where Maurice exchanged paintings for glasses of wine, and to restaurants that exchanged food for paintings. He inquired at Rosalie's and found what he already knew. Most of her paintings in the basement, priceless paintings by Modigliani, Utrillo and a wealth of Impressionists were eaten by rats. Maurice had done at least twelve hundred canvases during the war years, in and out of institutions. André had only to separate some of the frauds done by Gay, from the others, and by selling ten of his own paintings to purchase one Utrillo, he slowly built up a huge collection. I felt quite thrilled.

But my success as an artist continued. I was elected as the secretary of the Salon d'Automne where I had been exhibiting since 1909, and I was reelected as an associate of the *Société des Artistes Indépendants*, a great honor. My success inflated my ego, a fact that was difficult for André, to live with.

By 1921, André in his new role as businessman, arranged a group exhibition at Berthe Weil and success was sweet to me. It was a delicious feeling that I had not anticipated until the most exhilarating of emotions took hold and it made all other injustices suffered ultimately fade; it was far simpler to be generous to one's enemies for one could afford to be. Yet, what cold revenge it was to have Druet clamor for my son's pictures for his gallery.

In December I had a solo show at the International Exhibition of Modern Art in Geneva. I sent huge canvases, *The Casting of the Net*, and *Adam and Eve*, testaments to my early love for André.

The critic André Tabarant writing in *L'Oeuvre*,

" . . . *everything under her brush comes to life, breathing and pulsing, this extraordinary woman is passion herself and one seeks in vain for someone to compare her with . . .* "

The following year I painted my servant, Lily Walton. She had come to me from London and proved an excellent cook, far more outspoken than Catherine at Pierrefitte, and had an imperiousness about her which one caught immediately. I posed Lily in a chair beside a chest of drawers, and in her lap sat my cat, Raminou, in feline arrogance. I caught the essence of Lily, her intrinsic authority, the uncompromising Lily who claimed to have been a nursemaid and governess to a duchess in London. I depicted an Englishwoman of considerable abilities, quiet, humorless, capable, in her sensible shoes and discerning clear gaze.

When I finished I leaned back and scrutinized the work with a feeling of elation. Nothing I could feel was akin to it.

* * *

It was an inescapable fact that Maurice's alcoholism had reached a turning point for both of us. It seemed I relived the same nightmare over and over again, he always hovering in a shadow, his drinking making a blurred debilitating pattern of entrances and exits to hospitals and sanitariums with every new season. And the seasons turned into years . . . the momentum ever quickening, ever enveloping with its horror. And I repeated my cries, entreating him, beseeching him, an unending pattern. "Maumau . . . stop drinking, *merde*, let me paint in peace."

And Maurice would start to paint again, and then another incident, worse, much worse . . . and I would try again with an unreasoning blind optimism, a churning, unearthly force which propelled me forward, surprising even myself, dismissing his lunacies and his excesses, so that all I saw and felt was his talent. He rebelled and I rebelled as well. I was determined to keep him viable, painting . . . I picked up the paints, one by one as he threw them out the window, and I threw them back at him.

"You will paint, Maumau. No matter how many times you throw them out the window, it will do no good . . . I will get them again and return them . . . you will paint, Maumau, you *will*, for this is what I have taught you to do, this is what you have the genius to do, and this is what you must do!"

My insistent cry took hold, *"Paint, Maumau, paint, paint!"*

Finally, he picked up his brushes, and as before . . . many times before, starting over and over again . . . he began a canvas. And it didn't matter to me that his colors were suddenly different, strangely brighter, and it didn't matter that his paintings were maddening in their precision; that he used a ruler and a trisquare as though doing an architectural drawing and that postcards were clipped to his easel. I just wanted him to go on painting. Nothing else mattered. For in the end he always succumbed to some magnetic pull in my personality, my insistence and his idolatry of his mother. I had only to command, and ultimately he must of necessity obey. Here in No. 12 rue Cortot, I had become his jailer. Here he stayed confined again with the male nurse, Pierre, in a room with bars on the windows.

I turned to André for support but André seemed oblivious now to Maurice's alcoholism; and he had less respect for him as an artist. André continued to dress like a dandy and wore the most awful clothes, patent leather shoes, white spats, striped trousers and a boater. Was this the André who swept me off my feet? He drank more and more, dining in expensive cafés, and I heard rumors circulating of his mistress, Eveline. But I decided to shrug it all off, the terrors of an alcoholic son and the vagaries of a straying husband, and revel in my artistic success.

I drowned my problems with furs, tea gowns and Russian style clothes which were all terribly chic. I bought caviar for my cats and filet mignon for my dogs. I was driven about Paris in a shining Panhard equipped with a chauffeur in a spotless white livery that had to be changed twice daily. I used a taxi for the most trivial reasons and passed out money, and gave tremendous tips to waitresses. One only had to ask for my assistance, one only had to show one's need. It all made me feel important and benevolent. But I did wild, impetuous, unorthodox things, throwing everything in the face of respectability. One night, the old Madame of the lavish brothel at Rue des Moulins allowed me to have a soirée in the lounge. Something within me loved to shock, perhaps stemming from my earliest years on the streets.

I persuaded André to buy an old Château at Saint-Bernard. It proved to be a dilapidated almost uninhabitable structure three hundred fifty miles southeast of Paris; a hodgepodge of assorted architecture, unsafe staircases, and a mass of peeling paint. But the tower which was habitable was impressive and soared upward, beckoning to us. And as we purchased it, a mood of euphoria colored the transaction. It changed nothing. But it was at the Château Saint-Bernard that I threw my most lavish luncheons with Lily Walton to help prepare the meals. Premier Edward Herriot who had a deep interest in my paintings was a frequent guest. The happiness I reached for and the *joie de vivre* I longed for were elusive. A storm always threatened in the distance.

* * *

I sensed that something was wrong that summer morning of 1923 when I decided to drive back to the Château, and forget my troubles and paint a scene from the window of the tower. Maurice, André and I had gone to Saint-Bernard more frequently of late. The only unusual thing was that this time I was alone. I felt restless and uneasy in the afternoon blazing sun. I looked at the chauffeur who stood sparkling white in his livery, as he helped me out of the Panhard, and wiped a smudge from the gleaming black door. Then he went into the servant's quarters.

I looked about. The little Beaujolais town was quiet and the church near the Villefranche-sur-Saône was peaceful as the bells tolled four o'clock. I stood taking in the warmth of the sun. I walked inside the crumbling building breathing in the musty air of six centuries. The light was brilliant, filtering through the trees onto the façade of the château and coming through the misty windows. It was lush during the summer with the fields growing wild with an abundance of herbs, shrubs and colorful wild flowers and interrupted by feathery acacia trees.

I had taken a room to sleep in with André, and several large rooms adapted as studios for André, Maurice and myself. I passed by a crumbling staircase and cracked plaster which made desultory patterns on the wall, and entered our bedroom, a huge room facing the east where it caught the rising sun. I thought of the last time he had made love to me in this fantastic room.

My eyes swept the room to the bed where André and his mistress, the dancer Eveline, lay entwined nude in each other's arms.

It's odd, but at first I said nothing but stared and stepped backwards and I felt something hit me as my stomach tightened. Then, I screamed, "You unfaithful bastard! And you, *putain,* get out of my bed! Whore! Eveline! How could you use our room André, our precious room, our castle . . . yours and mine? You . . . you slimy dog! Take your naked fat carcass out of here, you bitch!"

I ran to the kitchen and got a broom. "Out! Out! You miserable whore! I'll sweep you out you slut!"

I slammed the broom across Eveline's bare buttocks. "Let me see what a dancer you are now!" Eveline looked about twenty, was of surprising Rubinesque proportions with bright red hair and a fair skin. I hit her again and again until the woman cried and bright red marks striped her buttocks. André jumped up and held me and I began to scream. My venom frightened him. I scratched his face and the blood ran down his cheeks.

"You're *fou* Suzanne, leave us alone," he faltered.

"I'm *fou!* So I'm *fou!* Yes, I'm crazy to be married to you and have you live from the sweat and toil of my poor son you force to paint, even in an asylum. You're like Libaude, no better. You make him paint so you can fuck whores."

"Don't speak to me of Maurice. Yes, he was once an artist . . .

not anymore. He fools the others but not me."

"You're a bastard to say that, a bastard! Don't you dare criticize my son or his art! I taught him to paint. Go fuck your whore."

Eveline stood up and turned her eyes on me with blazing raw hatred. "Shut up!" she shouted. "Shut up, old lady!"

"Old lady!" I screamed and lunged at her and we wrestled to the ground. I tore Eveline's chemise open which she had hastily thrown on, exposing a full breast. I spat on Eveline's bosom. We rolled on the floor and dust from weeks of neglect coated us.

"Your *bonne* should clean," she gasped out.

"I'll rip your hair out!" I snarled and grabbed a handful of curly red hair while Eveline howled. André tried to break us up and then sat on the bed in disgust patting his bleeding cheek.

Eveline got away, straightened her chemise and began to cry. "*Mon Dieu*, André, what a terrible woman."

I screamed, "Now get out of here!" I threw her dress at her.

They both left quickly and I sat down on the bed.

"Why here?" I said aloud shaking with emotion. I knew he had a mistress but why defile this place which was so precious to us? Why here? He had the money to have gone to any lavish hotel, and André spent money freely.

Somehow I couldn't cry. It seemed so hopeless to cry, too late for tears. I went to my studio and set up the easel before the afternoon sun and began to paint. I felt sick. This would calm me. But it didn't work.

Sweet bits of memory flew past me; flashes of myself making love to André in my studio while he posed for the Adam and Eve. There were those delightful days at the start in rue Cortot when I hung on every word he uttered, and held him in my arms during those rapturous nights. Yet perhaps it had all been some fantasy, some delicious illusion, a fevered product of the yearnings of a woman past her prime. Perhaps that's what it all was. Had there really ever been love between us? And this thing I called love. Wasn't it a delusion after all, the distorted edifice I had built in my mind to ward off an encroaching old age? Well, I had lost. He had finally seen that I had grown old and he looked for the youth of his youth. Why did I fight the losing battle and become a ridiculous prey for this terrible inevitable defeat? And

I fought this Eveline, so many years my junior. Was I mad? I would continue to fight for him. It was as though I was fighting the battle of every woman who loved a man much younger than herself. I would ward off my greatest foe, age. I would win.

I painted absentmindedly. Afterwards I threw up in the sink.

When I returned to my studio, André was figuring his accounts quietly with a sheepish look on his face. He said nothing at all about the scene at Saint-Bernard. He treated it as though it never happened, but his cheek bore two long scratch marks and when he stood he swayed from drinking.

He turned and embraced me through his drunken haze.

I drew away. "You speak to me after what you've done?"

"I still love you," he said, "and I'm miserable . . . why in the world are you so damn difficult? Why is our life so impossible with Maurice's insanities? Do you know what he's doing now?"

I turned away.

"No listen. You've got to listen. I'm going to tell you because you don't want to hear. He smears zinc white on all his paintings so they should look like his white period. They all clamor for his white period and the technique is gone. It's all gone. Even postcards don't help. Alcohol has destroyed what talent he had. Don't pretend, Suzanne. You've seen it. I'm living a lie, his lie."

"Shut up . . . I see nothing. Maurice's paintings keep you in fine suits and fine young mistresses. My poor, poor Maumau brings you thousands of francs so that you can have harlots like Eveline, and you can pay their bills . . . you think I've not found evidence? And by the way, your precious slut, Eveline, had the effrontery to send me a bill for her costumes. Perhaps I'll visit her and shove that bill up her . . ."

He cut me off. "No, she's a sweet innocent child."

"*Mais certainement!* I saw her sweet innocence. It was written all over her naked cunt. Oh, you poor fool. You think you're twenty like her but you're over forty and how long do you think you will satisfy a twenty year old whore who uses my bed like an alley cat?"

"I don't want to speak of it." His eyes suddenly blazed with frustration. "I've prostituted my painting to become a prosperous pimp of someone's fraud; I deal in art instead of flesh. My life will pass and I'll accomplish nothing," he began to weep.

I was touched. It was the first time I had seen him cry. What happened to the André I knew, the ever optimistic, ebullient, self confident André who espoused all the theories of art . . . to whom I turned for advice, ever rapt with what he had to say? Sympathy swelled within me. I felt I was a painter now in camaraderie with him, giving him solace, support like I had done with poor Modi, and my voice grew softer. "I never urged you to give up your painting, André. You're still a fine painter, your landscapes, the few that you've done, rival those of Cézanne or Van Gogh. Even the critics agree. Someday . . ."

"Why can't I sell? I, the great entrepreneur that I have become can't sell my own work, why?" His eyes were bloodshot.

"I don't know, André."

He put his head in his hands and wept uncontrollably.

"André, you've been drinking and you're not yourself."

"Oh, my God, I'm truly miserable. Tell me what to do. You've always been strong. Tell me. I never meant to hurt you, my Suzanne, *ma petite* Suzanne."

I embraced him and he cried into my bosom like a child.

20

André
An Aging Lover

"By God, she'll drive me mad! I've given up my own painting, but she wants more. And her obsession with age is absurd. I will always see her as young, always. My Suzanne will be eternally young. And she doesn't understand what business I'm trying to conduct. Neither she nor her drunken son know what's going on. Well the Bernheim-Jeune Gallery is considering signing a lucrative contract with us for one million francs a year. It doesn't matter to those two. Of course, I'm not appreciated for anything I accomplish, so what's the difference? Why should I even try to get them money?

Our relationship is becoming worse. The fact is that her little Maumau is a fraud. And to think I've sacrificed my own art to sell his. He's a despicable sick fraud. He can paint his endless streets and buildings with women who look like puppets, big hips and buttocks . . . he can do it until he's blue in the face, but why should I be obligated to sell them? I'm *un Alphonse*, that's all I am, a goddamn pimp!"

She can scream and defend him and call him a great artist but she knows, Suzanne knows what has happened to him and she can't face it. And she's become something worse and I told her the truth about herself one afternoon. It's something I have always hated in a woman.

"You've become a shrew, a shrew. There's never any peace. I don't know you anymore, Suzanne. Listen to yourself."

"Oh, how sure you are of yourself. I, a shrew? If I'm one, I blame you and your easy life with your whores. You certainly haven't been able to refuse their demands, have you, especially when you have a poor, tragic son and a wife who provides you with their upkeep. And how is your slut, Eveline? Has she been satisfying your needs in bed? Has she a young cunt, André . . . tell me what does it feel like to *foutre* her? You like them young that way, don't you, don't you? How you lie. Only a sniveling coward lies the way you do." She said these last words quietly and with a hatred more deadly than her shouting. I grew afraid.

I don't know what those two want of me. And about my mistresses, it's a fact of my wretched life which makes it bearable. I have them, and in numbers and I'm certainly not the first in Paris to be unfaithful. So what. I find that my love affairs are a vast adventure . . . each flirtation, each sexual conquest a tremendous experience as though another aspect of that love I had once with Suzanne was gratified. I'm forty but can still satisfy any woman so why must I be miserable?

But *sacrebleu!* The demands these women make on me. Their financial and emotional demands are exhausting. The bills they run up and send to me are positively indecent. And these bills flood us daily. They all need money, the whole lot of them, all aspiring actresses or dancers or artists' models who want me to do something for them. I can tell you that I pay dearly for their bodies. And if I don't oblige, they create the most ghastly scenes in public places with the intent of course to embarrass the hell out of me, forcing me to come through . . . it's blackmail, that's all it is, blackmail. They all converge on me, present and past loves and make my life totally impossible. It's an addiction I can't shake and for every new young vagina I pay dearly. But next to my Suzanne they all pale into insignificance.

I never meant to hurt my Suzanne . . . I never meant to hurt her. But what can I do?

21

Suzanne
The Blue Room

It was still warm that fall of 1923 and the windows were flung wide open to let in the faint breeze. The problems I was having with Maurice and André gnawed at my soul. But I drew my strength from the only way I knew, from my art. It always provided the courage to dissipate the bleakness which was gathering about me.

I contemplated a canvas about three feet high and four feet wide, and had a curious yearning to do something that would be a synthesis of all I felt, of all I knew, of all I had seen. I could feel the echoes of Gauguin and Cézanne and the influence of the Orientals whom I so admired, but I would depict my own way of observing life in all its reality, without pretense, without artifice, and without illusion.

What I wanted was to produce what I felt might be one of my best paintings. Was it always to be so that the greater the adversity, the more adamant I became to achieve? This persistence was my weapon. But what was I to paint?

Berthe Sourel was a cleaning woman who came into my studio on occasion. She was large, the way Paulette was large, with plump arms and full thighs and she smoked incessantly and cared little about anything. Her very nonchalance made her interesting.

"Pose for me, Berthe. You'll make the wages you would make cleaning."

"I wouldn't mind a change," she tossed out in a bored voice. "If it's for the same pay, it'll give me a rest and I'll lay myself down. How's this? These old striped pants have to be okay because I can tell you, Madame, I'm so tired I ain't going to change."

The resemblance between Berthe and Paulette ended there. There was no good humor about Berthe, no servile, obedient behavior. She was jaded, the daughter of a prostitute, and she had walked her mother's old beat near the Church de Lorette when she needed money. She had once worked briefly in a brothel on the rue d'Amboise. She had a child she had placed out with a country couple, but she was totally disinterested in her daughter, scarcely aware of her, mentioning her only briefly.

Frequently beaten and twice raped by her mother's pimp, she had grown impervious to violence, and blasé about villainy. She was 25 and could have been 50.

I pulled down a blue flowered hanging and threw it over a divan. I then draped fabric behind it. Two books, one smaller than the other lay on the divan.

"Can I smoke?"

"By all means."

Berthe thrust a cigarette into her mouth but didn't light it. "'Now, if this ain't the good life . . . I could do this more often I'll tell you. It sure beats cleaning or being fucked by a *miché* like I sometimes do."

"But you must stay still and not speak."

"It's okay with me. What a lark. Why didn't I think of this before. I once seen the artists looking for models down by the fountain."

I sketched her in her pink camisole and top which emphasized her bare full arms and her green striped pants. Her body was relaxed as she kicked off her shoes. I began painting Berthe as I saw life and according to my own passions.

And when it was done I put down my brush. I looked at my

work, held my breath and trembled.

The Blue Room, as I called my finished product was simply a woman lying on a blue divan. But it was more . . . it was a synthesis of all I felt and knew; it had the broad flat colors of Gauguin. My palette, now extended, included the bright green of the woman's striped pants. The painting had the decorative background of Matisse, infusions of bright printed hangings, and the emerald green of the trousers contrasted with the blue cloth of the divan. The figure looked unconcerned by it all, dangling a cigarette in her mouth. Was it an odalisque by Matisse? Was I influenced by Lautrec and a whore of his brothels? Berthe, this clothed, jaded *Olympia* of the streets was not Manet's pampered whore of 1865, a beautiful, slender, nude girl, not quite twenty who was innocent of the sordidness of the world, but rather my crude charwoman, occasionally a prostitute, whose hands were roughened by the lye in scrubbing soaps, and whose body was coarsened by repeated loveless sex with faceless men. But unlike Olympia, her cold eyes looked out in contempt at the world. Her clothes of the charwoman, the pink top and casual striped pajamas which Berthe wore to work, were in preparation for the drudgery of life, not her next paramour.

It was what I loved to do, to paint, looking at life with realistic eyes. It was the same unrelenting formula I tried to use in all my portraits, lyrical and spontaneous and mercilessly honest, my strident best. If it had overtones of Lautrec, he had put them there for I had learned well from him. I stood back and contemplated the painting and I knew it could be identified as unmistakably mine. The thrill of creation swept over me, only akin to the birth of a child!

André arranged an exhibit for Maurice and myself at Berthe Weill. A series of portraits including my *Lily Walton,* several nudes, still lifes, and landscapes of Montmartre were exhibited. And with the sale of my paintings and my recognition as an artist, with reviews by such critics as André Warnod and George Coquiot and with money flowing in which I couldn't seem to handle, luxury undreamed of became an integral part of my life.

And incredibly, the Bernheim-Jeune Gallery signed a lucrative contract with us for one million francs a year. Tabarant had a magnificent dinner at the Maison Rose, rue de L'Abreuvoir afterward. Our friends were present, André Warnod, Francis Carco, Georges Coquiot, Braque, Derain, Picasso, Pascin and George and Nora Kars. We also had rounds of wild parties at the Lapin Agile to which the young artists of Montparnasse and Montmartre were invited along with our more seasoned friends like Picasso. Wine flowed freely at the tables, wine of every variety, and champagne spilled down the throats of eager fledgling artists like so many glasses of water. "It's a wonderful life!" I said to André attempting to always be the coquette and attempting to ignore the fact that Maurice was being maintained by a keeper, Pierre, and bars on his windows.

I stood at the bar at the Lapin Agile in my Paris creation, helping to pour the drinks, and then flitting to a table where I fell on Picasso, hugging him and smoothing his unruly hair. It was a Picasso who was now at the height of his career. And then I half danced about, trying to balance my fifty-eight years with a petite slim figure sheathed in a pleated deep turquoise silk satin Italian gown by Fortuny which hung to the floor, simple and draped like a Greek statue, covered by a velvet coat. The gold locket with the tiny sapphire on its lid, Henri's precious locket, hung about my neck. I wove in and out among my guests and flattered the young struggling artists, giving them hope. Then before them I raised a glass and shouted, "*Vive l'amour!*"

I looked at André but what I saw was a growing coldness between us and he looked away.

I exhibited *The Blue Room* at the Salon d'Automne and an observer stood before it and said, "You know what you've painted, Madame Valadon?"

"What?"

"A masterpiece. It is truly a masterpiece."

Looking at me was the critic, Francis Jourdain.

"Of course," I replied very simply. "That's what I intended."

22

Maurice

The Turmoil

Even André is testing me. I've been watching him. He hates me and my painting. He thinks I'm a failure as an artist. And I don't trust Diaghileff, supposedly the great Russian impresario who had me work on scenery... deliberate, deliberate. He thinks he's fooling me but I see through all of their little tricks... all plotting against me, testing me, rest assured.

"I know what you're thinking, Maumau, you are so successful you should feel proud," Maman said. "Do you know your paintings are bringing in five times as much as mine?"

"It frightens me... it frightens me when people bow to me. They think I'm crazy. You'll see, they'll put me in Picpus again."

"*Mon Dieu*, why do you think that? They respect you... don't they call you, Monsieur Maurice, the artist?"

"They buy my paintings because they... they want to see how a crazy man paints. Why do you think, Maman, they all stare at me? It's because I'm losing my mind."

"It's absurd. You need a wife, that's all. If only Paulette would not have..."

"But you see... even she ran away from me."

"*Sacrebleu*, I can't talk to you. You have an answer for everything. You have the success that poor Modi wished he had."

"Can't you see? Can't you see that I'm losing my mind?"

"I'm not going to listen to your idiotic talk."

As I expected it all came to a head as a fearful climax to my drinking. I felt that my old sickness was back when I hurled profanities at pregnant women who passed on rue Cortot. That ass hole gendarme took me into custody and I became furious.

"Do you know who I am?" I hissed out.

"Yes, we know who you are, Maurice Utrillo, the *artiste-peintre*, drunk and crazy."

"I want a drink."

"No, you've had quite enough."

"I want a drink!" I clamored.

"That does it. You're going into a cell."

They dragged me, and I banged on anything in sight. I pounded my fists on the walls of the cell. "I want a drink, I want a drink, I want a drink!"

I started banging my head against the cell wall. A trickle of blood rolled down my brow onto my cheek and into my stained collar. "Stop!" the captain yelled out. But I continued, purposely, angrily, tasting the salty warmth of my blood on my lips. My eyes stung and were half hooded by swollen eyelids.

"I better stop him, captain."

"Just don't pay attention to him, then he'll stop."

"He could kill himself."

I continued banging my head on the cell wall and suddenly crumpled onto the floor. Vague shapes danced about me. Thousands laughed. The gendarme ran to the cell, unlocked the door and pulled me out. I felt myself sinking. "*Sacrebleu!*" swore the captain. "Call a doctor, *vite!* I don't want his death on my record. If he dies I'll have every mad artist in Paris after my hide."

He bent down and wiped the blood from my brow and head.

I lay partly dazed at home, my scalp laid open and bloody bandages wrapped my head. I heard muffled voices, "He'll recover, Madame Utter," a doctor said gently. "Have no fear, he will paint again. It will take time. But it's you who must take care of herself. You look as though you haven't slept for a week."

Maman sat by my bed looking so haggard those endless days

and nights, but her very concern comforted me. In the beginning, I couldn't form the words and just uttered sounds. Maman listened quietly to my senseless jargon and her eyes were filled with terror. She didn't eat, nor did she paint, but sat holding my hand as I lay staring at her, half seeing. And as I improved, she became thinner and more haggard with deep gray shadows around her eyes, and she who never prayed, prayed to my statuette of Joan of Arc to make me well.

"I'm becoming as mad as you are," she said.

Pierre was rehired to minister to my needs, but Maman never left my side. Finally, she bundled me up and took me to the Château Saint-Bernard in late June of 1924 together with André, Pierre, Lily Walton and a serving girl.

Maman stood on a little mound and suddenly she was beautiful, as beautiful as when she was young and her hair blew back from the wind. How I loved her.

"Breathe in the fresh air, my precious. Breathe it in. I stand here and feel as though I'm drowning in the lush fields. Look how the wild flowers bloom with such glorious colors. Isn't it beautiful *chéri*? I could look all day at these azure skies which we should paint together, and of course you'll put your own marvelous leaden skies into the painting. You will paint wonderful things, *mon vieux*. You will paint as you've never done before and your genius will shine through. You will see. Only I know, a mother knows. Don't you feel it my beautiful artist, my cherished Maumau? I will care for my son and make him well and we will paint all of it together, and all this will cure you."

So Maman supervised my meals, making special dishes which Lily Walton prepared. She fed me spoon by spoon like I was a child, telling me stories from both of our childhoods. I was the baby whom she had never raised. She had become my Grandmère. She kissed me on the cheek and combed my hair with loving care and trimmed my mustache.

"*Voilà*, you're so beautiful," she said. "And you'll get well and be the greatest artist in Paris besides myself, of course. And now is the time you always say, 'But you are immodest, Maman.' Say it, *mon vieux*." I smiled and scarcely mouthed the words, and I saw the lines around my mother's eyes, the deep furrows between her brows and the yellow color of her skin and said nothing.

She sat with me in the shadow of the tower and two easels with empty canvases were before us. I just sat and looked at the scenery. The Beaujolais hills left me cold. But one day I began to paint images of the streets which had been stored in my memory. I painted what I was nurtured on, the Montmartre. And the winter passed. And the spring of 1925 turned into summer and Maman and I painted and remained at Saint-Bernard. André arranged with Diaghileff for me to do scenery for the ballet, *Barabau*. I accomplished the assignment quickly.

One day in late summer, Lucie Pauwels drove up in a similar Panhard as Maman's, wearing a huge straw cartwheel hat. "My dear Suzanne," fluttered Lucie Pauwels. How I loved listening to her . . . almost as much as listening to Grand-mère.

"I heard about Maurice's terrible, terrible trial last year and just had to come. Where is my great artist?" She held her hand over her eyes to shield herself from the August sun. "Oh, it's so marvelous to have great painters for close friends, just wonderful to be a part of your life and its joys and tragedies . . . we've been to London, and I've brought you a vase of lovely blue Wedgwood, but wait until you see the marvelous cashmere sweater for my precious Maurice, as blue as his eyes . . . now, let me see all those wonderful paintings you precious artists have done. I'm just in the mood to buy you know. Dear heart, please get the gifts out of the car. Oh, my dearest husband . . . where is that man? I think he's fast asleep at the wheel . . . works so hard for me, dear lamb, to keep me in silks and satins. Oh, dear one," she called. "Wake up now."

It was hilarious how she went over to the automobile, shook her husband's shoulders, clapped her hands to wake him, scooped up the gifts, then came toward me holding the huge brimmed hat which was fluttering in the wind. "Oh, my darling Maurice, my marvelous painter . . . let me kiss you, dear boy." The woman was positively hypnotic. I felt my face burn and offered my cheek to her in a daze.

But Maman sat watching Lucie with a grim expression.

23

Suzanne

Love And Remembrance

Of course, it was inevitable that we would separate, and my life ended that awful summer, and when the season cooled into autumn at Saint–Bernard, there was little left. André felt resentment both as a painter and as an agent representing the two people who kept him on an allowance; and I retaliated by accusing André of infidelities. And finally, I put away my paints, took my staff and returned to rue Cortot.

André was given a liberal allowance and used the money to pay for his younger mistresses. I continued to find bills for medical treatment, high couture and living expenses for Eveline. After several explosive scenes with André, I hoped it would all pass. But in the aftermath of Maurice's attempted suicide, I spent wildly to submerge all my grief. Bernheim-Jeune Gallery, alarmed at my wild spending and André's dissolute life style decided to buy a house at 12 Avenue Junot in behalf of Maurice, and there the family would reside.

I found it difficult to leave the rue Cortot. There were memories of my early life with André, and the fantasy of those first idyllic, unbearably sweet moments. I had hung on every word he uttered, revered every opinion, cherished every gesture, and lived in a fevered pitch of longing for the very touch of his body during the nights so filled with unbelievable delight; it was all there inhabiting the rooms, dreamlike, poignant yet blurred . . . so many years ago and I was tired, so tired.

When Maurice and I left with our ménage for our new home on the Avenue Junot, André refused to go with us. It was something I never anticipated . . . it was unthinkable, it was unimaginable. I pleaded with him to come with me, but he answered with a stoic silence which was more deafening than any shouting he had done. The unreality of it seemed to crush me. What had happened? It couldn't be so.

I came over to him and reached up to embrace him. For a brief moment, my eyes filled with tears and the look beseeched him to come with me. For a brief moment he almost relented, but his eyes were at first cold, and then tortured and he shook his head. I was sure he would follow just given time. But he just stood in stoic silence and watched me leave, and he stayed behind in our studio where he and I, his petite Suzanne, had once been lovers. But although our marriage had virtually dissolved, something remained in the ashes. What was left couldn't be stamped out. The memory lingered and it hung by a tenuous thread.

The quiet Avenue Junot opened in 1910 onto the Montmartre "maquis" as the still unbuilt areas of the avenue were referred to. The little wooden shacks were replaced slowly by houses such as mine, a modern one, but a small distance from the rue Cortot. At the new house, Maurice's room on the first floor had iron grills on the windows. There was a large studio on the lower level where he painted, and upstairs, a dining room, kitchen and two small rooms. My studio was in the garden and when André repeatedly visited, we made love there, the spark rekindled for an hour.

After my bout with Eveline, after seeing her smooth young skin, I became obsessed with aging and I held onto whatever beauty I had with a desperation. I looked at my reflection and saw I had grown older, much older. It seemed as though I aged overnight, and the sight of the once rounded firm thighs now sagging with the flesh mottled and veined, and my belly losing its hardness, and the flesh of my arms loosening ominously, made my mouth run dry. Was this the body which once posed for Renoir's *The Bathers*? Why should André choose me if he could lie next to the smooth taut skin of a girl of twenty? That was my fate. This was my penalty for marrying a man twenty-one years younger than myself.

With the passage of time, lovers of my youth were also fast disappearing . . . my former lover, Erik Satie had died. My portrait of Erik with his battered hat, my early venture into painting hung in Degas' dining room until his death when it was returned to me; it was now in my studio. Puckish, eccentric Erik who never married.

After his death, his brother Conrad Satie found a bundle of letters Erik had written to me but never sent. Conrad wrote to me and we finally arranged for their delivery. When I read them the memories stirred up were both bitter and sweet. Dear Erik whose *Gymnopédie* with its lonely haunting melody evoked for me the familiar longing touched by sadness and terrible nostalgia for a fast fading era seemed all a fantasy. Slowly, the rekindled memory of him faded as well.

Adèle visited me one afternoon in 1927 and watched me paint. She was now exceedingly plump, and her gray hair powdered the last of a reddish blonde mane. I was working on an oil on canvas I simply called *Flowers in a Vase*. She was fascinated as she watched the painting's progress. When I painted my flowers, my brush tenderly stroked each stem, each calyx, each petal with a passion stemming from years at Pierrefitte working in my garden. We talked of the past and the present and of youth and of age.

"Who cares, Marie? It's sometimes too difficult to be young. I've had enough lovers sponging off me."

"Difficult? It's difficult to be young? You're mad, Adèle, or you've grown old. Just give me youth. How I would treasure every difficulty if I could be young again. I would sell my soul, what's left of it for youth. Age is death . . . in age there is no love, no passion of the flesh. There's no moment like that feeling of exquisite love, Adèle, nothing can equal it and it dies with age. Don't tell me you've already forgotten how it all felt? My body aches with a longing for passion. Sometimes I almost forget that joy and then André . . ."

"You see, you haven't changed Marie. You're the same wicked one you always were, standing by the Place Pigalle, waiting for the artists and sleeping with half of Paris. *Ma fois!* You haven't changed. We're over sixty, Marie. It's time to . . . now, what the devil is that?"

"My portrait."

"Well, it's awful Marie. It's certainly not you. You're still a beautiful woman . . . look at that. You look far too old and dull. If anything you are not dull."

"My poor, poor friend, you remember me as I was. Look again."

The sixty-two year old woman I painted stared at Adèle from the canvas and looked wistful, sad and determined, her hair cut short, mercilessly short . . . and she looked at the world accepting the inevitable.

Adèle reflected, "Why don't you marry again? Forget André."

"Before another man shares my bed, I would like to see Maumau married."

"Maumau? Maumau is in his forties. I can't believe he'll ever marry. And then, Marie, you know he might be . . ."

"He's not homosexual! And you've said that before."

"How can you be so sure?"

"I'm sure, but I'll see to it that he marries."

"Oh how you once told me that if you had a child you'd throw it away. Whatever happened to your carefree life? Your son is too goddamn close to you, Marie . . . it's not natural at his age."

"Isn't it ironic, dear friend, that the child I didn't want *is* now my whole life. I must get him a strong wife, Adèle."

"Let him take care of himself. Well, what you need is to buy something young and chic to cheer you up."

"I can't. I'm starting another painting."

"Forget that. This is more important. We'll go tomorrow and buy up all of Paris."

"Whatever for?"

"To be alive. Isn't that enough? You still don't know the most basic element in life is fashion."

"Fashion? *Dieu Merci*, Degas never heard you say that," I laughed, forcing a sad little laugh.

And for a brief interlude, for just a moment in which to catch my breath, for a measured hiatus in a morning in which I would steep myself in painting . . . on this morning, Adèle and I visited the House of Jean Patou on the Rue Saint-Florentin. We sat on posh gold velvet cushions dripping with tassels, and a host of boyish dresses were brought out by Patou himself.

"The bosom, where is the bosom? I cannot wear it," I moaned.

"*Tant pis!* You'll flatten yourself with a bandeau like I do," Adèle snapped back.

"Impossible. I could never look like a boy." I said.

"This dress is *très chic, Madame, très chic*," said Monsieur Patou. "The boyish look which I have designed myself, is all the rage; even Chanel is designing it. It takes a bit of getting used to, but it's definitely in all the better shops in Paris. These are the very modern twenties Madame."

The dress was a wraparound garment, mid-knee, with a sleeveless bodice of eggshell crepe and vertical black velvet bands on the skirt.

"It's so short, it's indecent," I laughed.

"Why hide such legs, Madame? All these years beautiful women have hidden them with long skirts, but now, *voilà*," Monsieur Patou laughed fingering his thin mustache and leaned over and brushed his spats.

"You know what they say," said Adèle, "the legs are the last to go in the end."

I looked down and picked up my skirt. My legs were still slim with shapely calves.

"She'll take the dress, Monsieur," said Adèle, "if I have to pay for it myself."

"Perhaps when André sees me in it . . . ?"

"There's no hope for you, Marie."

"I know," I said quietly. "Goddamn him."

I lived for the moment that he would change and return. I only existed for the hope that he would see me as I once was. And each time he visited, in a quiet lull between his denunciations of Maurice's paintings, his self-praise about his financial successes, and his recital of frustrations about not selling his own works; in these brief shining moments of calm I would act flirtatious with him to make him stay. It was an agonizing desperation for his love as it once was.

"But you're so good for Maurice. He has someone to turn to," I protested.

"No, I don't believe in him, anymore."

"Well, it doesn't 'matter," I said bitterly. "I have a lover myself." It was a last desperate ploy.

"Who?"

"Oh, an important official in Lyons."

"Then you don't need me," he replied with a playful smile.

I knew he didn't believe me.

* * *

Good God, I had been right all along!

Of course, I always knew it. Of course I always knew it even if André hadn't; even if Maurice just sat playing like a child with his electric trains; even if the cost had been so high from the time he began tossing the tubes of paint from the window and I retrieved them. I had always known.

Amidst my myriad of landscape paintings, and group exhibitions in Amsterdam and New York; amidst solo shows at the Galerie des Archers in Lyons; amidst it all, it happened, the grande fulfillment. And one morning in the autumn of 1928, André came up to Saint-Bernard where Maurice and I had been staying and told me.

"They want to give Maurice the Legion of Honor. Imagine, Suzanne, such an honor. And he sits there unconcerned."

Maurice sat on a bench under an acacia tree in the courtyard, and I sat with him, my arm about his shoulders. The sedation given by a doctor from Sainte-Anne had done its job well. He seemed in a daze, quite unaware of what was occurring when an official delegation of government representatives and artists from Lyons arrived at Saint-Bernard that morning for the ceremonies. I greeted them warmly using my old charm. I wore a simple plaid pleated skirt and stole to match, a cloche pulled low on my forehead and a dark high necked blouse adorned with Henri Lautrec's gold locket. But this time a tiny photo was placed inside, not of my lover and husband, André, but of my son, my precious artist son, Maurice.

André stood nearby with a prosperous air about him and a look of satisfaction on his face. This award undoubtedly would help sales of Maurice's art.

The ceremony for *le peintre* was simple. He was awarded the "Cross of the Legion of Honor." Maurice smiled and stroked the ribbon when he sat down. He sat on a low wall during the simple ceremony, played with the autumn leaves, and as the medal was pinned to his suit, smiled and lapsed into a reverie, lost.

I had been right all along but it was a Pyrrhic victory. It probably cost me my marriage. I, forcing Maurice to paint, an absurd thing to do; my terrible involvement in his bouts of alcoholism; my conflicts in my desire to paint and be a mother simultaneously; my fears and panic mounting with every sign of deterioration in his work . . . it all didn't matter. I had been right all along. I had been right. Dr. Ettlinger, now gone, would have been proud of what I had done. If Maurice had no will, he didn't have to because I had, because I knew what was best, I was the mother, not they. I knew what Maurice and his needs were, not they. Half man, half child, Maurice would never grow up, but I had instilled in him a life's purpose, and I would supervise him in all things, particularly his painting; his painting would fill the void between the boy and the man.

I watched the proceedings and then closed my eyes, overwhelmed, and two tiny tears rolled down my cheeks. It was a bittersweet joy, an elation mixed with pathos. I took my son's hand in mine and we both looked up at the autumn trees, at the thinning branches slowly shorn of leaves. Maurice stopped rubbing the satin ribbon and examined the leaves which fell lazily to the ground, turning his hat around and around.

"Come, Maumau, we're to attend the luncheon in your honor."

He rose, held my hand, and walked with me. A glass of wine had been prepared for him, one glass only, diluted with water. And I knew I would sell my soul so that he could have a clean slate on which to paint.

With the advent of the Great Depression, there was a slump which the artists called, *La crise*. American Museums and wealthy collectors stopped buying paintings of living artists, and competed among themselves for those of the dead ones. There was a scramble for the paintings of Modigliani, among others. Many of the French dealers canceled existing contracts. Living artists became impoverished. And André felt it sorely in the paucity of his sales of Utrillos and Valadons.

And still I painted, while Paris was still under a dark mantle and a voice within me kept urging me on, and one day I felt overwhelmed and almost collapsed from fatigue. There were virtually no sales. Perhaps I should stop for awhile.

I slept for hours and then awoke and painted. I was painting the truth and I felt myself resigned to it. I would paint the stresses and age which were taking its toll on my body.

I stood naked before the mirror and saw my beauty deteriorated. I painted a picture of myself, a brutal, unflattering portrait of a sixty-six year old woman with a contorted flat face without dimension, hair cut short above the ear and the mouth drawn up as though teeth were missing. My breasts were flaccid and an absurd string of beads hung around my neck as though the adornment mocked my lost beauty. It was almost a self-punishment for growing old. I painted until time became meaningless and the hours passed as in a dream.

And when I stopped painting I came to grips with the thing I wanted and that was André. I would have him back. I looked at my painting of myself. The beautiful woman André had married was gone, and this monster had taken her place. My natural vivaciousness, my feigned gaiety, my contagious laugh were all replaced by this caricature. In my mind I had fought the encroachment of age and lost. But it didn't matter. All this didn't matter. I wanted him back. My heart and mind cried out in frustration but I wouldn't be defeated. I suddenly was seized by an overwhelming fatigue and felt faint. What was happening?

André had been staying in Saint-Bernard quite frequently. From time to time he would stay for a month and then return to Paris. It was as though he was trying to come to terms with something within himself. One afternoon I had a strong desire to revisit Saint-Bernard. I knew André was there and that he had been avoiding me with the slump in sales.

When I arrived at Saint-Bernard, I saw a tired looking André sitting on a log with two dogs. I felt I needed an excuse to stay.

"I want to paint you, André."

"Paint me if you wish. As you can see I'm not your Adam."

I smiled. "You'll always be my Adam."

While I set up my easel and paint box from the studio in the Château, I was struck by his appearance. André was forty-seven, and looked sixty. An air of complete dejection, and hopelessness poured from his body . . . his failure as an artist, the failure of our marriage, and the maze of relationships with assorted mistresses. He sat looking very bourgeois in his white shirt and pants and slippers. He could have been a storekeeper, perhaps a bookkeeper, or a wine merchant, but never an artist. I bent over him when I finished sketching the canvas and kissed the top of his head, overwhelmed by a feeling of sadness.

It was early spring and the poplars swayed majestically. We sat side by side and I felt a kind of magic nostalgia which turned to desire; he felt it as well as he reached up and embraced me.

"I still love you, Suzanne, I still love you."

"Oh André," I whispered, "if only we . . . come back my dearest to Avenue Junot with me."

He didn't answer, but took my hand and together we went to the bedroom in the Château, our bedroom, to the dream of perfection that was to be ours. I thought I heard old vibrations of voices in a cacophony of sound pouring down the musty corridors and climbing the walls in a fearful din; it was all there waiting for us, poised to destroy; echoes of Maurice's screams and my shouts and retorts to André in petty quarrels.

But that night André was my lover again just as before. We

made love with a hunger, a mad delight we once felt early in our relationship, and there was an additional element for I groped for him in terrible loneliness and never had I given myself to him so completely in an abandoned frenzy. I begged him to stay with me with my mouth and body, carnally, tenderly, in shuddering pleasure, my vagina folding about him as though I were a cat. And as we lay entwined in each other's arms, I fought for him with a reservoir of past skills as a lover taught by Puvis and by all the ones who had come after; and by life itself and passion, if passion could teach. I drew upon this arsenal of past loves as weapons to enable me to fight; fight the specter of this Eveline who had lain in the same bed entwined with my André; but to battle Eveline was to fight youth with age, an unfair match, probably a battle already lost.

"André, come back," I whispered over and over again, and kissed his face and neck and golden hairs on his chest, his protruding paunch and his marvelous cock which had given me so much pleasure in the beginning, mine alone, my lover and still my husband and I was fighting a lost battle to hold him.

"I . . . we can't be together," was all he said at the end as I fell onto his chest, my cheek resting on its golden hairs.

"André, we'll work it out . . . you'll see . . . it will be as it was in the beginning.

He didn't answer and slept all that night in my arms And in the morning with light streaming into the windows across the bed, the illusion fled. He had already returned to rue Cortot. The bed was empty. It had all been a fantasy and it was as though a cold hand had touched me in admonition, and I took the painting of him from the easel. Amidst all the sadness of loss, when I looked at it a familiar exhilaration took hold.

I called the painting, *André Utter and His Dogs*. My Adam, my marvelous Adam was replaced by a plump middle aged man, unshaven with a wan sad look in his eyes; and one dog slept and seemed to reflect his master's expression.

It was what I had left.

George Petit Galleries held my most important retrospective exhibition which covered my work from my self-portrait in pastel in 1883 to paintings, drawings, engravings and lithographs. Sixty-five works were mentioned in the catalogue. At the last moment I entered *André and his Dogs,* a poignant reminder of our glorious night at Saint-Bernard. Edouard Herriot, former premier of France, wrote the forward to the catalogue in which I was compared to springtime itself. It was glorious praise. But even the acclaim by the art critics didn't help the sales.

André tried. He felt as though he lost his touch. In spite of this, he arranged a group exhibition of the wicked Utrillo-Valadon-Utter trinity at the Moos Gallery in Geneva; and I entered about a hundred paintings. A well executed book was published illustrating my engraved works with a forward and catalogue by Roger-Marx. But neither the book nor the paintings sold well. I found the exhibit both mentally and physically exhausting. The paucity of the sales drained me completely.

The seasons passed as in a blur, and the glorious sun again pierced the trees at Saint-Bernard which bloomed lush with the foliage browning into deep russets mixed with the gold and yellow ochre I put into my paintings. The branches with their interesting shapes lost their leaves in silent cadence to the rhythm of the changing season. The *Church of Saint-Bernard* was clearly seen now, and I could watch the waters of the Saône for hours on end and feel that tranquillity which wafted down through the centuries; I could always feel and hear the echoes of voices through the château, of its inhabitants long gone. These were voices neither frightening nor wraithlike but rather friendly, pervading a warmth throughout the vast rooms, an intimacy born of comfortable and languid living. I remembered the love I felt when I gazed at the lofty tower where I entertained my friends so lavishly, so proudly; the faces of Edouard Herriot, the Mayor of Lyons, who had become the Premier of France, George and Nora Kars, the Coquiots, and the Braques. I had elaborate wine tastings and luncheons alfresco, and the great personages of the theatre were there, Lugné Poe, Copeau, Mistinguett and Diaghileff who mingled with my friends from the art world. And it all eroded with years of turmoil and dampened by the Great Depression.

And now I virtually stayed in the small house on the Avenue Junot, a self-imposed prisoner. Was the old fight in me waning?

But sometimes Maurice and I returned to the château. It was a glorious afternoon in the Beaujolais hills and the structure glimmered in a tawny light, a monument to a past love I once shared with André. The trees were bare once again that November, and I traced the arched windows of the Church, the small houses before it, and the mountains hovering in the distance. Maurice sat near me and started painting but turned in anger.

"André treated you badly. I saw his mistress and I won't forget it. I should have killed him."

His eyes flashed sparks of purple rage, so like Miguel, so like Miguel, except that Miguel, once my lover was now dead. My Miguel who took me in the grasses of the Butte Montmartre and in his room, was now gone and he left behind three sons, two of whom made their way from Spain to my studio, and their resemblance to Maurice was startling. They came with news of their father's death, and offered me a small sum which I refused.

"You've traveled a long way," I said and they handed me letters I had once written to Miguel, tied with a red ribbon. My God, he had kept them all these years.

His sons smiled with the smile of Maurice.

"I have brothers," Maurice laughed. "I have brothers. My father is dead?"

"Yes," I answered. "Your father is dead."

And the incident was closed when Maurice watched his half-brothers, half-brothers with his face, leave the studio forever.

* * *

On a warm summer evening, I sat outdoors with Maurice on the small terrace of the little restaurant owned by Adèle.

"At last you've come out of your retreat, my friend. What in the world is wrong with you? I have some *boeuf bourguignon* today . . . a beef stew for a king, for your Maumau, made with Beaujolais, tiny boiled potatoes and a marvelous soufflé for you my friend, Marie, who is so elegant she calls herself, Suzanne."

"You work too hard, Adèle."

"Modeling didn't make me rich. What can I do? Well, first you're going to have some of my marvelous *bouillabaisse*. You see those young artists? They come here to the Moulin Joyeaux just for the soup . . . and I charge them next to nothing."

"You probably charged them nothing judging by their faces."

"If Rosalie gives out food for nothing, so can I . . . she won't outdo me."

"Rosalie gets paintings in return."

"Which the rats eat up in the basement . . . so why bother. Are you painting, Marie? What's wrong? You look dreadful."

"I'm well enough to consider exhibiting with women artists."

"I don't understand."

"Did you ever know me to exhibit with other women? An artist is an artist . . . not a woman or man. It all goes against my nature. But times are difficult now, Adèle, so what can one do? But I can tell you that I dislike the idea intensely."

"No matter, we'll have to celebrate. The soufflé is not for such an occasion. I have a special dish. Nothing less than my *Oie Braisée aux Marrons*. Magnificent, if I say so myself, and on the house. And by the way, I'm going to put a plaque where you and Maurice are sitting right now."

"How elegant. And what will it say?"

"You'll see when it's done. By the way, speaking of elegance, how is your friend, Lucie Pauwels?" Adèle asked rolling her eyes.

"Well, I'll admit she amuses me."

"If she buys your paintings, she's worth while putting up with . . . now don't keep me talking. I must get your dinner." And Adèle scurried off adjusting her huge white apron, still a woman of boundless energy.

Maurice murmured coming out of his reverie for a moment. "I like her."

"Of course you like Adèle. She's my closest friend."

"Not Adèle. I don't mean *her*."

"Who?"

"Lucie Pauwels. I really like her." His face flushed.

I laughed. "Maumau, where is your taste?"

My son was undoubtedly superbly naive.

Several weeks later Lucie Pauwels herself visited me, visibly shaken. Her husband, the Belgian banker had died.

"You don't know what it was to have been supported by such a wonderful man," she cried. "And then suddenly he's not here. I can't bear it," she wiped her eyes. "But, I must admit he's left me quite well off, you know, precious lamb that he was."

"I'm sorry . . ." I began.

"Because you're my dearest friend, I must confess something dreadful to you that you must never breathe to anyone. Monsieur Pauwels," she whispered, "never really swept me off my feet, not that he didn't give me all that I desired but as for the grande passion, I often wondered what it was and sometimes imagined it . . . that woman's feeling when you make love, I dare not utter the word, *orgasme,* there, I'm a naughty girl, but knowing you, Suzanne, I'm sure you had felt it. But it didn't matter to me. I've met so many married women who have never . . . the whole matter was a nuisance, anyway. But you know that I had what I wanted and I taught him to respect my person, and gradually eliminated . . . that cruder physical aspect of marriage. A woman must train a man, do you see?"

"*Vraiment!*" I said, amused.

"What will the future now hold for me, Suzanne? I went to a clairvoyant reputed to be the greatest clairvoyant in Paris. I didn't believe in such things, but anyway, she read both my hands and the cards, and she said, 'In two years you'll be married again and your marriage will be with one of the greatest men in France, and be surrounded by paintings.' Now who can that be?"

I caught my breath, but said nothing. Was the woman joking? Surely she must be joking. How could Lucie be so obvious? Then, slowly, my mind began to sort it all out. Lucie? Lucie and Maurice? It was all too absurd. This woman was ridiculous to intimate it and I dismissed the notion from my mind.

But Lucie was persistent in her schemes. As the months passed, now in her widowhood, she resumed the name, Lucie Valore she had used as an actress. She came repeatedly to my home, and I listened to her persistent monologues of self-praise, and was always amused by it. When it was over, Lucie usually purchased a painting.

"Oh, I almost forgot, I brought you a bottle of a new fragrance, Chanel #5, simply heavenly my dear, simply heavenly. And as for you, my dear young artist," she said as she drew a mature Maurice to her ample bosom, "you must do one of those delicious scenes for me of the Moulin de la Galette, dear heart."

"I have done so many," he muttered, breathing in her scent.

"But you will have to do another, dear heart, and don't drink, dear boy; I smell it on your breath." She kissed him again on the cheek, and wiped off the scarlet imprint of her lips with a lace handkerchief drenched in scent.

He grinned with pleasure.

"Oh did I tell you that I have danced in the theatre?" She executed a few dance steps and extended her plump arms. "You can see how very graceful I am."

"You *are* very graceful," I said, hardly containing myself. I watched Lucie fasten her plumed beret on her head and adjust a new sapphire blue cashmere cape trimmed with silver fox. She had become quite portly through the years and exuded an air of prosperity, well being, and authority. She kissed me on the cheek and strutted about chatting like a magpie and preening like a peacock.

"Now, this is the way one leaves the stage," Lucie eternally said, stretched out her arms and tossed the end of her cape across one shoulder in a dramatic gesture. Maurice gazed wistfully after Lucie, breathing in the trail of scent, mesmerized.

* * *

Time flooded Paris with new movements in art; they flourished for awhile and like kaleidoscopes, melded one into the other, each drawing its strength from the one before, some remaining, influencing the world of art for years to come. And suddenly with Adolph Hitler, politics shaded art, sometimes casting a dark shadow.

And my fatigue worsened.

"Is this what the passing years do . . . what old age is like?"

"Perhaps you should see a doctor," affirmed Adèle.

"I'm growing older, nothing more."

"I'm your age, Marie, and I feel healthy. See a doctor."

"I hate doctors. They're all quacks and I don't trust them."

But the fatigue sapped my strength at the easel. It was as though with the separation from André, something had died within me, something had crumbled. And I was so weary that every step seemed a chore. It was an unnatural fatigue. I could scarcely wake up in the mornings and felt a fever sweep over me from time to time. It seemed unbelievable that I, always so robust, always healthy and now . . . was it old age . . . was I so terribly old? Was I so terribly worn out? Perhaps if I drank it would help. I could take a small drink now and then to raise my spirits and it would give me the incentive to paint, the way it sometimes gave Maumau. What am I saying? I went to the cabinet and took a swig of brandy. It was the drink that Maman had thrived on. Maman must be laughing from her grave . . . oh how I could understand my mother now, her loneliness, her despair and her love for her Maumau. It all swept over me as tears rolled down my cheeks. *Mon Dieu*, what's wrong with me? I looked at my reflection in the glass and a tiny old woman of seventy, with short blunt cut hair and a sallowing skin and large glasses stared back at me. Where was the beauteous Suzanne who was painted by Lautrec, Puvis and Renoir . . . this was a tired old elf, a wizened face lined with the troubles of a lifetime. Who was she?

Oh yes, she was an artist.

"I am an artist," I said aloud as though attempting to affirm my identity. "I am an exceptional artist." I leaned back in the chair, my eyes closed, feeling the warmth of the drink as it glided down. I took another, and then another, but it didn't help. And I fell asleep for the first time during the day; my easel waited; my painting of my flowers unfinished, and when I awoke that afternoon in January, 1935, I felt very, very ill.

Ettlinger's son who had taken over his father's practice now lived on Boulevard Clichy.

"I'll have to make some tests, Madame Utter."

A feeling of dread swept over me.

I suffered through the battery of tests he administered and then decided that I wouldn't inquire about the results, and promptly disregarded the whole affair.

But he called me on the new phone installed in my studio.

"Don't you want to know the results, Madame Utter? I want you to visit my office."

I half blocked him out as I held my breath on the dark green leather chair.

"You have diabetes, Madame Utter. This is nothing to play around with. You're not handling your disease properly. You must watch your diet, positively no alcohol, not even brandy."

I wondered how he could know.

"And Madame, come to see me in a month. If there's no improvement, insulin can be given if necessary."

I never returned and resumed my occasional drinking. I was painting a still life of a vase filled with my beloved flowers when I felt a terrible nausea followed by repeated vomiting. I staggered outside and hailed a cab to take me to the American Hospital in Neuilly, near Paris. I felt feverish. And when I walked through the front portals of the hospital I collapsed, and was later diagnosed as critically ill with uremic poisoning.

Fear of the unsmiling doctors gripped me and I lashed out refusing to be examined, refusing to eat and dumping the pills down the toilet when the nurses walked away. I tried unappreciated dry humor on the doctors and I began to scream long enough for everyone to come running. I would show them. Most of all I resented being ill. They weren't going to get the better of me. This was not the way I was going to end up. Damn them all!

Dr. Ettlinger, a serious young man, with whom I found it impossible to joke, said quite sternly, "Madame, the doctors and nurses inform me that you are making it difficult for them. If you want to get well, you must follow their instructions."

"Take me out of here. I'm alright."

"In good time," he answered. "You've been very ill."

He promised nothing.

Maurice came, sat still looking sadly at me, and then he sent for Lucie. And for the first time I was overjoyed to see her, "Lucie, how in the world can I get out of here," I said half sitting up. Then I fell back on the pillow, exhausted, and became terrified by my own weakness, "Oh, Lucie, I'm so glad you're here . . . they're all killing me. I feel so weak and I confess I'm frightened. Adèle was here and Nora Kars and Berthe Weil, and they want me to stay. Please take me out, Lucie. Don't leave me here or I'll die for sure."

Lucie bent over and kissed me, her Chanel mixing with the antiseptic odors of the hospital. I felt comforted by the fragrance of her perfume. Lucie wore her familiar beret with a long ostrich plume jutting recklessly at a rakish angle, her arms were adorned with several dangling bracelets over her long black leather gloves and her body was enveloped by a very full mink coat, too full, the skins of which hid her portly figure. Clusters of rubies and diamonds were at her ears, and their brilliance punctuated her melodic insistent voice. She never ceased to fascinate me with her flamboyance and flashed a new cocktail ring which encircled a plump finger. Lucie's rings always had a decidedly baroque quality about them, intricately worked, dazzling in their profusion of gems. She removed the mink, and placed it carefully across a chair, smoothing the fur with an enormous pride. I somehow welcomed every jewel, every adornment, every exaggerated gesture of Lucie as balm for my soul. She stood out in sharp relief against the sterility of the hospital.

"You look lovely, Lucie, and you have a beautiful coat."

"Oh, my dearest friend, this mink is not new. It was a present from my dearest husband. My precious is gone for two years, and I can still barely think of it. What does the future hold for me? Another clairvoyant said I would definitely be married to a famous man. It was the same fortune the other two gave me. She said that I would be surrounded by paintings. What is it, Suzanne? You look dreadful. What do you want to tell me?"

Was it really possible that this strong self-assured woman would be good for my son? And Maurice liked her. There would be no nonsense with her; she wouldn't stand for tirades from her "man of distinction" a painter who had gotten the Legion of Honor. My mind worked quickly.

"Lucie, suppose I never get well?"

"Don't be silly, dear, of course you'll get well."

"No, I'm afraid, not just for myself, but for Maurice. What

will happen to him if anything should happen to me? Who will take care of him?"

Lucie looked at me and a faint flush passed over her face; she adjusted her earrings and smoothed her hair, startling me by her sudden coquetry.

"Suzanne," she said slowly and deliberately, "have no fear, dear, dear friend. You know who will take care of him. *I will*, dear friend. Of course you knew that."

I was astonished, but then why should I be? Lucie had known from the start that this was the inevitable. She had insinuated herself into the family for this; she had known it all along.

"You will?" I mouthed the words as though in a dream.

"Of course. Of course I'll marry him, Suzanne. It's the only way. Haven't you seen the way he has looked at me all these years with such admiration, such love, and after my poor lamb's death, Maurice sent me such passionate letters. Of course he wants me and I will have him. After all, he is truly one of the greatest painters in France. My dear, we'll be engaged shortly. I will be happy to be his wife."

"He has to agree," I whispered weakly, marveling at her sheer nerve and fabrications . . . passionate letters, my foot!

"Oh, he will, darling Suzanne, he will. Have no fear. I'm a woman he knows is quite exceptional." She smiled, opened her purse with an élan only possessed by Lucie, and removed a sterling silver compact, its cover engraved with her initials. She powdered her cheeks. In her sixties, her skin was amazingly youthful. "I had this powder especially blended to my skin tones by Coty, and this shade is simply luscious . . . called *blush of love*. It's quite appropriate for the occasion, don't you think?"

I watched, marveled at Lucie, her unwavering aplomb, her ability to discuss face powder and my son in the same breath. But a weight was lifted from my chest.

When February began, I left the hospital, and I felt extremely weak; but as I regained my strength, my feelings about the match became more uncertain. I could have controlled Paulette but I would never have the final word over Lucie. Lucie was practically my contemporary and arranged life as she saw fit, dominated by no one, least of all her future mother-in-law. And how could Lucie be so certain that Maurice would agree to the marriage? I began to devise little schemes to discourage her.

"You know, Lucie," I confided, "Maurice is impotent. I think you should consider that."

"As a matter of fact, my dearest Suzanne, I really don't care. That kind of intimacy is not high on my agenda. My dear departed husband and I had a pure relationship. You can try again, Suzanne, but you won't make a difference. *Au revoir,* dear one and of course you know that he isn't what you say." She sweetly smiled, leaving a trail of Chanel as she floated out of the room.

Lucie was certainly no ingenue. She was sixty-four, and Maurice fifty-one. Her first husband had been ten years younger than herself, so she, like I, was no stranger to the concept of being married to a younger man. But I found the match more and more distasteful. Why had I been so desperate? Lucie was not for my son. I didn't want her. I wanted a daughter-in-law I could instruct, correct and generally rule. Lucie was too old. She was overwhelming. Everything about Lucie overwhelmed, her perfume, her dress, her self-assurance, her amiability, her optimism and her ability to insinuate her way into any friendship and liaison she desired. She had a colossal aggressiveness in combination with a dramatic flair and incomparable coquetry and style uniquely her own. One made way for her verve.

Mais non, mais non, mais non. Go away, let him be, I silently screamed. Who are you to intrude in our lives? Who are you but a ridiculous old woman in a ridiculous match.

"I don't want you!" I screamed aloud to the empty walls and from somewhere a woman's laughter answered me, shrill, mocking, and strong in its power.

24

Lucie
The Grand Proposal

Confidentially, I must admit I'm very pleased with the way I've managed my life thus far. Undoubtedly, I am quite gifted. I can accomplish anything I make up my mind to do. For example, I had once decided to become an actress and as I have often told Suzanne, the great Coqueline heard me one day and said, "There's a girl who belongs on the stage." But, of course, Monsieur Pauwels saw me as the lead in Tartuffe, and was so smitten with my beauty and talent that he swept me off my feet. Being such a successful banker, he insisted that I give up the theatre. You must realize that he was a distinguished, aristocratic, art connoisseur, a wealthy man who spoke many languages and whose name was known in the artistic circles. Of course I would devote myself to a marriage of such real distinction. He was only fifty-three when he died but now I'm a widow and must plan my life accordingly.

From the first, my Maurice, my great artist, was smitten with me the way *mon cher mari* was. How could it ever have been different? His love letters are tied with a ribbon on my vanity. My grace and beauty made him defenseless. And when a fortune teller in Angoulême predicted that I would be married to one of the greatest men in France, it didn't surprise me. I was always destined from birth for great things. I was never ordinary like some others, always exceptional.

I planned it all very well but then this is all a part of my talent. I never fail to accomplish anything I set my mind to and I aim to be the wife of France's greatest painter, Maurice Utrillo. I was so destined from birth for great things.

Late in February, my precious Maurice sat across the table from me wearing a crisp new dark blue suit and wine colored tie in a foulard print, a tie I had given him straight from the shop of a famous clothier.

I took care that there was candlelight at our table so it would compliment my skin. I wore a deep blue silk dress draped to one side, a Dior creation with a triple strand of cultured pearls at my throat and hanging pearl and diamond earrings at my ears. In the mirror of my silver compact I saw my eyes glisten, and the sequins from my Dior caught the gleam of the candles. I had arranged the setting marvelously. I poured some of my Chanel into a handkerchief and wafted it about the table as I put a hand on Maurice's arm. He stared at the huge diamond on my finger, a priceless gem from my previous marriage, and at the diamond bracelet watch, its pattern intricately worked by the famous Marcel, my Parisian jeweler. Maurice sat in a contented daze, fascinated by the beaded Juliet cap on my head, encrusted with tiny sequins and the latest rage of Paris. It was commonly known that I always dressed with great chic.

I took his hand. He was startled at the sudden contact and sat immobilized. Poor dear, he was so helpless against my charms. "My dear, dear heart, I knew you wanted to dine out with me. Don't be upset, dearest *peintre* if I'm very forward and say what's on my mind."

He nodded, lost in a trance.

"I always knew there was a fate which threw us together. . . that I was destined for you. I knew you would want me . . . there . . . I'm a naughty girl for saying it. Will you forgive me dear heart?" I had to be gentle with him.

"I don't understand. What do you mean?" he said, still in his reverie.

"What I mean, dear, dear heart is I knew you would want to marry me."

"What?" My precious lamb loved to pretend.

"You would want to marry me, my marvelous artist," I said without hesitation.

"I would?"

"Yes, you would. You're playing naughty games with me, dearest one. I've always known it, Maurice, my love. It's our destiny. Even my clairvoyant told me that one of the most famous men in France would marry me. For years I saw you look longingly at me . . . but dearest, it couldn't be because I had my husband. I was already spoken for but now . . . " I held his hand tighter.

He sat still, staring at me with a look of sheer admiration. Look how he loves me, I thought. The precious lamb is so devoted.

"Oh," was all he answered. Oh he is the sly one.

"*D'accord!* I would be happy, no flattered to be your wife."

"You would?"

"Oh yes, my dearest one, I would. I would be proud and it would make your mother very, very happy." The use of Suzanne's sanction in this was a clever touch of mine.

I then withdrew my hand and removed the rings from the fourth finger of my left hand and slipped them into my purse. "*Voilà!* Now, if you notice, my precious Maurice, this finger is bare. And if you so choose to present me with an engagement ring, I would be more than overjoyed to help you purchase it. The finest jeweler in Paris is my friend." I stretched out my hand again. "You may kiss my hand, Maurice, to seal it."

"To seal what?"

How my precious lamb loves to tease me. "Our engagement, you dear boy. As if you didn't know, my precious."

"Oh!" He flushed and was completely entranced by me.

"Now, dearest one, I don't believe in long engagements. We have so many arrangements to make. I'll open my house in Angoulême . . . you know my husband had reverses but I'm not a poor woman."

Maurice continued watching me in utter pleasure, and grinned boyishly. How dear he was. What admiration I have for his talent.

"Eat some of your filet mignon, dear heart and then we shall toast our engagement with a bit of champagne. I don't want you drinking now on an empty stomach. It's such a special occasion we won't even water the wine like your mother does . . . not yet."

Maurice's eyes lit up and he smiled at the prospect of the wine. I took his hand again across the table.

"My dearest, dearest love," I said softly. "I'm honored, truly honored."

His hand felt sure, warm and safe in mine and I knew that in the soft candlelight I was quite beautiful.

My marvelous mission was accomplished, *voilà*!

25

Suzanne
The Legacy

Bitch! That miserable scheming bitch! Of course she hypnotized him. How I detest her for what she has done to him; and nothing can measure my contempt for her.

"What do you want from me? First you want me to marry Paulette . . . and now that I've chosen someone, you're trying to change my mind." Maurice's eyes were pleading with me, mute and pathetic.

"You didn't choose her . . . she chose you."

"And you chose Paulette. You don't know what you want. I'll make up my own mind this time . . . I'm of age."

"Oh, you've grown up have you? Not in my book. By all means go ahead. After all, what do I know? I only suffer, that's all. Don't you want children?"

"I don't need any children."

"That's what you think now. Oh, you'll be sorry that you didn't give me grandchildren. Go ahead and marry her, by all means. Do as you wish and you'll become a real bourgeois in her hands and never paint. Oh, she'll make of you what she made of her first husband, nothing. Just someone to support her, that's all."

"I think I love her, Maman . . . she makes me feel . . ."

"Love? You fool. You love her?" I laughed, but my voice grew hoarse from emotion. "Don't tell me that. And you'll get no sex from her with her proper ways. She'll train you not to expect any, like she trained her last husband."

"*Sacrebleu!* What is love? You loved André, so what. Lucie makes me feel safe. I want to feel safe."

"She's too old for you."

"You were twenty one years older than André."

"That was different. We were younger then . . . and I loved André. You'll have a cold bed with her, and *Mon Dieu*, she looks like one of those unsightly fat women you love to paint. Of course, that's why you like her no doubt."

"Leave me alone. I really love her," he said partly dreaming.

"You already have a mother. You make me sick."

But at the beginning of March, Maurice sat quietly before his easel and said slowly and deliberately to me as I was painting my now eternal flowers, "I'm going to marry Lucie. I have really decided, Maman. And she'll be good for me and I'll be out of your way. After all my trouble to you, you should be happy."

I began to weep, and a panic seized me, a terrible haunting emptiness that began to gnaw away at my soul. What had I done? First André gone, and now my Maurice. I remembered what aching loneliness was like when André left for the front and Maurice was in an asylum. But I knew both would return so it was bearable. But this . . . this was too much to bear . . . the hurt was too great. Why wouldn't he obey me, why?

"I'll lose you, Maumau . . . I'll lose you and I'll have nothing."

"I'll visit you often."

"If Lucie lets you."

"Lucie loves you and she'll do as I ask," he replied.

"Lucie will do as she chooses."

"Don't be foolish, Maman . . . she'll be a daughter to you like you wanted Paulette to be."

"That's ridiculous. She's too old for that. She's so near my age, I think you should call her Maman."

"Shut up!"

"Shut up? You talk that way to me? You see what she's done to you? You're destroying me. Please, Maumau, please, remember your mother all alone. You don't need another mother, you have me. I don't understand your decision. I don't understand it. It's true I wanted you married but to someone else, younger, who could give me grandchildren, another little Maumau."

"Are you serious? Another like me? Look, Maman, I'm over fifty, and I'm tired. I want a woman like Lucie to care for me, not some young girl. There's nothing to understand."

"If you need a keeper, we can get Pierre back."

"You don't understand. Lucie is charming and appreciates my painting."

"Of course, for the money it will bring, no doubt. In spite of anything she tells you, her husband left her destitute. She needs any money your paintings can bring. The whole thing is a farce."

"No . . . she loves me," and his eyes grew wistful and moist with an expression foreign to him.

"She loves you? She loves you? She loves no one but herself."

But he wouldn't listen. I searched my son's face for some remorse, some contrition . . . there was none. It was all unreal. This couldn't be Maurice who disobeyed me. There must be some mistake. That witch hypnotized him. *She hypnotized him.* I was right. That bitch! That miserable, scheming bitch!

And I knew that the fight to keep him was over.

Lucie operated like a whirlwind. She insisted that Maurice first be baptized because she wanted a church wedding as well as a civil one, and he was swiftly baptized and confirmed. His military card which I had disposed of, was duplicated to obtain a license. I withheld the money for a ring but it did no good. Lucie simply went into her collection of Utrillos and Valadons, took several of the paintings to an art dealer and obtained enough to purchase an ornate diamond wedding band.

Nothing fazed Lucie. It was the last day in March when she sailed into the Avenue Junot trailing her scent and greeted me.

"Oh, my dear, how exciting everything is . . . now that we finally did the correct thing and got this dear boy baptized. I'll have to think of what to wear at the wedding and Maurice must have a new suit of clothes. I know a marvelous tailor my dear husband used, but it will be expensive. Do you like this Chanel suit I'm wearing, darling Suzanne? I could wear it to the civil ceremony and change afterward at Angoulême. What do you think? You have such good judgment. Of course I've arranged a quiet reception at Angoulême, my home, our home, dear heart." She turned and smiled at Maurice extending a plump arm in a theatrical gesture. "The wedding must be quiet, or those wild bohemian artists will be there. What will you wear, Suzanne, dear? I'll go with you for a gown. I'd love to. What do you think?"

I mouthed each syllable slowly and deliberately, *"There will be no wedding."*

"What do you mean?"

"Just as I said."

"I just don't understand. You were my closest friend, like a sister, and now you turn on me ... and I've always had the kindest affection for you." She reached out her arms to embrace me but I pulled away, "What's wrong? What have I done?"

"You're taking my son away. You'll ruin him as a painter."

"That's not true. I love his paintings, you know that." I marveled in my anger at Lucie's calm.

"He'll be too comfortable, like a child."

"You watch him like a child," and Lucie motioned to the bars on the windows and his toy trains. "You know I'm very fond of him." She smiled at Maurice coquettishly.

"Oh, how you've ensnared him with your tricks. And you feel nothing but greed. Your only passion is money. You're only interested in what money can buy. You're not to take him away from me. I forbid it!" My voice grew thick with anger. But Lucie was prepared for me.

"Oh Suzanne, dear, I'm not taking him away ... we'll visit and you'll visit us. It will work out beautifully." Her voice was amazingly calm.

I had met my match.

For every insult I hurled at Lucie, for every accusation, there was a quiet answer. She had an impenetrable façade. It made me feel more desperate, an old panic mounting inside of me at being left alone. My Maumau always came back ... even from his commitments ... he always returned.

"Don't go with her, Maumau," I pleaded, "Don't go with her. She's a witch, can't you see it? How can you be so fooled by her?

It's no good. It's like it was with Mousis . . . she's too bourgeois for you. Stay, stay here in Montmartre with me and you'll paint. You'll stop painting with her or you'll paint what she demands, don't you see it's a trick . . . she doesn't really care . . . only a mother really cares."

"Oh, Suzanne, darling," Lucie smiled patiently, "every mother whose son marries feels like this, and let's face it . . . he's a big boy now."

I cut her off and in a low breathy voice, choked with passion, "Don't *compare* me to other mothers! Don't *ever* compare me to other mothers!" My voice cracked. "It was I who made him paint, made him an artist, made him what he is today. It was I who suffered through his mad binges and confinements, I, not you. Where were you then, Lucie, where were you then? And now you're coming in on the fruits, reaping the rewards of my suffering with your scheming ways. How dare you! How dare you! *Merde!*" My voice broke with a sob, "Don't go to her, Maumau. Stay with your mother."

He stood looking at me, a pitiful, tortured look in his eyes, a look which stemmed from childhood when he wanted me to be near him always.

"Well," I said, "now I'll see how much you love me."

"I'm leaving with Lucie," he said, his voice almost inaudible.

"I can't believe that you would do this to me. I can't believe it. What good were all those poems you wrote to me? They were all a fake. Well, well, don't stand there, answer me. If that's what you're going to do, Maurice, go on . . . go on . . . get out of here, both of you . . . get out of here! Out!" I shrieked.

Lucie turned white for a moment, then composed herself, straightened her beret, and adjusted the jacket of her suit. She took Maurice firmly by the hand. "We'll go on with the time arranged for the ceremony on April 18, not one day earlier or later . . . and if you want to come to your son's wedding, you're certainly welcome, Suzanne. If not, it will be a tragedy because Maurice will never forgive you. Come Maurice, come along . . . we'll take a stroll on the boulevard, dear heart." Lucie smiled up at him and brushed a lock of hair out of his eyes as a mother would to a son. "It's a bit chilly, love, so get your coat." Maurice walked sheepishly to a closet, quickly flung on a light tweed balmacaan topcoat and they left, Lucie leading the way. He avoided my eyes.

I slammed the door after them and watched them from the window, the plump matron and the lined, somewhat dissolute looking slim figure of a middle aged Maurice, the two walking like young lovers, hand in hand. Lucie's bright plumed hat fluttered bravely in the breeze as she chattered away incessantly. She laughed, flirted with him, hugged him from time to time, pushed him coyly away, played every inch the vixen as she swung her full hips and matronly body. She looked miraculously younger, and I caught a glimpse of the budding actress who vamped Pauwels, probably a much slimmer Lucie, but one with the same vitality and élan.

How could Maurice treat me in this manner? He had always done what I wanted, always. Yet, deep from some recesses of my inner consciousness, I breathed a psychic sigh of relief. He was, after all, finally getting married and being looked after. That counted for something.

Alors, I would attend the civil ceremony, only that. I decided that I wouldn't set foot in Angoulême nor in Lucie's home, not yet. It was about as far as I would go.

The civil ceremony of Maurice and Lucie was held at the Montmartre *mairie* of the 16th arrondissement that April in 1935, and at the service, Lucie stood extremely happy, in an eggshell colored silk and satin evening dress from Mainbocher with a hem line almost to the floor. In the back was a panel which formed a train, a style now popular in the thirties. She wore a large lace hat from Lily Daché and a double strand of pearls about her throat. Maurice was dressed in an elegant dark blue suit which was whipped up by the tailor of the late Pauwels. And I? I wore my well worn, well viewed turquoise velvet Fortuny, *tant pis*.

The ceremony was brief, with Lucie using her stage name, Valore, in the ceremony. Maurice was quite sober and he looked at Lucie from time to time for approval as he had once done to me. The civil ceremony was followed afterward by a religious ceremony in a church in Angoulême, Lucie's home and the

Bishop blessed their union. I came only to the civil ceremony. I never attended the church.

"There were archbishops at my son's wedding but there wasn't all that fuss when he was born, I assure you," I said to Adèle.

*   *   *

The simple fact was that Lucie was a genius. Her talent lay in a realistic adjustment to life. Having never conceived a child, Maurice would be both her son and her husband. All her life, she had been groomed for this grande chore. She had been saved for great accomplishments and caring for Maurice was the greatest. And if I were to admit it, she would succeed.

Maurice Utrillo V, the *artiste-peintre,* Lucie initially observed, was a handful. Neither I, nor André, nor his Grand-mère, nor Paul Mousis, had been able to control him. But If they couldn't do it, she could. Of this she was certain. She felt that in marrying this highly gifted man, she would have to pay a price. He was her challenge and she would succeed. So when she had settled down to connubial bliss in her home in Angoulême, Lucie began her life with Maurice as a wife, mother and police matron and something else, a business manager. She assessed the situation and saw that under Utter, Maurice's work had stalemated. We weren't selling.

Lucie formulated a new tactic. She allowed Maurice to paint a little and then permitted none of his paintings to be sold. André protested, but Lucie wouldn't budge. Word spread through the Montmartre that he was finished as a painter. The alcohol had ruined whatever talent he had. Was this her concoction or was it true? I cursed the very thought of Lucie.

But when I visited I saw Maurice painting. She had the gall and scheming wisdom to make him paint the white paintings she knew would ultimately sell. She spoke to dealers on her own and confirmed her actions with them. How slimy she was. When Maurice grew more difficult she watered his wine, got him a bodyguard, personally prepared his food and portioned out his drink. She placed bars on the windows. She held his paintings for a year longer and dismissed André Utter as a nuisance. This woman was a viper, a snake. André was dealt a terrible blow.

Collectors grew greedy. The prices of all existing paintings by Utrillo soared. Then, slowly, she began to release the stock of paintings he had finished. The paintings sold for enormous sums.

With their new affluence, Lucie purchased a villa and grounds in *Le Vésinet*, an expensive area on the outskirts of Paris. She called her new house *La Bonne Lucie*, became self-satisfied, shrewd and wealthy. Her garden with its 19th century sculpture and stone frogs, ducks and turtles, was a monument to Lucie's bad taste. She bought a Rolls Royce, employed a chauffeur, a cook, a secretary, and had a houseful of carved and gilded ornate furniture, thick Aubusson carpets as well as objects of art as a further testament to her ostentation. She wore the dresses of Dior, Chanel, Schiaparelli, Patou and other couturiers, and accumulated a wealth of diamonds. She purchased a diamond for every painting Utrillo sold. She had her hair done by a prominent hairdresser, Monsieur Claude and under her influence, I did likewise. She secretly footed the bill. But her arrogance was astonishing. It drove me wild. She considered herself the Empress of Montmartre and because of that she scoffed at bills presented to her in bistros and boutiques.

And occasionally she allowed my poor Maurice a trip into Montmartre where they would visit me and then to the Lapin Agile where he signed the guest book as a celebrity. On such excursions I wished the curses of the damned on my daughter-in-law, but Lucie kissed me affectionately and treated me with a gracious manner. Lucie was far too clever to be rattled by it all. She handled life with assurance and ease, and I heard about the extensive sale of Maurice's paintings, but the hurt was always there. Maurice had deserted the Montmartre and had become the husband of a rich bourgeois. He would become so content that he would ultimately never pick up a brush again. I cursed Lucie with my full hatred and bit my lip when Lucie said, "Come along, Maurice, it's time to go." It was an echo of the way she had once instructed her departed husband.

"You must take care of yourself, dear Suzanne. A Chanel suit would look marvelous on you. Let's remain friends my dearest Suzanne, the way we always were."

I suffered Lucie's kiss on my cheek and realized that of course Lucie was impervious to insult.

When Lucie didn't visit, I became apprehensive. In my mind, the dénouement had finally come about, that horror which Lucie had planned for my son, his final awful demise. He had stopped painting and was in some sort of catatonic stupor from which there was no return. She had finally ruined him. Visions of my Maurice being mistreated became an obsession, causing me sleepless nights. I had to find peace and I took a bus to Le Vésinet to see Maurice, *my* Maurice. I would rescue him, *I, alone*. I would storm this bastion of greed and pull him out of her hands and take him back with me to Montmartre. No guards or gates could stop me. My will was too great. I had suffered too much to promote his genius to let it rot away in this manner. Damn Lucie! Damn her! Damn her forever in hell!

Lucie greeted me warmly when I came to Vésinet one hot July afternoon. She was her customary self, flitting about, directing the servants and generally acknowledging her self-importance. "Oh Suzanne. I couldn't wait to tell you. I've started painting. Wait, I must show you one of my pictures."

She took out a painting of a Montmartre scene done in primitive style, an atrocity, an insult to my son's name. "Am I not a talent? Isn't it one of Maurice's streets? And I'm so clever that if you want to buy one of my Maurice's paintings, you must buy one of mine. I don't know how these marvelous ideas come to me, but how do you like my painting? Isn't it magnificent?"

"Have you shown this to Maurice?" I asked impatiently.

"Oh, he just stares and says nothing, but you can see he's very impressed. You see, we are all without training. I'm now one of your precious artists. Who knows, perhaps I will hang in the Louvre beside you and Maurice. I shouldn't be surprised. I sign myself, Lucie Utrillo, isn't that clever?"

"What!"

"It *is* my name. Now, have you any suggestions for my art?"

"None. Absolutely none. Where is he, where is my son?"

"Oh, my dear Suzanne. I haven't killed him yet . . . come I'll show you." She said this smiling good-naturedly, "I want you to see the amazing room I've fixed up for him." She led me down the gleaming cream corridor with flocked satin wall covering.

I stood at the threshold and gazed inside, taking a deep breath. The room was astonishing with its muted lighting and religious aura. On an altar were several statues of Saint Joan and before it, Maurice knelt in prayer.

"Isn't this room my act of genius?"

"Maurice," I breathed. He turned and greeted me.

"Doesn't he look well?" affirmed Lucie. "He has an exceptional wife."

This was directed to Maurice who didn't seem to hear her.

So he looks well this time . . . for how long? Oh she's a vixen that one, a slimy viper with her smiles and flattery, but if he doesn't produce, she'll destroy him.

"Isn't it wonderful for him here?" Lucie said. "I am pleased beyond my wildest dreams at how things are developing. You don't ever have to worry yourself, dear one, about him at all. What a change for my great artist, my genius, Maurice. And it is I, Lucie Valore, who has done it all!"

"*Not all of it.*" I felt a familiar fury well up inside of me.

Lucie ignored my answer.

"Of course *I've* done it all," Lucie contradicted with a smile and good humor. "Do you know what I really am in this place."

"I can't imagine," I said bitterly.

"I'm really his Joan of Arc, because *I've* delivered him. Yes, I've lead the troops and been his salvation. And he has done a painting for me, just for me called *The Birthplace of Joan of Arc*, see how he thought of me. You must read the inscription."

"Where?"

"Why in the lower left hand side of the painting, of course. I wanted it right on the canvas. He is so overwhelmed with my talents I'm right there for all to see. I'll read it to you, *À Ma Chère Femme, Lucie.* You see it's so marvelous to be worshipped in this manner . . . for me alone. It's a wedding present, my dear. Can you think of a better one? I'll be immortal like his Saint Joan."

No, no, no! I screamed inside. The wound was reopened by

Lucie's boasting. Every fiber in my being protested against this interfering stranger. Why couldn't Lucie understand that all those years I had given to my son . . . all that torment he had engendered in me, all the moments that I had forced him to paint, all this belonged to *me, me* alone. What Lucie did was superficial and unimportant. The glory was *mine*, not Lucie's, *mine*. Yet, this stranger was garnering and reaping the reward of a lifetime of my nurturing. *I, Suzanne*, instructing him, urging him to paint. *It was I*, mother of the great artist, Maurice Utrillo.

Now I had nothing, not Maurice, not André, and little money. Lucie had it all. She had everything except my talent but I was so tired, so weary but to rest was to die, for how much time was left? It was but an infinitesimal drop in an eternity . . . I felt it fleeting, faster, ever faster on wings, whirling crazily, the months into years . . . the sagging bosom, the wrinkled skin, ever testaments to its destruction and passage leaving in its wake a wasteland . . . so just paint the landscapes, the still lifes, the self-portraits, the drawings and the sketches, so cruel and unrelenting in their bitter strivings. Mine was the eternal search of a woman for truth, a woman who happened to become an artist, ever devoting her life . . . and there were those like Lautrec and Degas who really cared. Age is fleeting like beauty, so ephemeral one cannot hold it. But my art matters, nothing else, nothing else

And in the end after I'm gone, what I paint, will be left as a legacy.

* * *

The exhibition of European Women's Painters was held at the Petit Palais in which several of my latest paintings hung in addition to past works. The exhibit was to go on to the Metropolitan Museum in New York. When Maurice and Lucie joined me, I, in a rare generous mood toward her, greeted my daughter-in-law with all the feigned warmth and affection I could muster.

And Lucie responded in kind. "I bow before Suzanne Valadon, the artist," and she blithely kissed me on the cheek. "You know, my dears," she said to the group accompanying me, Nora Kars, Madame Coquiot and André, "I am doing painting myself, and am quite good at it, aren't I, Maurice, my love? I sign myself Lucie Utrillo and everyone buys my art."

"Your paintings are an abomination, oh great one," André muttered bitterly. There was a low ripple of laughter from my friends. Lucie turned away and totally ignored them.

My eyes went to Maurice who stood by silently and smiled, submerged in his own grayed images. He was lost in the world Lucie concocted, looking well nourished and prosperous, much older, and more wistful. I saw his eyes glance once at Lucie and then rove from canvas to canvas with an amused expression.

When I examined the paintings once again, I noted that the French women artists were well represented, there were paintings by Marie Laurencin, Saraphine Louis, Marie Blanchard, Vignée-Lebrun, Berthe Morisot, Maria Gonzales, who had died in childbirth and Mary Cassatt who died in 1926, a blind spinster. A section consisted of English artists, Dutch, Hungarian, Italian, Norwegian, Polish and others. There were in all five thousand fifty works from women artists from over fifty countries.

It was astonishing. "I'm truly amazed. André, look at that brushwork. It's marvelous," I said pointing to a painting by Morisot. I never realized how good she was . . . how honored I am to exhibit with these women, André."

He said nothing, but watched me flit excitedly from one canvas to another. I surprised myself that I was here at all. How could I be, I, the individualist, I was Suzanne Valadon, alone, who belonged to none of them. I had always scorned being called a woman painter . . . there was no gender to art. But I found myself practically floating about the room with an exhilaration I hadn't anticipated, sailing from canvas to canvas, examining, assessing, criticizing, admiring, passing over some, dwelling on others, occasionally stopping and staring with naked admiration at what women from some other country had accomplished, had painted. The exhibit had touched on something in me, the feeling for the underdog, the cry of women artists who in addition to affirming their art had the additional burden of gender. This is what my contemporaries and predecessors in art were doing when I thought myself so unique. I found myself flabbergasted at the enormity and range of the works. What amazed me was that women alone had painted all this . . . women.

"I never really understood," I said repeatedly.

I thought back to my own career. Consciously I knew that the same credence was never given to a woman artist. Puvis de Chavannes had disdained and resented me as an artist . . . but he was no different from others. There were books of art published without a woman artist's name mentioned in them. The world of Bohemia was essentially a man's world. *La vie de bohème* was the life of the male French artist . . . the world of Monet, Manet, Pissarro, Lautrec, Renoir, Cézanne, Gauguin, Van Gogh, Modigliani, and my son Maurice, and the world now of Picasso, Braque, Matisse, and the others, the world again of the male artist. Occasionally a woman's name would infiltrate that world, a name like Cassatt, Marie Laurencin, Berthe Morisot or Suzanne Valadon. But the women's names were few. It was the nature of the conventional life they led. And poor Eva Gonzales, who would have become a fine painter, lost her life in childbirth.

At the very least I lived with audacity and I knew that quality of boldness put its stamp on my work. I'm not humble about it. I don't regret one moment of it. And the work I painted was my own individual style . . . my paintings reeked of earthiness. But there must be others who were like myself. I wasn't sure.

I left overwhelmed and shaken by the paintings on so global a scale, yet convinced of my own uniqueness. Afterwards, I found Maurice sitting with an effusive Lucie at the Lapin Agile and I told my son, "You know *chéri,* I have often boasted about my art because I thought that was what people expected, for an artist to boast. I'm very humble after what we have seen this afternoon. The women of France can paint too, *hein?* But do you know, I think maybe God has made *me* France's greatest woman painter."

"You are immodest, Maman," said Maurice smiling.

I had almost forgotten that it was once part of a game we played. I hurriedly brushed a tear from my cheek and Lucie gave me a puzzled look. For once, Lucie was locked out of that world which once existed between a mother and son.

* * *

Several weeks after a young artist came up to me in the rue Norvins. I remembered him buying paints in the Montmartre. How he reminded me of Modi, with his handsome face and intense dark eyes. The young women ogled him, calling him a Mongol Prince, who had women falling at his feet.

He sat next to me and we talked for several hours. "I'll call you my little mother by adoption. Why are you surprised?"

"Modi once called me that . . . Modigliani . . . you're as handsome as he was."

"You knew Modigliani? By God, that's wonderful!"

"What's your name?"

"Gazi . . . and do you know, Madame Valadon, I knew you as a child. You were a friend of my aunt."

But if Gazi reminded me of poor Modi with his intensity and beauty, the resemblance ended there. He was deeply mystical in his beliefs, and when we met again on the Butte, he spoke endlessly about his revelations. "I've had so many mystical experiences since childhood, and now the Virgin Mary has instructed me," he said earnestly.

"And what in the world did she tell you?" I asked lightly.

"She told me, *Mémère* to take care of you."

"Oh, did she? How wonderful. I'll certainly not object."

"You don't take me seriously. You're not religious, I know, but you should pray. It will ease your soul."

"Why should I pray?"

"Because it will give you peace."

"Nothing will give me peace, nothing. I've lost too much."

"It's right that I should live with you."

I hesitated, and in my loneliness I agreed.

"Look at that scene down there, Gazi. I used to come here when I was a child. I would come and sketch a little cat which followed me, and I danced through those twisted streets when I could skip out of school," I laughed. "And that was often, Gazi, until I dropped out altogether, but it didn't matter. It was all quite marvelous. I would hand my little drawings to my mother who was always drunk, and she would push them away and say they were scribblings. My poor drunken mother," I said, and wiped my eyes. "Her name was Madeleine . . . you can see her in my drawings . . . I didn't understand her then but one has to be a mother for a while to understand a mother's grief, *hein?*"

"I know," Gazi affirmed.

He was a marvelous listener for my repeated monologues, .

The gossips of the Butte never changed, and there was laughter that a woman of over seventy passed by with Gazi. Would I never stop consorting with younger men? But I had been nurtured on the gossip of Madame Pinchot, now long gone, who had reported on my every move to matrons of the Butte.

Gazi took care of me, cooking for me, ever catering to my frail health. We sat together for many hours as he vainly attempted to indoctrinate me into his mysticism. Sometimes I attended mass at the Church of Saint-Pierre to placate him. But attending mass helped little. It couldn't bring back what I had lost.

"I have lost my son to her. He paints bad pictures with her, pictures for the vulgar money of the bourgeoisie. She has him painting anything without mercy just to line her purse. With me he produced masterpieces. I always his inspiration, not Lucie, but myself. Was I my mother all over again, Madeleine, lamenting my life and lamenting my past suffering?

But most of all I told him how I taught myself to paint, I, an urchin of the streets, my own teacher and my son's.

And Gazi listened. My joy instilling in my son the spark of glory, igniting that genius, was a concept Gazi could fathom.

My friends continued to visit me . . . Mauricia Coquiot, Nora Kars, Derain and George Braque, and of course Adèle, dear Adèle, once proprietress and now retired, having sold the Moulin Joyeaux, the small restaurant at the top of the Butte. When my friends visited, we talked and laughed, and recounted stories from years gone by, ablaze with figures now gone. And the women's talk was punctuated with shrill laughter, denunciations, and sometimes tears. And in the end, the women wiped their eyes and then dismissed the past.

But it was my present relationship with André which had become a weary one . . . tedious, unending, unresolved, remaining in a half-married, half-divorced state, and occasionally we came together as lovers, only to separate again. He stayed in the rue Cortot, but I eternally waited for a paunchy André to come walking up the path to my house, puffing on his pipe wanting me. André Utter was now a roué, a womanizer, a drunkard, and there were times that the caretaker at Saint-Bernard found him at his easel unconscious with drink. Painting full time now, he never sold. I traded my paintings to provide André with food and wine that he loved, but he didn't stay.

"We're not the same, Suzanne. We have both changed. Both of us live in the past . . . of what was and what might have been. This is no longer the world we met in. Is this the Montmartre we once knew? We were so young. Now why do you cry?" But I embraced him and let him go, and then wiped my eyes. I watched him walk down the cobblestone streets. His paunchy, middle aged figure advancing wearily toward the studio where we came long ago, once in the magic promise of love.

I painted less and less, and my paintings were confined to those of my beloved cut flowers. My friends visited infrequently now, and sometimes no one came, no one except André, who sometimes drifted in, looked at Gazi with heavily bagged amused eyes and hurriedly left. Lucie and Maurice visited, but the time between visits grew longer. The silent ticking of the clock cut through a terrible stillness and something in me was giving way.

And I finally reverted more to the past which overwhelmed and consumed me and I became a young gamine of the streets who modeled for Renoir. Oh, how sweet the days were then, I thought, and how young I was and how the heads would turn as I walked near the fountain of the Place Pigalle. How does one recapture the time gone by, the time forever lost like a wisp of sunshine which floats like a memory on a breeze.

The deafening silence answered me.

When I visited Le Vésinet to see Maurice that day in March of

1938, Lucie, as always, greeted me warmly, and took me to Maurice's chapel, "My dear heart," said Lucie, "What is it you always say to me?" she questioned Maurice.

"I love my Joan of Arc, my mother, and my wife," he replied dutifully.

"Isn't that sweet?" said Lucie, "and I've always insisted that your son place you before me in his affection."

I looked at Maurice long and lingering this time, as if attempting to indelibly stamp each beloved feature on my memory, the face I had painted countless times, the dear aging face, now with its deep lines and furrows, the face which I had first drawn.

Returning from Le Vésinet, the last of the bitter winds whipped around us and chilled me thoroughly as I stepped into Lucie's Rolls Royce, and I shivered the whole time her chauffeur drove me home. When I reached the Avenue Junot, Gazi made me repeated hot drinks and bundled me with warm blankets.

"*Mémère, Mémère,* be careful," he whispered.

"You have been a blessing to me, Gazi," I said, "a blessing. You are like a son to me. My own son could not have been more devoted. I know I will not live much longer. I came into the world with nothing and I'll leave with nothing. I finished my work and I rejoice that I never betrayed what I believed in. Someday, the world will see it if they care to, and at last recognize me more fully. When I die, Gazi, you will keep my soul in your pocket and take good care of it." Then, I patted him on his arm with the hand of my mother and my mother's mother before me. But with a childless Maurice, my line had ended; a grandchild existed only in a dream and my progeny evaporated into the breezes which whispered through the trees on the Butte Montmartre.

* * *

The warmth of April comes on suddenly, an unnatural warmth of an early spring promising a blazing summer. The chestnut trees are blooming along the Champ Élysées and the acacias shine through them, the scene Renoir adored. I think of this as I walk along the Boulevards and I will climb to the top of the Butte as I had done as a child and look down at Paris, and then I will sketch. Today I can scarcely catch my breath.

The hill of Montmartre climbs high above the Seine, and still overlooks the colorful, tortuous and still picturesque streets. How I remember this Montmartre as it once was, this country village which I had looked down at, alive with chickens, rabbits and pigs scurrying about, with manure making dank trails down the walkways, my very own and I would stand there as a child of ten and hug myself with joy. The landscape has changed somewhat from the time I first climbed to the top, yet it seems that the air this spring day of 1938 is clearer, purer than it had ever been when I was a child. It is as though all eternity rests on this hill, and I sit very still catching my breath . . . expectant, waiting . . .

And as I sit, a barefoot child dances toward me. She smiles briefly and sits next to me and sketches a small cat with a pencil she removes from her leather pouch. And then she puts the drawing away and stands looking down at the scene. She places her hands haughtily on her hips and bravely tosses back her sun kissed hair as she shouts down, "How I love you, Montmartre. Do you hear me down there?"

Oh, she is a beauty, that little one, a saucy beauty.

"Marie-Clémentine . . . where are you?" And then it seems I hear Maman calling her in a familiar voice thickened with drink. It is a voice that wafts through the twisted streets, seeps through the rocks and filters through the trees brushing the leaves with its hoarse timbre until it creeps its way to the top.

We never exchange a word as the child dances away followed by her cat as it sniffs and nibbles here and there on a blade of grass.

Epilogue

April 7, 1938
Paris, France

It is the spring of 1938 and she stands at her easel, at seventy three. Beneath the spectacles are deep sapphire eyes fringed with straight lashes, once the wonder of artists.

She feels the loneliness without André and Maurice while she is painting. And it happens. The stroke happens. Soon it will be over, all of it. It will all be behind her.

"My work is finished. I've said all that I need to say," she whispers to Degas, a Degas who had died long before in 1917.

She is dreaming now, a long languid dream of incredible sweetness. She dances along so easily and she is deliciously young. Henri calls her hair the color of sun-kissed cognac.

The world of Paris in the spring is the world of her girlhood. The world of the Impressionists is the world of glowing radiant color pulsating with the rays of the sun; the sun of Van Gogh capturing its brilliance on canvas; of Gauguin with his stained glass colorings; and of Lautrec who moves among the misbegotten and grotesque. Her Maurice sees and hears the dismal notes with his paintings of sordid streets. It is a lost world.

Yes, perhaps she might stand with the models at the fountains at the Place Pigalle, or perhaps go where the artists talk together. She might see Henri Lautrec painting with his carved cane resting against a table and he might nod as his gaze meets hers. It doesn't matter at all because she is safe now and she is among them.

A familiar voice comes through to her from the shadows. "You're going to be alright," Adèle says, holding her hands so tightly and looking down at her face. "Please, stay . . . for Maurice's sake . . . at least . . ."

For a brief second she opens her eyes with the mention of her son, and whispers his name and then she turns her head away.

It is only eleven o'clock in the morning.

And in the end it's her daughter-in-law, a competent Lucie who takes charge of the proceedings. Suzanne's tiny shriveled body is now in the parish church of Saint-Pierre in Montmartre; its corridors redolent with the timeless aura of centuries.

Edouard Herriot, twice Premier of France, delivers the eulogy for the artist who worked in Montmartre from the cradle to the grave. André Utter, once her lover and husband sits completely crushed. An aging Maurice sits alone in his lavish home and just stares into space, bewildered. He can't comprehend his mother's death. His eyes spot a canvas in a corner, a scene of Montmartre which he had struggled with in its mastery in the beginning. A large photograph of Suzanne sits on a mantel and he feels the full force of his mother's presence.

"Paint, Maumau, you must paint, *chéri*, you must paint . . ."

He picks up a brush and goes to the easel.

By Way of a Conclusion

A legacy of paintings by Suzanne Valadon and Maurice Utrillo hang in the Utrillo-Valadon room in the Musée National d'Art, CNAC, George Pompidou, Paris.

Maurice Utrillo painted his views of Montmartre until the very end with a life-size photograph of his mother in a white smock, palette in hand placed before him. On the anniversary of the deaths of his grandmother, Modigliani, Monsieur Gay and of course, his mother, he went into solitary prayer. He died on December 6, 1955, of pulmonary congestion, and his funeral was held in Montmartre's Saint-Pierre chapel. He was buried in Saint-Vincent cemetery next to the Lapin Agile, which he frequently painted.

André Utter died in 1948 at 62, a broken man. He stayed at the château after Suzanne's death and lead a life of carousing and dissipation. His futile attempts at artistic recognition led him to paint and drink furiously. He was still thought of as a fine artist causing him frustration at not being able to sell. At the end, he was buried beside Valadon and her mother at Sainte-Ouen cemetery.

Lucie Valore died in 1965 at the age of 94. She garnished a long life of affluent self-aggrandizement. Her home was filled with photographs of her illustrious friends such as Prince Ali Kahn and Rita Hayworth. To purchase a painting from her done by Utrillo, one was required to buy one of her own crude canvases. She unbelievably obtained a commission from the City of Paris to do a floral panel. A subject for gossip she became "engaged" well into her eighties to an Italian writer of 40.

Louis Anquetin who had a lofty opinion about his destined fame, died virtually obscure in 1932.

Émile Bernard joined Cormon's studio in the early 1880's, was dismissed by him in 1886 for painting a nude in emerald green and vermilion. He went to paint in Brittany where he joined Gauguin and they formed a new movement. He never achieved what he wanted and died in 1941, forgotten for his contribution to modern painting.

François Gauzi was basically a talented artist, born in Toulouse and was a cheerful close friend of Lautrec for many years. He was to write about Lautrec, "He had the gift of endearing people to him and his friends were devoted to him." Gauzi died in seclusion in 1933.

The Rue des Moulins, the notorious brothel painted by Lautrec, was sold in 1946. A Parisian secondhand dealer put an elaborately decorated copper bath on display. One afternoon, two old women stopped to look at it. "Do you want to purchase it?" asked the dealer. "Oh no!" they replied. "It brings back so many memories." They were two old prostitutes from the brothel.

And as for this writer, I have never abandoned the idea that the locket which Lautrec presented to Suzanne so many years ago would someday fall my way. I'm still looking for it.

Acknowledgements

I am deeply grateful to those who assisted my research in Paris namely, Gilbert Pétridès of the Galerie Gilbert et Paul Pétridès and its director Jeanette Anderfuhren. I wish to thank Anne-Marie Zuchelli, Documentalist of the Musée Nationale d'Art Moderne, CNAC George Pompidou and Danièle Devynck, Conservateur en Chef of The Musée Toulouse-Lautrec in Albi. My thanks as well to Henri Loyrette, Conservateur en Chef, and the Directeur du Musée d'Orsay in Paris. I want to note the kind interest shown by Daniel Marchesseau, of the Musée d'Art Moderne de la Ville and his marvelous catalogue of Suzanne Valadon connected with his exhibit.

I wish to note the sincere interest in my project shown by Jean Stone, widow and editor of Irving Stone and Patricia Coughlan, photographer, widow of Robert Coughlan, author of Wine of Genius (Utrillo) and her insights into Lucie Valore, wife of Maurice Utrillo.

Among the New York City institutions, I wish to thank the staff of the Museum of Modern Art in New York City for information provided as well as the New York Public Library for the *Catalogue raisonné (Pétridès)* and other documents.

I truly appreciate my daughter Professor Lori A. Todd, at the University of North Carolina at Chapel Hill, for her assistance in locating, gathering and duplicating important articles about Suzanne Valadon.

And to my husband who lived through the birth pangs with me of producing the manuscript. His insight, support and love proved invaluable.

Credits

Letter of Erik Satie to Suzanne Valadon: Musée National d'Art Moderne, CNAC, Georges Pompidou, Documentation Department, Robert Le Masle Collection, Paris.
VOLTA, ORNELLA: *Satie Seen Through His Letters;* Marion Boyars, London, 1989, pp. 44-47.
HARRIS, ANN SUTHERLAND, and, LINDA NOCHLIN: *Women Artists, 1550-1950;* Alfred A. Knopf, Inc. New York, and Museum Associates of the Los Angeles County of the Museum of Art, 1976.
GREER, GERMAINE: *The Obstacle Race;* Farrar Straus Giroux, New York, 1979. Use of quote on back cover courtesy of Aiken, Stone & Wylie, Limited, London.
POEM: *To My Mother;* by Maurice Utrillo, New York, SPADEM, Paris. 1995 Artists Rights Society, New York.

Notes

ABSINTHE: The *Green Muse* or the *Green Fairy* was a pale green anise flavored drink. It proved lethal and was banned in 1915.

HONORS: The marble plaque at the Moulin Joyeaux reads, "*Dans ce restaurant La Grande Artiste Suzanne Valadon a dîné de 1919 a 1935, accompagnée de son fils, Maurice Utrillo.*" The city of Paris also designated, a *rue Valadon*.

LA GRANDE CELINE : She was a part-time prostitute who was said to have modeled for Bartholdi's *Statue of Liberty*. However, it was also said that Madame Bartholdi Senior the mother of the sculptor, a tremendously bigoted domineering woman who caused the madness of a son, ironically was given the facial features of Bartholdi's *Liberty*.

LAUTREC: His *Madame Poupooule at Her Toilette* was painted in 1900 at the Rue des Moulins brothel. He focused mainly on her long reddish hair rather than her features. Partial to redheads he used them frequently in his paintings.

LIFE OF MODELS: What many of the Parisian as well as the Italian models from Naples were looking for was a permanent liaison or marriage. Several artists such as Monet and Renoir married their models.

MARRIAGE OF SUZANNE VALADON AND PAUL MOUSIS: A thorough search of the *mairies* both in Montmartre and Pierrefitte failed to produce any record of marriage or divorce.

MODIGLIANI: His oil of *Jeanne Hébuterne* (1919) was one of many paintings and drawings Modigliani did of his mistress.

PUVIS DE CHAVANNES: In one theory, he loved a married Princess Cantacuzene. Another theory married him to the Princess and he kept two studios, running from one to the other to dodge her.

THE BETROTHAL OF MAURICE: According to *Suzanne,* Lucie asserted, "I have decided to take care of your son since you won't be able to." According to *Lucie,* Suzanne begged her, "Who will take care of my poor Maurice?" (I confess, I used Lucie's version.)

THE BROTHEL: A brothel of any quality had a routine *visite* (inspection) by a doctor of the prostitutes for venereal disease. Lautrec did a graphic painting of the *visite* in 1894 called *The Inspection*.

A Selected Bibliography

WORKS USED IN THE TEXT

Beachboard, Robert: *La Trinité Maudite, Utter, Valadon, Utrillo;* Amiot-Dumont, Paris, 1953.
Bouret, Jean: *Degas;* Tudor Publishing Company, New York, 1961.
Coughlan, Robert: *The Wine of Genius;* Harper & Brothers, New York, 1951.
Fitfield, William: *Modigliani;* William Morrow and Company, Inc., New York, 1976.
Gauguin, Paul: *The Writings of a Savage;* The Viking Press, New York, 1974.
Greer, Germaine: *The Obstacle Race;* Farrar Straus Giroux, New York, 1979.
Harris, Ann Sutherland and Linda Nochlin: *Women Artists, 1550-1950;* Los Angeles County Museum of Art, Alfred A. Knopf, New York, 1977.
Jourdain, Francis; *Utrillo;* Les Éditions Braun & Cie, Paris - E.S. Hermann, New York, 1948.
Mack, Gerstle: *Toulouse-Lautrec;* Alfred A. Knopf, 1953.
Myers, Rollo H.: *Erik Satie;* Dover Publications, Inc. New York, 1968.
Perruchot, Henri: *Toulouse Lautrec;* Perpetua Books, London, 1962.
Rosenberg, Charles and Carroll Smith: *Sex, Marriage and Society-Birth Control and Family Planning in Nineteenth-Century America;* Arno Press, New York, 1974.
Salmon, André: *Modigliani a memoir;* G. P. Putnam's Sons, New York, 1961.
Shattuck, Roger: *The Banquet Years, The Origins of the Avant Guard in France, 1885 to World War 1;* Vintage Books, New York, 1968.
Stone, Irving: *Depths of Glory;* Doubleday & Company, New York, 1985.
Storm, John: *The Valadon Drama;* E. P. Dutton & Co., New York, 1959.
Valore, Lucie: *Maurice Utrillo, Mon Mari;* Joseph Foret, Paris, 1956.
Vollard, Ambroise: *Recollections of a Picture Dealer;* Dover Publications, Inc., New York, 1978.
  Degas, An Intimate Portrait; Dover Publications, Inc., New York, 1986.
Volta, Ornella: *Satie Seen through His Letters;* Marion Boyars, London - New York, 1989.
Warnod, Jeanine: *Suzanne Valadon;* Crown Publishers, New York, 1981.
  Maurice Utrillo V.; Crown Publishers, New York, 1983.

Werner, Alfred: *Maurice Utrillo*; Harry Abrams, Inc., New York, 1981.
Wilenski, R. H.: *Modern French Painters*; Harcourt, Brace and Company, New York, 1945.

OTHER READINGS

Bonnat, Yves: *Valadon*; Club d'art Bordas, Paris, 1969.
Châtelet, Albert: *Impressionist Painting*; McGraw-Hill Book Company, New York, 1962.
Cooper, Douglas: *Toulouse Lautrec*; Harry N. Abrams, Inc., New York, no date given.
Desanti, Dominique: *A Woman in Revolt, a Biography of Flora Tristan*; (grandmother of Paul Gauguin); Crown Publishers, New York, 1972.
Diehl, Gaston: *Modigliani*; Crown Publishers, Inc., New York, 1969.
Dumont: *The Montmartre Colony*; Collection du Musée Du Vieux Montmartre, Paris, 1963.
Fermigier, André: *Toulouse Lautrec*; Frederick A. Praeger, Publishers, New York, 1969.
Gatley, Charles Neilsen: *Gauguin's Astonishing Grandmother, A Biography of Flora Tristan*; Femina Books Ltd., London 1970.
Gauzi, François: *Lautrec et son Temps*; David Perret, Paris, 1954. (Collection, La Bibioteque des Arts)
    English Edition: *My Friend, Toulouse Lautrec*, Spearman, London, 1957.
Huisman, Philippe: *Morisot Enchantment*; French and European Publications, Inc., New York, 1963.
Huisman, P. and M. G. Dortu: *Lautrec by Lautrec*; The Viking Press, New York, 1964.
Jacometti, Nesto: *Suzanne Valadon*; Éditions Pierre Cailler, Geneve, 1947.
Klüver, Billy and Julie Martin: *KiKi's Paris Artists and Lovers 1900-1930*; Harry N. Abrams, Inc., New York, 1989.
Lethève, Jacques: *Daily Life of French Artists in the Nineteenth Century*; Praeger Publishers, New York, 1972.
Lewis, David: *Prisoners of Honor, The Dreyfus Affair*; Henry Holt, 1994.
Mann, Carol: *Modigliani*; Oxford University Press, 1980.
Mathey, François: *The Impressionists*; Frederick A. Praeger, New York, 1961.
Muller, Joseph-Émile: *Toulouse-Lautrec*; Leon Amiel, New York, 1975.
Polnay, Peter de: *Enfant Terrible, The Life and World of Maurice Utrillo*; William Morrow and Company, New York, 1969.
Renoir, Jean: *Renoir, My Father*; Little Brown and Company, Boston, 1958.
Rewald, Alice Bellony: *The Lost World of the Impressionists*; Galley Press, New York, 1976.
Rosinsky, Thérèse Diamond: *Suzanne Valadon*; Universe Publishing, New York, 1994.
Senefelder, Alois: *A Complete Course of Lithography*; Da Capo Press Inc., New

York, 1977.
Skinner, Cornelia Otis: *Madame Sarah;* Houghton Mifflin Company, Boston, 1967.
Stone, Irving: *Lust for Life;* Methuen, London, 1989 Edition.

ARTICLES

Bailey, Martin, " Edgar Degas" *Smithsonian,* Oct.1996,Wasington, DC
Beauz-Arts; "Special issue on Suzanne Valadon," April 15, 1938.
Besson, George; "Hommage to Suzanne Valadon," *Lettres françoises,* 1948.
Bond, Constance, Van Gogh*Smithsonian, Oct. 1998, Washington, DC*
Coughlan, Robert; "The Dark Wine of Genius," *Life* #28, Jan 16, 1950 (Utrillo)
Fels, Robert, "Suzanne Valadon" *In L'Information,* Paris, 1961.
Guenne, Jacques; "Suzanne Valadon," *Art Vivant,* Paris, April, 1932.
'Maria of Montmartre," *Time* No. 67, May 28, 1956.
Valadon, Suzanne and Germain Bazin; "Suzanne Valadon par elle-même," *Prométhée,* March 1939.
Schiff,, Bennett, "Modigliani" *Smithsonian,* Jan., 1984, Wahington, DC

CATALOGUES

Fondation Pierre Giannadda: Marchesseau, Daniel, Commissaire,; *Exposition de Suzanne Valadon,* Martigny, Suisse, 26 Janvier 27 Mai, 1996.
Galerie Georges Petit; *Exposition de Suzanne Valadon,* 1932.
Los Angeles County Museum of Art: *Women Painters:* 1550-1950, Ann Sutherland Harris and Linda Nochlin, Los Angeles, 1976
Musée Toulouse-Lautrec, *Maurice Utrillo, Suzanne Valadon, Rencontre de Trois Peintres,* Jean Alain Meric, 1959, Albi, France.
Pétridès, Paul; "Catelogue raisonne de l'oeuvre de Suzanne Valadon et Avant propos, *Compagnie française des arts graphiques,*" Paris, 1971.

MUSEUMS

Galerie Gilbert & Paul Pétridès, Paris.
Musée Municipal de Limoges.
Musée de Menton.
Musée d'Art Moderne de la Ville de Paris.
Musée de Nancy.
Musée National d'Art Moderne, CNAC, Georges Pompidou, Paris.
Musée d'Orsay, Paris.
Musée Toulouse-Lautrec Albi.
Los Angeles County Museum of Art.
Museum of Modern Art, New York.
National Museum of Women in the Arts, Washington, D.C.

Paintings in Text

SUZANNE VALADON (1865-1938)

1883: *Portrait of the Artist*; Pastel. Musée National d'Art Moderne, CNAC, Georges Pompidou, Paris.

1886: *Maurice Utrillo at the Age of Two*; Red Chalk on Paper. Musée National d'Art Moderne, CNAC, Georges Pompidou, Paris.

1891: *Miguel Utrillo Smoking a Pipe*; Drawing. Private Collection.

1892: *Portrait of Erik Satie*; Oil on Canvas. Musée National d'Art Moderne, CNAC, Georges Pompidou, Paris.

1894: *A Nude Utrillo with a Sitting Grandmother*; Black Pencil. Collection Paul Pétridès, Paris.

1895: *Utrillo Nude Sitting on a Couch*; Black Crayon. Private Collection.

Maurice Utrillo Playing With a Slingshot; Crayon. Private Collection.

1896: *My Son*; Black Crayon. Private Collection.

1910: *A Tree at Montmagny Quarry*; Oil on Canvas. Museum of Art, Carnegie Institute, Pittsburgh, Pennsylvania.

Adam and Eve; Oil on Canvas. Musée National d'Art Moderne, CNAC, Georges Pompidou, Paris.

Grandmother and Grandson; Oil on Cardboard. Musée National d'Art Moderne, CNAC, Georges Pompidou, Paris.

1911: *The Joy of Living*; Oil on Canvas. Metropolitan Museum Of Art, New York City.

1914: *Casting of the Net*; Oil on Canvas. Musée National d'Art Moderne, CNAC, Georges Pompidou, Paris.

1915: *Portrait of Madame Coquiot*; Oil on Canvas. Musée de Menton, France.

1916: *Sacré Coeur Seen from the Garden of the rue Cortot*; Oil on Canvas. Musée National d'Art Moderne, CNAC, Georges Pompidou, Paris.

1919: *Maurice Utrillo Painting*; Oil on Canvas. Musée d'Art Moderne de la Ville de Paris.

1921: *The Utter Family*; Oil on canvas. Musée National d'Art Moderne, CNAC, Georges Pompidou, Paris.

The Abandoned Doll; Oil on Canvas. The National Museum of Women in the Arts, Washington, D.C.

1922: *Portrait of Miss Lily Walton*; Oil on Canvas. Musée National d'Art Moderne, CNAC, Georges Pompidou, Paris.

1923: *The Blue Room*; Oil on Canvas. Musée National d'Art, CNAC, Georges Pompidou, Paris.

1927: *Self-Portrait, The Artist at 62*; Oil on Canvas. Lefevre Gallery, London.

Flowers in a Vase; Oil on Canvas. Private Collection.

1929: *The Church of Saint Bernard*; Oil on Canvas. Musée National d'Art Moderne, CNAC, Georges Pompidou, Paris.

1931: *Portrait with Bare Breasts;* Oil on Canvas. Private Collection.
1932: *André Utter and his Dogs;* Oil on Canvas. Private Collection.

MAURICE UTRILLO (1883-1955)

1905: *Butte Pinson at Montmagny;* Oil on Cardboard. Private Collection.
1907: *Guingette at Montmagny;* Oil on Cardboard. Private Collection.
1909: *Rue de la Jonquière;* Oil on Cardboard. Private Collection.
1910: *Rue des Abbesses;* Oil on Cardboard. Private Collection.
  Rue Norvins; Oil on Cardboard. The Brooklyn Museum, N.Y.
  Rue Ravignon; Oil on Canvas. Metropolitan Museum of Art, N.Y.
  Renoir's Garden; Oil on Canvas. Private Collection, New York.
  Factory at Saint Denis; Oil on Canvas. Museum, Tokyo.
1911: *Street at Montmartre;* Oil on Cardboard. Private Collection.
1912: *Rue du Mont-Cenis;* Oil on Canvas. Musée National d'Art Moderne, CNAC, Georges Pompidou, Paris.
  Place du Tertre; Oil on Cardboard. Albright-Knox Gallery, Buffalo.
1913: *Le Lapin Agile;* Oil on Canvas. Private Collection.
1915: *Rue à Asnières;* Oil on Canvas. Nelson Gallery-Atkins Museum, Kansas City, Missouri.
1922: *Le Petit Palais;* Oil on Canvas. San Francisco Museum of Art.
1935: *The Birthplace of Joan of Arc;* Oil on Canvas. Metropolitan Museum of Art, New York.

HENRI DE TOULOUSE-LAUTREC (1864-1901)

1885: *Portrait of Suzanne Valadon,** Pastel. Ny Carlsberg, Glyptotek, Copenhagen.
1887: *Portrait of the Comtesse A. De Toulouse Lautrec In The Salon At Malromé;* Oil on Canvas. Albi Museum.
1888: *Au Cirque Fernando: The Equestrienne;** Oil on Canvas. Art Institute of Chicago.
  *The Laundress,** Ink. Cleveland Museum of Art, Ohio.
1889: *La Buveuse-,The Drinker;** India Ink and Blue Chalk. Albi Museum, France.
1890: *Madame Poupoule At Her Toilette;* Oil on Panel. Albi Museum.
1894: *The Salon In The Rue Des Moulins,* Oil on Canvas. Albi Museum, France.

PIERRE-AUGUSTE RENOIR (1841-1919)

1883: *The Dance At Bougival;** Oil on Canvas. Museum of Fine Arts, Boston.
1885: *The Braid;** Private Collection, Baden, Switzerland.
1887: *The Bathers;** Drawing. Art Institute of Chicago.

* *Starred paintings (above) are posed for by Suzanne Valadon.*

Meet the Author

As a "woman of a certain age" like her heroine, *Suzanne*, Elaine Todd Koren has defied time by consistently bucking the tide. A renaissance woman who modeled, acted and studied art with Moses Soyer, she is both an accomplished painter and a writer. A divorced single mother of two, she worked in the New York inner- city school system both as a teacher and guidance counselor, and at night she wrote. Her mystical short stories of the children she met won first prize in both the Educational Press and International Labor Press Association awards. Her guidance book for the elementary school teacher (Prentice-Hall) was successful, well reviewed and widely used in colleges. She left the educational field to write full time and has published articles, contributed to anthologies and then worked on the biographical novel, *Suzanne*. For many years she researched, in the United States and in France, the life of *Suzanne Valadon*, the French painter and the people she touched. Ms.Koren presently resides in New York City with her husband where she is working on a memoir.

-Another work from Maverick Books-

The WORLD OF CORNELIUS MAGEE

Tales from the School

Magical, Hilarious, Outrageous and Heartbreaking

From the author of *Suzanne,* Elaine Todd Koren has deftly interwoven a series of tales of an inner city school in New York City in the sixties. "The World of Cornelius Magee" and "James is Gone, Thank Heaven" won first prize in the International Labor Association Press Awards and the Educational Press Awards

Laugh, cry and live with such stories as the author's memoir in the tale *"The Divorced Ones"* and in the farces, *"Sex on the Staircase"* *"*and *"Don't Go Near the Window, Dr. Fallek,"* the latter a psychiatrist's nightmare.

For additional information contact:

Maverick Books
Box 897
Woodstock, N.Y. 12498
or
email: maverickbooks@aol.com

Schoolhouse image adapted from *Art Explosion 250,000.*